An Invitation To Sin

D0027688

Jo Beverley
Vanessa Kelly
Sally MacKenzie
Kaitlin O'Riley

ZEBRA BOOKS
KENSINGTON PUBLISHING CORP.
http://www.kensingtonbooks.com

Books by Jo Beverley

AN ARRANGED MARRIAGE
AN UNWILLING BRIDE
DANGEROUS JOY
FORBIDDEN
TEMPTING FORTUNE
THE SHATTERED ROSE
CHRISTMAS ANGEL

Books by Vanessa Kelly

MASTERING THE MARQUESS
SEX AND THE SINGLE EARL

Books by Sally MacKenzie

THE NAKED GENTLEMAN
THE NAKED MARQUIS
THE NAKED DUKE
THE NAKED EARL
THE NAKED BARON
LORDS OF DESIRE
THE NAKED VISCOUNT

Books by Kaitlin O'Riley

SECRETS OF A DUCHESS
ONE SINFUL NIGHT
WHEN HIS KISS IS WICKED
DESIRE IN HIS EYES
YOURS FOR ETERNITY

Published by Kensington Publishing Corporation

CONTENTS

Forbidden Affections

JO BEVERLEY

Anna Featherstone sat up in bed and fumbled urgently for her candlestick. Grasping it, she slipped out of bed to light it at the night lamp on the mantelpiece, then held it high and turned to study her peculiar new bedroom.

Her sleepy thoughts had been right. The Gothic monstrosity was exactly like Dulcinea's prison in the novel, *Forbidden Affections*! When the notion had come to her at a point between sleep and waking she had been sure she must have been mistaken, but now she wandered the room, convinced she was correct.

It was a wonderful discovery, but also very puzzling.

Anna had spent her sixteen years in the Derbyshire countryside and knew she was not *au fait* with the latest fashions, but even if dark, heavily carved Gothic furniture was the rage in London, surely such morbid motifs as deadly nightshade and coffins were not. In the novel, Dulcinea's cruel uncle had caused her room to be decorated with symbols of death to remind her of her probable fate if she did not surrender to his evil passions.

Anna was not the least alarmed by the grinning skeletons and contorted gargoyles in the carvings. She was sadly lacking in sensibility. When her sister Maria had once demanded to know what Anna would do if actually confronted by a skeleton in a monk's robe, Anna had replied that she'd inspect it to find out how it held its bones together without ligaments or muscles.

Smiling at the memory of Maria's shudders, Anna wandered the room, appreciating the fine attention to detail. The heavy armoire boasted ivory knobs carved as skulls, and the rather pretty design in the wallpaper turned out to be a coffin shape. As best she could remember, it was exactly as in *Forbidden Affections*.

She wished she had the novel with her so she could check each detail, but she had not been permitted to bring many books on this trip to London. Allowed only five, she would never choose *Forbidden Affections* over, for example, *Cruel Matrimony,* an earlier novel by Mrs. Jamison. Anna had always thought there was something unsatisfactory about *Forbidden Affections,* which had apparently been the lady's last work. Perhaps she had been ill.

Anna longed to know the history of this room for it must have been created by a wealthy and devoted admirer of the novel, and not that long ago. *Forbidden Affections* had first been published less than ten years ago, though Anna had only read it last year. After all, at the time of publication she had scarce been out of the nursery.

Would the servants know the house's history?

Number 9, Carne Terrace was just a house hired for the spring Season—part of a handsome row of houses in an excellent part of London. Her parents and sister had been delighted with it until this bedroom had been discovered. At that point, they had almost left to stay at an inn. The Gothic marvel was clearly the master bedroom, but Lady Featherstone had declared most absolutely that nothing would persuade her to sleep beneath a canopy of gargoyles.

Maria, who always copied Mama, had declared the same, adding that she could never even open a drawer if it involved touching a skull. She had gone so far as to collapse into a convenient chair to make her point, and had required a sniff of laudanum to overcome the shock.

Since there were only three good bedrooms in the house, and Maria and Anna hated to share a bed, there was only one solution. Anna and her father had shared an ironic glance and Anna had made the noble sacrifice, secretly delighted to have such a room.

Now she was even more so. Imagine having Dulcinea's chamber all to herself. Heavens, it might even turn her into a romantic heroine!

Anna caught sight of herself in a mirror surrounded by grotesque carved heads and laughed. Dulcinea she was not. Dulcinea—like all Mrs. Jamison's heroines—was slender as a willow-wand, had a complexion of pearly hue, and silky golden tresses. Anna possessed thick, dark hair which always fought the constraint of her plait, full rosy cheeks, and a round body that was the despair of her fashionable mama.

She remembered then that when Dulcinea had first seen her reflection surrounded by gargoyles she had screamed and fainted. Dulcinea—again like all Mrs. Jamison's heroines—tended to faint quite often. Anna had never fainted in her life.

She had always wanted to, and had tried various tricks to achieve it, including putting scraps of silk in her shoes, but she had never achieved so much as a slight sensation of dizziness.

With a grimace at her robust reflection, she hoped that sturdy nerves and common sense didn't rule out all possibility of a handsome hero one day sweeping her off her feet.

Still delighted by the room, Anna began to return to bed, but then she turned back to contemplate the huge carved stone fireplace guarded by armored skeletons on either side.

Surely not!

In the book, evil Count Nacre had constructed a secret

doorway in the fireplace so that he could sneak into Dulcinea's room at night. One of the things about the book that irritated Anna was that Dulcinea's escape from his wicked plans was not of her own doing. Anna could think of any number of ways the silly creature could have escaped, but of course Dulcinea had waited for handsome Roland to find the secret door and rescue her.

Just before ancient, rat-infested Castle Nacre crumbled to the ground during an earthquake.

Now Anna eyed the ridiculous fireplace, refusing to believe that anyone had actually gone so far as to construct a secret door in a modern London town house. Where could it go, after all? Number 9, Carne Terrace was solidly bounded by number 8 and number 10.

But she could not resist trying.

The lever, if it was there, would be the spear of the skeleton to the right of the grate. The spear was held across his body and extended into the chimney so that it wouldn't be accidentally moved by a servant.

In the book.

This was real life. This wasn't a book.

Anna seized the spear and pulled it toward her. At first—as she expected—nothing happened. Then it began to move.

Anna snatched her hands away and stared at the spear as if it had come to life. This was taking replication to extremes! After all, on the other side of this fireplace there assuredly was not an abandoned, rat-infested, ivy-covered tower.

Was there?

Her heart began to thump.

For the first time, Anna's very practical mind was toying with the fantastic.

On the other side of this fireplace, she told herself firmly, was number 10, Carne Terrace, a respectable modern house.

Well, not precisely respectable.

That had been another shock for her parents—to realize that Carne Terrace was named after the Earl of Carne, who had built it, and that number 10, the large end house next door, belonged to the notorious fourth earl.

Their housekeeper had revealed that fact when asked who their neighbors were. Mrs. Postle had hastened to explain that the house stood empty and had done so for over eight years—ever since *the incident*.

Those two words had been said with the sort of meaningful glance that Anna knew all too well. It meant that young ladies were not to hear about it, and of course that had left Anna in a ferment of curiosity. What on earth had the earl done? It was probably to do with carnal relations. *Incidents* always were.

She'd followed the subsequent conversations very closely, but all she had learned was that after *the incident* the earl had left England and had not been seen since.

Anna was surprised. She'd heard of a number of young ladies who had traveled abroad as a result of *incidents*. Gentlemen, on the other hand, never seemed to suffer the full consequences of their follies.

She had been delighted by this hint of murky mystery, however. Though her parents had brought both their daughters to London, only Maria was to make her curtsy this year, and Anna had expected to be a little bored. Digging out the whole story of *the incident* would definitely enliven her stay.

Now it seemed she had other amusements—if she dared pull the lever fully.

Was it truly possible that it would open a door into the house of the wicked Earl of Carne?

Curiosity was Anna's greatest weakness, and she knew it. She generally kept it under control, but she could never return to bed and sleep without finding out if the door was there or not. After all, if Count Nacre could creep into

Dulcinea's chamber, perhaps the wicked Earl of Carne could creep into hers!

She might be in danger . . .

But that was sophistry, and she knew it. She wanted to try the lever just because it was there.

She grasped it and pulled it all the way. It made only a slight grinding sound, but it clearly had done something. She took a deep breath, went to the right-hand part of the fireplace, and pushed.

Just as in the book, the panel swiveled slightly.

Anna stopped to consider. No, she was not dreaming. No, she had not been plunged into the pages of a novel. But there was, assuredly, a secret door.

Even Anna's prosaic heart was beating high and fast as she pushed the panel fully open. She told herself it had to open the way into number 10 . . .

But a small, less rational part of her brain was prepared for it to open into a rat-infested, crumbling castle.

Anna, therefore, was prepared to scream.

Once the door was open she cautiously peeped through. She laughed shakily and her heart rate began to steady. The room beyond was a perfectly ordinary bedroom shrouded in Holland covers.

The secret door, as expected, simply led into number 10, Carne Terrace.

Of course, that meant that it led into the home of the wicked earl. A proper young lady, assuming that she hadn't already fallen into the vapors, would at this point have run to Papa to have the door firmly nailed shut. Anna Featherstone, fairly bubbling with excitement, walked through to explore.

After all, the earl was not here, and had not been here for years. In confirmation, this room—which was probably the master bedroom—had the feel of a place long unused.

Anna turned to look at the fireplace and found it to be

much more normal than the one on her side, though rather ornate for a bedchamber. It was of carved wood and had the heavy side panels necessary to disguise the moving parts.

Whatever the reason for this construction, there had obviously been a conspiracy by the residents of both houses, and she'd go odds it was all to do with *the incident*. Anna was not naive, and secretly connected bedchambers told their own story. Although she still wanted to know why the bedchamber in number 9 was so peculiar.

Being a careful person, Anna checked the mechanism before moving away from the door. Once she was sure she could return at will, she prepared to enjoy herself.

She was wickedly at large in someone else's house, and it was an adventure impossible to resist, especially when the risk was so small. Since the house was unused it was unlikely that she would be found out. And if she did meet anyone, she would hardly be thrown into prison. A young lady of sixteen in her nightgown could not be mistaken for a housebreaker.

Anna crept barefooted across the carpet and gingerly turned the knob. It made no sound. She eased the door open and peeped out into a corridor rather wider than the one in number 9. This corner house, a nobleman's residence, was at least twice the size of the other houses in the terrace.

She was struck by the silence.

It took Anna a moment to think why this was so strange, and then she realized that there was not even the ticking of a clock. She'd never before been in a house which did not have a clock ticking somewhere.

She detected no smell of decay or mold, though. The house might be unused but it was not neglected. In fact, now that she searched for it, there was the faint smell of polish in the air. This meant there had to be some servants and so she must be careful.

It did not mean she would give up her exploration,

though. This was like having an enormous playhouse all to herself.

She walked the corridor, shielding her candle and glancing at the pictures on the walls. They were not particularly interesting—mostly rather nondescript landscapes with no indication of the places they represented.

She peeped into the various rooms along the hall, but they were not interesting, either—some bedchambers and dressing rooms and a moderately sized drawing room.

Then, in a large sitting room or boudoir, she caught sight of an intriguing painting. She wasn't sure at first why it had caught her eye, as it was only half-lit by the flickering candle. When she went closer, she decided it was a simple matter of quality. She did not know a great deal about art but surely this portrait had been painted by a master.

Even in the candlelight the young man's skin tones glowed with vitality and his dark curls sprang crisply from his brow. His expression was quite sober and yet she could *feel* that he desperately wanted to laugh. Perhaps it was the way his bright blue eyes were crinkled slightly with the humor he was trying to suppress. Was he trying to appear older than he was? She didn't think he was a great deal older than her own sixteen years. He reminded her in many ways of her brother James and his friends, full of the joy of life and ready for mischief.

Of course, she reminded herself, by now this young man could be ancient.

She didn't think so, though. The high collar and plain cravat fitted recent fashion.

Anna realized she had been staring at the portrait as if expecting him to move and speak, so skillfully had the fleeting expression been captured. With a smile of farewell, she made herself leave the room, feeling rather as if she abandoned someone to dark neglect.

When she had looked in every room on this floor, she

came to her Rubicon, the stairs to the lower floor. A prudent miss would now return to her room and forget about this place. Anna had to admit as well that it was probably morally wrong to creep about someone's house like this, peeping and prying. It was almost like reading a private journal.

On the other hand, there were no secrets here. It was just an empty house and she wanted to see all of it.

She went cautiously down the stairs to the main floor.

All the windows she had seen had been curtained, presumably to keep the sun off the unused rooms, but here a handsome fan light over the door spilled moonlight into the hall, making it seem more alive, more as if someone might suddenly appear.

She stood still, her feet chilling on the tiled floor, listening for any sound.

She heard only silence. Any servants were fast asleep.

All the same, Anna decided to hurry through the rest of her exploration and get back to her bed.

A breakfast room, shrouded. A reception room, the same. A dining room, a library . . .

Anna halted, faced temptation, and succumbed.

Anna loved books. She loved novels, but they were not her only reading. Her father said she would read anything, even a sporting journal if desperate, and he had always encouraged her. He had not, however, allowed her to bring more than a small box of books with her and to her dismay the library in number 9 was a skeleton of a room with empty shelves. She supposed no one would want to leave books for unpredictable tenants, but she had been disappointed. After all, her consumption of books was so large that trips to the lending libraries were going to take most of her days!

Here, however, was a supply, to hand and neglected. The books seemed to call to her, begging to be read.

No, no, her conscience argued. To borrow without permission would be like stealing.

Yet Anna was soon cruising the glass-fronted shelves almost without thought, drawn like iron to a magnet. Rows and rows of matched volumes—bound magazines, philosophical classics, eminent sermons. But also rows and rows of mismatched books likely to have been bought for love.

And organized. Here was travel. Here was science. And here were novels.

Just one row.

In fact, just the novels of Mrs. Jamison. That was intriguing, to be sure.

She opened the case and ran her fingers over the glossy leather covers, pausing at the three volumes that comprised *Forbidden Affections*. She wanted to read it again in Dulcinea's room to check the accuracy of the simulation. She wanted it so much it was agony to resist.

But Anna knew that if she took the books she would have gone beyond an intrusion of privacy to theft. She found the strength to close the bookcase doors and leave the chamber of temptation.

Frightened that she would weaken, Anna ran up the stairs and back to the secret door. Her candle blew out, but she knew the way. She groped toward the fireplace and squeezed through the door, easing it shut behind her. Then she was back in her own room again with that door firmly closed.

She jumped into bed and pulled up the covers, then lay there, wondering if what she had just done had been real. But she knew it had, and she knew she desperately wanted to explore again another day.

Anna awoke the next morning when Martha, middle-aged maid to the Featherstone daughters, drew back the curtains to let in sunlight. Anna's first thought was that she had had the most interesting dream.

It took only seconds to realize that it had actually happened.

The room was still the same, and in daylight assuredly Dulcinea's chamber.

"What a room this is!" declared Martha, setting the jug of hot water on the washstand. "You're a braver lass than I am, Miss Anna, to sleep here so sound."

Anna sat up to hug her knees. "I don't mind. I like it."

Martha just shook her head. "Up with you, miss. I'll be back in a little while to button you up and fix your hair."

Anna popped out of bed and washed, then put on her stockings and petticoat. She was just working into her light stays when Martha returned to help her.

"How do you like it here, Martha?" Anna asked, holding her long plait away from the buttons down her back.

"Seems a decent enough house, miss. Sit you down now. Breakfast'll be ready in a moment."

Anna sat in front of the gargoyle-guarded mirror. "Have you found out anything about this place?"

"About it?" Martha was quickly unraveling the plait and brushing it out. "What do you mean, miss?"

"Well, about this room. It is a little strange."

"Who knows what they do in Lunnon, miss? The regular staff haven't said anything, but then, by the time we were here and unpacked, it were pretty well time for bed."

"I suppose so."

The Featherstones had arrived at nearly eight in the evening and had only taken time for supper before retiring. They were here until June, however. Time enough for Anna to unravel the mystery this room presented, and to find out all about the wicked Earl of Carne's *incident*.

As soon as Martha was finished, Anna ran down to the breakfast parlor and kissed her parents. Lady Featherstone, slender and blond, smiled in a slightly pained way at her younger daughter's high spirits. Sir Jeffrey hugged her warmly.

"Sleep well, Pippin, in your Gothic chamber?"

Anna had to suppress a giggle. "Very well, Papa."

Lady Featherstone shuddered. "Anna, you have no sensibility."

"Which is as well, my dear," said her husband, "or the girls would have had to sleep together, and you know they hate that." Sir Jeffrey was ruddy-faced and robust. It was from him that Anna got her looks and temperament.

"Maria tosses and turns all night," said Anna.

"Only in a strange bed," said Maria, drifting in wanly. "I declare I have not had a moment's rest! The mattress is decidedly hard."

If Maria was poorly rested, it had not affected her looks. She, like Dulcinea, was a pale blond beauty with pearly skin and a slender, elegant figure. Lady Featherstone fussed over her, commiserating on her sensitive nature and plying her with tea.

Sir Jeffrey grinned at Anna. "Well, what plans for today, Pippin? Let me guess. An attack on the book emporiums of the Metropolis?"

Anna grinned back as she helped herself to eggs. "Most certainly. I am hoping you will direct me to the best lending libraries in town, Papa."

Since Sir Jeffrey was a Member of Parliament, he knew London quite well and obligingly wrote out a list of the best book suppliers while his wife and older daughter planned their assault on modistes and haberdashers.

Folding the list, Anna asked casually, "What was Mrs. Postle referring to when she mentioned an incident concerning our neighbor, Papa?" She had reason to hope that her liberal-minded father would give her a straight answer.

However, his only response was, "Never you mind, Pippin. London isn't like the country. It is quite possible to ignore neighbors."

"But Papa, the doors are only feet apart. What if we encounter people coming and going?"

Her mother had picked up on the conversation and now a look flashed between her parents. Anna's curiosity expanded to a bursting point. What *had* the earl done?

"Anna," said her mother, "if you should happen to encounter any of our neighbors, a distant nod will suffice until you have been formally introduced. Which is unlikely since you are not here to *be* introduced."

It was Maria who let the cat out of the bag. "Martha said that number 10 had a murder there some years back. Can you imagine? It makes me feel quite faint to think of it!"

Lady Featherstone began to say something sharp about the maid, but her husband overruled her. "It is perhaps as well, my dear, that the girls be prepared. Maria, Anna, it is true that an irregular death occurred at the Earl of Carne's house some years ago, but it was suicide, not murder. It is an old matter and need not disturb you at all, but you should know that the earl, despite his rank, is not the sort of man who is introduced to young ladies. I am assured that he lives abroad, but if you should encounter him, you will ignore him entirely."

Anna stared. "Cut an earl?"

"If the man has a scrap of decency that will not be necessary. But if he should turn up and approach you in any way, yes, you must refuse to acknowledge him."

This was hardly the sort of talk to calm Anna's bubbling curiosity, but she could see she would get nothing more out of her parents. She would have to hope the servants would be more forthcoming. It was typical, though, that Martha had told more to Maria than she had to Anna. It was so tedious being a schoolroom miss.

Immediately after breakfast Maria and Lady Feather-stone embarked on matters to do with Society. Sir Jeffrey warned Anna to go nowhere without both maid and foot-man, then went out to Parliament. Anna obediently sum-moned Martha and a footman and set out for the best lending library in London, her main intent being to bring home a copy of *Forbidden Affections*.

As they walked, Arthur, the footman, pointed out the sights, and the occasional famous person passing by.

Anna was interested in London, but she could not stop puzzling over the matter of number 10. "London seems so crowded," she said at one point. "I'm surprised the house next door to us is allowed to stay empty."

"Criminal waste of a house, I'd say," Martha remarked with a sniff.

Arthur shrugged. "It's the earl's to waste, Miss Anna, and he's rich enough not to care."

"But there must be servants," Anna probed.

"Just a couple who keep the place up. The Murchisons have got it easy, and that's the truth. The whole place is under covers, they say."

Anna waited, hoping for more, but it became clear that if she wanted more information, she'd have to dig for it. "And no one has lived in it for years?"

"That's right, miss. Ever since the earl's ladybird was found dead there."

"Arthur!" exclaimed Martha. "I'll thank you to remem-ber that Miss Anna is still a schoolroom miss!"

Anna could have strangled Martha. Just as the conversa-tion was becoming interesting!

The earl's ladybird? That meant lover. So the earl's lover had committed suicide in number 10? Embarrassing, certainly, but enough to send a peer of the realm into exile?

Hardly.

And why had Maria reported it as murder?

These thoughts tumbled around in Anna's head as she gathered an armful of books at Hatchards. She did not find a copy of *Forbidden Affections* so asked a clerk for assistance. He consulted the large book which served as their catalogue. "I'm afraid we no longer have a copy, miss."

"What? Why on earth not?"

At her sharp tone he looked rather harried. "It is eight years old, miss. Possibly one of the volumes was lost or damaged . . . May I recommend this one?"

Anna listened politely as he recommended a number of the latest romantic novels, and even took one to allay suspicion. She knew it was irrational to think that Martha and Arthur, who were standing by chatting, would read anything into her desire for a copy of *Forbidden Affections,* but she felt compelled to disguise her feelings.

She wanted no one to discover her secret until she had solved the mysteries of Carne Terrace. And she wanted to solve them on her own.

She would have liked to go to another library to continue her search for the novel, but how could she with Arthur already burdened with at least two days' reading? Seething at the stupidity of a library that didn't have multiple copies of every one of Mrs. Jamison's novels, Anna returned home.

Releasing Martha and Arthur to their other duties, she sat down to read. The books she had selected were interesting, but she could not concentrate on any of them. Her mind was full of Lord Carne, his dead lover, and the Gothic chamber of Dulcinea. In fact, Anna knew she was merely passing time until that night when she could explore again.

By mid-afternoon she could restrain her curiosity no longer and wandered into the kitchen where the cook, Mrs. Jones, and two maids were preparing dinner.

"Hungry, miss?" asked the wiry woman pleasantly enough. "There's maids-of-honor there that could do with testing."

Anna grinned at the cook and sat at the table to nibble an almond tart. "They're delicious," she said honestly. "Alas, I don't think my stay here will increase my chances of becoming thin and interesting."

"Let's not have any of that nonsense, miss. Some healthy padding serves a woman well. And there's many a gentleman likes an armful." Mrs. Jones pushed another cake over to Anna.

Anna did not actually want another one, but she took it with a smile. "I certainly hope so, since I am to have your cooking. I'm sure they should charge extra for this house if you come with it."

The cook preened. "Been here nigh on ten years, miss, and there's been no complaints. Maggie, stop beating those eggs now and put the water on."

A rather slack-faced maid put aside a big bowl of eggs and went to haul a copper pot onto the stove.

Anna decided on a direct approach to one part of the puzzle. "Were you here when my bedroom was made?"

The woman rolled her eyes. "That Chamber of Horrors? Aye. It was a fancy of the mistress of the time, Lady Delabury . . ." The woman broke off what she was about to say. "Maggie, the *big* pan!"

With a clatter, one pan was put down and another picked up.

"She must have been very fond of novels," Anna prompted.

The cook looked at her in surprise and with a touch of suspicion. "How did you know that, miss?"

"Oh, there are rooms like that in many novels." Anna dropped her voice and made it sound mysterious. "Usually in the less-frequented parts of moldering castles, hung with cobwebs and infested by rats . . ."

Both the cook and the two maids were staring at her.

"Well, there's no rats in this house!" declared Mrs.

Jones. "It makes a bit of sense, though," she added more moderately, "since Lady Delabury wrote those sorts of books."

"Wrote them?" Anna almost choked on a pastry crumb.

"Not under her own name, of course. Mrs. Jamison, that was the name she used, even when she were a single lady . . . All right, Maggie, stop gawking and add those bones . . . ! She was a lovely lady, miss, very like your sister. Lord Delabury would have done anything for her, so when she wanted that room he had it made. Dreadful upset, he was, about her death."

A Dulcinea, in other words. No wonder Mrs. Jamison's heroines were always of that type. But then why the doorway into the other house? Lady Delabury had her Roland.

Perhaps. Perhaps the poor lady had been married to Count Nacre and had dreamed of escape.

"What was Lord Delabury like?" Anna asked.

"Oh, a very handsome young man and a good employer. He gave up living here, though, after the death, and stays at his estate in the north nearly all the time. A sad tale . . . Maggie, come cut up these turnips . . . Look, miss, we've got to get on with dinner now."

Anna took the hint, but instead of returning to the house, she chose to wander out into the garden, her mind churning with speculation. For Lady Delabury to have a room made in the image of a chamber in one of her books was eccentric but understandable. For her to incorporate a secret doorway into the house next door was another matter entirely. For one thing, it would surely require the consent of the owners of both properties.

And if the secret door was part of *the incident,* and Arthur had been right in what he said, then Lady Delabury had been the Earl of Carne's ladybird even though she was quite recently married to a pleasant young man who adored her. And she had killed herself.

It was all deliciously intriguing.

Anna played with ideas as she wandered the uninspired garden, pulling up a weed here or there. At the limit of the garden she turned to look back at the row of houses. They told her nothing, however. Number 10, with its blinds drawn, was particularly uncommunicative.

There was a gate in the back of the garden and Anna saw that it opened onto the mews. There was a gate from the mews into the garden of number 10, too. She resisted the temptation to explore. The garden was unlikely to hold the key to the mystery.

She returned to the house and her unsatisfactory books, and waited for night.

To Anna's frustration, her family was no longer tired from the journey, and they would never believe it if she claimed to be. If she tried to go to bed early, they'd send for the doctor.

It was very pleasant to play whist and read a little, but she was desperate to go adventuring.

The only progress she made with her mystery came from one comment by her father.

"I don't think we need worry about the earl. The general opinion seems to be that he died on one of his wild adventures. In fact his heir, a cousin, has started a court case to have him declared dead."

"I think that's rather horrid," Anna said, thinking of the young man in the portrait, for she suspected he might be the earl.

"It's practical, Pippin. Servants are all very well, but a large estate should not be left unsupervised for so many years."

Conversation turned then to another case of neglect and Anna learned nothing more.

At half-past ten, Lady Featherstone declared that it was

time for her daughters to get their beauty sleep and they obligingly went to their bedrooms.

Martha came and went, Anna was officially in bed, and at last the adventure could begin. Even if the earl were dead, there was a mystery to be solved. She needed to do some research, and the library of number 10 was the place to do it. Anna had persuaded her conscience that if she didn't take the books away it was not very naughty, and so she slipped through into the next house. Once there, she crept quickly, carefully, down the stairs to the library.

Safely behind the closed door, she placed her candle on the marquetry table and surveyed the bound copies of magazines and journals. Somewhere among them would be mention of *the incident.*

She looked first at the yearly report called *The Annual Register.* It did not take her long to find a reference, though it was frustratingly brief.

May 25, 1809. On this night a great uproar was heard in the handsome environs of Carne Terrace, when a lady of gentle birth and fine family was found to have done away with herself by means of laudanum. This tragic event was made bewildering because the lady, wife of Viscount D******y, died not in her own bed, but in the bed of her neighbor, the Earl of C****.

Heavens! That certainly would have set the cat among the pigeons.

The noble earl, however, was not in residence at the time, being at his estate in Norfolk.

And that must certainly have saddened the scandal mongers. Still, many had clearly deduced that the lady was his mistress.

Unless it had been well-known before.

The circumstances were made yet more mysterious by the fact that the earl's heir, Lord M********le, was hosting a bachelor party on a lower floor. Neither he, his well-born

guests, nor the servants saw the lady enter in her nightgown.
A doctor was summoned, but life had long since departed.

Anna stopped to ponder that. Who was the present earl?
The one whose bed the lady had chosen to die in, or the heir
carousing downstairs? She suspected the latter, and a glance
at Burke's confirmed it. The current earl was now thirty
years old and there was no Lord Manderville. What was
more startling was that the earl had acceded to the title in
May 1809, only days after Lady Delabury's death.

Anna returned the Burke's to the shelf and searched
other publications for more details. She had almost given
up when she found more in the *London Report*.

The account of the event was similar to that in *The
Annual Register*, but this one continued to cover the inquest.

*. . . a doctor brought in by the lady's grieving husband
stated that certain bruises on the arms suggested that the
lady could have been compelled to consume the cause of
her death, but since it was equally impossible that a murderer sneak into the house, and as Lord M********le and
his friends all vouched for one another, that none had left
the room during the evening, and in view of the fact that the
lady was found clutching a farewell note to her poor be-
reaved husband, a judgment of suicide was made.*

Anna closed the book. No wonder people thought the
worst of the current earl, the then Lord Manderville. The
death had been suspicious, and it was more than likely that
he and his cronies would stick together.

What puzzled her was that no one seemed to know
about the secret door or they would not wonder how Lady
Delabury gained access to this house. It was particularly
strange that Lord Delabury not know of it. Could he, in
fact, have been the murderer?

She would dearly like to know what was in that note.
What reason had the beautiful, talented young woman

given for taking her life? Guilt because she was Lord Manderville's mistress?

But why had a recently married woman sought a lover? Anna assumed Lord Manderville was the young man of the portrait, so she could see the appeal, but it did seem strange behavior, even for London. It suggested that her husband must have been a monster beneath his charming exterior.

But what of Lord Manderville, the prime suspect? Anna could believe that the young man of the portrait—a few years older—would have taken a neighbor's wife as lover. She could believe he had spent an evening carousing with his friends. She could not believe that he would have callously forced his mistress to drink laudanum.

She sat at the table, chin on hands, to ponder it all. What else might have happened? If Lady Delabury had been Lord Manderville's mistress, then she might have been at his party. Had it been some kind of orgy? Anna had read enough ancient history to know about orgies. She understood that quite sensible people could be carried into extremes of vice and passion.

Perhaps the young man had gone into exile out of grief and guilt because his wild party had turned into fatal disaster—especially if the events had led to the death of his father, perhaps from shame . . .

The candle was shrinking and it was time for Anna to return to her own room. She replaced the books thoughtfully, informed but dissatisfied. There was surely a great deal more to *the incident* but she was no longer sure what questions to ask.

Before leaving, she turned to the shelf of novels, wondering if there might be answers there. There clearly was some connection between *Forbidden Affections* and the unfortunate death, since the author had caused that room to be made.

Anna opened the glass door and hesitated. She would

have to take the volumes back to her room to study them, and that was the line she had drawn for herself—she would not remove anything from the house.

But she needed to know the truth. She reached out for the first volume of *Forbidden Affections*—

With a click, the door behind her opened.

Anna froze, wondering in wild irrationality whether staying very still would make her invisible. But it wouldn't, so she turned slowly to stare, appalled, at the man staring back at her.

She was caught.

And surely she was caught by the wicked earl himself. Tall, dark, and authoritative, it was the young man in the picture some ten or more years older.

The astonished silence stretched, and then the earl closed the door and approached. "I was not aware that the Murchisons had hired staff. You do know you are likely to be on the street in the morning, girl?"

He thought her a servant intruding where she had no business to be. "Beg pardon, sir," Anna mumbled, thinking furiously. If she could just get out of this room without revealing her identity, he might never know who she was.

She was going to die of embarrassment if this got back to her parents!

He came closer, and her heart raced with even more immediate fears. Gracious, but he was tall and broad. Of course, that could be the effect of his heavily caped greatcoat. But then he shrugged it off and dropped it on a chair and was still tall and broad. His dark jacket and leather riding breeches did not soften him one bit.

She remembered the portrait wistfully. That young man had seemed a friend, but this person was entirely different. There was no laughter in those blue eyes now and the lines of his face spoke of experience and ruthless ways. He even bore a scar down one cheek. Wicked or not, Anna feared the earl was most certainly a dangerous man.

Was he a murderer, though?

If he discovered that she had been looking into the death of Lady Delabury, would he kill again?

Anna was not of a nervous temperament, but she liked to think she knew when it was reasonable to be afraid.

She was afraid now.

He sat in a winged chair, stretched his legs as if he owned the place, and eyed her thoughtfully.

He does own the place! Anna told her mind, which was turning giddy with fear. *Think. Think. We have to get out of here!*

She considered running for the door but had no doubt that he could stop her. If she was to conceal her identity, she had to persuade him to let her leave peaceably.

He slowly pulled off his black leather gloves, watching her every minute. "Since you're here, girl, you can make yourself useful. Pour me some brandy." When she did not move, he added, "I suppose it's to your credit that you don't know where it is. In that table there. Raise the lid and there should be glasses and a full decanter unless my orders have been ignored."

Anna swallowed and went to the table to do as he said. Other reasons for fear were occurring to her. She was here alone with a gentleman—a wicked gentleman—in her *nightgown.* With not a stitch under it! Even though it was of thick cotton, high-necked and long-sleeved, she felt as if he must feel her nakedness as she did, open to the breeze of her movements across the room. He would know from her bare feet that she wore no stockings.

Just see what a bramble-patch your curiosity has led you to, Anna Featherstone! And you knew all along it was wrong and foolish.

Anna's hands shook as she opened the table to lift the

heavy-based tumbler and the cut-glass decanter. She managed to pour the brandy without spilling any, then put the decanter down and turned.

His brows were raised. "Do you think you're serving a dowager? Fill it up, girl!"

Anna looked at the glass, at the modest amount she had poured, the amount her father would drink. A full glass would surely deprive a man of his wits. But that might be good. She filled it almost to the brim.

Then she had to take it to him. She wished her arms would suddenly become ten feet long, but they didn't and so she had to walk over to stand by his chair.

She waited, but he made no attempt to reach for the glass, and so she had to press against his stretched legs to put it in his right hand. His boots rubbed against her calves through the cotton and something—almost an emanation— set her nerves jumping with panic. As soon as he took the glass she stepped back but his left hand shot out to seize the front of her nightdress.

"Oh, no, you don't. What's your name?"

Anna leaned back, desperate that his hand not brush her body. "Maggie!" she gasped, plucking the first name that came to mind.

He gathered in more of the cotton, pulling her closer, bringing her body close to his fist. "Well, Maggie, were you going to steal the books, or can you actually read?"

"I can read, sir!"

He drank from the glass in his right hand. "My lord," he corrected. A glint in his eye told her he knew just how uncomfortable she was.

"Sorry, milord," she muttered, though she wanted to do the wretch a very painful physical injury. What right had he to tease a poor maid this way, even if he had found her in his library? And more to the point, what were his true intentions? Anna knew how the wicked part of the world behaved.

"You'll have to prove it," he said.

Anna jumped. "Prove what, milord?"

He abruptly released her. "That you can read. Choose one of those revolting novels and read me a passage."

Anna thought again of running, but knew it was pointless. Instead she accepted the test. Once he saw she was in here in search of reading material, perhaps he would let her go even if he did intend to dismiss her in the morning. Once she was out of this room unescorted, she could be back in her bed in moments.

She returned to the shelf. Avoiding *Forbidden Affections,* she chose *Cruel Matrimony.*

When she opened it, she realized with surprise that it had never been read. The pages weren't even cut. She could read the first page, however.

"Was any woman so profoundly miserable as beautiful Melisande de La Fleur when the dreadful news descended upon her? She was to wed the dread lord of Breadalbane? Never!"

"Enough," said the earl disdainfully, swallowing more brandy. "So you *can* read, and with an educated accent, too. Who the devil are you?"

Anna cursed her carelessness in letting her servant's tones drop, and knew she was turning red with guilt. "I was raised gently, yes, my lord, but have no choice now but service."

"Plunged into dire poverty, are you?" His voice gentled as he said, "Perhaps we can find you an alternative to base service, my dear. Loose your hair."

It took a moment for Anna to guess his meaning, but then her breath caught. "No. Please, my lord——"

"Obey me." It was said without great emphasis, yet it chilled her protests.

Anna heard a whimper, and knew it was her own. She should scream, but who would hear?

What would happen if she told him who she was? Would the wicked Earl of Carne continue his vile seduction when he knew she was the gently bred daughter of his neighbor?

If he did, said the logical part of her, then he'd care as much later as now. Perhaps he was just playing with her and would let her go in a little while. After all, she was hardly the sort of girl to drive men wild, especially a man like this.

So Anna took off her ribbon and fingered her dark hair loose, knowing her naturally rosy cheeks were apple red.

He eyed her over the rim of the glass, studying her dispassionately from tousled head to naked toes. "Very pretty. How old are you?"

"But sixteen, milord."

"There's no use putting on that servant's burr again, sweetheart. Sixteen's a good age." He drained the glass and placed it on a table by his elbow. "Come here."

The slight slur in his voice alarmed her. She suspected he'd not been entirely sober when he came in, and was now worse. Any belief that he would be rational was weakening and she glanced around in search of a weapon. There wasn't so much as a penknife.

"Please, my lord, let me go. I'm sorry for having intruded—"

"But having done so, you must pay the toll." His eyes were hooded. "A kiss," he said with wicked softness. "No more, Maggie, or not yet. My word on it. Come here."

Anna discovered that her feet simply wouldn't carry her over to him. "I can't . . ."

He raised his brows. "I could threaten to dismiss you tomorrow. Yet why do I feel that wouldn't sway you? So, I'll make another threat. If you don't come here and be kissed, my sweet mysterious Maggie, I'll come to you and do much worse. And you have my word on that, too."

After a moment, he added, "That trembling innocence, the hands over the mouth, the eyes wide with panic, will not sway me. It's actually quite arousing, you know. We men are such perverse creatures. You'd do better to appear bold and willing. I'd probably dismiss you on the instant."

Anna realized she was reacting exactly as he said, but she *was* a trembling innocent. "I wouldn't kn . . . know how to act bold, m . . . my lord," she stammered. "Have mercy."

"Damnation, girl," he said without heat, "it's a kiss I'm demanding, not a life of sin. You'll be the better for getting over these nervous tremors. *Come here.*"

The snapped authority in the last words had Anna walking toward him before she thought. He caught her nightgown before she could retreat and pulled her onto his lap. She did scream then, and struggled, but it did no good. He just laughed. "Squirm away, Maggie. It's quite interesting, and in moments your legs will be naked as the day you were born."

Anna went very, very still.

"Wise girl," he said, and even smoothed her nightgown back around her legs—a touch that sent a jolt right through her.

He ignored it, and spoke soothingly. "There, see, the heavens haven't fallen. Satan hasn't appeared to drag you off to hell. Kissing is not a cardinal sin. You might even enjoy it. I suspect I will." He caught her chin, smiling as a thumb rubbed along her jaw.

Anna twitched. "My lord!"

"Oh, do stop my lording me, girl! If we're to share a kiss I'll make you free of my name for a while. It's Roland."

"Roland?" Astonishment temporarily overwhelmed even fear.

He continued to rub along her jaw, gently, confusingly. "Why the amazement, sweetheart? Perhaps my parents had high hopes of me."

"It . . . it's an unusual name, my lord. You are called for Charlemagne's hero?"

He grinned. "No. I'm called for a rich great-uncle who obligingly left me his all." His finger was tracing the edge of her lips now, as if learning of them.

Or perhaps he knew the extraordinary effect it could have on a woman . . .

"Roland was a noble character, though, my lord," Anna said desperately. In a moment she was going to have to tell him who she was. "*Roland est preux . . .*"

"She speaks French, too! *Chérie,* you are wasted in the kitchens. Let us proceed with your metamorphosis to a higher order." He deftly moved her more intimately to his body and dropped a light kiss on her tingling lips. "You're as tasty as a rosy apple, sweetheart. I think I'll call you Pippin."

At that use of her father's pet name, it was as if he were here, witness to her shame.

Anna burst into tears.

The earl froze, but did not let her go. To her astonishment, after a moment he held her closer and even rocked her a little. "Hush, Pippin. What the devil's the matter with you? We're talking a kiss here. It'll go no further today if you're not of a mind to it. I'm no rapist and we've plenty of time . . ."

His very reasonable and rather bemused tone calmed Anna's worst fears. She peeped up at him cautiously, sniffing.

But perhaps seducers always behaved like this . . .

"That's better," he said soothingly, thumbing tears from beneath her eyes and stroking strands of hair off her face. "Just a kiss, a taste, Pippin. And then I'll let you leave. This time."

Heart pounding, Anna held on to that. One kiss and she could go.

And she would never come back here again!

But when his lips brushed over hers—a gentle, brandy-flavored roughness—she flinched away instinctively. He was ready for it and trapped her head, preventing all effort to avoid the deepening of the kiss.

Anna tried to protest, but since her mouth was now covered by his, it came out as only a mewling sound. Her hands were trapped against his body and she truly feared that if she squirmed she would reveal all.

God help her, what would happen if her parents ever found out about this?

He ignored her struggles and protests, but released her mouth long enough to say, "You've the sweetest-tasting mouth I've known in a long time, Pippin."

"My lord, please—"

But then he was kissing her again, pushing her mouth open, touching her tongue with his so she squeaked and struggled violently. But then, abruptly, like a wave crashing over her, Anna realized there was pleasure in it.

There couldn't be.

But there was.

It was like the first time she had eaten oysters. She hadn't liked the thought of it at all, and hadn't liked the first attempt much. But then, somehow, she had overcome the thought that the shellfish were alive, and that they were a little slimy, and had discovered they were delicious.

She had never liked the idea of this kind of kissing, and hadn't liked the first mingling of his mouth with hers, but now she found that he, too, was delicious—sweet and spicy beneath the tang of brandy.

In moments the moist heat of his tongue seemed as natural as her own, and that acceptance spread downward through her body, relaxing her . . .

He released her mouth with slow, parting kisses, smiling more warmly now, more like the youth in the portrait. "That's it, Pippin, my rosy, juicy little apple. You see what's in store? You needn't fear I'll mistreat you. I'll take care of you . . ."

Anna suddenly realized that his hand was sliding *under* her nightdress and took in the meaning of his words.

She kicked against his touch. "No, my lord! Truly, I cannot be your mistress!"

Despite her squirming, his hand ventured slightly higher, up to her knee. "You didn't think you'd like kissing, Maggie. Let's see how you like this . . ."

"No . . . *Help!*" Anna tried to put the full force of her healthy lungs behind it but he clapped a hand over her mouth and laughed at her struggles.

So much for his promises!

As he looked down with interest at the leg her struggle was exposing, Anna saw the glint of the glass he had set down. She stretched out, seized it, and swung it with all her strength to crash against her ravisher's head.

With a cry, he relaxed his hold.

Anna tore herself free.

He was cursing now and holding his head. Anna was dreadfully afraid that she'd done him some terrible injury, but that was even more reason to flee.

She raced into the hall and up the steps, her heart thundering, her breath mere gasps of panic. In moments she was through the door and back in her bedroom.

She slid to the floor in limp relief, offering earnest prayers of thanks to the deity who watched over foolish virgins.

Which made her think of lamps.

Which made her realize a terrible thing.

She'd left the candlestick!

At that moment, Anna Featherstone nearly fainted.

She wanted to huddle under her covers and pretend none of the recent events had happened but if she didn't retrieve the candlestick, it would be obvious she'd been there. Quite apart from the fact that she would be short a candlestick, it was probably identifiable as from this house.

What on earth would happen to her? What if she'd done some terrible injury to the earl? What if he was lying on his library floor breathing his last?

Would they hang her?

At least, said a voice, if he's dead he can't identify his assailant.

But the candlestick could.

There was only one thing to do.

Anna's legs felt weak as wet paper, but she forced herself to her feet. Still shaking and struggling not to sob, she opened the secret door again to re-enter the Earl of Carne's cursed house.

She staggered out onto the landing, listening carefully for any hint of what was happening. She heard a voice. It was the earl, apparently calling for a servant.

Anna almost collapsed with relief again. He didn't sound at all dead. But in that case, how was she to retrieve the evidence?

Then she realized that he was heading for the lower floor, shouting for his servants. She leaned over the stair rail and saw him, holding a white cloth to his head, disappear in that direction.

It almost demanded too much courage, but Anna forced herself. She ran down the stairs, tracking that distant voice all the time, dashed into the library, grabbed the candlestick, and raced back to her own room.

Once there, she flung herself into bed, pulled the covers over her head, and swore that she would never, ever, give in to curiosity again!

"Miss Anna! Miss Anna! Wake up."

Anna stirred, resisting the call to wake. She'd been

sleepless half the night worrying over the consequences of her actions.

"Miss Anna! Are you all right?"

Anna forced her eyes open. "Yes, Martha. Of course I'm all right."

Martha frowned at her in grave concern. "I've never known you to be a slugabed. Are you sure you're not sickening or something?

Anna struggled up, trying to appear her usual cheery self. "Of course I'm not! I must have just stayed up reading longer than I intended."

"The state of the candle tells *that* story, miss," said Martha with a glance at the candlestick.

Full memory rushed back and Anna winced at the thought of the story that candlestick could tell. Along with memory came anxiety. What would Lord Carne have done when he couldn't find Maggie? Had he called in the Bow Street Runners?

One thing was certain, Anna must make sure the man never set eyes on her. She leaned back against her pillows. "Perhaps I might be catching a cold," she said in a suffering tone. "My head aches a little . . ."

Martha came back to the bed and studied her. "You don't look yourself, Miss Anna, and that's the truth. Why, you've even taken off your ribbon and got your hair in a tangle. You must have been fevered in the night." She shook her head. "You'd best stay in bed for now. I'll bring you breakfast here and tell Lady Featherstone."

Martha left and Anna groaned. Her hair ribbon. She'd left evidence after all!

It wasn't a disaster, though. A candlestick was one thing, but a plain white hair ribbon could belong to anyone. It fretted her, though, so she was in danger of becoming truly ill through anxiety.

She took refuge in planning. The first thing was to stay

out of sight for as long as possible, and being sick was an excellent excuse. It would be tedious, but far better than bumping into Lord Carne on the doorstep!

What was she going to do, though, if he intended more than a brief visit to his London house?

She rubbed her hands over her face. She should have known her mad behavior would lead to disaster. At the thought of what might have been, she shuddered. If that glass hadn't been to hand, she might have been ruined beyond all repair!

To a young lady raised in the country, known by all and well-guarded, it scarce seemed credible that a chance encounter—no matter how peculiar—could have ruined her life, but it was so.

Lord Carne could have stolen her virtue by brute strength. Truth obliged her to admit that he might have managed to steal it by clever seductions.

Anna stared sightlessly at a grinning gargoyle and absorbed the fact that she had almost been seduced by a stranger.

Lady Featherstone was no believer in innocence as defense against ruin. She had informed her daughters about carnal matters, and warned them that the perils of the flesh sometimes included the temptations of pleasure. Her instruction was to avoid occasions of intimacy in case their consciences turned weak on them.

"And that frequently happens," she had said. "Not many unfortunate girls *intend* their ruin. They are caught unawares and either forced, tricked, or seduced into depravity. And seduction means that they succumbed to pleasure. So be on your guard and avoid the very occasions of sin, girls. Prudent, well-behaved young ladies do not come to grief."

Anna had never really believed that she could be forced, tricked, or seduced into ruin, but then she'd never anticipated anyone like the Earl of Carne. Cautiously, she allowed her memory to bring to mind the man she had met last night, trying to decide what made him so dangerous. Handsome, yes. But not in a smooth, gentle way. He was lean, hard, and had proved to be alarmingly strong.

Anna shuddered at the memory of being as helpless as a struggling toddler.

Perhaps, however, that very strength was part of the seductive appeal that lingered even now as a spicy sweetness beneath anxiety. Certainly something about him had speeded her pulse and weakened her knees in a way she had never experienced before, and it hadn't entirely been fear.

Unless it was fear of the wantonness he had so easily summoned in her.

Yet another reason to avoid the earl. Anna was no fool.

Sometimes it was best not to put one's willpower to the test.

She sat up straighter and turned her mind to assessing her situation and making plans.

With luck and caution, Anna decided, she might escape the consequences of her folly. She was not ruined, and it did not seem Lord Carne was seriously injured. He was doubtless puzzled as to the identity of Maggie, but if Anna stayed concealed for a day or two, all could be well. The earl would surely move on, either to travel again or to inspect his neglected estates.

Martha returned with a breakfast tray and Lady Featherstone, who laid a cool hand on Anna's brow. "You do not seem fevered, my dear. Are you in pain?"

"Just the headache, Mama."

Anna's mother studied her with intent concern and Anna felt sure she would read every secret. But eventually Lady Featherstone said, "I don't think there is anything much amiss. Perhaps it is just the excitement of the city. Or this horrid room. Do you want to share Maria's room?"

"No, Mama!"

With a shake of her head, Lady Featherstone dropped the subject. "Rest today, then, and I am sure you will soon be more the thing. But if you feel the need we will send for the doctor."

When her mother had left, Anna settled to her breakfast, then asked Martha to help her dress, saying she would sit quietly on a chaise by the window. It was true that she had no desire to spend the day in bed, but she had other reasons. Her room looked out onto the street, and she wanted to be able to observe the comings and goings at number 10.

Preferably the goings.

What she hoped to see was the Earl of Carne entering a well-piled coach, clearly headed for foreign lands, or at least for the provinces. What she actually saw were two fashionable gentlemen stroll up and be admitted. Since they stayed about an hour, and neither looked like a doctor, Anna felt able to assume that the earl was not on his deathbed.

When two coaches arrived, Anna experienced a moment of hope, but then the chests and boxes were taken *into* the house. "Oh, no," she muttered. "The wretch is taking up residence!"

Anna looked at the fireplace in alarm, then hurried over to push a solid bench in front of the secret door. It might not prevent a forcible entry, but it would prevent a silent one.

But how was she to avoid a meeting if the earl was to stay next door?

When Martha came to offer her lunch, Anna said, "There seems to be some activity at number 10. Has the earl leased the house after all?"

Martha put her tray on the table and started to lay out the meal. "Nay, miss. Believe it or not, his lordship's come back. Arrived in the night without warning! And," she added in a whisper, "it's to be feared he's mad."

"Mad?" Dear heaven. Had her blow deprived him of his wits?

Martha looked around as if expecting an angel to come and silence her, then leaned closer. "He came knocking at the kitchen door this morning, miss."

"The earl?" Anna's heart started to flutter with panic. He knew! How did he know?

Martha leaned even closer. "The wicked earl himself! And the Lord knows what wickedness he'd been up to, Miss Anna, for he'd a mighty wound on his temple, all swollen and bruised-like. I tell you true, miss, none of us thought we were safe!"

"Whatever did he want?" Anna whispered back, wondering why the heavens had not already fallen on her.

"You'll never believe it . . ."

"What?"

"He wanted Maggie! Poor little Maggie, who might be a bit slow, but hasn't a scrap of bad in her!"

Anna didn't know what to say.

"Mind you," said Martha, straightening to rearrange a mustard pot on the small table, "the earl did come to his senses after a fashion. As soon as he clapped eyes on her he looked right bewildered. Apologized for disturbing us and took himself off.

"Sad, really," she said with a shake of her head. "Mrs. Postle says he was a right promising young man once, before . . . well, before. Certain it is though, Miss Anna, that you must keep out of that man's way. I'm sure your parents are going to be very concerned to know that he's settling in next door."

Lord and Lady Featherstone certainly were concerned, the lady rather more than the lord. Over dinner that evening she said, "You must be very careful, girls. Very careful. He has already shown his true flags."

Lady Featherstone left it there, so Anna decided to stimulate discussion. "You mean him crashing into the kitchen covered with blood demanding Maggie?"

Unfortunately, Maria had not heard the story. She shrieked and assumed her ready-to-faint posture, hand to heart.

Anna's father frowned. "Don't exaggerate, Pippin. And Maria, don't get into a taking. I am assured he knocked at the door and inquired after her in a fairly normal manner."

"Normal?" demanded Maria. "Papa, how can it be *normal* for an earl to turn up at the kitchen door asking after the scullery maid? He must be mad. We'll be murdered in our beds like that other woman!"

"Nonsense," said Sir Jeffrey. "I will not have such exaggerations, girls. Lady Delabury took too much laudanum and it was years ago. As for Maggie, though I did not like to do it, I called on the earl and asked an explanation. It appears he surprised an intruder in his house last night, a young woman who called herself Maggie. When he attempted to apprehend her, she hit him on the head, which accounts for his wound. When his servants told him a maid called Maggie served next door, he naturally assumed she would be the same."

"Then an honest man," said Lady Featherstone, "would have sent for a Runner!"

"A charitable man might not, my dear. I did not expect it, but I gained the impression that the earl was motivated by compassion. He admitted that he had frightened the girl into attacking him, and he thought she might have been lacking her wits . . ."

Anna almost choked on a piece of chicken. The wretch!

"So he decided to discover her," her father continued, "and speak to her superiors on the matter. Of course, since our scullery maid turned out not to be his quarry, he is no further forward in solving the mystery. And he did apologize for any upset he might have caused."

"So I should think!" Lady Featherstone declared.

"I must confess, my dear, that I was pleasantly surprised

by the earl. He seems a man of sense. We know he indulged in some youthful follies, but time can heal. I gather he has spent his recent years in the Eastern Mediterranean and he speaks intelligently of matters there. I suspect he may have been engaged on the King's business."

Her father might be quite in charity with their neighbor; Anna was not. She did not believe for one moment that Lord Carne had been moved by compassion. He either wanted revenge, or wished to continue his wicked plan to set "Maggie" up as his mistress.

Perhaps both.

Perhaps he had been intending to blackmail the poor, powerless maid into surrendering to his vile lust.

"Is the earl to stay in London, Papa?" she asked.

"It would appear so, my dear. His cousin's efforts to have him declared dead have obliged him to return and prove his existence. It seems that he intends to stay for some time."

"I cannot like it," said Lady Featherstone. "It will stir all those old stories, and since there is a connection to this house, it will cause the kind of attention I cannot like."

Anna was hard put not to roll her eyes at the word "connection." If her mother only knew!

"Nonsense, my love," said Sir Jeffrey with a twinkling grin. "The earl's presence and those old stories will assure you an excellent attendance at any entertainments you care to give."

And so it proved. When Lady Featherstone held a small, informal musical evening a few days later, her rooms were gratifyingly full, and it was astonishing how often conversation turned to neighbors, past and present.

As it was an informal affair, Anna had been allowed to attend in her one good silk gown to listen to the music. She knew she was not to put herself forward in any way, and was quite content to sit quietly, watching people and keeping her ears pricked for any snippets of information about the wicked Earl of Carne.

Unfortunately, no one seemed to know more than she. In fact she could, if she wished, give them a clearer story than they had.

She heard one person murmur that he was crippled by debauchery, and another report that she had been reliably informed that he was hideously scarred.

It was clear, however, that the *ton* was fascinated, and Anna suspected that the supposed wickedness of his past would easily be whitewashed by curiosity about his present. Add to that his status as a wealthy, unmarried peer of the realm and she had the sinking feeling that the dreaded earl would soon be accepted everywhere.

That was the last thing Anna wanted. Sitting in her corner listening to Mozart, she seriously considered taking up her investigations again in order to prove that Lord Carne really had murdered his inconvenient mistress. It would serve the wretch right . . .

"Miss Anna Featherstone, I believe?"

Anna looked up to see a young man bowing before her. She glanced at her mother, unsure how to handle this, but Lady Featherstone was deep in conversation with another guest.

Anna took refuge in good manners, smiled, and admitted her identity.

The pleasant-looking, brown-haired young gentleman took a seat beside her. "I know I am being a little bold, Miss Anna. My name is Liddell, by the way, David Liddell, and I am completely respectable."

Anna met his eyes. "You would be bound to say so, though, wouldn't you, Mr. Liddell? However, since I cannot imagine being the victim of seizure and rapine in my mother's drawing room, I will not have the vapors just yet."

After a startled moment, he laughed. "What a shame you

are not making your curtsy, too, Miss Anna. You would set London by the ears."

Anna twinkled at him. "I think that is what my mother fears."

She held her smile even as her amusement faded. Her mother was clearly wise, for Anna had almost created disaster already. Perhaps bandying words with Mr. Liddell was a mistake, too.

He patted her hand. "Don't grow nervous with me. Truth to tell, I wish to speak to you about your sister."

"Ah," said Anna, relaxing. This was familiar ground. "Have you fallen in love with her so quickly?"

He blushed. "Hardly that. We have only met a few times. But I would like to know her better."

"Then I suggest you speak to her, not me, Mr. Liddell."

"But I am being cunning, Miss Anna. If you will tell me the subjects that most interest Miss Featherstone, then I will be able to use my precious time with her to greatest effect."

Anna considered him approvingly. "Initiative should certainly be rewarded, sir. Maria is interested in fashion, Keats' poetry, and, on a more serious note, slavery. She is, of course, opposed to it. But I must warn you that we Featherstones are distressingly practical. Maria will not marry solely for money and title, but she is very unlikely to marry for love in a cottage. I do hope you have a comfortable situation."

His face rippled under a revealing flash of pique before he controlled it. "I have expectations," he said vaguely as he rose. "I must thank you, Miss Anna, and hope that perhaps one day we may be closer."

Anna watched him cross to where Maria held court, feeling mildly sorry for him. He seemed pleasant and intelligent, but she feared his expectations were not equal to the occasion.

Then Lady Featherstone swished to Anna's side. "And what, pray, were you doing conversing with a gentleman?"

"I could not avoid it, Mama. He introduced himself."

"Gentlemen do not introduce themselves!"

Anna grinned. "They do when they want to know the way to Maria's heart."

"Ah." Lady Featherstone frowned, but not at Anna. "It is unlikely to do, for all Maria seems to look kindly upon him."

"Why? What is wrong with him?"

"He's a Liddell. Which means he's related to the Earl of Carne. That cannot be to his favor."

Anna stared at Mr. Liddell with new interest. In her examination of Burke's, she had scarcely noted the earl's family name. "Is he the cousin, then?" she asked. "The heir?"

"Yes. Which now means he is a gentleman of limited means. 'Tis a shame, perhaps, that Lord Carne resurfaced, for as an earl Mr. Liddell would make an eligible *parti*. Without the title he is too small a fish."

"But if Maria favors him, Mama?"

Lady Featherstone patted Anna's head. "I will not force either of you to marry against your inclinations, dear, but nor will I permit you to follow some romantic fancy into hardship. It will be easy enough for a girl as pretty as Maria to find a husband who is both congenial and comfortable. Off to bed with you now, Anna. And tomorrow you are to cease this moping about the house or I will assuredly send for the doctor."

Anna considered David Liddell before she left. Any resemblance between him and the earl was very slight, though he was handsome enough in his own way. She was surprised by the fact that she had not the slightest wish for the earl to die so Mr. Liddell could be earl in his place.

Not the slightest.

Not even if Maria did favor him.

Not even if the earl had committed murder.

Anna feared she was a sad case.

She was finding it impossible to forget her encounter with Lord Carne, who was not marked by debauchery, and whose scar enhanced rather than diminished his appeal. Nor could she forget the feel of being in his arms, of his thumbs gently wiping away her tears, of his mouth exploring hers.

These were not suitable thoughts for a sixteen-year-old schoolroom miss. Anna was painfully aware that her parents would be appalled if they could read her mind, and that saddened her for she loved them very much.

For she now knew she was wicked.

Every night when she went to her room she had to fight the temptation to open the secret door and venture once more into the territory of the wicked Earl of Carne.

The next day Anna did venture outdoors, for otherwise her mother would send for a doctor and it was Anna's experience that doctors never admitted that a patient was healthy—there was no money in that. They always prescribed some medicine or treatment, invariably unpleasant. She had no mind to be dosed with tonic or worse, blistered, purged, or have blood let.

What Anna wanted to do was to attack the lending libraries again. She had long since finished the books from her last trip, and more than ever she wanted a copy of *Forbidden Affections*. She quailed, however, at the thought of walking down fashionable streets where she might come face-to-face with the Earl of Carne.

Instead, she gathered Martha and Arthur and announced a walk in the park. She was sure wicked noblemen did not walk in the park at this unfashionable hour. The dangerous moment would be leaving the house when there was the slight possibility that the earl might be doing the same thing. All Anna could do to lessen that hazard was to wear her deepest-brimmed bonnet.

As it happened, her precaution was unnecessary and she and her escort left the house with no incident at all.

Anna delighted in the brisk walk in the summer sun after so many days of idleness. It was almost like the country. Trees were in heavy leaf and bright splashes of blossom broke the smoothness of daisy-speckled grass. Ducks and swans cruised the small lake, while at the edges children pushed out toy boats. She also had Arthur's gossip to enliven the day.

"Setting in for a regular stay," Arthur said. "New staff and all. The Murchisons don't much care for it if you ask me, Miss Anna. They've had an easy life all these years, living in comfort with no one breathing down their neck.

"Not but what they haven't done a good job," he added quickly. "And what a business about that young woman! Had a word with Jack Murchison myself, I did, and every word is true. They did think, as we did, that perhaps the earl had had a bit too much and imagined it, but Jack said he had clearly been hit a mighty blow on the head. And what's more, there was a ribbon. A female's hair ribbon!"

"Heavens!" gasped Anna, thinking such a response appropriate. In truth, she'd hoped that scrap of silk had been overlooked.

"No way to tell whose, of course. It'll be a mystery till Domesday, if you ask me, for she was doubtless just a sneak thief, thinking the house was empty. For all we know, she'd been in the habit of prowling the house, snitching things, for years . . ."

Anna stopped listening at that point because she was pondering the fact that the earl did not appear to have told anyone that the intruder was in her nightgown. It was true the weather was warm, but it was hard to imagine any woman going thieving dressed like that.

She wondered uneasily what the earl *was* imagining.

Then, as if summoned by her thoughts, she saw Lord Carne, elegant in blue jacket, buff breeches, and tall beaver, strolling along the path toward them.

Chilled by panic, Anna swung away from the path to stare at some trees. "Look, a kingfisher. How peculiar to see one here in town!"

"A kingfisher, Miss Anna?" asked Martha, shielding her eyes. "You must be mistaken."

"Oh, I could have sworn . . . Are there other birds of such bright color? It was a flash of the most remarkable blue! What other bright birds are there? Parakeets? Might one have escaped . . . ?"

She maintained this ridiculous chatter as long as possible, but eventually was forced to turn back to the path. With a wash of relief, she saw that the earl had passed them and was well ahead on the path.

She wished the wretched man in Hades. What possible business had a gazetted rake to be in the park at this time of day when only doddering ancients and nursemaids with children were supposed to use it?

And why did he have to look so very elegant . . .

"Miss Anna! Are you all right?"

Anna snapped her wits together. "Yes, Martha. I just had a thought, that's all. But it is doubtless time to return home."

By the time they arrived at Carne Terrace, Anna was well into the blue devils. She could not go on like this, afraid to step outside the door, gabbling about kingfishers in Green Park! Perhaps it would be best to confess all to Papa and have done with it. She wouldn't have to confess to that kiss, after all, for surely the earl must be as ashamed of it as anyone.

But her courage failed her.

Her parents would be so shocked by the fact that she had invaded someone's home, never mind her brutal attack. And how was she to justify the attack without revealing the kiss?

No, she told herself, the chances of meeting the earl again were really quite slight since she didn't move in fashionable circles. Her mother had assured her that now the Season was well underway, the hours kept by the *ton* would not be those of ordinary people. The fashionable throng rose at midday and returned to bed in the early hours of the morning.

If Anna kept her outings to the morning, she should be safe.

It was most irritating that the Earl of Carne did not keep fashionable hours.

At least, as far as Anna knew, he danced the night away with the rest of Society, but it seemed he often rose at an early hour as well. Her careful observation of the front door of number 10 showed him leaving to walk or ride at nine or ten of the morning.

She was beginning to wonder if her mind were disordered, for it did seem to her that no matter what time she chose to leave the house, the earl was likely to appear, forcing her to hurry in or out to avoid giving him a clear view of her face.

And she was extremely tired of wearing her coal-scuttle bonnet.

She was also concerned for her sanity because she had a disturbing tendency to study the man when she could do so secretly.

At first, she had tried to persuade herself that she was merely studying the enemy, but she was not in the habit of deceiving herself. The truth was, she liked to look at him.

There was a presence to Lord Carne, an unconscious

authority in every movement. He moved with remarkable grace, and she had the impression that at any moment he could respond to danger if need be.

From behind her curtains, Anna studied his features and was forced to conclude that they were completely perfect. Not perhaps as smooth as some gentlemen's, and there was that scar, but in her opinion they were everything a man's features ought to be. His bones were excellent, his nose straight, his lips well-shaped and neither thin nor pouty . . .

She was inclined to linger on the thought of those lips and how they had felt against hers. She very much wanted that sensation again.

But not, she told herself firmly, at the danger of exposure or ruin!

Her obsession was not improved by the fact that she now had a copy of *Forbidden Affections* to study. There could be no doubt that Roland—Lady Delabury had even used his first name!—was the earl. Or Lord Manderville, as he had then been. If Anna took the youth in the picture and merged him with the man living next door, she had an exact representation of Roland of Toulaine, Dulcinea's gallant lover.

That this merely confirmed the fact that Lady Delabury and Lord Manderville had been lovers was depressing indeed, especially when it suggested that the earl might have caused the lady's death, even if only by driving her to suicide.

There was nothing in *Forbidden Affections* to cast light on Lady Delabury's death, however, and Anna returned the book to the library and read Mrs. Jamison's other five novels. The rereading confirmed that she enjoyed them more, and it puzzled her.

The heroine was always the same—a variety, Anna supposed, of Lady Delabury herself, or Miss Skelton as she had been before her marriage. The heroes, however, were varied. Anna thought them a rather unrealistic lot. She had never known men to be so inclined to protest their extreme unworthiness to even touch a lady's hand, or to weep with grief at having dared to steal a kiss.

All this did rather incline Anna to remember a gentleman who would never weep over that stolen kiss, and would never for a moment imagine himself unworthy. She touched her own lips, remembering another touch, and was alarmingly aware that it would not take much for her to say to the Earl of Carne, "Kiss me again, please."

Lady Featherstone was not always right. Sometimes young ladies *did* plot their own downfall.

Perhaps it was just that the constant avoidance of the earl was so wearing, or perhaps it was a secret wish for ruin. One day, when Anna returned home and encountered the earl leaving his house, as close to face-to-face as two people twelve feet away could be, she did not duck her head and scurry. Instead, she stared at him, chin up, daring him to summon the constables.

He was startled, then a slight smile moved his lips before, with the slightest nod of acknowledgment, he went on his way.

Anna went into the house in a daze of horror and relief. He knew!

It was as if he'd spoken to her and told her that he knew, and had known all along.

She was horrified that anyone knew what Anna Featherstone had done. At the same time there was tremendous relief. Clearly he was not going to call in the law, was not even going to inform her parents. And she didn't think the composed gentleman she had encountered today was going to lie in wait to have his wicked way with her.

She was just the tiniest bit disappointed about that.

By the time Anna had her bonnet and spencer off,

reaction had set in, threatening tears. The great drama of her life had proved to be as substantial as a . . . a soap bubble! Rather than spending the past weeks searching for a mysterious, dangerous intruder, the Earl of Carne had known all along that it had been a mere schoolgirl neighbor, and had been amused.

It was intensely mortifying.

Anna would have liked to flee to the country or fall into a convenient fatal decline, but this being reality rather than a novel, she had to go on with life and try to put the whole matter out of her mind.

When she began to pay attention to events around her, she found that the wicked earl was being received everywhere. No one seemed to care anymore about *the incident,* and Lady Delabury's death was being politely ignored.

Maria was a great success, and though she had not made her choice, it was likely that she would accept an offer within weeks. Mr. Liddell was still a constant attendant, but his chances of success seemed slim. Now that Lord Carne was back, his heir had no prospects beyond a small estate and a government post.

Anna returned to spending her time as originally planned, visiting historic places and educational exhibitions. In fact, she should perhaps have acted this way all along, for she never encountered the earl in these activities.

Then he began to show a marked interest in Maria, causing a great fluttering in the Featherstone nest.

"I have grave reservations," said Lady Featherstone at luncheon one day. "For all that the earl behaves quite properly, I cannot forget his past."

"Time heals," said Sir Jeffrey. "Morals as well as hearts. Since there is no evidence of anything but wildness in his past, I think Lord Carne should be judged on his present behavior. What do you feel, Maria?"

Maria raised a hand to her head as if dizzy. "I must be

sensible of the honor, Papa. But I am not sure I can forget his past. Mr. Liddell has told me such things . . ."

"Mr. Liddell has his own ax to grind," Anna pointed out.

"I know that," said Maria, her expression a blend of irritation and complacency. She did enjoy being fought over. "But it is generally accepted that he . . . that the earl had an improper relationship with the woman who died. I cannot overlook that in a man."

"Then you'd best get yourself to a nunnery," Anna muttered.

Maria gasped, and even her father raised his brows in surprise.

"Anna!" exclaimed Lady Featherstone. "Go to your room at once, and study Bishop Stortford's sermon on unclean thoughts."

Anna flushed with mortification as she rose and curtsied. What had possessed her to say such a thing? "Yes, Mama. I beg pardon, Mama."

In her room, however, Anna didn't study the sermon—which she knew almost by heart—but contemplated the terrible reason for her outburst.

Jealousy.

She was jealous of Maria, and could not endure the thought of the Earl of Carne being her brother-in-law.

Which led to the next incredible step.

She wanted him for herself.

Anna laughed out loud. It was impossible, and exactly the sort of silly infatuation girls seemed prone to, but that did not make it any the less powerful at the moment. She ached with the loss of something she had never had, or had hope of.

She was honestly convinced, however, that Lord Carne and Maria would not suit. There was nothing wrong with Maria, but she needed a husband who appreciated sensibility and delicate feelings. The Wicked Earl would find Maria's airs a dead bore inside a month.

There was nothing a schoolroom miss could do about this, however, except be miserable and intensify her efforts to avoid the man. It would be the last straw if she made a fool of herself by acting like a lovesick moonling over him.

Anna thought avoiding the earl would be easy, but she hadn't considered the consequences of his interest in Maria. He now had the entrée to number 9.

In fact, he appeared at a small tea party Lady Featherstone gave two days later. It appeared he had been invited, though no one had expected him to attend. After all, it was an informal affair, so much so that Anna was in attendance.

When Anna heard him announced her heart began to pound, blood rushed to her head, and though she focused all her attention on old Lord Threpton, who was droning on about his problems with poachers, she didn't hear a word he was saying.

Once again she had this longing to become invisible, and that carried her thoughts straight back to a night in the Wicked Earl's library, and the things he had done to her then.

She knew color was flooding her face.

She wanted to die.

The mere sound of Lord Carne's voice—the first time she had heard it since that night—was interfering with her breathing, causing a perilous light-headedness.

Lord Threpton peered at her. "Hey, missie, I didn't mean to upset you with these matters!" He patted her knee. "You're a good girl to listen to an old man rambling on."

Anna kept her eyes fixed on his rheumy ones. "I don't mind, my lord. You are very interesting."

He pinched her cheek. "Some man's going to be very lucky in you, my dear. Now, why not go and find that plate of jam tarts and offer me another one. Very good, they are."

Thus Anna was forced out of hiding and set to walk across the room on unsteady legs. Which meant that her mother had to introduce her to the earl. "My youngest daughter, Anna, my lord. She is not yet out."

He bowed with his typical grace. "Miss Anna. Charmed to make your acquaintance." He acted as if she was a total stranger, but Anna shivered as if he had stroked her back.

She wanted not to look to him, but couldn't help herself. He was even more perfect up close than he was at a distance. And what an actor he was. There was no hint of anything untoward about him except perhaps for a hint of intimate humor in his blue eyes, humor fighting to escape, just as it had in the portrait.

Anna wished desperately that he wouldn't look at her like that. It touched her heart and made her think of kisses.

Then she realized she was standing there red-faced and speechless, a picture of a schoolgirl *gaucherie*. She hastily dropped a curtsy and he moved on to be introduced elsewhere.

Maria came over to hiss, "For goodness sake, Anna, there's no need for you to look at him as if you thought he'd eat you! You were the one defending him before!"

"I didn't!"

"Yes, you did. Oh well," she said with a superior smile. "I suppose you are unaccustomed to meeting earls. Don't worry, dearest, he won't expect much from a schoolroom miss."

Maria switched on a warmer smile and went off to greet new guests. Anna marched on in search of jam tarts, wishing fiercely that she were at least out and able to compete on equal terms.

Compete? she thought, as she picked up the plate. It was hard not to laugh like the madwoman in Mrs. Jamison's *Lord of the Dark Tower*.

Maria was a diamond of the first water, and Anna was

a . . . mildly pretty pebble! Crossing the room with the plate, she flickered a glance at the earl. He caught her at it. Almost imperceptibly, he winked, and his mouth moved in a secret smile.

Anna jerked her gaze away, and hurried back to Lord Threpton. If she didn't know better, she'd think the Earl of Carne was *flirting* with her!

Nonsense, she told herself firmly. What he was doing was playing a rather cruel teasing game just to make her uncomfortable. Perhaps it was his way to pay her back for her assault.

Anna found herself busy handing out tea and passing plates of cake, and was glad of it, but inevitably this led to her offering a plate to Lord Carne. She had to stand quite close and was sharply reminded of the time she had brought him that glass of brandy.

And of all that had followed.

She watched him warily and prayed her hand wouldn't shake.

Again he met her eyes, but with no special expression. "Thank you, Miss Anna. I am spoiled for choice. Which cake would you recommend?"

Anna's throat went dry as if he had asked something private and significant. She swallowed. "The lady-cakes are very good, my lord."

He studied the plate, and Anna saw it start to tremble slightly with her nerves. "I wonder if a lady-cake would meet with me . . ." He appeared to trail off as if in thought.

Anna's heart skipped a beat. Had he really said, "me" rather than "my"? And had he swallowed the word "cake" so that he seemed to say, "I wonder if a lady would meet with me?"

Surely not!

"I doubt it, my lord," she mumbled. It had to be her imagination. Even the Earl of Carne could not be so bold.

She remembered telling Mr. Liddell that she did not fear seizure and rapine in her mother's drawing room. Now she was not so sure.

He looked up at her rather seriously. "What a shame there are no maids-of-honor here today."

Anna flushed at the rebuke and the injustice of it. But inside here there was also a spark of delight at the sheer wit and effrontery of the man. He was using the name of the almond cakes and giving it another meaning.

"Perhaps there are maids-of-honor," she retorted. "Gentlemen-of-honor might be a little harder to find."

The lady sitting beside the earl tittered. "Miss Anna, you are too young to attempt barbed witticisms!"

Lady Featherstone came over quickly. "My lord, is there a problem?"

"Not at all, Lady Featherstone. I was merely inquiring as to maids-of-honor. I am particularly partial to them."

"Oh. No, I'm afraid we do not have them today, my lord."

"Alas. But as I like my maids-of-honor for a late supper, perhaps I can still order some for tonight. At about midnight, I think." He took a jam tart. "And, Miss Anna, I think you are quite correct. If we have maids-of-honor, we should have gentlemen-of-honor as well. I wonder what sort of cake they would be?"

Taking up his meaning of "cake" as "fool," Anna replied, "I don't see how any gentleman of honor could be a *cake,* my lord."

"Then it seems unfair that maids-of-honor be cakes, when it clearly is not so."

"Unless it means that they take the cake, my lord," said Anna, switching the meaning to that of victory. She was enjoying this clever wordplay immensely, but Lady Featherstone interrupted.

"You must excuse Anna, my lord. She is bookish."

As her mother steered her away, Anna heard him say, "I suspected it from the first."

Anna hated letting him have the last word.

Lady Featherstone drew Anna to the far side of the room. "It is most inappropriate of you to be bandying words with the earl, Anna, and it is fatal for a girl to become known as clever. Moreover, I still fear there is something strange about that man. Going on about his supper, indeed. Keep away from him."

"Yes, Mama."

Anna dutifully passed the cakes around the other side of the room, but her mind was running back over that conversation. She had just been invited to a midnight tryst with the wicked earl, and promised that he would behave as a gentleman of honor, and that he held her in the highest regard.

And he'd done it in front of a room full of people!

She couldn't help but admire a man like that.

She slid a glance over to him, and he smiled in a way that reminded her that she was a foolish, infatuated girl.

But how could a foolish, infatuated girl be expected to refuse such an invitation?

By the time she prepared for bed that night, Anna was still not sure what she would do, and she spent the next two hours pondering it.

Despite that talk of honor, logic said that it was more than likely that the earl was inviting her to a wicked encounter where he would kiss her again and try to do even more.

The alarming thing was that the idea was very attractive.

On the other hand, her instinct told her that the man she had met today had had no such intent, but some other reason for requesting a meeting. It was certainly true that there was little chance of them having a private *tête-à-tête* in a normal manner.

Of course, a silly little part of Anna's mind was dreaming that he had fallen desperately in love with her during that one encounter. If that was true, then perhaps he would go on his knees and protest his undying love for her even as he declaimed his extreme unworthiness to so much as touch the hem of her gown, just like a hero in a novel by Mrs. Jamison.

"Fustian!" Anna said out loud as she struggled back into her gown, muttering about buttons that were never designed for a lady to do up by herself. In the end she put on a short spencer jacket to cover the undone buttons at the back.

The mirror assured her that she was covered neck to toe, and decidedly not the sort of apparition likely to drive a man mad with love or lust.

As the clocks in the house struck midnight, she told herself that was how she wanted it and, heart thudding, moved the bench so she could return to number 10.

The lever worked without a sound, and the door opened smoothly. She almost screamed, however, to find the earl awaiting her in the bedroom.

"Ah," he said, investigating the doorway, "I thought it must be in here, but I couldn't find the secret to it."

Anna sidled away from him, shockingly aware of the intimacy of being alone with an unrelated man for only the second time in her life, and certainly for the first time in a bedroom! At least the place was still shrouded in Holland covers, which in some irrational way made it less dangerous.

"Does the room make you nervous?" he asked calmly. "Don't be. I have no wicked intentions. But there are servants now, and to be wandering around the house would be very dangerous."

Anna put down her unsteady candlestick, placing it

beside his on a bureau. "What if the door had not been in here, my lord? Then I would have had to search the house for you."

He smiled. "You are charmingly forthright. I gambled, but I also hedged my bets. There is a note in the library asking you to come here. Will you take a seat?" He indicated one of the two chairs bracketing the screened fireplace.

Both relieved and disappointed that there was no sofa, Anna perched on the chair. He relaxed into the other one and stretched his long legs so that his boots came perilously close to her skirts. "Damned uncomfortable, these chairs. I like ones with lots of padding. I see you feel the same."

"Me?" It came out as a squeak. Anna tried to relax, but it was impossible when this man was sitting so close, making her feel rather breathless. "I am just somewhat apprehensive, my lord. Do you intend to tell my parents?"

His brows rose in surprise. "What! That you sneaked into my house, where I mistook you for a serving maid and did my best to have my wicked way with you? Hardly."

"Oh. Then I don't suppose you are going to try and blackmail me, either."

"Is that what you thought? What was I going to blackmail you into doing? Oh, dear. Not into succumbing to my wicked way. You've been reading too much Mrs. Jamison, Pippin."

Smarting from his tone, Anna snapped, "Don't call me that! It's my father's pet name for me."

"Ah. I'm sorry then. It does suit you, though. And I have the greatest appreciation for juicy apples."

Anna could feel herself turning as hot as if there was a roaring fire in the grate. "Are you flirting with me, sir?"

His smile turned wry. "That would be most dishonorable, wouldn't it, after I'd given you my parole. Very well, to business. The reason I requested this meeting, Miss

Featherstone, is because you clearly know things that I do not. Such as the location of that secret door. I've been trying to find a way to speak with you for weeks, and have had to resort to this. Would you explain it, please?"

Anna felt very loath to tell him, loath to share her secret with anyone, but made herself say, "It's in one of the novels. *Forbidden Affections.*"

He sat up. "In a novel?" he said blankly. "Read by thousands?"

"Yes. You see, Dulcinea is kept in a room exactly like the one I have—it's very horrid—and Roland . . ."

He winced as if in pain. "Did that dreadful woman actually name a hero after me?"

Anna tried to assimilate the word "dreadful." It seemed to her that no one could refer to a lover as dreadful in quite that tone. "I'm afraid so. Roland of Toulaine."

"No wonder you reacted to my name the last time we met. And what did the noble Roland look like? Or can I guess?"

She nodded. "Just like you, I'm afraid. Or rather, more like you in that portrait."

His blue eyes opened wider. "You *have* been prying, haven't you, my dishonorable maid."

Anna was blushing again, this time with mortification. "I do beg your pardon. It was inexcusable."

"Hardly," he said, recovering his equanimity. "I doubt I could have resisted the temptation, especially at . . . How old *are* you?"

"Sixteen, as I said."

"I was hoping you'd lied. *Hélas.* So, are there other aspects of this novel that relate to reality?"

"How should I know, my lord? You might read it for yourself. You do own a copy."

"The woman gave copies of all her works to my mother,

who was too polite to refuse them but has never read a novel in her life."

"How sad for her," said Anna militantly.

Humor flickered in his eyes. "She has often declared that they turn young ladies into weaklings, inclined to faint at the slightest thing. I will delight in telling her how wrong she is."

"She's still alive?" Anna immediately regretted the question, but she was startled to find that the earl was not alone in the world.

"Yes, though she has not been hearty for years. She resides in Bath. So, come, tell me more about this novel so that we can see what parallels there might be."

"Why?"

"You are not a particularly biddable girl, are you? Because, Miss Featherstone, I am still suspected of having murdered Lady Delabury, largely because no one ever believed that she could have gained entry to this house in her very revealing nightgown—for, unlike you, she favored diaphanous silk—without me knowing. Since my friends vouched for me, this casts a shadow on their honor, too. I want the matter cleared up."

"After all these years? And . . ."

"Yes?"

Anna looked down. "I feel horribly selfish, but how can you tell the world about the door without involving me?"

She looked up to see him smile quite gently. "I'll find a way. You must trust me."

And she did. Yet again, relief was tinged with a little disappointment. She trusted him with her reputation, but she feared she could also trust him with her virtue. He wasn't going to seduce her, after all.

Oh, dear, she was a perilously wicked creature!

"Anna?"

She started at his use of her name.

"Anna, tell me about the book."

And so she did, not making a great deal of it because it was quite a silly story. She told how Count Nacre had trapped poor Dulcinea on the very eve of her wedding to Roland, and hidden her in the deserted tower of his castle, where he intended to ruin her, thus forcing her to marry him instead.

"And each night he would come to her, intending"—she was blushing again—"intending the worst. But something would always happen to disturb them." She found the courage to look at him. "It is a little like Scherazade, my lord, except that stupid Dulcinea does *nothing* to change her fate. She just faints and weeps."

His lips twitched. "Unlike you."

Anna's face was heating again. "I did. Weep."

"True, and most disconcerting it was, child. But you also smashed me on the head with a heavy glass. I'm sure Dulcinea could have done the same."

"Yes, she could. If I'd been her I would have waited by the door and hit him with a poker as he came in. In fact, I saw nothing in the book to suggest that Dulcinea couldn't have opened the door from her own side any time she wanted. But you see, she was afraid of the rats."

He laughed out loud. "Oh, the scorn! Are you not afraid of rats, Anna?"

Something in his manner was causing a new kind of heat, a warmth that came from his relaxed manner and smiling eyes, from his admiration. "I don't like them, my lord, but if it were rats or Count Nacre, I'd chance the rats."

"I'm sure you would. And so the fainting maiden waits patiently for Roland to arrive on his white charger and throw her over his saddlebow."

"Hardly at the top of a tower, my lord."

"True. So what did happen?"

Anna settled to telling the story. "Roland confronts

Count Nacre in his hall, where they engage mightily with their swords. The contest is equal . . ."

"How old is Count Nacre?"

"Oh, quite old. At least forty."

"Ancient," he remarked dryly. "But then the contest is unlikely to be equal. He probably has the gout."

"The count is a mighty warrior, my lord, champion of the king. May I continue?"

"I do beg your pardon," he said unrepentantly. "So they engage mightily with their swords. Do they batter themselves to simultaneous exhaustion?"

"Of course not."

"Why not? Ah, she frowns at me . . ."

Anna was indeed frowning, though she was hard-pressed not to giggle. "Because, my lord, the count suddenly comes to a realization of his own wickedness and throws himself upon Roland's sword."

He blinked. "How very disconcerting."

"Hush, my lord!" She bit her lip and pushed gamely on. "Roland races up the tower to Dulcinea . . ."

"Despite his wounds?"

"Heroes are *never* wounded. Or not seriously."

"Then they are hardly very heroic, are they?"

"Have you ever been wounded?" The words popped out before she could control them, fracturing the lighthearted atmosphere. Her eyes fixed on his scar.

"I'm no hero, Anna."

"You didn't answer my question."

"Villains get wounded, too. Proceed with your story or I'll show you my other wounds, which would move this meeting out of the field of honor, Miss Featherstone."

Anna was crushingly aware of having been relegated to formality, and swallowed a hint of tears. "Where was I, my lord?"

"Your hero was racing up the tower steps despite his

many wounds, and muscles that burned and ached from the mighty battle."

"So he enters Dulcinea's chamber, causing her to swoon."

"Twit. You would have tended his wounds, wouldn't you?"

"My lord, he *wasn't* wounded!"

"How could she tell? He was doubtless covered by the evil count's blood."

Anna paused. "That's true, isn't it? I didn't say it was a *good* story, my lord."

"Just as well. So, what next? I suppose he has to carry her down the winding stairs. Tricky, that, I should think."

"Doubtless, especially as an earthquake starts just then . . ."

"An *earthquake?* The very earth protesting at the count's demise? Then he must be the hero, and Roland, vile Roland, a wastrel and a murderer."

"Nonsense. Roland is the very epitome of a hero. But the stones do begin to tumble around them, and the steps crumble beneath their feet . . ."

"Whereupon, he slaps her awake and makes her use her feet as they race to safety?"

"Of course not! In fact, she does come out of her swoon . . ."

"Thank heavens . . ."

". . . But by then they have rats swarming around them, which sends her off again. Please, my lord, don't make me laugh or I will never finish!"

"There's more?" he asked, straight-faced, but with eyes full of hilarity. He looked exactly like the portrait.

With difficulty, Anna gathered her wits. "It can hardly end then!"

"I don't see why not. They can be entombed together as an eternal monument to folly."

"They manage to survive. Just as they emerge, the tower crumbles, leaving only a heap of stones . . ."

"And a lot of homeless rats."

"I don't think that was mentioned," she said severely. "The king then arrives . . ."

"George III?" he queried in astonishment.

"No! King Rudolph of . . . Oh, I've forgotten the country. It's all made up."

He raised one brow. "You astonish me, Miss Featherstone."

A giggle escaped, but Anna struggled on. "The king has found out that Count Nacre is plotting treason and has come to execute him . . ."

"How very unlawful. Due process, my dear."

". . . But now he makes Roland Count of Nacre . . ."

"Whereupon Dulcinea breaks off the match because she refuses to live in a rat-infested castle."

"The *castle* wasn't rat-infested, my lord!"

"It will be now the rats don't have their cozy tower to live in. Where do you think all those rats went?"

Anna succumbed to laughter. "Oh dear! It is all . . . all so silly, isn't it?"

He leaned over and passed her a handkerchief. "Very. Are you truly addicted to these novels, Anna?"

Anna controlled her laughter and wiped her eyes. "Most of them are not as bad as that. Even Mrs. Jamison's earlier ones were much better, though her heroines did tend to swoon at the drop of a pin."

"From the little I know of her, Lady Delabury was of much the same temperament."

Anna made a business of drying her cheeks, considering yet another statement that indicated that the earl and Lady Delabury had not been intimate. Then why on earth had the woman committed suicide in this very room?

He leaned back, sober again and thoughtful, and echoed

her thought. "I see nothing in that silly story to explain why the author decided to commit suicide, or why she chose to do so in this room."

"Perhaps because she'd written such a terrible novel?" Anna clapped her hand over her mouth. "Oh, how uncharitable!"

He focused his serious features and amused eyes on her. "Quite. And Margaret Delabury thought every word she wrote absolutely perfect. She had just married Delabury, an excellent catch for her, and the poor man was besotted. She had everything."

He lapsed into thought, and Anna chanced a question. "What was in the note she left, my lord?"

"Some stuff about despair because she could not hold her husband's affection."

"He was unfaithful?" Anna asked, knowing she was turning pink at discussing such matters with a gentleman.

"Most unlikely. As I said, he was besotted. One reason I left the country was because fool Delabury was convinced I was his wife's lover and murderer. Having failed to get me sent to trial, he was intent on calling me out."

"Oh, my."

"I did hope that by now he'd found a new bride and no longer felt so keenly on the subject. I have just heard that he is on his way to town with dueling on his mind."

"Oh, dear!"

"Quite. Which is why I want to solve this mystery."

"I wish I could help. Truly. But I think I've told you all I know."

He rose to his feet. "I think so, too." He was suddenly standing quite close to her. "I have enjoyed this, though."

She looked up at him, delight at their shared amusement still fizzing in her. She had never known an instant bond such as this. "So have I, my lord," she admitted shyly.

For a moment she thought he had something important

to say, but then he turned sharply away. "Would you permit me to glance into your room, Miss Featherstone?"

Anna swallowed her disappointment. "By all means, my lord. I've wandered all over your house, so it seems only fair that you should see a little of mine."

As they went through the door, he said, "It is not at all the same. You should not invite men into your bedroom."

She glanced back over her shoulder. "For fear that the very sight of my virginal couch will turn them into ravening beasts?"

"Something like that," he said vaguely, but he was staring around the room. "Good God. The solution is obvious. The woman was mad."

"A convenient assessment, my lord, but hard to prove."

"This room is proof." He poked a finger into the grinning mouth of a gargoyle. "I suppose one could keep small coins and buttons in places like that."

Anna giggled, but placed her fingers over her lips. "Hush, my lord. I'm not at all sure your voice cannot be heard in other rooms!"

"And that would set the cat among the pigeons, wouldn't it?" he said softly. He turned to look at her. "Farewell, Anna."

Her heart skipped a beat. "No more secret meetings?"

"No more secret meetings. It would be very foolish."

"No one need know . . ."

"Except us."

Anna gripped her hands tight together. "I . . . I like you, my lord."

There was the merest twitch of his lips, but his eyes looked rather sad. "I like you, too, Anna Featherstone."

"Well," said Anna, after swallowing a lump in her throat. "I suppose if you marry Maria, we will meet occasionally."

"I have no intention of marrying your sister. I've only been paying court to her to get access to Maggie."

"Oh. And that was just because you wanted to know about the secret door."

"Exactly."

It was all rather deflating, but that magical time of intimacy and laughter could not be entirely dispelled. Anna gathered her courage and looked up at him. "If you were feeling grateful for my help, you might perhaps . . . might kiss me once, my lord, with kindness, before you go."

"Kindness? Was I not kind the other night?"

"It was hard for me to tell. I was very frightened."

"It may be hard for you to tell now. Why aren't you frightened?"

Anna considered it. "I trust you."

"If I were truly kind and trustworthy, Anna, I would leave." But he held out a hand.

Breath catching in her throat, Anna placed her hand in his, touching him for the first time in weeks. His hand was firm, warm, smooth . . . All in all, it would be extraordinary if it were anything else, and yet it seemed remarkable to her.

He drew her into his arms and inside she melted into a blend of sadness and wonder.

"It is so unfair," she said.

He tilted her chin. "What is?"

"That this is wrong."

She could not read his expression at all. "You do at least know that it is wrong?"

"To be kissing a man in my bedroom? And such a man? I'd have to be perfectly fluff-witted not to."

"And fluff-witted is the last description I would put to Anna Featherstone. Too clever by half . . ."

He kissed her simply on the lips. She was about to protest that the kiss was too brief when he returned to deepen it, teasing her mouth open and bringing the pleasure that had heated her dreams.

When he started to draw away from her, she tightened her arms around him. "Oysters," she said.

"What?"

"Kissing is like oysters. A bit unpleasant at first, but quite delicious when one is accustomed."

He laughed then, struggling to be quiet. He rested his head against hers, his shaking running through into her.

She moved her head so her lips found his and swallowed his laughter so that it changed into something else, something even better than before. Her body became involved in the kiss, moving against him as her hands explored—

He pulled away.

When she resisted, he used force.

Anna was abruptly mortified by her behavior, but at least he was none too calm either.

Then his expression became kind, and he brushed some hair from her face. "I do wish you weren't sixteen, Anna Featherstone." With that, he slipped back through the doors.

"I will get older," she whispered, but it was to a closed panel.

Anna undressed, aching with needs she had never imagined but understood perfectly well. He was right, though. The world would be shocked by such a match, and an eligible earl couldn't be expected to wait years until she was older, and "out." He would marry someone else, and Anna's heart would break. But at least it wouldn't be Maria.

That was cold comfort. Anna sniffed a few tears as she changed into her nightgown and climbed into her chilly, virginal couch.

In the next days, Anna could only be glad that her parents and sister were busily engaged in the height of the

Season, for it was beyond her to behave entirely in her normal, prosaic manner.

She was foolishly, idiotically in love. Daydreams filled her head, wild sensations flooded her body, and she could hardly think of anything but the Earl of Carne. She attempted drawings of him, and wrote his name endlessly on pieces of paper—which were hard to dispose of in warm weather when there were no fires except in the kitchen.

She spent entirely too much time sitting by windows hoping to catch a glimpse of him entering or leaving his house. Once or twice he looked thoughtfully at number 9, but she wasn't sure she could read anything significant into that.

To try to bring some order to her mind, she began again to consider the mystery of Lady Delabury's death. After all, if Carne was to be believed, the lady's husband could already be in town looking for an excuse to call the earl out, or perhaps planning to kill him in cold blood!

She was sitting in the drawing room one day scribbling random thoughts on a piece of paper when Maria came in, untying the ribbons of a very fetching blue silk bonnet.

"I confess I am beginning to weary of this constant social round," she said, with feeling. "We meet the same people everywhere, and everyone talks of the same things."

"It must grow tiring," Anna commiserated. "But it will be worth it if you find the ideal husband."

Maria sighed. "What is an ideal husband? This one is handsome, that one is rich, another is clever, another has exquisite taste . . ."

"Have you not found anyone to love?" Anna asked. It seemed to her that falling in love was alarmingly easy.

"Oh, *love.* You are such a romantic, Anna! If you talk of that sort of foolishness, I perhaps favor Mr. Liddell, but he is impossible now his cousin is home, hale and hearty." She drifted over. "What are you writing?"

Anna said the first thing that came to mind. "A . . . novel."

When Maria picked up the piece of paper, Anna almost snatched it back, but she realized in time that to do so would alert her sister to a mystery. She hoped the scattered words would be meaningless. She hadn't used "Carne" or "Delabury." In fact, the names she had used had been mainly from *Forbidden Affections*.

"I'm trying to come up with the plot for one," she said. Maria did not read novels. She hardly read anything. Surely she wouldn't recognize the names.

Maria scanned the sheet and suddenly frowned. "It's not a *roman à clef*, is it, Anna?"

"No. Why would you think that?"

Maria lost interest and returned the sheet of paper. "Just the name of your hero. Count Nacre. It's an anagram of Carne. Count Nacre—the Earl of Carne. Since you seemed to take the man in aversion, I thought you might be planning a novel in which he came to a dreadful end. Mother would have the vapors." With that, she wandered away leaving Anna stunned.

Her brain must have been muddled for weeks not to see that the villain of *Forbidden Affections* had been the Earl of Carne, the present earl's father. She wondered if they looked the same, for that would clinch it.

She hurried down to visit the cook, and though it took time to turn the conversation to the old earl, she eventually confirmed her suspicions. The Wicked Earl's father had been a tall, barrel-chested, dark-visaged man who up to the time of his death had enjoyed hard riding and pugilism. He had been Count Nacre.

She retreated to her room to ponder the implications. Had Lady Delabury been in love with Lord Carne's son,

Roland, and thwarted by the father? Had *Forbidden Affections* been a novel of revenge?

Or had the lady been trying to reveal to the world that the earl was creeping into her horrid chamber to terrorize her?

But that was nonsense! Lady Delabury herself had ordered the chamber made, and if the earl had come through the secret door—that peculiar secret door—she could easily have complained or nailed it shut.

So what if . . .

Anna's mind began to wander strange paths which seemed unlikely but were the only ones to fit the facts.

One thing was clear. She had to discuss this with the earl.

Anna could not be sure of the earl being in his house at any particular hour. She could only plan to take up vigil once her family left for the evening, hoping to see Lord Carne come home before she fell asleep.

A snarl in this plan developed during the afternoon as her family sat together in the drawing room.

Her father addressed Maria. "We are well into June, my dear; and must soon be returning home. Is it not about time I started to encourage one of your eager suitors?"

Maria blushed. "I am undecided, Papa."

"I can quite see that you're spoiled for choice," he teased. "But the old saying is 'Out of sight, out of mind.' If we return home with you unspoken-for, they might turn their eyes elsewhere."

"If I am so easily forgotten, perhaps I should be."

Anna so heartily agreed with that sentiment that it took her a moment to realize how strangely it sat on Maria's lips, who thought no one should ever forget her. She looked up from her book and realized that Maria was quite agitated.

"Now, now, my love," said Lady Featherstone. "We do

not intend to pressure you. But you must have some notion of where your favor lies."

Maria looked down and said nothing so that an awkward silence developed.

It was as much to break that silence as to tease that Anna said, "It seems to me that Maria favors Mr. Liddell if she favors anyone."

Maria's delicious color blossomed even as Lady Featherstone's face became pinched. Sir Jeffrey merely looked thoughtful.

"Maria!" exclaimed Lady Featherstone. "You have an *earl* seeking your hand. Surely you cannot be so foolish . . ."

"Hush, my dear," said Sir Jeffrey. "We do not look only at rank, surely. Maria, do you favor Mr. Liddell?"

Maria's fingers were knotted in the trim of her embroidered tunic. "I truly don't know, Papa. But . . . but I cannot seem to find interest in any of the other gentlemen, excellent though they are."

"Well, really!" snapped Lady Featherstone. "I never thought you to be so . . . so ungoverned in your affections! I have told you over and over that a girl can fix her affections where she should if she but puts her mind to it. I forbid it! I forbid you to even speak to the man again."

Maria leapt to her feet. "How can you be so cruel! If his horrid cousin had been dead, you would have been delighted to see me wed to him. How is it different?"

"It is a title and eighty thousand a year different, my girl! Believe me, Maria, you are not cut out to live in a cottage doing your own laundry."

"It would hardly come to that. David has nearly a thousand pounds a year."

"David, is it?"

"Hush, my love," said Sir Jeffrey. "Let us not wrangle over it. This requires thought and calm debate. Maria, I am saddened that you have tried to conceal the state of your feelings."

Maria was weeping now, very prettily. "Oh, Papa, I have not been deceitful. Truly I haven't. I thought I could grow fond of Lord Whelksham, or Lord Harlowe. It is only now in talking of it that I realize how I feel about David."

Her father rose to hug her. "It is well that we know the truth. Now, I'm not saying I will consent, for like your mother I have qualms. But we will all think over it. I am sure it will be wise for us to make our apologies and stay home tonight, and perhaps you and Anna would be better for having a quiet meal in your rooms."

Anna met her father's eyes with a quizzical expression, and humor tugged at his lips before being controlled. She dutifully accompanied her sister upstairs.

Maria collapsed into a chair. "Oh, Anna, what will become of me?"

"I suspect you'll end up married to Mr. Liddell if you truly want it."

"Mama will oppose it with all her strength!" Maria declared, reminding Anna all too much of Dulcinea in despair.

"Mama will come to see reason once the first shock is past. But have you truly considered the practicalities?"

"I love him!"

Anna felt like Horatio facing overwhelming odds, but she set herself to trying to lead Maria into a logical consideration of her future. "You have always wanted a fine country estate, Maria."

"I am sure David will have one in time."

"How?"

Maria's eyes shifted. "If his cousin should die . . ."

Anna's heart tightened painfully. "Lord Carne seems very healthy."

"Healthy men die. In duels, for example. I understand there may be a duel."

Anna moved slightly backward. "Maria, you *can't* wish for someone's death. That is wicked!"

Her sister's lips tightened. "He was supposed to be dead. And he is a murderer."

"Oh, nonsense."

"You can't know that. Why are you so hot in his defense?"

Anna controlled herself. "I feel sure that old story is mostly rumor and exaggeration. Maria, if you marry Mr. Liddell you must accept that you will be marrying him as he is, and as he can be. He seems personable and intelligent. I'm sure he can work his way up to a comfortable situation, perhaps even into being awarded a title one day."

Anna had not actually intended this to be a daunting speech—it wouldn't have daunted her—but Maria paled. "That could take years!"

"Yes."

"Oh, go away! I don't see that you have any right to lecture me so. You think you are so clever but you know nothing about the way the world works. Nothing!"

Anna saw that her attempts to help could drive Maria into the vapors, so she left and took up her post by her window watching number 10. More than ever she wanted a word with the earl. It clearly was important to try to solve the death of Lady Delabury, but she also wasn't sure it was beyond Mr. Liddell to plot his cousin's murder.

Lord Carne must be warned.

Unfortunately, what she saw was the earl leaving his house with a friend, dressed for the evening.

The two men waited at the curb, presumably for his carriage, for the earl wore only light shoes. He must be going to a ball later, perhaps after the theater.

Anna sighed, wishing she were going with him, trying to imagine what it would be like to dance with him. He was very agile and graceful, so he must be a good dancer. She imagined spinning in a waltz with him and then, at the end, being wickedly pulled into his arms and kissed. She was sure he was bold enough to defy convention in that way . . .

She sank her head in her hands, alarmed at the physical response she felt at the mere thought.

When she looked up, he was gone.

Doubtless he'd be out until the early hours. Anna took her dinner by the window; then when she was ready for bed she sat there to read a book, just on the chance that he would come home.

When he did, she almost missed him. He didn't return in the carriage, and she was absorbed by *Mr. Arnold's Travels in North Africa.* Some sixth sense, perhaps, made her look up just in time to see Lord Carne turn toward his house and go in.

Anna's heart immediately started to pound and her hands went clammy. There was nothing she wanted more than to be with the earl again, but she feared he wouldn't be best pleased to see her, and wouldn't like the subject she wanted to discuss.

She must be resolute, though. She slipped into her gown and spencer, not forgetting the armor of stockings and shoes, and went to open the secret door.

The door did not move.

The other side was blocked!

She pushed harder and the door gave a little but was reinforced by an obstacle. The earl had done as she had once, and placed something against it. What, though? If it was an armoire, she would never get through.

She had blocked her door in fear of her virtue. She stifled a giggle at the thought of the earl barricading the door for the same reason. Then she decided it wasn't funny. He'd doubtless blocked the door because he did not want her to use it. He would not be pleased to see her.

Anna pushed again, increasing the pressure until the obstacle moved. Ah, not too substantial an object. Probably a very solid chair. As with her bench, its main deterrence would be noise, but unless the earl had moved into this room there was a chance that no one would hear it.

She pushed as hard as she could, and with a trundling noise the chair moved enough to let her through.

"Hah!" she said, and triumphantly moved the chair to another spot farther down the wall. Then, breathing heavily from her exertions, she stopped to listen. She didn't think that noise would have alerted anyone, and in a moment, peace told her it had not.

Now her only problem was to decide how to find the earl in a house still awake and equipped with servants. She thought of returning to her room to wait for later, but she was afraid that Lord Carne might have only returned home for a short while.

So, she would have to be brave and venturesome.

Anna opened the bedroom door a tiny chink, feeling very different from that first time when it had all seemed like a wonderful game. The dangers were greater now, and she also knew this wasn't a game. She very much feared she had passed over into a new world, an adult world, where what one did could have grave consequences. With a sigh, she looked out into the corridor.

The landing around the central stairs was completely deserted, but the feel of the house was different. It was inhabited now. She heard the ticking of clocks and, faint in the distance, noise of the servants in the basement. On the end posts of the staircase, oil lamps flickered against the time when the setting sun brought gloom.

This part of the house seemed safe, but the earl was probably in his library, which meant she must go down to the lower floor. Anna crept along the carpet runner, praying that no board creaked. As she passed one door a noise froze her in midstep. Faint, slight, unidentifiable, it told her someone was there.

She let out the breath she had been holding. From her previous exploration she knew this was one of the major bedrooms, and likely to be used by Lord Carne. If someone was in it, it was either the earl or a servant. The chances were that it was the earl, though it easily could be both . . .

She contemplated the mahogany panels and decided that she must either open this door or return to her own room. No other choice was logical.

She turned the knob and walked in.

"What is it?" asked Lord Carne sharply, and turned.

They stood frozen for a second, he by her unexpected appearance, she by the fact that he was only wearing his tight dark pantaloons.

Then he moved swiftly past her to shut the door. "What the devil are you doing here?"

"I had to speak to you!" Anna swiftly turned her gaze to a still life on the wall, but the image of his body was imprinted in her brain. She'd never seen a real muscular male torso before in her life, and the wonder of it had her dizzy—golden, contoured like the finest classical statue . . .

"Why?"

She had to turn back. When she did, he had pulled on a shirt. That helped her equanimity, but no one could think he was pleased with her. "I . . . I've been thinking about Lady Delabury, and the novel, and everything . . ."

"Yes?" Then before she could answer, he said, "Damnation. It's not much past nine. Surely someone might check on you."

"Not usually."

"It would be just our luck." He grasped her wrist and pulled her toward the door.

"Stop! What—"

"Be quiet and come along."

Since he'd already towed her into the corridor, Anna had little chance but to be quiet; however, inside she was seething. He was going to throw her back into her room and nail the door shut without giving her a chance to explain her thoughts.

At the secret door he stopped and let her go. "All looks well."

"I told you so!" she snapped, rubbing her wrist.

"Did I hurt you? I'm sorry. But I've no mind to be entangled in another scandal." His tone was courteous, but merely the courtesy he would give a stranger.

An intrusive stranger.

Anna felt rather sick, but she spoke up. "I do need to talk to you, my lord."

He leaned back against the wall. "Talk, then. But keep your ears open. If it seems anyone might enter your room, dash in and shut the door. If they see the door you can claim to have just discovered it."

Though she was still rather cross with him, Anna had to admit that made sense, and moved into her room. "Count Nacre is an anagram of Lord Carne," she whispered.

"Of course."

She stared at him. "Why didn't you say so?"

"It didn't strike me immediately."

Anna frowned at him. "And perhaps you didn't want anyone to know?"

He looked at her sharply, and he may even have colored, though that could just be the setting sun shining through her lace curtains. "You really are too sharp for your own good, Anna."

She swallowed and said the awful words. "Your father was Lady Delabury's lover."

After a moment he said, "Then why did she make him the villain of the book?"

Anna had worked out a rationale. "I think the affair must have been over, and it was a kind of blackmail. She was threatening your father that she had merely to direct her husband's attention to the novel for him to guess the truth. But she couldn't make him the hero. He was too old. So she made him the villain. I realized that was what was wrong with the book. Even though Count Nacre is supposed to be the villain, Dulcinea is . . . is too drawn to him. It's difficult to believe she truly wants to escape."

"Too clever by half indeed. How do you come to understand these things?"

"I read a lot."

"I always knew it was a mistake to allow women to read." But he smiled slightly and the barriers between them were lower.

"Did your father kill her?"

"It was looked into. He was in Norfolk at the time."

"Oh." Anna had forgotten that. Also, she felt she had walked into a wall, the wall of his reticence. She chipped away anyway. "Was it a true suicide, then? There was the note."

"A dose of laudanum and a note was exactly in Lady Delabury's style. Suicide wasn't. She thought herself much too important to leave before her time. Look, Anna, I know this must tantalize you, but I want you to leave it alone."

"But what of Lord Delabury? He's going to call you out!"

"He already has. That's why I came home. He threw a glass of wine at me in White's."

Anna gasped and clutched his shirt. "No!"

He touched her cheek fleetingly. "Hush. Our seconds did their appointed duties for once. We managed to have a discussion and it is all sorted out."

"Oh, thank God. But how? How did you convince him? Did you tell him about your father?"

He sighed and freed his shirt from her grasp. "He knew. Or suspected." He had not released her hands. "Delabury's belief that his wife was unfaithful had been a source of contention throughout their marriage, though his suspicions had naturally fallen on younger men such as myself, especially as such types were always the heroes of her novels. It was only after her death that he began to wonder about my father. He didn't want to accept it. He, too, is a bit of a romantic and he doesn't much care for the fact that his wife preferred a man twice his age, and . . . My father was a hard-drinking, hard-riding old rip, if you want the truth. Delabury found a journal of hers. It named no names but made it clear that part of the charm of her lover was his domination and roughness . . . Good Lord, I should not be speaking of such things to you!"

He began to move away, but Anna held on to his hands and he did not fight free. "Don't worry, my lord. I have read Greek tragedies. I suppose this explains why she was in your father's bedchamber. She wanted to frighten him back into the affair. Or perhaps just experience more of his roughness," she added thoughtfully, causing Lord Carne to raise his brows. "But this still doesn't explain why she died."

"Perhaps she simply miscalculated her dose . . ."

"Or perhaps someone forced her to take more. But who . . . ?"

He switched his grip so he was holding her hands, controlling her. "The main thing is that Delabury accepts that I lacked sufficient reason to kill her."

"Sufficient? You lacked *all* reason!"

"Did I? The woman was flirting with me, and generally doing her damnedest to make it look as if we were having an affair. This and possibly other suspicions were upsetting my mother, who was not well even then. That in turn was upsetting my father, for in his own way he cared for my mother. I suspect that was the reason he ended the affair, and that was why Lady Delabury staged her suicide. He was expected back that night and should have found her in his bed. But he took ill just before leaving home. My mother came back alone, since she had commitments in town. It was she who found the body."

A blinding certainty struck Anna. She stared at him, and even opened her mouth, but then balked at putting it into words.

"Wise Anna," he murmured.

She remembered the blithe young man of the portrait and wanted to cry. "But you went abroad. For so long!"

"It was no great hardship. In fact," he added with the ghost of a boyish grin, "I enjoyed it immensely. But you are right. In the beginning I left England to avoid Delabury, who was a lot less rational then than now."

"Because you knew that in such a case your mother would come forward—"

He laid his fingers over her lips. "Remain wise, Anna. It's over now. All it will ever be is an unsolved mystery."

"People will still talk."

"A fig for gossips." He moved away then, and began to leave.

"Can I ask just one more question?"

He halted warily. "Yes, though I don't promise to answer it."

"How did your father die? It was within days of Lady Delabury's death."

His features hardened. "The event killed him. Perhaps his sickness had been more serious than we thought, but I don't think so. As soon as he had word of Lady Delabury's death, he rushed to London. His heart gave out on the way."

"I have another question."

His lips twitched. "Why doesn't that surprise me?"

"I don't understand Lady Delabury. Her husband was apparently young, handsome, and in love with her. Why was she having an affair with an elderly man? And what did she hope to gain from her mock suicide?"

"I'm pleased to see that some human behavior still perplexes you, Anna. My father at the time was only forty-five. That may seem ancient to you, but he was a fine figure of a man. One could ask rather why she married Delabury at all." He looked into the distance. "She wanted marriage, I think. She wanted a title. I suspect she was rather naive. She lived quietly with her parents before her marriage, then married someone very like the heroes of her novels. I'm sure she thought she would find the blissful happiness that occurred at the end of her stories, but instead was rather disappointed. Then she met my father and discovered she was a woman who finds older men attractive. Moreover, she found adoration boring and challenge stimulating."

"That seems very strange to me."

He smiled at her. "So it should. You, of course, have daydreams about handsome young gallants with pure hearts and the most noble of intentions."

She had daydreams about him, but she muttered, "I suppose so."

"Is the mystery solved to your satisfaction?"

Anna touched the door. "I'm still not quite sure how they had this made without raising suspicion."

"Delabury still has no idea about the door, but I asked him about the room. Apparently Lady Delabury asked that such a room be made and he agreed. She even specified the firm to do the work. That firm was the one regularly employed by my father, so it must have been collusion. He was clearly infatuated beyond all sense . . ."

When he broke off, she feared he would not complete the tale, but he carried on. "At the same time that this room was made, he had renovations done to his house, including his bedroom. I talked to the builder, who still has responsibility for the maintenance of the terrace. It was simply a matter of keeping mouths shut about a little extra detail in the work. Straightforward enough for the builder in return for the job of looking after all the earldom's property in London."

"Oh. It is rather disappointing that in the end everything turns out to be so rational and lacking in drama."

He shook his head, smiling. "There's been enough drama for me, I assure you. You would rather I be meeting Delabury at dawn?"

"No."

"Then what?"

"I suppose I'd rather there was a wicked villain to suffer an appropriately grisly fate."

"But this is life, not a novel, Anna, and there's trouble enough in the world without looking for more. Certainly no good would be served by dragging my invalid mother before the courts." He stepped backward. "Now, this time it really is farewell, Anna. I don't want to risk suspicion by having the builders in to seal this door, but I will if I have to. I want your word that you will not use it again under any circumstances."

Anna gathered her courage. "I love you, you know."

He met her eyes. "I hope you don't. It is—"

"Just infatuation," she completed bitterly. "A girl of my age is *capable* of love, you know. In the past, girls were married younger than sixteen!"

He put his hand hard over her mouth. "Hush. Unless it is your plan to have us discovered."

Anna went hot and red. "How dare you!" she whispered when he released her. "I would never sink to that."

"No, of course you wouldn't. My apologies, Anna. But you must recognize that the world would have a collective case of the vapors at the thought of our marriage. I'm fourteen years older than you, theoretically old enough to be your father, and have lived those fourteen years to the full."

"And do such things matter to you?"

"They would matter to your father, I'm sure."

"Are you saying you would marry me if my father consented?"

She did not see him move, but it felt as if he had stepped farther away from her. "Anna, stop this. There is no question of marriage between us. Our meetings have been pleasant, but that's as far as it goes. You will get over your current insanity and in time you will meet a suitable young gentleman and be—"

To salvage some of her pride, Anna stepped back and closed the door in his face. Then she sat down and won a battle with tears. He was doubtless right. In time it would not seem so tragic. Thank heavens that she, unlike Maria, would have a few years to recover from her own forbidden affection.

She got up and blew her nose fiercely. In two years time when she entered Society with marriage in mind she would have entirely forgotten the Earl of Carne. It would be much more sensible anyway to marry a man closer to her own age. When she was in her prime, Lord Carne would be a gouty ancient.

She blew her nose again.

Then she heard the screams.

She dashed out into the corridor, then headed toward the noise coming from downstairs. A servant, she assumed, but in some terrible distress.

It was Maria—a tattered, bruised, hysterical Maria.

Lord and Lady Featherstone were already with her, helping her into the drawing room.

"He hit me!" she gasped between sobs. "He *hit* me!"

Sir Jeffrey glanced around. "Anna, get some brandy." He looked back to his older daughter. "Who hit you? Where were you? What have you been doing?"

"Hush, Featherstone," said his wife, dabbing at Maria's

dirty, bruised face with her lace handkerchief. "Oh, poor darling. Water. We need water. Who did this to you?"

Maria stared at her mother a moment as if lost for words. Then she said, "Lord Carne! It was Lord Carne. I went out into the garden, and he tried to . . . I fought him . . . Lord Carne."

There was a gasp from the hovering servants. Anna gasped, too, then dazedly brought over the glass of brandy. Sir Jeffrey made Maria drink a little.

Anna studied her disheveled sister, wondering what on earth was going on.

Maria coughed as the fiery spirit went down, but it seemed to calm her, so that she could lie back on the sofa. With a chill, Anna saw that one of the sleeves of her sister's gown was hanging loose, and it seemed someone had slashed the front so that it gaped, almost showing her breasts.

A servant arrived with a bowl of warm water and a cloth and Lady Featherstone began to wipe her face. "Now, Maria, you must tell us exactly what happened to you."

Maria's eyes were still wide with what looked like terror. "He attacked me!"

"Lord Carne?"

Maria closed her eyes and nodded.

"When?" Anna demanded urgently. She couldn't believe he had done such a thing.

"Just now," Maria said. "What a stupid question!"

Anna had a moment to consider, to contemplate keeping silent. A moment to consider all the consequences. She swallowed. "Then it wasn't Lord Carne."

"Oh, do be silent, Anna," snapped her mother. "You can know nothing of all this."

"Yes, I can. Because just now Lord Carne was with me."

Everyone stared at her. Then her father said, "Anna, this is no time for fairy stories."

"It's not a fairy story, Papa. He was with me."

"Where? I do see that you are dressed for the outdoors rather than for bed."

Anna thought she'd considered the implications, but the avid looks on the faces of the gawking servants made her want to hide.

Her father went swiftly to close the doors. "Where, Anna?"

"In my bedroom," she whispered.

Lady Featherstone gave a small scream, and Maria said, "To speak of liars! How on earth would the Earl of Carne get into your bedroom, you foolish girl?"

"There's a secret door."

Her father shook his head. "Anna, my dear, I fear you are letting your imagination run away with you. This is not a novel but a very serious situation . . ."

"I'm telling the truth! If you come up to my room, I will show you. As for the earl, you will have to believe me. We did nothing wrong. We were discussing the mystery of Lady Delabury's death."

"Discussing . . . ?" Her father rose to his feet. "Very well, miss, I will come and see this secret door. But if it is not there, there will be no more novel-reading for you."

Anna knew that proving the door was real was the least of her problems, but she led the way through huddled, whispering servants to her room.

Having a man in her bedroom was enough to ruin her. It was enough to force a marriage . . .

Was her tiny thrill of excitement at that thought very wicked?

Yes, it was. She had never thought to trap the earl like that, and she would not let it happen.

Once in her room, Lady Featherstone shuddered. "Poor Anna. It is this room that has disordered your wits! I knew I should never have allowed you to sleep here."

"My wits are not disordered, Mama. This room is a

replica of one in a novel called *Forbidden Affections* by Mrs. Jamison, who was also Lady Delabury . . ."

This summoned fresh exclamations from Lady Featherstone. Maria, however, was looking paler, and even more frantic.

"Oh, this is such nonsense," she gasped. "Don't listen to her . . ."

"In the novel," Anna continued, already having some terrible thoughts about her sister, "the heroine's room had a secret door. I looked to see if this one had the same door." She went to the fireplace and used the lever, then swung the door open. "And it does."

"Good Lord!" said her father. "But surely it doesn't . . ."

"It opens into the room where Lady Delabury died." Anna pushed open the door, noting sadly that the earl had trusted her word and not replaced the chair. At least he wasn't there.

Maria had collapsed onto the chaise, and both she and Lady Featherstone were staring at Anna in horror.

"How long have you known about this?" Anna's mother demanded.

"Since the first night we were here," Anna admitted.

"And you have left a way for that man to creep into this house without saying a word? You foolish girl. We could all have been murdered in our beds!"

"He didn't murder Lady Delabury!"

"Oh, you poor, misguided child. What has he been doing to you?"

"Yes," said Maria spitefully. "What has he been doing to you, since you seem so eager to lie to protect him."

"Well, Anna?" asked her father quietly as he closed the door.

"He's done nothing," Anna protested, determined to avoid entangling Lord Carne in just the scandal he'd wanted to avoid. "The earl didn't know about this door himself until I told him. And he didn't want me to use it. He even put a chair to block it, but I pushed it out of the way tonight because I wanted to talk to him about Lady Delabury's death. He made me promise never to use the door again."

"If true, that shows some sense. It would have been rather better, however, if the earl had come to me to tell me of this foolishness." He turned to Maria. "So, what does this make of your story, miss?"

"I've told the truth," said Maria stubbornly. "It's clear to me that Anna has been behaving most improperly. She's become infatuated with the earl and will say anything to protect him from the consequences of his wickedness. I don't believe for a moment that tonight was their first meeting."

Sir Jeffrey turned to Anna. "Well?"

Damn Maria. "I never said it was. I . . . I know it was wrong, Papa, but I couldn't resist exploring a little. When we first arrived here, number 10 was empty. Then the earl returned and caught me."

"Maggie!" exclaimed her father. "Did you really hit him with something, Anna?"

Anna hung her head and nodded, praying desperately that no one would ask why she had hit him.

"Why did you do such a thing, Anna?" asked her mother.

Anna tried desperately to think of a clever story that would cover all the elements of the situation, and failed. All she could do was mute the truth. "He . . . he thought I was a servant, and he was a little foxed. He tried to kiss me . . ."

"There, see?" said Maria triumphantly. "He is in the habit of attacking defenseless females. When I think on it, I smelled brandy about him tonight."

"Maria, he wasn't in the garden tonight," Anna said.

"So," said her father, "having escaped, you never went into the house again until tonight?"

Anna tried to pronounce the lie, but couldn't and knew her color was betraying her.

"Anna. The full story, please. What has been going on?"

Anna sat down, for her legs were beginning to feel rather unsteady. "I did go into number 10 one other time to meet him. He asked me to."

"How, pray?" demanded Lady Featherstone. "How could you speak to such a man, or receive messages from him?"

"It was at the tea party when he was talking about maids-of-honor." She could see her mother did not understand at all, and looked at her father. "It was a sort of code, Papa. But I understood."

"But why would you think of going, Anna, when he had assaulted you?"

"He told me I could trust him."

Lady Featherstone exclaimed, but Anna saw some understanding in her father's eyes. "And what happened?" he asked.

"The earl had realized who Maggie must be, and that there was a secret door. He was trying to find out what had happened to Lady Delabury." Anna meticulously went through their discussion and conclusions.

"And that was all?" her father asked at last.

Anna nodded, but she could feel the betraying heat rise in her cheeks.

"Anna?"

She looked up. "He kissed me." When her mother exclaimed, she added, "I asked him to!"

"And is that all he did?" her father asked.

"Yes. Truly, Papa!"

He nodded. "I believe you. You have been very foolish, my dear, but the blame goes to him, a man old enough to know better who has taken advantage of your innocence."

Anna thought this dreadfully unfair, but knew that to say so would make matters worse.

"But you do see, Papa, that Maria must be mistaken, for tonight I was speaking to the earl here, in the doorway, when she thought he was attacking her."

Sir Jeffrey turned to Maria. "Well?"

"She's lying," said Maria mulishly. "She's lying about everything. He's probably ruined her."

Lady Featherstone added to this. "What reason could Maria possibly have for lying? And it is clear that someone assaulted her."

Anna didn't want to do it, but she had to speak up. "I think it is something to do with Mr. Liddell."

Maria's face gave her away.

"Maria?" asked her father.

Maria sat in silence, hands clasped tight together.

"Maria?" asked her mother, disbelievingly. "Did Mr. Liddell do this to you?"

"It was Lord Carne . . . It was!" But then Maria took refuge in hysterics, and with an aghast look at her husband, Lady Featherstone led her away.

Sir Jeffrey looked at Anna. "You've been playing in deep waters, Pippin."

His disappointment brought tears to prick at her eyes. "I'm sorry, Papa."

"Are you really? If you had your time again, would you change your behavior?"

Anna considered it and sighed. "No, Papa."

"I suspect you fancy yourself in love, Anna."

Anna blew her nose. "It's all right, Papa. The earl thinks me every bit as much of a foolish child as you do."

"I doubt that, Pippin. If he did, he would surely have spoken to me about this."

Her father turned to leave, and Anna said, "Papa! You won't say anything to him, will you? It wasn't his fault!"

"I hardly think Lord Carne needs your protection, Pippin. This is a man's matter. I certainly will have to speak to him, since you unwisely spoke up in front of the servants. Moreover, I fear he may be in danger of mischief."

"Oh, yes, do warn him, Papa! And I thought Mr. Liddell quite a sensible sort of man when I met him."

"Young women like Maria can deprive the wisest men of their senses. It seems you have that power, too." He opened the door, then turned back, truly stern. "And you are not to use that door, Anna. Not even to warn the frail and sensitive earl of the impending visitation of an irate father. Yes?"

"Yes, Papa." They shared a smile, since it was ridiculous to think that the earl could not handle her father's annoyance.

She ran into her father's arms. "Papa, I do love you so. Many fathers might not have believed my innocence."

He hugged her back. "I know you, Pippin, and I'm sure you're a match for any man, no matter how rascally."

"He's not a rascal, Papa."

"We won't argue about that, if you please. But he is not the man for you, my dear. You must believe that."

"Very well, Papa."

As she prepared again for bed, Anna fought against tears. She knew there was no hope that Lord Carne would marry her, but that didn't stop her heart from bleeding. She also felt as if she had betrayed their secret, no matter how good the reason.

Moreover, she and Lord Carne had parted coolly, with him out of patience with her. This turn of events would hardly improve matters. She did want him to like her at least . . .

But thankfully he would be warned about his perfidious cousin.

The next day, the Featherstone establishment was as somber as if a death had occurred. Maria remained in her room, attended by her mother and Martha. Sir Jeffrey paid a visit to number 10 and then retreated to his study. Anna attempted to lose herself in reading and failed miserably. A careful watch of the street did not catch Lord Carne leaving his house.

As the hours passed she lost patience and went to knock on her father's door. At his permission, she entered.

"Did you speak to the earl, Papa?"

Her father appeared abstracted and solemn. "Yes, Anna. He freely admitted his fault in encouraging you to use that door, and he was deeply shocked by his cousin's behavior."

"What will he do?"

Her father raised his brows. "He had no need to tell me that, and I no cause to ask. I am sure he is a man capable of handling these matters."

"Oh, poor Maria."

"Oh, poor Maria if she were to marry Liddell, Anna. Sit down."

Not liking his tone, Anna sat gingerly on a hard wooden chair.

"Anna, I have told the servants that you were out in the garden with Maria, and that you ventured into the mews and met the earl there. He agrees to support that story. Your rashness in speaking up before the servants could have caused a scandal, though."

"I'm sorry, Papa. But I could not let Maria's accusation stand."

"I realize that. With a little thought, however, you could have held your tongue until we were private."

"But then the servants would have believed her."

Sir Jeffrey shook his head. "The earl's reputation could bear another dent, I think. And if we continued on good terms, no one would believe the worst."

"But that wouldn't be fair, Papa!"

"Oh, Anna . . . Fighting for justice is very dangerous, you know."

"Do you say we shouldn't?"

He smiled. "No, I cannot say that. But any parent wants a smooth path for their children's feet. However," he said more briskly, "you need a stern talking-to, young lady. You are too trusting. The earl, had he been a different sort of man, could have abused you quite dreadfully, and your rash behavior would have largely been to blame."

Anna was inclined to argue on both counts, but decided submissive silence was the wise course.

"Mr. Liddell is a handsome man with a smooth social manner, and thus both you and Maria found him attractive and pleasing. The earl could well have been another of the same stamp."

"I wouldn't say Lord Carne had a smooth social manner when I first met him."

"The less said of that, the better, miss."

Anna blushed, wondering just what her father knew, or guessed. "I would like to know exactly what happened this morning, Papa."

"I'm sure you would, Miss Curiosity." He flashed her an intent look. "The earl expressed a wish to meet with you in more normal circumstances, and he seemed to feel you were entitled to an explanation of it all . . ."

Anna's heart began to beat a little faster.

"I have been considering the matter, and cannot see that it will do harm. Do you wish to meet him?"

Anna suppressed a wild *yes* and said demurely, "I would dearly love to know exactly what went on, Papa."

Her father was clearly not bamboozled, but he wrote a brief note and rang for a servant to deliver it next door.

In a few minutes, Lord Carne entered the study.

Anna stared at him anxiously, wondering if he would be

angry, but he smiled. "I understand I have to thank you for defending my honor, Anna."

Anna glanced between the two men, feeling the strangeness of the situation. "I'm sorry if it caused trouble."

"I'm sure it caused less than it saved. Your father was quite forbearing in the circumstances."

"Largely," said Sir Jeffrey, "because of my belief in Anna's good sense. Please be seated, Carne."

The earl sat quite close to Anna, reminding her of that meeting in the bedroom, when they had shared laughter and a depth of understanding that still lingered in her heart. She lowered her eyes to her clasped hands. *Don't make a fool of yourself, Anna. This is the earl.*

She looked up. "So, my lord. You are going to explain it to me?"

"Can anyone explain the insanity of love? My cousin, desperate for your sister, decided to do away with me. His clever plan was to incite poor Delabury to challenge me. When that failed, he rushed over here, where he had arranged a tryst with your sister."

"Maria had arranged to meet him in the garden? She must have been besotted."

"How true. He needed some way to re-agitate Delabury, and hit upon the notion of having me supposedly attack Maria. David would inform Delabury, pointing out that my rank would prevent justice being done, but that he could rid the world of a villain. We'll never know if it would have worked, thanks to you."

"I could almost feel sorry for your cousin if he hadn't hit her."

"It does show a baser side, does it not? But it had a good effect in that it truly shocked your sister. She stuck with her story at first because she could see nothing else to do, but I gather she no longer wants anything to do with my cousin. You'll be pleased to know he is to leave England. I have some business interests in Morocco and he will take care of them for me. If he does well he could make his fortune. If he tries any tricks, I fear he will come to a sticky end. As he will if he returns to England in the next ten years."

"You're ruthless . . ."

"When I need to be, yes."

Anna stared at him, storing him in her heart, for she could sense the farewell approaching like a cloud on a summer's day.

The earl rose. "Any more questions?"

When will I see you again?

Do you care for me at all?

Are you hurting now as I am?

Anna shook her head and stood, too. "No, my lord. I think all is finally explained."

"As I gather from your father that you will shortly be leaving town, I think this is farewell."

Anna glanced at her father, who said, "There is no purpose in staying, Anna, and Maria needs the peace of the country, I think."

Anna turned back to the earl, and despite her watching father said, "We have said farewell before, my lord."

"This time, it is real." He took her hand and kissed it lightly. "Good-bye, Anna. One day, a hero is going to be very fortunate in his heroine." With that he nodded to her father and left.

The next day, as the hired chaise rolled away from number 9, Carne Terrace, Anna refused to look back, but she allowed herself to imagine the Wicked Earl emerging disheveled from number 10 to stare haggardly after the departing vehicle.

It helped Anna's sanity to be back home. There was nothing to remind her of Lord Carne, and if memories intruded, she could push them back with summertime activities.

She had her friends to visit again, and to tell of the excitements in London. Though it was tempting, she did not tell any of them—not even her closest friend, Harriet Northam—about the secret door and the earl. She did tell her that the house had once belonged to Mrs. Jamison, author of some of their favorite novels, and that was enough of a thrill in itself.

Since it was July, her brothers were home to bother and distract her, and the garden provided work. The Featherstone children were expected to help there, doing such things as picking fruit and weeding. Long days and good weather bred abundant social activities such as walking, riding, angling, and parties both formal and informal.

Maria soon regained her bloom, and being Maria, soon forgot the less fortunate parts of her London experience. Her spirits revived amazingly when Lord Whelksham contrived a visit to a nearby house, clearly with the sole intention of pursuing his ardent courtship.

Anna believed she had put folly behind her and achieved a return to her pleasant, unadventurous life until she was summoned to her father's study one morning.

"Yes, Papa?"

He was standing by the window, hands clasped behind his back, in his serious-consideration pose. He turned slowly. "Anna, we have a visitor."

Anna looked around, but saw no one.

"He is in the garden. It is the Earl of Carne."

Anna's heart immediately began a mad dance that threatened to deprive her of her senses. Six weeks of conscientious common sense were wiped away in an instant.

"What does he want?" she asked, compelled to sink into a seat.

Her father laughed and shook his head. "For an intelligent, mature man he was remarkably confused upon the subject. He claims to be only passing by, though I am not clear as to his destination. He wants to speak with you, though I don't know about what."

Anna bounced up again. "Then I should go into the garden?"

"I doubt that will do you any harm, my dear."

"Oh." Suddenly nervous, Anna straightened her skirts. She wished she were in something better than an ordinary printed muslin. She wished her hair wasn't in a plait . . . But her encounters with Lord Carne had not been marked by elegance, and he presumably didn't care what a schoolroom miss looked like.

She caught a twinkle in her father's eye and blushed. "What should I say, Papa?"

He frowned as if in heavy thought. "You could try, 'Good day, Lord Carne. How kind of you to call.'"

Anna giggled. "Papa, what does he *want?*"

"You'll have to ask him, Pippin. But if he asks you to marry him, you should know that I will not oppose the match, even though you are so young."

"Marry . . ." Anna whispered, her suppressed hopes bubbling wildly and turning abruptly into blind terror.

"You have been very sensible about it all, Anna, but I have no doubt you formed an attachment. The fact that the earl is here—and we are not on the road to anywhere of significance—implies that perhaps he has, too. You are young, but in many ways you are more mature than Maria. I leave the decision up to you. And I may be wrong, Anna. He may not put such a question at all. Off you go, my dear, and find out."

Anna wandered out of the room in a daze, half-tempted to run and hide under her bed to avoid a meeting for which she was ill-prepared. She didn't even know anymore if she wanted to marry the earl, who had become an almost dream-like person in her mind. Perhaps he wasn't as handsome.

Perhaps they didn't share the same sense of the ridiculous. Perhaps he would seem old . . .

On such a sunny day, she really should find a bonnet, but a part of her was so anxious to see him again that her feet found wings all of their own and fairly rushed her out into the gardens.

She found him in the rose garden by the sundial, standing quite still and gazing into the distance.

He was dressed very like he had been at their first meeting, without the greatcoat—in dark leather riding breeches and a dark jacket. He wore a beaver on his head and carried a crop. He must have ridden . . .

Anna was frozen, heart pounding, unable to move closer.

Suddenly, he turned and saw her. He looked rather rueful, but just as wonderful as always, and the feelings she remembered blossomed as freshly as the roses all around them.

At the slightest encouragement she would have run into his arms, but she would not make a fool of herself and walked forward calmly. If he had come, all confused, to ask for more information about Mrs. Jamison's novels, she would hide her hurt for later.

A few feet away she cleared her throat and cropped a curtsy. "Good day, my lord. How kind of you to call."

His eyes were intent as they traveled her. "Anna," he said at last, slowly, as if the word had great meaning. "Sunlight and roses become you."

She pushed some straying curls out of her eyes. "I should have a bonnet . . ."

"Do you fear for your complexion?" He looked around. "There is a seat beneath that beech tree, if you would prefer it."

They walked over to the rustic seat built around the trunk of the spreading tree, and sat in the shade there, a proper few feet apart. Anna's rainbow exhilaration was fading to grey. He didn't seem confused. He doubtless was here on a very practical matter.

And there was nothing less practical than a marriage between a sixteen-year-old schoolgirl and a thirty-year-old rake, as both he and her father had so clearly pointed out.

She made herself look calmly into his face. "How can I help you, my lord?"

"I wanted to thank you again for stepping forward to deflect my cousin's malice. It must have been difficult."

"Not very. My parents are not ogres."

"No, they are not. But I am in your debt." He, too, appeared calm. Even bored. Was that truly why he was here? Obligation?

"Consider the debt forgiven, my lord. I am only sorry that Maria lent herself to such a scheme."

"My cousin can be a clever cozener."

"Has he left to take up his punishment?"

"Yes, appearing genuinely shaken by his own villainy. Perhaps he was turned mad by love."

Anna was beginning to feel rather bitter, and lashed out. "And what of your mother, my lord?"

"What of her?"

"It seems to me that she has avoided the consequences of murder."

He shook his head. "She suffered. She lost my father far more absolutely than she would have done through his affairs with such as Lady Delabury. It is doubtful he would have died so soon if not for that disaster. And she lost me, both physically when I went abroad, and spiritually when I realized what she had done, and that she never made any attempt to clear my name. Will it distress you if I tell you that my mother has always been a selfish, small-minded woman?"

Something in his tone made Anna reach out to touch his hand. "I wish for your sake it had not been so, my lord."

"And for your sake?" He turned her hand to hold it. "A

selfish mother and a philandering father. What does that make me?"

Anna felt the heat rise in her face, summoned perhaps by the look in his eyes. "I once confessed to . . . to finding you admirable, my lord."

"You might have come to your senses."

"I might," she said, unwilling to open herself to ridicule.

He released her hand and rose to swing his crop at an innocuous dandelion. "I have argued with myself about this for weeks, Anna. You deserve better. You deserve a young man with the bloom of innocence still on him, someone you can learn about life with, hand in hand. You deserve more years of girlhood before settling into domesticity. You deserve more balls, more parties, a Season in London, and the chance to have dozens of adoring suitors vying for your hand . . ."

Anna bit her lip. "My lord, are you saying you're not worthy of me?"

He flashed her a glance. "I suppose I am."

The laughter escaped. "Oh, I'm sorry, but I remember thinking that you would never act like a hero in one of Mrs. Jamison's novels. If you would care to get down on your knees and kiss the hem of my garment, the picture would be complete."

A flash of appreciative humor entered his eyes. "If I get down on my knees and raise your skirt, minx, it will be to enjoy the sight of your lovely legs. I was serious about what I said, though."

"I know. And it is very kind of you, but . . ." Anna grasped her courage and placed her heart before him. "It would be a dreadful waste of time to go through all those experiences when I only long for you."

He stared at her for a moment, then dropped his crop and drew her to her feet. "Are you sure? I am convinced I'm being a selfish brute."

"I'm sure. Even if you will be gouty when I'm in my prime."

His brows shot up. "What?"

Anna rested her hands on his chest, delighting in the fact that such intimacies might, perhaps, be no longer improper, and remembering a naked chest she very much wanted to see again. "I have already considered the practicalities, you see," she teased. "When you are fifty, I will only be thirty-six, and with luck I will still be in full vigor. But I will be most careful not to overexert you, my lord—"

Her mischief was silenced by his demanding lips, and she responded enthusiastically. When he finished, however, she rested against him, clinging to his lapels. "I am not sure I will be in full vigor after twenty years of kisses such as that."

"I hoped you'd realize that, minx. I will eat moderately and exercise frequently so as not to be a disappointment to you in my dotage."

"Oh, good." She ran her hand up over his starched cravat to his neck. "You're very hot."

"Quite natural in the circumstances, I assure you. Anna, you do realize that Society will raise its brows at our marriage."

"A fig for Society. Anyway, I am hoping that you will revive your love of travel and take me to Greece."

He captured her hand and kissed it. "It will be my delight to take you to Greece, and to Rome . . ." He turned her hand and kissed her palm. "And to heaven."

"Heaven?" Her knees were weakening again.

"You will see."

"Oh, you mean bed." Anna tried to sound prosaic, but it came out as a squeak.

He nipped the base of her thumb. "Yes, I mean bed, you outrageous child. And though it will be beyond me to deny myself your delights entirely, I will try not to get you with child for a while. I will try to give you some years of freedom."

Anna stared at him. "I didn't even know that was possible. How—"

He covered her lips with his fingers. "I will educate you after the wedding."

When he moved his fingers, Anna said, "But if there are such ways, everyone should know! When I think of the suffering some women experience through unblessed or unwanted babies . . ."

He was looking rather harried. "Lord, I should have learned to keep my mouth shut with you, Anna. Don't go babbling of such matters. When you know all, perhaps you can pass the information on, privately. Many men do not approve of women having such knowledge."

"Many men are villains, too." But then social issues were swamped by other thoughts. "Are we engaged to marry, then?"

He smiled, and there was a glow to it that warmed her heart. "I consider us to be so."

"Oh, good." Anna began to tug him back toward the house. "We must tell my parents. How soon can we wed? I have this great thirst for education."

He laughed. "Soon, Anna. Very, very soon. I'm afraid that if I hesitate my better nature will resurface and I'll let you escape."

"Escape!" Anna halted to frown into his wonderful blue eyes. "If you try to renege, my lord, after raising my hopes so high, I will hunt you down and take terrible revenge upon your body!"

"Now that," said the Wicked Earl with a mysterious smile, "is almost sufficient enticement . . ."

The Pleasure
of a Younger Lover

VANESSA KELLY

Chapter 1

The Archer Mansion
London, 1813

"This is the worst idea you've ever had," Clarissa moaned. "I can't believe I let you talk me into wearing this scandalous gown! I look like a demi-rep on display at Covent Garden."

Her best friend, Lillian, Lady Montegue, gave an irritated huff. "Nonsense. You look absolutely beautiful. That dress is divine, and your hair and jewels are exquisite. Everything is just as it should be except for that grimace you call a smile."

Clarissa, better known to the *ton* as the widow of Captain Jeremy Middleton, felt the muscles in her jaw contract another notch. It seemed like forever since she'd last attended a ball. She'd never been enamored with large crowds and overheated, cavernous rooms, and this particular event was proving to be worse than anticipated. But Lillian had refused to listen to Clarissa's excuses, roundly declaring that it was time, after a year and a half, to come out of deep mourning.

Clarissa cast her friend a reproachful glance. "You told me to look happy. That's what I'm trying to do."

"Well, you certainly don't look happy," Lillian replied. "You look ready to murder someone. I wish you would stop it."

Clarissa gratefully dropped her feeble pretense. If only she could cover her bosom as easily as she could transform her face with a smile—or the lack of one. It would be a miracle if she didn't pop out of the top of her gown before the evening was over.

Resisting the urge to tug the gauzy muslin up over her breasts, she wondered again how she had allowed Lillian to persuade her to wear so revealing a gown. Or, for that matter, to attend the biggest crush of the Little Season. After all, it wasn't as if she *had* to attract a husband. She had a substantial widow's portion and still had the funds Jeremy had settled on her when they were married. Over a year had passed since her husband's death, and the initial, searing pangs of grief had finally subsided. But Clarissa couldn't escape the dull ache that filled her chest every time she thought of Jeremy.

She swallowed hard, forcing down a childish rush of tears. A sea of scarlet uniforms and vibrantly colored gowns swam before her blurred vision, a dazzling display of gaiety and wealth set off to advantage in the splendid ballroom of the Archer family mansion on Brooke Street. But to Clarissa, the red of the soldiers' uniforms throbbed and pulsed under the blazing chandeliers like a gaping wound—a sickening reminder of all she had lost on the blood-soaked ramparts of a Spanish fort.

Even in the heat of the ballroom, cold prickles raced over her flesh and her heart thudded with a stuttering rhythm. She found it hard to catch her breath.

"What am I doing here, Lillian?" she forced out, barely able to keep her seat. Every muscle in her body urged her to flee to the quiet safety of the town house she shared with her elderly father-in-law, Colonel Middleton. "I'm too old for this kind of thing. It was very kind of you to invite me tonight, but I'm just coming out of mourning. And everyone is staring at me. I'm sure I'm making a complete fool of myself."

Lillian shook her head in gentle reproof.

"Clarissa, you must stop thinking like that. You're thirty-two—the same age as me. You don't see me wearing those wretched gowns you've grown so fond of. It's time to stop dressing like an old widow with one foot in the grave."

"Sometimes I think I *was* buried in that grave in Spain," Clarissa sighed. "Right alongside Jeremy."

Lillian's blue eyes grew misty.

"I know you feel that way, darling. But you're very much alive, and more beautiful than ever. That's why people are staring. You cast every other woman in this room into a complete shade—especially in that gown."

Clarissa rolled her eyes, but the tight feeling inside her eased. Her friend rewarded her with a teasing smile.

"Jeremy used to love it when you dressed up," Lillian said. "Do you remember? He was so proud of you, forever telling me how lucky he was that you chose him over all the fashionable young bucks who vied for your hand."

Clarissa smiled at that, even though the memory of Jeremy's ardent admiration brought her as much pain as pleasure. "I remember. He used to tease me about it, and tell me that he could never understand why I fell in love with such an ordinary fellow. But Jeremy was anything but ordinary. I've never known such a kind, wise man—before or since."

Lillian nodded. "If he were here now, he would tell you not to spend the rest of your life pining for him. You're still a young woman, Clarissa. You deserve to love, and to be loved again. That's what Jeremy would want for you."

Clarissa drew in a deep breath, the ache blooming in

her chest. "I don't know if I can love again. Not after what happened to Jeremy."

Lillian studied her through narrowed eyes. After several considering moments, she seemed to reach a decision. "He would certainly not want you to molder away in that gloomy house, turning yourself into a nurse for his invalid of a father. Colonel Middleton is as rich as Croesus. He could hire ten nurses to attend him, if only you would agree to it."

Clarissa shook her head. "But—"

Lillian waved away her attempt to protest. "You know it's true. And you know part of you wants it, too, or you wouldn't have come here tonight."

Clarissa let out a grudging laugh. "I never could hide anything from you, could I?"

"Nor can you resist me. I've known what's best for you since the day we met. I was the one who introduced Jeremy to you, wasn't I? You must trust me to know what you need."

Clarissa tamped down a flare of irritation. People always claimed to know what was best for her. And they never had any compunction about telling her what to do.

Not that she could blame her friends and family. Always, she'd been painfully shy. A milksop, her father used to call her. Only Jeremy Middleton had made her feel confident and happy. But her husband had gone off to war and to his death, leaving her alone and frightened once more.

Meeting Lillian's troubled gaze, Clarissa dredged up a brittle smile. She hated it when her friends fussed over her. It made her feel resentful, and that resentment made her feel guilty and ungrateful.

"You're right, Lillian," she replied in an apologetic voice. "I'm sorry for being so petulant. Jeremy would be upset to see me sulking in a corner, pouring out my troubles to you. And I'm sure you're longing to dance with Richard. I see him mooning at you from the other side of the ballroom."

Lillian scoffed. "He always looks like that. He does it to keep me from flirting with other men."

Clarissa smiled. "But it never works, does it?"

"Heavens, no!" Lillian said, giving her husband a cheerful wave. "What's the good of being married if you can't flirt? It's just a bit of harmless fun, and Richard knows it."

Suddenly, Lillian switched her assessing gaze to Clarissa's face.

"No, Lillian," Clarissa said firmly, recognizing that look. "Whatever it is, I'm not interested."

Lillian gave her a sly grin. "You will be, once I'm through with you. I'm agreeing with you, Clarissa. You don't need a husband—you need a flirtation."

Clarissa gaped at her, rendered speechless. "Have you lost your senses?" she finally choked out. "I haven't the faintest idea how to flirt! I never did."

"For someone who never flirted, you always had a long line of suitors. It practically snaked round the block of your house in St. James's Square," Lillian replied dryly.

"It wasn't because I flirted with them. It was because of Papa's wealth."

Lillian batted aside that objection with a wave of the hand. "There were a great many rich girls when you were out, but none held a candle to you. What's more, you're the sweetest woman in London."

Clarissa grimaced. "Sweet, meaning boring."

"Absolutely not. There are dozens of men in this room who would kill for your notice."

"But I have no conversation," Clarissa protested. "Truly, I don't think I could flirt to save my life."

"You've forgotten how, but it's like riding a horse," Lillian replied, scanning the room for likely prospects. "It will come back as soon as you climb into the saddle."

Clarissa resisted the urge to drop her head into her hands and groan. "Lillian—"

"Oh, look," her friend exclaimed, jumping up. "Christian's finally arrived."

Casting a silent prayer heavenward for the timely interruption, Clarissa rose and shook out her skirts. "Rather late, isn't he? After all, this ball is in his honor."

"I know. He's a dreadful boy. But he was staying with friends in Kent and sent word he would be late. Apparently, he had a bit of an accident with his curricle."

"Why does that not surprise me?"

Lillian wrinkled her nose at her. "Don't be like that, darling. The only reason Christian agreed to this ball was to lure you out of that tomb of a house. He knew you couldn't refuse to see him. Not after all these years. And especially since he'll be returning to the Peninsula in just a few weeks."

Clarissa frowned, finding it hard to believe that Lillian's brother would spend any time thinking of her. Though she had known him all her life, she hadn't spoken to him in years. Not since he'd joined the army at the age of nineteen. He had returned to England on and off over the years, but she and Jeremy had spent most of their time in Devon, more than happy to avoid the social rigors of the London Season. Their occasional visits to town had never coincided with Christian's.

"I'm sure Christian rarely thinks of me," she said.

"You're wrong." Her friend seized her hand in a firm clasp. "Chris specifically said to make sure you came. He's always been very fond of you."

Clarissa allowed Lillian to tow her through the press of bodies until they reached the edge of the dance floor. "I can't imagine why. All we ever did was snipe at each other. He was the most rag-mannered boy I ever met. You said it yourself a thousand times."

"That was years ago. Just look at him—he's grown into such a handsome man. Doesn't he look splendid in his uniform? He's now an aide-de-camp to General Pakenham, you know. One of the youngest ever appointed." Lillian leaned over, continuing in a confidential voice, "He's up for a promotion—to Wellington's command, no less. But don't say anything. No one's supposed to know. He expects to find out before he returns to Portugal."

Clarissa could readily agree to Lillian's request. The last thing she wanted to do was talk to a soldier about his military career, even if that soldier was Christian Archer. The scarlet-coated officers swirling about the ballroom reminded her far too much of Jeremy, lost forever to the random cruelty of a French bullet. But she bit her tongue and went up on tiptoe, trying to see over the dancers and the cheerful, gabbing mob on the perimeter of the room.

After a few moments of craning her neck, she gave up. Her short stature prevented her from seeing anyone but the guests in front of her. Papa had always called her a sad dab of a female, too small to catch the notice of any man worth his salt. That hadn't proved to be the case, but the stinging memory of his words retained the power to make her cheeks burn with humiliation.

Lillian voiced a pleased exclamation and waved. The crowd parted in front of them, and a broad-shouldered man in an officer's uniform appeared in the gap.

Clarissa's eyes widened and her mouth dropped open as she gazed up into eyes the color of sapphires, so striking in a tanned, lean face. She would recognize those eyes anywhere—the eyes of the scrappy hellion five years her junior who had teased her mercilessly when she was a young miss. But the powerful, hard-looking man who loomed over her now was no boy, even though his eyes still glittered with devilment.

Her breath died in her throat as Christian's gaze roamed

leisurely downward, pausing to linger on her low-cut bodice before moving back to her face. His eyes caught and held hers, and her heart kicked into a racing gallop. She watched, dumbfounded, as his sensual mouth curved up in a roguish, devastating grin.

Clarissa had seen the same look on Christian's face so many times before in the past—a look of unbridled mischief. But now he was a man, and a battle-hardened soldier at that. Whatever his game was, she instinctively knew it would involve a great deal more than pulling on her braids or putting a frog in her jewelry box.

That knowledge made her nervous, indeed.

Chapter 2

Clarissa stared into Christian's deep-set eyes, unable to utter one sensible word. His smile slid into an amused grin, and she realized her mouth was open—wide enough to catch flies, if the look on his face was any indication.

Clamping her jaw shut, she inwardly cursed the flood of heat rushing to her cheeks. Blushing over Christian? What in the world had come over her?

"There's no need to pink up on my account, Ladybird," Christian said. "But I'll be happy to take the reaction as a compliment."

His words came out in a masculine rumble, warmed by a hint of laughter. In response, something fizzy shot down her spine. Surprise turned to alarm as she realized her body had turned traitor, responding to Christian on a purely physical level. Not since Jeremy marched off to war had she felt anything remotely similar. She had thought never to feel it again, nor had she any desire to.

Or so she had thought.

Fortunately, before she could do something truly stupid—such as continue to gape at Christian like a bird-wit—Lillian whacked her brother on the arm with her closed fan.

"Why in heaven's name would you refer to Clarissa by

that silly nickname? You know she has always hated it. You really are the most dreadful, annoying boy, Christian."

He laughed—a rich, entrancing sound. As if by magic, the tumult of the ballroom faded away, and Clarissa found herself transported back to a time when the world was bright and peaceful. To a time when she and Lillian had romped through the woods on the Archer estate with a pack of frolicking spaniels on their heels, and a rambunctious, teasing boy always at hand to make them laugh.

"She hates it?" Christian asked. "She never said anything to me. But if that's the case, certainly I'll call her Clarissa from now on."

"Now you're being disrespectful," Lillian scolded, sounding like her mother. "Her proper name is Mrs. Middleton, as well you know. Did you lose all your manners in the Peninsula?"

Christian's vibrant eyes turned serious, although a shadow of a smile still lingered on his lips. He executed a faultless bow, looking every inch the dashing officer in his regimentals. "Mrs. Middleton, please forgive my shabby ways. I have been too long away from the civilizing influence of the ladies. You may blame my bad manners on the fact that I spend most of my time in the company of soldiers—an uncouth lot at the best of times."

Clarissa forced herself to rally. It *was* only Christian. What did it matter that he had turned into perhaps the most handsome man she had ever seen? Besides, it was foolish for a widow to act in so ninny-headed a fashion over a younger man.

"There's no need to apologize, Captain Archer," she replied, trying to strike a note of friendly disinterest. "We're the oldest of friends, are we not? I was simply surprised at how . . ."

She trailed off, running a quick glance over his tall, impressive physique. How to explain her reaction without sounding like a flustered schoolgirl? Her cheeks began to heat again as she struggled to find the correct response.

Although the devil was back in his eyes, he took pity on her.

"I imagine you're surprised at how I've grown," he said. "I believe I was little more than a callow youth the last time you saw me."

Lillian rolled her eyes. "A beanpole, more like it. I never knew a boy as tall and skinny as you were before you joined the army. Father used to say you should have picked the navy, instead. They could have used you as a mast on a frigate."

Clarissa smiled with relief as brother and sister bantered back and forth, finally understanding her strange reaction. The last time she had seen Christian he'd been a gangly boy, his body giving no hint yet that he would grow into such a powerful man. In his dress uniform, he was a handsome, intimidating giant.

"You certainly are quite large," she interjected into a pause in the conversation. "I'm sure I'd have to stand on a chair if I wanted to box your ears again. It was so much easier when you were a little boy."

Christian's ready laughter sent a ripple of pleasure humming through her body. Clarissa couldn't help laughing, too, but more from surprise that she was actually enjoying herself than from the humor of her silly joke. A few nosy guests turned and leveled their quizzing glasses at her, but for once she didn't care. It had been a long time since she had felt this at ease.

Christian's eyes gleamed. "If you ever think I need my ears boxed, Mrs. Middleton, I'll be happy to escort you to a chair and hand you up. I should be most happy to receive a correction from you."

"Really, Christian, the things you say," huffed Lillian. But for all her scolding, Clarissa's friend was a complete fraud. Lillian gazed at her brother, pride and love shining in her eyes. Clearly, no regrets for Christian's chosen profession diminished her enjoyment of his company. No fears for his future frayed the edges of her happiness. Lillian and the entire Archer family had sent Christian off to war with their blessings, never doubting that he would cover himself in honor and glory. They seemed happy to make the sacrifice, even as the war dragged on year after year, the casualties mounting ever higher.

One of those casualties had been Jeremy.

At the unbidden thought, Clarissa pressed a hand to her stomach, willing the sick feeling that suddenly tightened her insides to subside. Unlike the Archers, she had begged her husband not to join the army. What were king and country to her if the war meant she might lose the man she loved? But Jeremy had gently but firmly overruled all her objections, telling her that every man must do his duty. She had almost hated him then, as she had in the months that followed his death.

Taking a deep breath, she cast her gaze around, trying to distract herself. But everywhere she looked, she saw only red coats and gold epaulettes. The room overflowed with officers—except for one. The only one who mattered to her, and who was lost forever.

A gentle hand touched her shoulder. She jerked her head up to meet Christian's gaze. His too perceptive eyes inspected her.

"Mrs. Middleton, are you well? It's very hot in here. Perhaps you should sit down."

"Goodness, no," she replied with a forced laugh. "I'm perfectly well, thank you."

"You do look rather odd, dear," said Lillian, peering at her with concern. "It's no wonder, since it's a terrible crush in here and getting worse by the minute. Are you sure—oh, blast! There's Mother waving at me from the door, looking ready to pitch a fit. No doubt some kitchen disaster has struck, or we're running out of champagne."

She flashed Clarissa an apologetic smile. "I'd better see what's wrong. You stay with Christian and catch him up on all the on-dits. I'll see you both at supper."

Before Clarissa could even think to object, Lillian slipped away, leaving her alone with a man she felt she no longer knew. And whose presence had thrown her disconcertingly off balance. As she looked into his eyes—so vibrantly blue—the room and the crowds wavered and dimmed, fading away. The strange sensations left her breathless.

Christian's angular features registered mock alarm. "Good God, Mrs. Middleton. Left to your own devices with the dreadful boy! Shall I take you over to a chair now, so the boxing of my ears can commence? Or would you rather we stroll about the room and make cutting comments about the other guests? Either way, I promise I'll do my best to entertain you."

His lighthearted jesting eased her tension, and she cast him a smile. "Captain Archer, you're under no obligation to entertain me. This is your night, after all. I'm sure you'd much rather spend it in the company of a beautiful young debutante than reminiscing with a quiz of an old widow."

When he frowned, she inwardly winced. She hadn't meant the words to come out bitterly, but it had become an old habit. An ugly one, borne of months of anger and grief.

Christian took her elbow and gently steered her to a shallow window alcove.

"Mrs. Middleton," he said, "you must allow me to offer my condolences on the loss of your husband. He was a good and kind man, and the world is a poorer place without him. I'm sorry I haven't had the opportunity to express my sentiments in person until now."

Clarissa shook her head. "You needn't apologize. I was

most grateful for the letter you sent me after we received the news. It was a comfort knowing that you spoke with Jeremy only a few weeks before . . ." She let her voice trail off.

He slipped easily into the verbal gap. "I was grateful to have had the opportunity to speak to him, and hear the news from home. I'm rarely in one place long enough to receive letters in a timely fashion. Of course, Captain Middleton spoke mostly of you. He was devoted to you, as I'm sure you know."

A flash of raw anger burned in her chest. "But not devoted enough to stay home with me, where he belonged," she said in a clipped voice.

He looked startled. Hesitating for a moment, he responded in a gentle voice, pitched so only she could hear.

"Mrs. Middleton . . . Clarissa . . . your husband was a man of honor. He did what he believed was right. But it was clear to me, and to everyone who knew him, that his heart remained in England. With you. Why would you ever doubt that?"

Because I begged him not to go, and yet he did.

Out of habit, she swallowed the bitter words that came to her tongue, knowing how selfish she would sound. How could Christian, a battle-tested warrior, ever hope to understand what she felt?

"He should never have gone," she managed to say in what she hoped was a rational voice. "He was far from strong. Physically, I mean. His doctor told him not to go, but he wouldn't listen."

Christian studied her face in silence, his keen eyes thoughtful. That in itself was surprising. She had expected him to deliver a lecture about duty and honor. Everyone else had chastised her when she had tried to stop Jeremy from transferring from the local militia to the regular army. No one had listened to her, or tried to understand.

"I believe Captain Middleton was stronger than you

realize. At least in spirit," he finally answered. "But he loathed every second that the war took him from your side. Whatever you think about his reasons for going, you must never doubt that."

"Thank . . . thank you," she stammered. She looked at him uncertainly, not sure what else to say. The familiar, confusing mix of anger, sorrow, and guilt whirled within her, but it seemed muted, as if the individual emotions had lost some of their power.

Christian waited patiently for her to recover her countenance. Standing with his back to the cheerful mob, he used his body to protect her from the crush. She gazed into his handsome face, and a seductive warmth began to steal through her limbs, along with an oddly familiar sense of something else. Was it belonging?

Clarissa frowned and took a step back. That couldn't possibly be right. She didn't belong anywhere. Jeremy's death had pitched her into an obscure landscape, and she hadn't yet begun to find her way back to where life had been before.

As she struggled to understand the elusive emotions, Christian moved closer. His muscular thigh, encased in form-fitting white breeches, brushed the skirts of her gown. She shivered, and the soft warmth of only a few moments ago fled, replaced by feelings of both panic and excitement. Sucking in a breath, she willed her racing heart to settle.

She stared at the medals and ribbons on his broad chest as she gave herself a silent scolding. There was nothing to be afraid of or excited about. Not in conversation with an old friend.

But then why was she so tongue-tied?

A mist of perspiration beaded her neck as she searched for a harmless topic of conversation. Christian began to look amused again, and not the least bit awkward. Fortunately for her nerves, he broke the embarrassing silence.

"Lillian tells me you have just come out of deep mourning. I'm honored that you chose this event to grace with your presence."

She blushed, wondering if he was teasing her.

"Truly, it . . . it was nothing," she stammered. *Blast!* What the devil was wrong with her?

She tried again. "I was happy to come. You know how persuasive Lillian can be. She would have had my head if I refused. Your mamma, as well. She was quite insistent."

Splendid. Now she was babbling. Anyone would think she was a debutante in her first season, instead of a widow approaching her middle years.

His gaze sharpened. "Clarissa, I'm not teasing you. I am genuinely honored."

Her face flamed with the belief that she was making a complete fool of herself.

"How did you know I thought—" She broke off. "Oh, never mind. I don't want to know. Shall we talk about something else besides me?"

"Of course," he said. "What would you like to talk about?"

"You," she blurted out.

His eyebrows went up and his grin returned. It took all her willpower to repress a groan. Without a doubt, she had truly forgotten how to make polite conversation.

He leaned back against the curving alcove wall and settled his arms across his chest.

"What would you like to know?"

"Lillian said you were wounded. Shot through the shoulder. Was the wound very bad? Has it healed?"

He shrugged, and the muscles of his upper arms flexed under the smooth fabric of his scarlet coat. The gold epaulette on his uniform shimmered in the light of a nearby wall sconce, drawing her reluctant gaze to his brawny shoulders. The moisture in her mouth evaporated.

"I've had worse," he said. "At least this one gave me an

excuse for a furlough. It's been almost two years since I returned home."

Clarissa resisted the impulse to lick her parched lips. She would die before she would let Christian see the extent of her nervousness.

"You must be very happy to see your family again," she said brightly.

His eyes grew dark and knowing as he gave her an appraising inspection. Heat danced across her skin when his gaze fell to her bosom, swelling almost indecently over the edge of her low-cut bodice.

Clarissa bit her lip, trying not to breathe too heavily as she cursed Lillian for persuading her to wear such a scandalous gown. What must Christian think of her?

His next statement made the answer crystal clear.

"There are others I'm just as happy to see," he murmured in a husky voice. "One of those I'd like to spend a great deal of time with. Alone, if possible."

She stifled a gasp. Was Christian actually flirting with her? How could that be possible?

Dumbfounded, she took in the wicked gleam in his eyes and the seductive curve of his mouth. Her mind tried desperately to refute what she sensed with every fiber of her being.

But her mind failed. Christian *was* flirting with her. Even worse, she feared he was trying to seduce her. Why, she couldn't begin to fathom. But what she *could* fathom was that it scared her half to death—for more reasons than she could count, starting with the fact that he was a soldier. She had vowed never to love another soldier.

Not to mention the fact that Christian was five years her junior.

"Well, Clarissa," he purred. "What do you think? Would you like to spend some time with me, starting with the next dance?"

He moved then, pushing away from the wall to close the distance between them. He loomed over her, forcing her to tilt her head back to look into his face.

Clarissa sucked in a startled breath, both terrified and fascinated by the blatant invitation in his eyes. It made her legs tremble and her body grow weak. His gloved hand moved down the bare flesh of her arm, trailing shivers in its wake. He took her hand in a gentle clasp, weaving their fingers together.

"It's only a dance, Clarissa," he murmured. "What's the harm?"

She let out a sigh—almost a whimper—as some part of her addled brain urged her to give in. To lean into his big, hard body and allow him to sweep her away. He made her feel alive again, full of sparkling energy and heat. Part of her welcomed it with a burning need to escape the cold that had wrapped itself around her heart and soul for so long.

Almost without thought, she returned the pressure of his hand. He smiled, his eyes flaring with something like triumph. His hand closed around hers, hard and possessive.

With a thump, Clarissa fell to earth. A thousand voices in her head urged her to flee before she made an even bigger fool of herself. Christian had no business treating her this way. Like a woman to be desired, not a widow sworn never to love again.

She snatched her hand away. "You must forgive me. I promised Lillian I would help her with something."

He frowned, puzzlement chasing away some of the heat in his eyes.

"I'm sure Lillian would prefer you to stay here and enjoy yourself. I will be glad to provide any excuse you need to avert her irritation."

That was exactly what she was afraid of.

"That won't be necessary," she said, backing away from him.

She bumped into a stout dowager, who promptly dropped her fan. Rolling his eyes, Christian scooped it up and handed it back to the protesting matron. Clarissa seized the opportunity to escape into the crush of guests.

As she wove her way to the door, she chanced a glance back in Christian's direction. He stood where she had left him, hands on his lean hips, his stern gaze locked on to her across the room. She froze like a rabbit before a fox, and his mobile eyebrows lifted in enquiry. Then he gave her a slow, satisfied curve of the lips.

With that, she turned and fled. But a quiet, inner voice whispered that whatever his game was, Christian would not let her escape so easily the next time.

Christian eyed Clarissa's barely restrained dash to freedom. She held her slender back ramrod straight, but her shoulders, hitched up around her ears, spoke of how thoroughly he had unnerved her.

Biting back an oath, he started after her. He'd made several unforgivable blunders, any one of which would have given her ample reason to flee. No wonder, because his first sight of her had knocked him back on his heels, and years of repressed desire had come roaring to the surface. What little caution he'd had—and he'd never had much when it came to her—evaporated like morning mist under a blazing Spanish sun.

Clarissa disappeared behind a group of preening dandies, but a moment later he caught a glimpse of her guinea-gold hair, pulled back in a simple chignon. God, she was lovely. So lovely it made his chest ache with a pain he'd spent years trying to banish. He would never have thought it possible, but she was even more beautiful than she'd been eight years ago. Perhaps her suffering and grief had harrowed her body and spirit down to their perfect, essential elements, for there was no artifice to Clarissa. Everything she was and had ever been could be read in the pure lines of her face, and in the honest clarity of her amber-colored gaze.

He remembered the last time they'd met, on her wedding day. Clarissa had been twenty-three—almost on the shelf, by the standards of the *ton*. But no one who watched her walk down the aisle could think that. For years, dozens of suitors had vied for her hand, attracted by her pale beauty, her kind nature, and her generous fortune. She had refused them all, including the high-borne lords.

But then she met Jeremy Middleton, a scholarly young gentleman from a good but not particularly fashionable military family. In his own quiet way, Jeremy had swept Clarissa off her feet. They were married two months to the day after Lillian introduced them.

A week later, Christian had persuaded his father to purchase his commission in the regulars, not the militia. Having to remain in England while seeing Clarissa in the arms of another man would have driven him mad. Yes, he was five years her junior and had never stood a chance with her, but he'd adored her since he was a stripling. The gap in their ages hadn't made a damn bit of difference to him. And not the years, the miles, or the other women in his life had ever fully erased her presence in his heart.

He studied her sweetly rounded figure as she made her way through the ballroom, smiling and nodding to acquaintances, but allowing no one to stop her. She thought to escape him. Perhaps if he were a better man, he would let her go.

But fate had intervened in the form of Jeremy Middleton's tragic death and given him another chance. Not that Christian would have wished that tragedy to befall her. He would have gladly spared Clarissa that terrible loss—even given his own life for Middleton's—if he could have. But

God and Napoleon's army had deemed otherwise, and Christian wouldn't turn away from the opportunity presented to him.

Not that it would be easy. He had obstacles to overcome, starting with their age difference. She would see that as an insurmountable difficulty. But eight years in the army—most of it at war—had taught him patience and determination. It had made him a man, and Clarissa's equal.

She finally managed to reach the wide, arching doorway. Passing through it, she turned left. Christian was tall enough to peer over the heads of the dancers and see Clarissa hurrying toward the marble staircase leading down to the entrance hall.

Perfect.

If he didn't miss his guess, she would slip downstairs and cut through his father's study to the back terrace overlooking the garden. He had escaped more than one boring dinner party by slipping out the same way, often to indulge in a solitary cigar.

Christian made his way through the crowd at a leisurely pace. No need to hurry, now that he was sure where his quarry would seek refuge. In fact, it made sense to give Clarissa time to compose herself. The darling girl needed kind and careful handling, and he had every intention of giving her exactly that.

Or so he thought until a few seconds later, when a tall, dark-headed officer adorned with a major's chevrons emerged from the cluster of guests near the head of the stairs. The man cut through a knot of chattering women, obviously intent on following Clarissa. Even as far back as he was, Christian could see greedy anticipation on the officer's blunt-featured countenance.

Blundell.

Expelling a frustrated breath, Christian picked up his pace, moving quickly around the perimeter of the ballroom.

The last person Clarissa would want to see was Lord Everard Blundell, a major in the same regiment as Jeremy Middleton. But where Jeremy had perished at Badajoz, Blundell had returned home without a scratch. Not surprising, given he had a politician's talent for avoiding danger to himself.

Years ago, Everard Blundell had been Clarissa's most persistent suitor. Her father had exerted tremendous pressure on her to marry him—after all, Blundell was the son of a powerful marquess. But Clarissa had firmly resisted. As a consequence, she had incurred her father's verbal wrath, and probably a slap or two from him in the process. But she had held her ground, convinced, so Lillian had told him, that Blundell was a bully and a cad. Her assessment, as far as Christian was concerned, was dead-on.

Blundell charged down the stairs in Clarissa's wake. Christian dodged a large, turbaned matron, determined to catch up with the bastard before he could reach Clarissa, alone and vulnerable, on the terrace.

"Captain Archer, hold fast there," exclaimed a familiar voice from behind him.

Christian bit back a curse so foul his mother would have swooned if she heard it. He halted and turned to see General Sir Arthur Stanton trundling down the hallway toward him. At any other time he would have enjoyed reporting to the old warhorse, but not tonight. Not when Clarissa might be in trouble.

"Well, my boy, I finally track you down," said the general, planting himself firmly in Christian's path. "How go things with the First Foot? How is my old friend General Pakenham? Don't spare me any details. I have all night, and I want to hear everything."

Chapter 3

Clarissa leaned over the stone balustrade of the terrace and peered at the shadow-filled garden below her. The chill of the October evening made her shiver, but she welcomed the cool air on her overheated skin.

She'd been so eager to escape the ball she hadn't thought to retrieve her wrap from one of the servants. Flustered, with conflicting thoughts skittering about in her head, she'd been intent only on retreat—mostly from Christian, but also from anyone else who might stop her. She'd always been like that at social functions. Her father had lamented what he called her fatal lack of charm, saying only her looks and his money had made her even passably acceptable. A man wanted a companion, he'd complain. Someone to entertain and amuse him, not some timid mouse of a girl who would bore him to death.

She breathed out an unhappy sigh, resting her forearms on the stone ledge. Jeremy had rescued her from that glittering but nerve-wracking world, but he couldn't rescue her now. Not from herself and her stupid fears, nor from well-meaning friends determined to push her back into a life she'd never wanted.

Unnerved by the fine tremors coursing through her fingers, Clarissa stood tall and flexed her hands. Blast Christian for flirting with her like she was just another pleasant diversion whilst on furlough. Still, he was young and handsome and would soon return to the front, so why shouldn't he entertain himself? Any man in his position would. But why did he pick her, for heaven's sake?

Her cheeks prickled with shameful heat as she acknowledged a possible explanation. Christian was probably taking pity on her, offering a brief flirtation because he felt sorry for the lonely widow uncomfortable in polite society. Perhaps Lillian, so obviously worried about her, had put him up to it. The very notion that her friend might have persuaded Christian to do such a thing—to make Clarissa the recipient of misguided charity—made her stomach churn.

Carefully gathering her skirts, she sat down on one of the wrought iron benches scattered around the terrace. The cold of the metal seat quickly penetrated her gown and chemise, but despite the chill she couldn't bring herself to return to the house. Not until she could regain at least some semblance of composure.

And certainly not until she understood her own confused reaction to Christian's attentions. That was the heart of the matter, wasn't it? Regardless of his intentions, and what it all meant to him, how did *she* feel about it?

After several useless minutes fidgeting with the lace trim on her fan, Clarissa had to admit the truth. Christian had frightened her, but she'd been flattered by his seductive flirtation. More than flattered. Entranced. She'd actually wanted him to take her in his arms and kiss her senseless.

That impulse had lasted only moments, but those moments had been enough. Enough to forget she had been standing in a crowded room full of chattering gossips. Enough to forget she had vowed never to fall in love again, and certainly never with a man like him.

Even worse, when Christian had stared at her, his gaze so hot and knowing, she had forgotten about Jeremy. What respectable woman—a widow, barely out of mourning—would so easily betray the memory of her beloved husband?

With an irritated sigh, she rose. Either she could hide like a coward, or she could go back inside with her head high and act like the sensible person she knew herself to be. Whatever disturbing emotions plagued her right now, their cause would soon take himself back to Portugal. All she had to do was keep Christian at a safe distance until he departed. Then life would return to its quiet, safe routine, exactly as she wanted. She owed that to Jeremy's memory.

She crossed the terrace toward the study. With a little luck, she could find Lillian and Lady Archer immediately and make her excuses for the night. It wouldn't be a lie to claim she had a headache, since all this fruitless rumination had indeed set her temples throbbing.

As she reached the French doors to the study, a bulky shape loomed out of the darkness. Surprised, she gasped and took a quick step back, catching her heel on the hem of her gown. A beefy hand shot out and took her by the elbow, squeezing it tightly.

"Careful now, Mrs. Middleton," said an oddly nasal voice. "We can't have you tumbling down and cracking your pretty head on the paving stones, can we?"

Clarissa let out an involuntary hiss, jerking her arm away. That voice belonged to a man who never failed to make her skin crawl.

Swallowing hard, she forced herself to appear calm. "Lord Blundell, what a surprise. Have you tired of the party?"

He moved forward into a stream of light from the ballroom windows above them. Her stomach took a sickening flop when she saw a lascivious smile lifting his thick-lipped mouth. Brandy fumes wafted over her as he stepped closer.

"I was following you, my dear. I was certain you saw me as you descended the stairs, and divined my intention to speak with you. Unfortunately, that old blowhard Lord Sobey waylaid me, preventing me from joining you until now."

She frowned, startled by his impertinent assumptions. "My Lord, I only stepped out for some fresh air, but I find it's much too cool without a wrap. I'm returning to the ball this very instant."

The smile congealed on his face, but only for a few seconds. Then a smug look settled on his features as he moved a step closer.

"Ah. You hope to tease me. You always were a minx, Clarissa. I remember your father warning me about that when I first proposed to you. I've always regretted that I didn't take a stronger stand. By the time I realized you needed a firm hand, you had already accepted Middleton's offer." He cast her an oily smile. "I assure you, I won't make the same mistake twice."

She choked, outrage closing her throat, but he ignored her reaction.

"You wish to punish me just a little for making you wait out here on the terrace, don't you?" he asked. "But now that I'm here, surely we can dispense with silly games. There's no need for you to keep me at arm's length a moment longer, now that you have returned to society."

He moved forward again, forcing her to retreat to the balustrade. Every nerve in her body shrieked at her to run, but he blocked her only exit. Unfortunately, she was never very good at putting bullies in their place. Still, she tried to muster up a cutting tone.

"You are talking nonsense, sir. Please move aside. It is most improper for us to be out here without a chaperone."

He crowded her against the parapet, thrusting forward until their bodies almost touched. Even without looking directly down, she could see a bulge in the front of his breeches. She swallowed, willing her dinner to remain in its proper place.

"Ah," he rasped. "Fortunately, you're no longer a maiden, but a widow and an experienced woman."

His queer voice scraped along her nerves. Though a bulky, coarse man, Lord Blundell spoke in a thin tone that seemed to strain his throat. When he courted her years ago, anxiety had slithered through her whenever he opened his mouth. No one had understood how she felt but Lillian. Certainly not her father, whose punishment for refusing Blundell's suit had left her with painful bruises.

"You offend me, sir," she said, fighting to keep her voice steady. "I am the widow of an officer who fought by your side—one of your own men. That alone should be reason enough to treat me with more respect."

To her surprise, he flinched. Even in the dim light she could see the blood drain from his face. But he soon recovered, staring at her so intently she felt like a cornered animal.

"I do respect you, Clarissa, so much so that I intend to make you my wife." He inspected her bosom with a lustful gaze. "Now that your period of mourning is over, you must recognize how advantageous it would be for you to marry again. If your father were still alive, he would surely urge you to accept my offer."

Anger rose in a hot, welcome flare, infusing her with courage. "You honor me, sir," she said coldly, "but I have no desire to marry. Now, if you will excuse me, I must return to Lady Montegue."

She attempted to force her way past, but he grabbed her arms. His thick fingers squeezed her in a pinching grip.

"Let go of me," she gasped.

She tried to yank away but he held fast. His nails dug into her flesh, sending lancing pain down her bare arms. She struggled, but he pulled her close, rubbing himself against her.

Black spots danced in front of her eyes as panic welled

in her chest. She clamped down hard, forcing her vision to clear. A scream bubbled up in her throat, but a shred of reason sealed her lips. The scandal if they were found like this would be overwhelming, and there was no predicting the consequences. To be discovered alone together, in so secluded a place, whomever was finally blamed—and Blundell might very well accuse *her* of improper behavior—her reputation would be irreparably damaged.

He bent his face close, leering at her. The reek of alcohol and the disgusting grind of his hips made her want to vomit.

"Don't play the innocent with me, Clarissa. Not dressed like this. Not when you engage in open flirtation in front of half the *ton*. I saw you upstairs with Archer," he sneered. "Why waste your time on a boy when you can have a man? You made that same mistake when you married Middleton. You would be wise not to do it again."

He might as well have thrown a pitcher of ice water in her face. Her head cleared and her spine straightened.

"Unhand me, Lord Blundell, or I shall scream loud enough to wake the dead. You are a vile man, and I would rather die than marry you."

A murderous fury darkened his gaze. He dug his fingers into her hair and yanked her head back. A strangled cry almost escaped her throat, but he cut it off with a hard, slobbering kiss. His lips mashed hers and his tongue invaded her mouth, choking her. Unable to breathe, she struggled with a desperation born of terror.

Blundell crushed himself against her, bending her over the hard stone of the parapet as he locked her in an unbreakable grip. Tears leaked from her eyes when she felt his hand dragging up her skirts.

But more than fear rose up in a welling tide. Fury rose, too, pushing out the fear. She had to stop him. She'd rather be exposed to all of London and shunned by everyone she knew than allow the brute to molest her.

When he took a breath, she bit down hard on his lower lip. He gave a shocked cry and jolted back, letting her go so suddenly she could barely keep from toppling over the barrier behind her. Quickly righting herself, she slipped past, dodging his clumsy attempts to grab her.

"Come back here, you bitch," he spat out in a snarling voice.

She dashed for the doors leading into the darkened study, only to collide with a rock-hard body coming through them. A pair of strong arms snaked around her, keeping her from crashing to the ground.

"Clarissa," exclaimed Christian, holding her close. "What the hell is going on out here?"

She stilled in his arms, gazing up at him, trying to see his face in the dark. Her brain went blank as relief wiped out every other emotion. She sagged, her limbs weak and trembling. He cradled her in a gentle embrace, one hand splayed securely across her back.

With an effort, she managed to calm her pounding heart, breathing in the clean, masculine scent of him. Her brain stopped tumbling around in her skull and her reason returned.

"Better?" he asked in a quiet voice as he rubbed a soothing hand down her spine.

She nodded.

"Good. Then please explain why you were running as if your life depended on it."

A painful rush of blood heated her cheeks. How could she explain without causing a scene? Christian would be furious, and God knew what he would do then. She had to defuse the situation before a scandal erupted right there in the middle of the largest ball of the Little Season.

"Ah . . . nothing . . . nothing was happening," she stuttered. "I was just . . ."

She trailed off as he arched his eyebrows in disbelief. Then he lifted his gaze and stared out at the terrace, where Blundell still stood, muttering curses under his breath. Christian's face grew stern, anger tightening his features into sharp angles.

"Never mind," he said in a quiet but lethal voice. "I see the problem." His flinty gaze switched back to her face. "Did that bastard hurt you?"

Clarissa loosened her fingers from where they clutched the front of Christian's coat and shook her head.

"I'm fine," she said in a firm voice. She gave his chest a gentle push, forcing him to let go. He did, but reluctantly.

"It was nothing," she continued. "Really. I'd be grateful if you escorted me back inside. I'd like to find Lillian."

He ignored her request, his eyes narrowed on Blundell. "It doesn't look like nothing to me. What happened to your lip, Blundell?"

"That is none of your business," sneered the other man. "And you will address me as Major Blundell or my lord, *Captain* Archer. If you know what's good for you."

Christian appeared unmoved by the threat. In fact, he took a menacing step toward Blundell, despite Clarissa's attempt to pull him in the opposite direction.

"If I find you laid a hand on her," he said in a harsh voice, "I'll make you regret the day you were born."

Blundell stopped dabbing at his lip—Clarissa was very glad to see it was bleeding quite profusely—and glared back at Christian.

"Fancy her for yourself, do you, Archer? Well, I suppose you're welcome to her. I've already had a taste, but I've discovered that aging widows aren't really in my line, after all."

A growl rumbled up from Christian's throat. Then, in a

blur of motion, he surged forward and drilled his fist into Blundell's face. The man went crashing to the ground with a muffled cry of pain. Christian reached down with one hand and took hold of his collar, then hauled Blundell up as he cocked his fist again.

Clarissa leapt forward, grabbing Christian's arm and tugging on it with all her might.

"Are you insane?" she hissed. "You can't do this in the middle of a ball. Think of the scandal! Your mother will be mortified."

Sluggishly recovering from Christian's devastating punch, Blundell began to struggle and thrash. Clarissa dug her fingers into Christian's arm and shook it.

"Let go, Christian," she commanded. "I don't want this."

He glowered at her even as he continued to hold the struggling Blundell at arm's length—apparently with very little effort, since the other man couldn't break loose.

Clarissa glared back. "I mean it," she said in the same voice she'd used when he was a disobedient little boy. "Let him go."

Shadows played over his stone-hard face. His lips twitched. Opening his hand, he dropped Blundell to the terrace pavement.

"Very well. But in return, I want you to explain what happened out here," he said.

"I will not," Clarissa retorted, taking his arm. "Now, will you please escort me back to the party?"

One corner of his mouth curved into a lazy half smile, replete with a masculine sensuality that stole the breath from her lungs.

"Will you dance with me if I do?"

She huffed. "Your sister was right. You really are the most impertinent boy. But yes, I will. Now take me away from here."

He glanced back at Blundell, who had crawled over to one of the benches and hauled himself onto its seat.

The banked anger in Christian's eyes flared back to life. "Are you sure about this, Clarissa? I won't have him bothering you again."

"I feel sure he won't," she said earnestly.

He didn't look convinced.

She sighed. "And if he does, I'll tell you. I promise."

He gave a reluctant nod as he took her elbow and began to lead her away. And not a moment too soon, as far as she was concerned. The longer they stayed on the terrace, the better the chances of being discovered. Then the gossips would truly have something to say.

She scampered across the paving stones, trying to hurry Christian along. As they stepped inside the study, Blundell's nasal voice—even more nasal now, thanks to Christian's punch—halted them in their tracks.

"Stop right there, Archer," he barked. "Don't think you can run away from me."

Under Clarissa's fingers, the muscles in Christian's arm turned to iron. She stifled a groan. Could things get any worse?

Christian carefully disengaged her hand and turned to face Blundell. "Are you calling me a coward, *Major?*"

Blundell staggered to his feet, his thick features distorted with rage, his eyes burning with hatred. Clarissa shivered, her insides pulling into a knot. She'd always known Everard Blundell had a vile temper, but now something sick and disturbing seemed to emanate from his hulking figure.

She tore her gaze from him and looked at Christian, who was inspecting the other man with a mild curiosity.

"I'll have my satisfaction," Blundell barked.

Christian replied as calmly as if he were ordering ices from Gunter's. "Name your seconds."

Clarissa's heart crashed into her ribs. A duel? Over her?

She detested dueling—the very idea of men shooting at each other in a senseless display of violence, all for their so-called honor. She'd had enough of that to last a lifetime.

"You will not," she interjected, stepping between the two men. "I absolutely forbid you to engage in that barbaric, outdated, *illegal* practice."

Christian expelled an impatient breath, reaching for her. She evaded him.

"It's not up to you," he said. "At this point, it has nothing to do with you."

She stiffened. "It has everything to do with me. I don't want it. I won't have it."

He rolled his eyes, opening his mouth to argue with her.

Blundell beat him to it. "I won't be insulted without redress."

He put his head down like an angry bull and stalked toward them. Clarissa took a hasty step back, fetching up against Christian's chest. His hands settled at her waist, resting lightly but possessively on the curve above her hips. Somehow, that felt right, even though she knew how wrong it was.

"I suggest you not come closer, my lord," drawled Christian. "You've distressed Mrs. Middleton quite enough for one night."

Blundell's lips peeled back into a taunting sneer. "Hiding behind the lady, Archer? Wonder what your fellow officers in the Fifth will have to say about that?"

All along Clarissa's spine, Christian's body went rock hard. Tension and anger radiated from him, enveloping her in a hot wave. In front of her, Blundell glared at Christian with murderous intent. So much belligerent male energy crackled around her, it was a wonder her hair didn't stand on end.

She had to do something.

"And what will your fellow officers do when they hear

you tried to force yourself on me, Lord Blundell? What will your father, the marquess, do when I recount your behavior tonight?"

Christian's fingers dug into her hips and she flinched. He loosened his grip, murmuring an apology in her ear.

Blundell's sneer twisted into an ugly grimace. "I doubt anyone would believe you. After all, I'm the son of a peer. And perhaps you forget that my father is a member of the government."

At one time, she would have accepted that. But with Christian at her back, his strength surrounding her like a shield, her courage returned. "I assure you, sir, I am quite convincing when I put my mind to it."

Blundell shook with rage. "I will have my satisfaction, I tell you!"

"You'll have nothing of the sort," Clarissa retorted. "Please leave, my lord, or I will be forced to relate this unfortunate incident to our host. You may consider yourself untouchable, but I will make it my business to tell everyone about what transpired here tonight. Your father, I suspect, will not be happy about that, no matter how powerful he is."

Clarissa wouldn't have been surprised if Blundell had started foaming at the mouth, but he managed to throttle back his rage. He stormed to the French doors, giving the two of them a wide berth. But before he disappeared inside, he rounded on them.

"This isn't the end of it, Archer. Be sure of it."

Behind her, Clarissa felt Christian shrug, his hands still clasped lightly on her hips.

"I'll look forward to our next meeting, my lord," he said in a bored voice.

Giving them a last, enraged look, Blundell stomped across the floor of the study, and then the door to the hallway slammed shut.

Clarissa stood frozen in Christian's embrace, trying to quell the trembling of her limbs. Muted sounds from upstairs—the chattering of voices, the scrape of violins—began to filter into her consciousness. She heaved a sigh as life began returning to normal.

With a reassuring murmur, Christian turned her in his arms. She couldn't look at him. Now that the crisis had passed, shame was fast replacing outrage. Her cheeks flushed with the knowledge that her urge to flee from Christian had placed her in this humiliating situation.

With a gentle hand, he tipped her chin up, and she met his gaze. The rugged angles of his face, only partly obscured by the shadows of the night, emanated masculine authority and determination. She had no doubt he was going to be overly protective and pigheadedly male, when all she wanted to do was go home and forget this night had ever happened.

But then he brushed a stray lock of hair from her cheek, sending tingles racing across her skin. When he smiled, his eyes crinkling at the corners, it sucked the air out of her lungs.

Clarissa realized with a blinding flash of insight that life had most certainly not returned to anything approaching normal.

Christian studied her, his eyes warm and full of concern. His penetrating sapphire gaze held her captive, and the glow she had felt earlier in the ballroom—when he first looked at her that way—surged through her veins. A foolish part of her wanted to stand there all evening, absorbing the heat of their silent exchange.

Blinking, she looked away, determined to break the mysterious connection that had sprung up between them. It frightened her, but she couldn't worry about that now. A more pressing problem had to be dealt with, namely, preventing Christian from challenging Blundell to a duel.

She braved a look at his face. No trace of anger remained on the clean lines and sharp-cut features. But that didn't fool her.

He caressed her cheek again, and she repressed a delicious shiver.

"Are you sure he didn't hurt you?" he asked in a husky voice.

She nodded, intensely aware that his hands still rested on her hip bones. In fact, his fingers were stroking her, lightly and soothingly, through the delicate fabric of her gown. This time, she couldn't repress the shiver.

He frowned. "Are you cold?"

She shook her head, disengaging reluctantly from his embrace. He let her go, allowing his fingers to trail a path of heat as she stepped away.

"I'm fine," she said, inwardly cursing the break in her voice.

"You don't seem very steady on your feet, and you're trembling. Do you want me to send for Lillian, or my mother?"

It wasn't only Blundell who had pitched her into her current state of unease, but Clarissa would die before admitting that.

"No!" she responded a bit too loudly.

Christian looked even more concerned. She clamped down on her nerves and tried again. "Really, Christian, there's no need to call anyone. Lord Blundell hardly touched me."

His lips turned down in a disapproving curve. "His mouth was bleeding, and you were running like you had the devil at your heels when you charged into me. That sounds rather more than *barely touching*."

She crossed her arms over her chest, remaining silent.

His mouth twitched up in a wry smile and he relented. "At least tell me what happened to his lip. Did you bash him with your fan?"

Her fan? What was he talking about?

"That," he said, glancing at her hand.

She stared in surprise at the fan she still clutched, now a tangled mess of broken sticks and torn lace. It must have been crushed in her struggle with Blundell.

"No. I . . . I bit him," she blurted out, instantly regretting it.

He looked puzzled. "You bit him?"

Unfortunately, his puzzlement didn't last. Enlightenment dawned, and a ferocious scowl descended on his brow. He grabbed her hand and began towing her into the study.

"I'll kill the bastard," he muttered under his breath. "I swear to God, I'll kill him."

Clarissa panicked. "Christian, stop," she exclaimed.

He ignored her. She dug her heels into the thick carpet in front of his father's desk and jerked him to a halt.

"What?" he snapped. His eyes blazed with fury. He looked ready to go to war.

She glared up at him. He glared right back.

"Stop. It. Now." She ground out each word.

He gave an impatient shake of his head. "You needn't worry about it, Clarissa. I'll take care of this."

"Don't patronize me. Whatever stupid male thing you're planning, I won't have it. I insist that you stay away from Blundell. He didn't hurt me, and I'll make sure I never go near him again."

"You insist?"

He gave her a sweeping inspection, his features etched with a barely controlled savagery. Clarissa hated angry men—hated the raised voices and the stinging slaps that often came with the anger. But Christian, even in a rage, would always be Christian. He would never do anything to harm her.

She propped her hands on her hips, meeting him stare for stare. But just looking at him made her knees quake. He was so impossibly handsome and so intensely masculine that she wanted to shriek with frustration. How infuriating that the boy she had known had grown into a man who could tear her so easily from her moorings.

"You said he forced himself on you, Clarissa," he growled. "I thought you might be exaggerating to get rid of him before I beat him to a pulp, but clearly I was wrong."

She sniffed defensively. "I said he *tried* to force himself. It was just a kiss, which was certainly bad enough. The man is a disgusting pig."

His eyes turned into chips of blue ice.

"Besides," she added hastily, "he came out much the worse for wear, thanks to you. I'm certain he won't come near me again."

Christian's anger didn't appear the least bit assuaged. "He needs to be taught a lesson."

"Not by you," she said firmly. "I absolutely forbid it."

His eyebrows arched with arrogant command, and he looked every bit the hardened soldier. If she didn't know him so well, she would be shaking in her kid slippers. Although, if truth be told, his imperious look made her stomach flutter with a girlish excitement, which suggested she didn't really know him very well at all.

"In case you haven't noticed, Clarissa," he said in a voice both dangerous and seductive, "I'm no longer a boy for you to order about. As one of your oldest family friends, I'm responsible for you. Your honor has been insulted, and under my own roof. I cannot allow that to go unchallenged."

The flutters in her stomach turned to pangs of frustration. *Honor.* He meant *his* honor. For men, that was always what it came to. She was sick to death of it.

"I don't care about your blasted honor," she retorted, her temper finally shredding. "All this talk of honor leads to only one thing—women crying alone in the night. I've had enough of that to last me a lifetime. I won't be the cause of anything happening to you, Christian."

She jabbed his chest with her index finger for emphasis. "Or even to Blundell, for that matter. My honor is my own to defend. I don't need you or anyone else to do it for me."

As she poked at him, he stopped looking angry and started looking amused. His blasted lips twitched again, a sure sign he was holding back laughter. As brawny as he was, she still longed to box his ears.

"And don't you dare issue Blundell a challenge," she ground out, determined to put him in his place. "I'll find out if you do. And . . . and I'll tell your mother!"

For a moment, she was sure he was going to laugh, and she vowed to murder him if he did. But he managed to school his expression into one of polite interest.

That made it worse. He was obviously going to ignore everything she said. She closed her eyes, breathing through her anger—and fear, apparently, because once she closed her lids a horrifying image came to life in the darkness. With chilling clarity, she saw Christian stretched out on the ground, a bloody wound in the center of his chest.

Jeremy had died from a bullet to the chest. In all her nightmares, he looked exactly like that.

She gasped, opening her eyes. The room whirled about her and she staggered. Christian's hands shot out to keep her from falling.

"Clarissa! What the devil—"

With a quiet oath, he swept her into his arms. She knew she ought to protest, but she couldn't even muster a squeak.

Striding across the room, he gently deposited her in a leather armchair by the fireplace. He hunkered down in front of her, taking her cold hands in a comforting grip.

"It's all right, sweetheart. If that's what it takes to make you happy, I won't challenge Blundell."

Sweetheart?

She ignored the shock of pleasure that one little word gave her, focusing instead on her anger to restore her strength.

"I don't believe you," she said, tugging her hands away. Whenever he touched her like that, her mind went sideways in the most disconcerting fashion.

He gave an exasperated shake of the head.

"Oh, ye of little faith," he replied sardonically. "I give you my word."

She snorted, and his eyes narrowed with a dangerous intensity. A prickle of apprehension slithered down her spine. Perhaps she had challenged him enough for one night.

"Oh, very well," she said in a grumpy tone. "I believe you."

"I should hope so," he said dryly. "Not that I won't be keeping an eye on Blundell. And if he touches you like that again, I won't be answerable for my actions."

Her frustration spiked. "Christian, I already told you—"

"Hush," he said, laying a finger across her lips.

All rational thought fled her brain.

His finger left her mouth and traced a soft path along her chin. He touched her with such tenderness that it brought a sting of tears to her eyes.

"I know how difficult this last year has been for you. And I know how much you hate violence," he said quietly. "I would not add to your distress. If Blundell makes any trouble, I promise I'll tell you before I take any action."

She stared at him, at sea in a swirl of conflicting emotions.

"It's just that I miss Jeremy so much," she tried to explain. "I can't help seeing him . . . all alone on that battlefield. If anything were to happen to you . . ."

"Nothing's going to happen to me. I'm as tough as boot

leather." Rising to his feet in one fluid motion, he said, "Now, you must promise me something in return."

"What?" she asked suspiciously, trying to ignore how big and handsome he looked as he stood over her.

He pulled her to her feet. "You must promise to drive in the park with me tomorrow. Just the two of us."

She started to protest, but he cut her off.

"It's my condition for capitulating to your wishes. I won't take no for an answer."

She bit her lip, buffeted once more by those annoying emotions. As ridiculous as it sounded, he threatened her peace and security in every way possible. He shouldn't be able to make her feel so unlike herself, but he did. It was mortifying, as was her overwhelming impulse to say yes.

"What are you afraid of, Clarissa?" he taunted softly. "It's just a spin around the park with an old friend."

"I'm not afraid," she scoffed, determined to reassert herself. "But I don't want people to gossip about us."

"Then we'll go earlier in the day. That way, only the nursemaids and the children will see us."

He grinned—a beautiful, boyish grin. One she remembered all too well. "Give over, Clarissa. It'll be fun. Just like the old days. You do remember having fun, don't you?"

Her inner defenses collapsed. She did remember, and *that* was exactly the problem.

Chapter 4

Clarissa strolled along the meandering path through Hyde Park, intensely aware of Christian beside her. He cast a mocking glance her way, then nodded at a group of nurse-maids and their charges—a cluster of little boys and girls pelting about the lawn of a nearby sheltered grove.

"See, Ladybird? Not a gossip or an old biddy in sight. Just a few nursery maids and their innocent darlings. No one who could be bothered to take notice of little old us."

She only just managed to hold back a sigh of relief. He was right, of course. No person of fashion would be seen in the park at this hour of the morning, which was precisely why she had insisted on it instead of a drive later in the day. Christian hadn't been pleased that she preferred a walk to a drive, but she'd stuck to her guns. The thought of sitting up next to him on the high perch of his curricle in a public display made her shudder. Even Blundell, who had been in his cups last night, had noticed Christian's flirtatious behavior. God only knew what the gossips would say if they saw her tooling about town in his dashing carriage.

A penetrating shriek from the direction of the grove interrupted her thoughts.

Christian jerked his head around in search of the source

of the commotion. "That's the most appalling noise I've ever heard. Who's getting murdered?"

Clarissa pointed across the lawn. "I believe the culprit is that little girl. One of those grubby boys yanked on her braids."

He snorted. "You never screeched like that when I pulled your braids, did you? I think I would have remembered if you had."

"I didn't, but only because most of your crimes were so much worse. Shrieking about the occasional hair pulling hardly seemed worth the effort."

A wicked gleam lit up his eyes. "Crimes such as?"

"Hmmm," she murmured, pretending to think about it. "There was that time you put salt in my tea. Quite a lot of it, I remember."

"I would never do anything so underhanded," he protested, trying to look innocent.

"You would and you did. And what about that time you snuck over from your estate to our manor house—which you did on a regular basis, as I recall."

"Our houses were only a few miles apart," he said. "I liked to come by and visit you."

"Torture me, you mean. Like the day you got into my bedroom and stole all my shoes."

He laughed, a deep, rolling sound that shot thrills of pleasure all the way to the soles of her feet. The morning sunshine picked out flecks of gold in his light brown hair and gilded his tanned skin to bronze. He looked like a young Greek god—so full of vibrant life that it made her head spin.

"I didn't steal them," he said with a grin. "I just hid them for a little while."

"In the stables, as I recall. It took me days to find them. I wanted to kill you."

Actually, his ridiculous prank had made her laugh,

especially since it infuriated her father. Not that Christian gave a fig about that. He'd been on the receiving end of her father's wrath on many occasions, but had always shrugged it off. His fearlessness as a young boy had astounded her, and she had admired him for his courage.

"But you didn't kill me," he said, gently brushing his hand down the length of her spine. His touch and his warm smile created an air of intimacy around them, as if they shared a delicious secret. It made her feel youthfully awkward, and she had to resist the urge to pull away from him.

Instead, she cleared her throat and adopted a tone of matronly disapproval.

"The worst was when you put a toad in my jewelry box. My heart stopped when I opened the lid and it jumped out at me. If I could have laid hands on you at that moment, I most certainly would have killed you."

He laughed outright at that. "But that was my way of showing you how much I liked you."

She frowned and came to a halt in the center of the path. "You liked me? What do you mean?"

He arched an eyebrow. "What do you think I mean?"

She stared up at him. His gaze, flaring with laughter and warmth, flickered over her. Tiny crackles of energy danced along her nerves. "You were only fourteen," she exclaimed in a breathless voice.

He gave her a lazy and utterly sensual smile. "I was a very mature fourteen."

She gaped at him, bewildered by the sense that she was tumbling through a strange landscape—one both terrifying and wonderful. He held her gaze, his eyes no longer laughing, but still full of a heat that made her skin prickle.

"Ladybird," he murmured in a husky voice.

"Stop calling me that!" She snatched her hand away from his arm and fled down the path, heading in a blind rush in the direction of Grosvenor Gate. In seconds, Christian had caught up with her, grasped her hand, and placed it back in the crook of his elbow. She wanted to pull away, but he held her firmly against his side. Heat flowed between them, thickening the air in her lungs, trapping the words of rejection in her throat.

But what was there to reject? He hadn't offered anything.

She managed a weak protest. "This . . . this is ridiculous."

"What is, sweetheart?" he asked quietly.

The simple endearment drove a spike of longing and pain through her heart. Only Jeremy had ever addressed her like that. Jeremy, the only man she had ever loved. And yet, when Christian spoke to her in that low, rumbling voice, and held her close to him, surrounding her with his seductive, masculine strength . . .

She pulled in a frustrated breath and threw her free arm out in a circle.

"*This*. Us. You, acting like—" She broke off, trying to find the right words, the words that would make him stop doing whatever it was that made her wish for things she could no longer have.

Gritting her teeth, she ordered her pounding heart to settle, then met his gaze. He looked calm and watchful, completely in control. For some reason she couldn't explain, that frayed her temper until it broke into pieces.

"Christian, why are you wasting time with me?" she snapped. "Don't you have better things to do than toddle around the park with boring old widows?"

He drew her to a halt, turning her to face him. She suddenly became aware that they had walked into the shade of a secluded stand of trees, away from the open lawns of the park. The playful shrieks of the children had faded, a peaceful silence taking their place. The bustle of the city seemed distant. Only the coo of a mourning dove calling for its mate intruded on their solitude.

Christian tilted her chin up with a gloved finger. His features were stern, even remote, but his eyes smoldered with a fierce emotion, an intensity that unnerved her, making her stomach flutter.

"You mustn't talk about yourself that way, Clarissa." His low voice held a note of command. "Not to me. I won't allow it."

She stared wretchedly up at him, at a loss for words. The hard lines of his face gentled. He stroked his finger along the edge of her jaw, the texture of his leather glove a whisper of velvet across her skin.

"Shall I tell you why I won't allow it?" he murmured.

She struggled to find her voice. To find her wits. "Yes . . . no. I . . . don't know," she replied, cringing at her awkward response.

He studied her, then shook his head, looking rueful. "Maybe later. You're not ready to hear what I have to say."

She blinked, deflated by his answer. Whatever it was that he wanted to tell her, she knew it would frighten her. But a part of her brain—her heart—yearned to hear it.

Yearned for him.

Transfixed and horrified by the thought that had popped unbidden into her head, Clarissa didn't resist when he guided her back along the path. Silence fell between them, weighted and full of meaning—for her. She hadn't a clue what Christian was thinking.

After waiting minutes for him to say something, she could no longer stand the silence. If one of them didn't speak, she might very well succumb to a fit of the vapors and run screaming from the park.

Or box Christian's ears.

Taking a deep breath, she blurted out the first thing that came into her head. "Captain Archer, when do you return to Portugal? Very soon, I would think."

As soon as the words were out of her mouth, she wanted

to sink into the ground. Could she possibly have made it any more evident that she wanted him gone?

He muttered a quiet oath. It was not the kind of thing he would normally say in polite company.

She lifted her eyebrows. "I beg your pardon?"

He shot her an irritated glance. "Don't start calling me *Captain Archer,* Clarissa."

"And don't make a fuss over such a little thing," she retorted, feeling defensive. "Please answer my question. When do you return to Portugal?"

"In a few weeks, at most. My shoulder is healed, so I don't have any reason to remain in London, do I?"

He sounded enough like a disgruntled schoolboy that she was tempted to laugh. She suddenly felt on familiar ground, with everything back in its proper place.

"Do you miss the Peninsula?" she asked, genuinely curious. "Even though it's dangerous, it must be very exciting, especially since you're an ADC to a general."

He shrugged, a graceful movement of his powerful shoulders. "Sometimes. Especially when we're out on campaign. But mostly it's hard, slogging work. Through rain and mud in the winter, and heat and dust in the summer. Often without decent food, or precious little of it, anyway. It's not the grand adventure people think it is."

Startled, she sucked in a breath. Had that been Jeremy's life? His letters had always assured her that he was comfortable and well. But his health had never been strong, and more than once she had suspected he lied for her sake. But, selfishly, she had always tried to avoid the pain of knowing what his daily life had been like.

"I hate to think of our men suffering like that," she said.

"It's not all bad. There's hunting when we have time, and even the occasional party or ball, especially when we're in Lisbon. The officers' wives make the best of everything, no matter how dreary the conditions."

She shuddered. "The women who follow the drum . . . they're so brave. I couldn't imagine doing that. All the hardship, the deprivation . . ." She let her voice trail off.

He ducked his head to inspect her face. "Not even to be with the man you loved?"

She flushed, reluctant to admit the truth. Besides, Jeremy would never have allowed her to join him, even though she knew several women of good standing who had gone to the Peninsula with their husbands.

Of course, it had never even occurred to her to ask.

"I don't think I could do it," she admitted. "I'd be too afraid."

He pressed her hand, giving her a warm smile. "You only think that because you can't imagine it. I've always known you had more pluck than you gave yourself credit for. You survived all those years with your father, didn't you? Don't you remember how you stood up to him when you decided to marry Jeremy? The old bastard blew his top, but you refused to back down."

"Christian! Your language," she spluttered, even though his praise brought a welcome warmth to her cheeks. She'd always thought of herself as ridiculously timid, but apparently Christian didn't see her that way.

"In fact," he continued in a musing tone, "if you were in the Peninsula, I'm sure you'd be the toast of the regiment. You have your own sort of courage, and you're the kindest woman I know. There isn't a lady over there who can hold a candle to you, Clarissa, once you put your mind to it."

A sudden, intense wave of shame washed through her. No matter what he thought, she wasn't brave. She was the cowardly one who had begged her husband to abandon his duty to country and king because she was afraid to let him go. A wife who blamed her husband for his own death—for doing what he thought was right.

She turned her head, blinking away the sting of tears.

"Clarissa, what's wrong?" he asked in a puzzled voice.

"I'm none of those things, and it's wrong of you to tease me," she choked out.

He gripped her by the shoulders and spun her to face him.

"I'm not teasing you," he exclaimed. "Why the hell would you think that?"

Suddenly, she couldn't take it anymore. "Christian, why are you doing this? It doesn't make any sense!"

His gaze burned through her. "I should think it would be obvious by now."

"Christian—" His fingers tightened on her shoulders, pulling her fractionally closer. Her heart fluttered like a trapped bird.

"No, Clarissa," he said gently. "I won't let you hide behind the wall you've built around yourself. Tell me what you're thinking."

A scorch of anger and humiliation drove her to throw the ugly answer back in his face. "I think you're bored, and I'm convenient."

His expression went dark. "Convenient for what?"

"You know exactly what I'm talking about," she retorted, hating herself even more than she hated him for making her say it. "I'm a widow and will probably never remarry. Perfectly *convenient* for a soldier on leave."

He gave her a prolonged stare, his features so grim that she considered pulling herself from his grip and making a dash for the gates. But now that he had forced her to this point, some impulse held her in place, refusing to let her back down.

"Ladybird," he finally growled. "What kind of loose screw do you take me for? How in God's name could you place so little value on yourself?"

His answer mystified her. "Then why, Christian? Do you

just feel sorry for me because you're my friend, and I'm a lonely old widow?"

He abruptly released her, but then grabbed her by the hand and drew her behind the shelter of a towering shrub.

"Christian!" Her voice came out on a startled squeak. "What are you doing?"

He backed her against a gigantic oak, caging her by placing his hands on either side of her shoulders. "Showing you that you're the furthest thing possible from a lonely old widow."

He swooped down and took her mouth in a ravening kiss. She whimpered under the onslaught. Her fists came up to his shoulders but, to her amazement, she didn't push him away. Instead, as his mouth devoured hers, tasting her with a hot passion, she felt her fingers open and then dig into the wool of his coat with a desperate grip. When his tongue slid along her lips, teasing, silently asking for her to open, she moaned and melted into him, hanging on with all her rapidly fading strength.

He took her hands and moved them up and around his neck. Their bodies melded together. Need simmered through her veins, eager—even greedy—and his kiss ignited a sweet, painful emotion that had lain dormant. She threaded her fingers through his thick hair, pulling his head down to nuzzle his mouth.

His groan of approval vibrated against her quivering lips. Again, his tongue danced across them, seeking entrance. Swept up in the rising tide of desire, she opened for him and he surged inside. A sweet fire, dark and scorching, burned through her limbs and settled deep in her core. Everything inside went soft as their tongues tangled, playing a delicious and forbidden game. He pressed against her, his solid body gently pushing her against the hard trunk at her back.

She flinched as the rough bark dug into her spine. With a murmur, he eased back, teasing her mouth with a slow, impossibly gentle kiss, so tender and sweet that tears gathered under her closed eyelids. That sweetness undid her. The memory of Jeremy, and the last kiss they had shared, forced its way back into her mind.

Her eyes sprang open. Horror and shame flooded her veins. Bad enough she was letting Christian kiss her like this, but out here in the park? In public?

She jerked back, knocking her head against the trunk of the tree.

Startled, Christian broke free. "Jesus, woman," he gasped. "What are you doing? Did you hurt yourself?"

"Let me go," she panted. She pushed against him, frantic.

He stepped back immediately. His cheekbones were glazed with a dark flush and his eyes still smoldered, but he looked wary. And worried.

"Sweetheart," he began.

She cut him off with a sharp chop of her hand. "No, Christian. Don't say anything more. This never should have happened."

With trembling hands, she set her bonnet on straight and dodged around him, heading back for the path. He caught up to her, fell in step beside her. The intensely humiliated part of her took comfort in the fact that he was breathing as hard as she was.

"Clarissa, I'm not playing with you," he said in a low voice. "I'm dead serious about this. I want to be with you. And not because you're convenient. I've felt this way for a long time."

Anxiety and a strange, sorrowful yearning squeezed the air from her lungs.

"No," she choked out. "We can't do this. It's absurd."

He grasped her elbow, forcing her to slow her headlong rush out of the park. She sensed the restrained strength in his grip, the desire to drag her to a halt.

"Why not?" he asked in a frustrated voice.

"Do I really have to explain it?"

"Yes."

She stifled a curse. "You're young, Christian." She could feel his gaze bearing down on her, but she refused to meet it. "You have your whole life ahead of you. And I'm—"

"Don't you dare say you're old. I swear I'll do something drastic if you do."

His voice held a note of warning, but something else, too. He sounded hurt.

She stopped and looked up at him. His eyes blazed with a complex mix of emotions: desire, anger, and pain. The pain of rejection, of not being good enough. She had seen that pain before. Years ago, when he had compared himself to his athletic and dashing older brothers and found himself wanting.

She sighed, both the fight and the fear draining out of her.

"Christian, you honor me. But I'm not ready for what you're asking of me. I still love Jeremy, and I'm not ready to let him go."

He towered over her, like a baffled giant. "Will you ever be ready?"

She briefly closed her eyes, letting her guilt and the love she felt for Jeremy bleed through her. "I don't know," she finally said. "But I don't think it could ever be with you. Whatever you might say, you are too young for me."

His face hardened into an austere mask. In that moment, he looked anything but young.

"You're wrong, Clarissa. Why do this to yourself?"

"Because I want peace and quiet. Is that so much to ask for?"

He began to argue, but she grasped his arm and gave it a little shake. "Christian, no. I'm begging you. I can't give you what you want. Please, let's just be friends, as we have always been."

She stared up at him, making no effort to hide the desperation behind her plea. His eyes went bleak, but he nodded.

"As you wish."

Without another word, he took her arm and led her from the park.

Chapter 5

Pressing her hand against her bodice, Clarissa fought to quell the mad fluttering of her heart. Christian and Lillian had come to call and now waited for her in the snug drawing room of the Middleton town house. Four days had passed since that devastating kiss in the park, and Clarissa had carefully avoided any contact with the Archer clan during that time. But as much as she'd been tempted to send the footman downstairs with a message to Lillian and Christian that she was unwell, neither of her friends deserved such shabby treatment. She had to face the consequences of her foolish behavior sooner or later, and delaying a meeting with Christian wouldn't make that any easier.

Gritting her teeth, she opened the door. Her guests rose to their feet. Christian's sapphire gaze locked on hers, boring into her with a smoldering intensity that halted her faltering steps. Her wafer-thin composure evaporated. If Lillian hadn't been in the room she would have turned tail and fled.

Her friend hurried across the room to greet her. Lillian enveloped her in a sweetly scented hug, then drew her over to sit on the sofa.

Christian bowed, then retreated to the fireplace. He looked

handsome and powerful, every inch the proud soldier. His leather boots and buckskin breeches clung to his muscled legs, and his beautifully tailored uniform showcased his brawny shoulders. With an effort, Clarissa turned her attention on Lillian.

"I've been so worried about you," Lillian said with an anxious smile. "When you didn't come to the Framinghams' ball last night I thought you must be ill."

Clarissa flushed. Bad enough that she had to lie to Lillian now. Even worse that the reason for her lie stood only a few feet away.

"I'm sorry. I should have sent you a note. My father-in-law has been unwell, and I was reluctant to leave him."

Lillian hesitated, casting a worried glance at Christian. A silent communication passed between them, one that sent a prickle of warning across the nape of Clarissa's neck.

"I hope the colonel feels more the thing very soon," Lillian replied. "But Christian and I thought we should call on you today. To ask if you'd heard, ah, any unusual gossip lately."

Clarissa frowned. "What do you mean? I haven't heard anything."

As soon as the words left her mouth, comprehension surged through her in a sickening rush. Had someone seen her in the park with Christian? Backed up against a tree while he devoured her mouth? Her gaze flew up to meet his. He gave a slight but decisive shake of the head.

A sigh of relief escaped her lips, and Christian's mouth thinned into a grim line. She winced, hating that she possessed the power to wound him.

Lillian briefly closed her eyes, as if in gratitude. "Thank goodness," she murmured.

Clarissa directed a questioning glance at Christian as her relief gave way to puzzlement. To her dismay, he gave a slight grimace, then dropped his gaze to the fire burning in the grate. Foreboding seeped through her veins.

"Lillian, whatever is the matter?"

Her friend took her hand. "Christian and I need to tell you something, and it's going to distress you. But please remember that the entire Archer family will do everything we can to help. And the rumors will die down soon enough."

Clarissa's heart gave a frightened thump. "What are you talking about?"

Lillian rolled her eyes at her brother, silently pleading for help. Still looking grim, Christian left his station by the fireplace, grabbed an armchair, and pulled it over to sit in front of Clarissa. He reached over and swallowed her hand in a warm, massive grip.

"Clarissa," he said gently, "rumors about Jeremy are circulating through the *ton*. They are without foundation, but of course that won't stop them from spreading. You and Colonel Middleton will surely hear of them soon enough."

Her mind went blank. What could anyone say about Jeremy that she didn't already know?

"What . . . what rumors?"

A muscle pulsed in his lean jaw. Her heart beat even harder in response.

"It's being whispered that Jeremy failed to act appropriately during the Battle of Badajoz," he replied in a carefully neutral voice.

She blinked, caught off guard. Jeremy had been one of the officers of the Forlorn Hope, the company assigned to lead the infantry attack on the besieged fortress. The company that obviously sustained the heaviest losses. Colonel Middleton had been told later that Jeremy had volunteered, thereby consigning himself to an almost certain death. Her husband's decision had eaten away at Clarissa for months, as she had struggled to understand why he could have made that choice.

"Did he make some kind of mistake?" she asked.

Christian squeezed her hand, and she saw pity in his eyes. That more than anything caused a bubble of fear to rise in her throat.

"Clarissa, it's being said that Jeremy froze at a decisive moment, and did not fulfill the duties of his command," he answered.

She gaped at him, her mind rejecting his horrifying words.

"Are they calling him a coward?" she finally choked out.

Christian gave a terse nod, his gaze sparking with anger.

Lillian put an arm around her shoulders. "No one who knew Jeremy will believe so foolish a story. We just have to ignore the rumors and they will eventually fade."

Clarissa snatched her hand away from Christian's grasp and twisted sideways to glare at Lillian. Fury rose within her in a blinding rush.

"How can you say that? You know very well that most people will believe that kind of rumor—they always do. Whoever started it is lying, and I'm going to find out exactly whom it is."

She was desperate to move, to get away from them. But Christian, seated in front of her, was blocking her way. Still, Clarissa tried to jump up, but he took her by the arms and held her in a gently unyielding grip.

"No, sweetheart. Wait," he soothed. "Let us finish telling you what happened."

Clarissa felt Lillian's start at his term of endearment, but right now she didn't care. Christian could call her whatever he wanted if only he would let her go.

"Let me up," she snapped. "I must go straight to the Horse Guards. Surely I can talk to someone there. One of Jeremy's commanding officers. I won't allow anyone to tell lies about my husband."

She struggled, but Christian held her as easily as he might hold a newborn kitten.

"I've already been to the Guards," he replied. "Father and I went this morning to speak to the commander of Jeremy's brigade. Stop struggling and I'll tell you exactly what he said."

She froze at the note of command in his voice. Some part of her wanted to strike out at him, but the rational part of her mind told her to listen. She gave him a grudging nod, and he eased his grip.

"My father and I heard the rumors yesterday, as did Lillian," he said. "By last night, we realized they were spreading, and we needed to ascertain the source."

"And deny the rumors for the vile untruths they are," Clarissa interjected hotly.

"Of course. Father and I felt it best to track down the source before speaking to you and Colonel Middleton. We wanted to squelch the rumors, if at all possible, and save you unnecessary pain."

Her stomach clenched at the thought of breaking such news to her father-in-law, especially given his weak heart.

"I'm assuming you weren't successful," she said bleakly.

"Unfortunately not. We spoke with Lieutenant-Colonel Harcourt this morning. At first, he tried to put us off, but he eventually revealed that he knew of the rumors."

Christian hesitated, and Clarissa's heart sank.

"Just say it," she said, bracing herself.

"After some discussion, the lieutenant-colonel admitted that they had surfaced once before. Immediately after the battle, and from a credible source. Jeremy's battalion commander at Badajoz was an old friend of Colonel Middleton's. For the colonel's sake, he ordered the matter hushed up. Harcourt swore he hadn't heard another word about it until this week, and now it's too late to do anything about it. To his way of thinking, the damage has already been done.

In fact, he flat out refused to deny the validity of the rumors, saying it was best not to talk about them at all."

Clarissa fought to pull in air as the muscles in her chest contracted into a crushing band. A hundred thoughts buzzed in her head, but none made any sense.

"Who accused Jeremy of being a coward?" she asked.

Christian glanced at Lillian, who slid her arm around Clarissa's waist.

"Dearest, does it really matter?" Lillian murmured. "We know it's a lie, as will everyone who ever knew Jeremy. Eventually it will all die down."

Clarissa stared at Lillian, stunned by her friend's response. Did she really not see why they had to fight back?

"Of course it matters," she retorted. "The cad spreading these lies must be held to account. For Colonel Middleton's sake, if for no other reason. Jeremy was his only child, and this will likely destroy him."

Lillian transferred her gaze to Christian. Again, a silent message passed between them, one they obviously didn't want to share with her.

Instantly, Clarissa knew why.

"You know who it is, don't you?" she demanded of Christian.

He sighed, deep grooves of unhappiness bracketing the corners of his mouth. She suddenly noticed that he looked like he hadn't slept well in days.

"Believe me. You're better off not knowing."

She grabbed his arm, digging her nails into his sleeve. "Tell me right now, Christian, or I'll go to the Horse Guards and find out for myself."

He looked mulish, but she refused to back down and glared at him.

"Very well," he finally said. "I'm almost certain it's Blundell. I suspected him from the moment I heard the rumors. A few other things I managed to find out confirmed my suspicions. He was one of Jeremy's superior officers at Badajoz. Given what happened the other night, the timing makes perfect sense."

Clarissa slumped against Lillian as the ugliness of it all seeped into her bones. Christian had to be right—it was too much of a coincidence. Blundell had threatened to punish her, and what could be more effective than tarnishing her husband's name? Especially since Blundell had always hated Jeremy for winning her hand.

But what should they do about it? What *could* they do about it?

Lillian hugged her but directed a quizzical glance at her brother. "What happened the other night?"

He gave an impatient shake of the head. "It's not important. What is important is how we're going to handle this."

Clarissa sat up, forcing back the leaden weight of despair that sought to overwhelm her. She had to fight back. Jeremy had sacrificed his life for his king, and she could not allow his honor to be trampled into the dust by a pig like Blundell.

"Did you reveal your suspicions to Lieutenant-Colonel Harcourt?" she asked.

Christian's mouth flattened into a disapproving line. "I did. And received a sharp reprimand in return. He told me in no uncertain terms to leave Blundell's name out of it. He ordered me, in fact, to leave the whole thing alone."

"How can he expect that of you?" she cried. "Didn't your father say something? Harcourt would have to listen to him, wouldn't he?"

"My father is only a baronet, Clarissa," he replied in a dry tone. "Not nearly as influential as Blundell's father, who, as you know, is both a marquess and a member of government. Harcourt made it clear he would take it up with my commanding officer if I didn't leave the matter alone."

Clarissa balled her fists into his shoulders and pushed. "Let me up," she snapped.

That muscle in his jaw ticked again, but he stood and drew her to her feet. She jerked away and began pacing the room.

After several rapid turns, she felt able to speak again without shrieking. She came to a halt in front of Christian, challenging his steady gaze. "Could you talk to other soldiers you know . . . officers who were at Badajoz? Get them to tell the truth?"

He grimaced. "I'd like nothing better, Clarissa. But I can't—not when Harcourt gave me specific orders. The lieutenant-colonel truly believes it's best for everyone to let the matter die down. He reasons that if the brass ignores it, everyone else will, too."

"That's nonsense," she retorted. "The man obviously won't risk angering Blundell's father."

He shrugged, not bothering to deny her accusation.

"Can't you do anything?" she whispered. "Even for me?"

His face turned to stone, but his eyes flashed with the evidence of a bitter internal struggle. Guilt speared through her for trying to manipulate him, but she had to, for Jeremy's sake.

"I would if I could. You know that. But I can't," he replied in a husky voice. "Not in the face of a direct order."

Lillian joined them. "Dearest, there's nothing Christian can do. He can't possibly disobey such an order, especially now that Wellington has his eye on him."

Clarissa swallowed around the constriction in her throat. "Can't anyone go talk to Blundell, at least? Tell him to stop spreading these horrible lies?"

Christian blew out a frustrated breath. "I intended to do just that, but Harcourt warned me away from him. And he did it in front of my father, making it quite clear that a duel to settle the matter was also not an option. Father agreed. Strongly, I might add. "

Clarissa stared at him, dumbfounded and despairing. She

felt utterly boxed in, and unable to do anything to protect the reputation of the best man she had ever known. Grief seared her soul, almost as intense as it was on the day she'd learned of her husband's death.

"So, there's nothing we can do," she said in a dull voice. "Nothing but listen and watch as Jeremy's reputation is trampled on in every drawing room in Mayfair."

Christian broke away and strode to the window. He stood with his back to them, quiet and still, but a furious tension vibrated in the atmosphere around him. Clarissa sensed his frustration, his need to take action, but too many forces were lined up against them. Even though grief held her immobile, some part of her yearned to comfort him.

"We've been discussing that," said Lillian, breaking into Clarissa's gloomy thoughts. "Father thinks it best that you leave town for at least a few days. He and Mother will try to refute the charges—quietly and in private conversations. But your presence will give the gossips more fodder. He suggested you and I spend a week or two at our estate in Kent. We could leave today and arrive by nightfall."

She cast a speculative glance at her brother's back, then gave Clarissa a tentative smile. "Christian will come, too. Won't that be nice?"

At any other time, Clarissa would have blushed. But despair and frustration leached through her like a poisoning mist, smothering the fragile peace she had achieved in these last few months.

"I couldn't possibly leave Colonel Middleton," she said. "Especially not now."

Christian turned to look at her. Clarissa didn't know what he saw in her face, but it brought him back to her side.

"You needn't worry about that, Ladybird," he said. "My mother sent a message to Colonel Middleton's sister in Russell Square. Mrs. Parker agreed to stay with him until your return to London."

He curled his hand around her cold fingers. She gazed helplessly into his eyes, which had grown dark with the shadows of her own reflected pain.

"It seems you've thought of everything," she said in a wretched voice.

Lillian gave her an encouraging smile. "Don't worry, Clarissa. Everything will turn out right in the end. I just know it will."

Clarissa nodded, even though her friend's reassurance was nonsense. Nothing would ever be right again.

Not unless she took matters into her own hands.

Chapter 6

With a surreptitious tug, Clarissa adjusted her bodice, exaggerating the swell of her breasts over the trim of her neckline. Less than a week ago, she'd been horrified to wear a gown that revealed so much flesh. But if she wanted Christian to help her she had no choice. She *had* to make him fall in love with her using whatever tools were at her disposal, including her bosom.

Sighing, she shifted on the old trundle bed, trying to get comfortable—although most of her discomfort sprang from her guilty conscience. She hated that she had to be so ruthless. But Christian was the only person who could assist her in clearing Jeremy's name, and clear it she would, no matter the cost. But first she had to entice him to disobey his orders and search for the information she needed. If she could transform his passing infatuation with her into something she believed was real, he might then be persuaded to help her.

There would be consequences when Christian learned the truth about her actions, but she couldn't think about that now or she'd lose her nerve.

Sitting cross-legged on the floor of the attic, Christian glanced up from the battered trunk in front of him. Sunlight slanted through the window at the south end of the low-pitched room, gilding his thick hair with glints of amber and casting a glow over his rugged, handsome features. His heavy-lidded gaze skimmed over her figure, lingering on her breasts.

A forbidden thrill rippled through her. It didn't matter how many silent scolds she gave herself every night as she tossed restlessly on her crisp linen sheets. Whenever he looked at her that way—whenever she remembered his impassioned kiss—her insides quivered.

He cast a lazy smile that made her want to purr like a kitten. "Did you say something, Clarissa?"

"Ah, no," she replied. "I simply cleared my throat. It is rather dusty up here."

He arched a brow and glanced around the tidy, well-dusted room that made up the attic of the Archer country manor, but forbore to comment on the idiocy of her remark.

"Would you like to go back downstairs?" he asked politely. "I'm beginning to suspect Lillian is leading us on a wild goose chase, although I can't imagine why. I'm fairly certain that if there were love letters from Charles II to one of my ancestors, someone would have found them long before now."

Clarissa choked back a dismayed groan. This was the first opportunity she'd had to get Christian truly alone since they'd arrived at Rosedell Manor yesterday. It was during the short journey into Kent that she'd hatched her desperate plan, but she could hardly launch it with Lillian sitting in the same carriage, right next to her brother. And since then, her friend had stuck to her like glue, clearly trying to distract her by telling one amusing story after another until Clarissa wanted to scream.

Fortunately, while they were lunching this afternoon, Lillian had mentioned an old family tale regarding an ancestral Lady Archer, and her association with the great Stuart king. Letters from the king had apparently survived, but no one had seen them in years. Lillian had mused that they were likely buried somewhere in the attic.

With an inspired flash born of desperation, Clarissa had asked Christian to help her search for the letters. Feigning a boldness that made her stomach hurt, she had pointedly neglected to include Lillian in her invitation. To her surprise, her friend had simply shrugged, claiming she had errands to run in the village.

Clarissa stared morosely at the whitewashed floorboards of the attic. Lillian would be furious that she was manipulating her beloved brother. God only knew if their friendship would even survive.

She sucked in a huge gulp of air as remorse squeezed her heart in an unforgiving grip. Christian looked up from a pile of documents in his lap.

"You need a rest," he said, looking worried. "We can do this later, after you've had a nap."

She scowled. "I'm not an old lady who needs her afternoon nap."

A muscle pulsed in his cheek, and she could tell he was trying not to laugh.

"That's what I've been saying all along, Ladybird. But, very well. Since you're intent on doing this, why don't you come over here and help me go through this bloody great trunk. It's full of documents, although I have my doubts we'll find any love letters."

She started to comply when a better idea popped into her head. Sinking down onto the bed, she threw him what she hoped was a sultry look.

"You don't really expect me to sit on the floor, do you? Why don't you drag the trunk over here and sit on the bed beside me?" she said.

His chin jerked up, and he studied her for a long moment. She held her breath, hoping her smile didn't look as false as it felt. God help her if he said no.

Relief coursed through her when he finally gave a slow nod and unfolded his long legs. He rose, then dragged the heavy trunk across the floor to the bed. He loomed over her, his face guarded, the wings of his eyebrows pulled together in an aggressive, masculine slash.

She patted the mattress and gave him an inviting smile. "Sit."

He hesitated, then came down beside her, careful to keep several inches between them. The bed creaked, but the sturdy old frame accepted the added weight of his brawny physique.

"Now," she murmured, "let's see if we can find those love letters. If we do, perhaps I can read them to you."

He blinked and a light flush glazed his cheekbones. "I wouldn't get your hopes up," he replied in a puzzled voice.

She wriggled across the mattress, closing the gap between them. He tensed, muscles flexing in his broad shoulders.

"But wouldn't it be fun if we did?" she prattled, trying not to show her nervousness. "One can only imagine what the king wrote. He was apparently quite a romantic and imaginative lover."

He shot her a startled glance. "Where the hell would you learn about something like that?"

For a moment, she forgot she was trying to seduce him.

"Really, Christian," she huffed. "It's not a secret that the king had several mistresses. And I was married, after all. I'm quite aware of what can happen in the bedchamber."

Oh, Lord. She hadn't meant to blurt that out. His eyes turned a smoky blue, and waves of heat raced under the confinement of her stays. Well, that was exactly the reaction she was hoping to elicit from him, wasn't it?

"I'm sure you are," he murmured. "But I never expected to hear you admit it."

"I don't see why not," she said lightly. "We're both adults."

She leaned forward to peer inside the trunk, giving him a generous view of her breasts. She blushed, shocked by her own behavior, but she couldn't suppress a niggle of excitement. And a surge of satisfaction when she heard the breath hitch in his throat.

Carefully removing a stack of papers, she gave him ample time to inspect her bosom before slowly straightening up. She turned to look at him, surprised to find she was beginning to enjoy playing the role of seductress. She had never been that kind of woman. One who was confident and sensual, and who could hold a man in the palm of her hand. It was intoxicating, especially when it involved a man as strong and masculine as Christian.

Her enjoyment died a swift death when she met his hard, suspicious gaze.

"What are you up to, Clarissa?"

Flinching at the steel in his voice, she fought the urge to bolt. She must be making a mess of it by confusing him. After all, just a few days ago she had begged him to leave her alone.

She tried again, giving him what she hoped was an adoring smile as she tentatively rested her hand on his thigh. The muscles in his leg felt as unyielding as stone, but the heat flowing into her fingers practically scorched her.

"I thought this was what you wanted," she whispered, gliding her hand upward.

He hissed out a breath, his fingers engulfing hers and holding them still. "It is. I suppose I'm a fool to question it, but this doesn't make any sense. You asked me to stay away from you, Clarissa. Have you really changed your mind, or is this some kind of game?" He looked angry, baffled, and . . . ready to rip her clothes off.

She called up every ounce of internal fortitude and held

his gaze, refusing to shrink away from his penetrating inspection. Quelling her fear, she tossed her head and pretended to be as bold as the other widows of the *ton*.

"A lady can change her mind, can't she? You were right about me, Christian. I *have* locked myself away, too afraid to let anyone near. Well, I've realized I'm sick of it, and sick of being alone."

She broke off, stunned to hear the words that tumbled out of her mouth. Stunned to realize those words were true.

The disapproving line of his sensual mouth eased fractionally. "Go on."

With a terrifying plunge, she finally voiced what she had been denying to herself since that day in the park. "I want you, Christian," she whispered. "I don't understand it, but I do."

He stared down at her, a warrior with a hard, predatory gaze—a gaze that sought to bare all the secrets of her soul. Her heart kicked into a racing gallop and she shrank away, knowing in a brutal flash of clarity that she couldn't go through with her scheme. Not when he looked at her like that.

But then, as if by magic, the angry warrior disappeared and Christian came back to her. A gentle hand cupped her cheek, and his lips curled into a rueful smile.

"Believe me, Ladybird, I'm not complaining. I want to be sure, because once we start this—once I touch you again—I'll be lost. I have no defenses against you."

She swallowed around the lump in her throat, awash with guilt and an astonished, almost fearful, tenderness. Christian was everything that Jeremy wasn't: confident, sometimes reckless, and full of energy and health.

And yet, he was much like Jeremy, too. He had the same kind and loving demeanor, the same devotion to family and friends, combined with the courage of a man of honor. That's what terrified her. Not that Christian was so different from her husband, but that he was so much the same.

Wretchedly, she stared back at him, conflicting emotions swirling about inside her. But in all the chaos, she was able to grasp one essential truth. In this moment she wanted to be with Christian, no matter the consequences.

Gently, he held her face as his mouth covered hers in a soft, sweet kiss. She clutched at him with trembling arms, telling herself to push him away. How could she betray him like this? Betray herself, and everything she knew to be right? She had to tell him the truth, had to let him make the decision for himself.

But when his tongue parted her lips, taking hot possession of her mouth, all her guilt and good intentions fell away. Only sensation remained. The tingling feel of his long, muscular thigh flexing against her leg, the exciting roughness of his calloused hands on her cheeks, the wet sweep of his tongue into her mouth. Nothing else mattered but the imprint of his hands on her flesh, the mark of his mouth on her body.

He released her face and lashed his arms around her, crushing her against his chest. Her breasts, spilling over the top of her skimpy bodice, pressed into the soft wool of his coat. The brush of fabric across her sensitized skin made her shiver, and her nipples, barely contained by her stays, contracted into hard little points. He devoured her mouth, licking and nibbling at her lips, sucking on her tongue as if she were a juicy sweet to be consumed. And that's exactly how she felt—like a hot, honeyed morsel, ready to be eaten.

And, God help her, that's exactly what she wanted him to do.

She opened up to him, sucking his tongue into her mouth. They tangled, and she relished the taste of him—sweet yet scorching, and powerfully male. His energy streamed into her, filling up the sad, empty places where all had been silent for so long. Tears leaked from the corners of her eyes and she gripped his shoulders, struggling to get closer, to plaster every inch of her body to his.

He broke the kiss, lifting his head to look at her. She gasped an incoherent protest, then buried her head in his cravat, overwhelmed and mortified, her need for him robbing her of strength.

"Shh, sweetheart," he murmured, moving one hand in a soothing glide down her spine.

"Why . . . why are you stopping?" she quavered, unable to still the tremors racing through her limbs.

He uttered a low laugh that sounded more like a feral growl. "I'm not. But I've got to slow down. I'm only seconds away from having you flat on your back with your legs spread wide and me deep inside you."

She jerked back to look at him. His eyes blazed with lust, and his crude but exciting words made the soft flesh between her legs throb and grow moist.

"Oh, I . . ."

She trailed off, too entranced by the way his hands were now roaming over her body to speak. His long fingers briefly shaped her hips and waist, then moved up the bare flesh of her arms, leaving a velvety heat in their wake. Her eyelids half closed as he stroked across her collarbones and brushed his fingers up her neck, tilting her head back so he could kiss the shivery spot below her ear.

She sighed with voluptuous pleasure. How could those hands—so calloused and hard from years of soldiering—be that tender against her skin? So able to send shudders of pleasure along her nerves?

"What were you saying, my love?" Christian murmured against her neck. He pushed her hair back and carefully set his teeth to her skin, giving her a tiny, tingling bite.

She jerked in his arms, a hard throb pulsing deep in her womb.

"I—ah, I wouldn't mind if you did that," she managed.

He suckled her neck, his tongue soothing the place where he had just set his teeth. She went boneless in his arms, her head falling back. Sensation stormed through her. Never had she felt so much, even during her marriage. She and Jeremy had enjoyed relations, but nothing like this. Christian's touch made her blood rush and her heart pound. Her limbs trembled, and she had to repress the urge to beg for more, like some helpless supplicant.

"Is that an invitation?" he asked, easing her down onto the trundle bed.

"Yes," she whispered. The bed was so narrow he had to lie half on top of her, one leg between her thighs as he propped himself up on an elbow.

She gazed up at him through half-closed lids, enthralled by the passion that carved his features into a wild, rough beauty. His lips pulled back in a sensual smile as his fingers busied themselves in the lacings of her bodice. Carefully, he tugged down the delicate fabric, exposing the flesh that plumped up over her stays. Clarissa's mouth went dry as she watched him draw one finger over the tops of her breasts, skimming the dusky flesh that ringed her nipples. She shivered, sparks of heat dancing along her skin.

"Are you sure?" he whispered.

He looked up, their eyes locking on each other's. Need flowed between them, linking them with a single, overwhelming hunger. She nodded, too overwhelmed by desire and trepidation to utter a word.

His gaze flared with a possessive heat, his unleashed passion rolling over her like a wave. With a swift movement, he yanked at her stays and her breasts spilled free. Christian hissed out a breath, a harsh, triumphant sound that set her heart pounding with a tiny jolt of panic.

But then he bent and pressed a reverential kiss on her chest, just over her racing heart.

"Christ," he muttered, his voice thick with emotion. "You're the sweetest thing I've ever seen. I swear I'm not worthy to touch you."

She heard it, then. The doubt in his voice. The fear that he would never be good enough. It had dogged him all his life, living as he did in the shadow of his older siblings.

With a murmur, she stroked his hair.

"Please, Christian," she pleaded. "I want you. Don't make me wait any longer."

He placed another gentle kiss between her breasts, but then his hands were on her, shaping and kneading with a masterful touch. Fire sizzled through her veins. She moved restlessly beneath him, craving more.

"Christian," she moaned.

He stroked her breasts, tweaking the hard, rosy nipples. The calloused pads of his fingers tortured her until she squirmed with excitement.

It wasn't enough.

As if he knew, he cupped her breasts in his big hands, plumping them. Then he fastened his mouth on the tight point of one nipple. A hot thrill streaked along her nerves and she arched her back, eagerly pushing her pelvis against his hip, pressing hard through the layers of their clothing. A small, sharp contraction pulsed in her womb, the pleasure so intense she gave a strangled cry.

Christian played with her, languidly moving from one breast to the other. His body pressed her down into the bed. The sense of being captured and restrained drove her wild. A luxurious, tormenting ache that she had almost forgotten these last several months throbbed between her thighs.

He lifted, pulling back with a hard suck, letting his teeth graze over the rigid tip of a nipple. But still, as if he couldn't help himself, he dipped again and dragged his tongue across her breast one last time before shifting away. She moaned, arching to follow his mouth.

He held her down.

"You have the loveliest breasts," he murmured as he stroked the tight points. "I could do this for hours."

She stared up at him, stunned that he would say something . . . so . . . so exciting.

His lips curled back, wolflike, exposing strong white teeth.

"Would you like that?" he asked with a wicked grin.

"Ah . . ." She was at a complete loss. It had never occurred to her that people talked about these things while they were doing them.

He gave a soft laugh. "Another time."

Swiftly, he unlaced her stays and pulled them from her body. Her chemise came next and then she lay before him, clad only in her stockings and shoes.

Clarissa blushed from head to toe as he gazed at her. But she felt only shyness, not shame. Christian's face bespoke adoration as much as lust, and his hands were gentle as he settled her more comfortably on the bed. She waited quietly while he stood to strip off his clothes.

As his body was revealed, her breath snagged. She saw a godlike, brawny, and powerful man. But a man who had experienced all the brutalities of war. She couldn't help clapping one hand over her mouth.

Christian's head came up and his eyes filled with concern.

"What's wrong, love?" he asked, sitting on the edge of the bed.

She touched the barely healed bullet wound on his shoulder, and then ran her fingers along the ridge of a cruel scar that bisected the left side of his torso. "Do they still hurt?" she asked.

He carried her hand to his lips. "I'm fine. There's nothing to worry about. I promise."

An echo of sorrow rustled in her chest. "I hate that you have to be a soldier."

He drew her close. She shuddered, loving the feel of his hot, hard body blanketing her limbs.

"Shh," he murmured. "Don't think about that. Not now."

He nuzzled her mouth as one hand shaped the globes of her bottom. Her aroused nipples brushed against the coarse hairs of his chest, forcing a groan from her mouth. Hunger and need poured through her veins, and her thighs dampened.

"Christian," she panted, breaking free from his tender kiss. "I need you. Now."

"Patience, love," he crooned as he trailed kisses along her jaw. "I don't want to hurt you."

She grabbed him by the ears and yanked his head up, bringing them nose to nose.

"Ouch," he yelped. For effect, she thought, since his eyes were gleaming with laughter.

"Now," she gritted between clenched teeth.

He made a quick, ravishing foray of her mouth, and then settled in the cradle of her thighs. She pulled her legs up around his hips to accommodate his muscled girth.

"As my lady commands," he said in a rumbling voice.

He flexed his hips, nudging the broad head of his erection into the opening of her body. Holding her head between his hands, he gazed into her eyes as he surged into her. She gasped at the scorching invasion that stretched and filled her to the limit. He stilled, and his head dropped to her shoulder, his breath a pant on her skin.

"Clarissa—" he choked out.

"No," she breathed. "It's all right." She wriggled a bit, and pleasure lanced up from the place where they were joined. It was more than all right. It was wonderful.

With a satisfied hum, she arched her spine, rubbing her breasts against the hardness of his chest. He began to move in short, hard nudges. She greedily absorbed every sensation, running her hands over the broad contours of his shoulders, tracing the rippling of muscles down his back and across his lean flanks.

Her touch spurred him on. He tilted her hips, moving deep, setting off a delicious, fevered ache in her most sensitive flesh. His mouth locked on hers, his tongue hot and caressing between her lips.

Clarissa pulled her knees up, opening herself as wide as she could. She was desperate, sobbing against his mouth, yearning for completion.

Breaking the kiss, Christian lifted on his elbows. She whimpered a protest, needing all of him—on her, in her, bringing her to rapture. Murmuring comfort, he brought his hand down between their bodies, slicking two fingers through her damp folds. She dug her heels in his thighs and cried out as a shuddering release trembled through her limbs.

In response, his muscles began to spasm. He lunged into her, pressing down as he shook with his release. A deep groan broke from his throat, and he collapsed, curling around her.

As they lay there, a panting tangle of arms and legs, Clarissa slowly came back to herself. The pressure of Christian's body lifted from her chest. She opened her eyes to look at him.

Her heart lurched. What she saw on his face wasn't some temporary infatuation. It was love—selfless, adoring, and full of joy.

Her plan, God forgive her, had worked.

Chapter 7

Christian propped himself on his elbows, relishing the feel of Clarissa's lush body lying beneath him. God, how he'd stormed into her, unable to hold himself back. He'd spoken the truth when he said he had no defenses against her. And it scared the hell out of him. But he could no more turn away from her now than he could cut out his own heart.

She stared up at him, looking dazed—flustered, even. Not that he could blame her. He had acted like a brute—taking her with no ceremony on an old trundle bed in the attic of his family's house. And in broad daylight. His parents would see him hanged for a scoundrel—after making sure he married Clarissa first.

Which he had every intention of doing.

He brushed his mouth across her kiss-swollen lips and she whimpered, her small hands fisting into his shoulders as if to push him away.

"Poor sweet," he murmured. "Am I crushing you?"

She gave a jerky nod in response.

With a deep sigh, he pulled out of her warm body and rolled onto his back, taking her with him. The damn bed was so small he almost fell out as he tried to arrange them on the mattress. That earned him a muffled giggle, one so girlish and sweet his heart turned over in his chest.

She wriggled on top of him, trying to get comfortable. His shaft twitched with renewed interest.

"Careful, love," he groaned. "You might get more than you bargained for."

She lifted her head from his chest and frowned. "What do you mean?"

He caressed her luscious bottom and she blushed, dropping her gaze.

"I don't think that would be a very good idea," she replied in a strained voice.

Christian frowned, trying to see her face, but she kept it turned away from him.

"What's wrong, Clarissa?"

"Nothing," she said tightly.

He knew that voice. Knew it meant she was hiding something. "Yes, there is." He rubbed the bunched muscles between her shoulder blades. "You can tell me anything. I won't be angry."

She gave an unhappy sigh that stirred the hairs on his chest. "It's just that . . . this will take some getting used to. I didn't expect it to happen."

He smiled, relief flooding through him. As long as she didn't regret what they'd done.

"Try not to think about it right now. There will be plenty of time to mull it over later."

She looked up, scowling. "You always say that. But sometimes things can't wait."

He stroked the glorious tangle of golden hair back from her face. "You know me, Ladybird. I'm a simple soldier. We don't like to think too much."

She made a scoffing noise and settled onto his chest. But even though she lay quietly for a few minutes, he could practically hear the cogs and wheels turning in her head. He gave her leg a gentle nudge with his foot.

"Tell me what it is," he said.

She stirred but kept her head down. "All these years you've called me Ladybird, and I never once asked you why."

An obvious feint, but he'd play along for now. "I called you that because you were always flying away home, just like in the nursery rhyme. We could be in the middle of anything—like fishing on the lake, playing cards—and you would drop everything and dash home as if the devil himself were at your heels."

She blew out a pensive breath. "I suppose in a way he was. Father would be so angry if I was late for afternoon tea or dinner. And I was late quite a lot, because I never wanted to leave Rosedell Manor. I loved it here."

Anger pierced his gut at the memory of Clarissa's mistreatment. "I know he used to hit you."

She seemed to shrink into herself. "Sometimes."

He hugged her close, the old anger warring with an aching regret. "No one will ever hurt you again, Clarissa."

"You can't possibly know that," she said in a hollow voice.

In a swift move, he rolled her underneath him. Her eyes widened in surprise as he took her face between his hands. "Yes, I can. Because you're mine, now. I won't let anyone hurt you, ever again," he vowed.

Panic seemed to flare in her eyes. She struggled, trying to push him off. "Christian, let me up."

He blinked, stunned by her reaction. "Clarissa—"

"Now!"

He rolled off her and sat on the edge of the bed. She grabbed her chemise and began wrestling it over her head. When he tried to help her, she batted his hands away.

Resisting the urge to swear, he reached for his breeches. Apparently, she was already regretting what they'd done. No doubt for myriad foolish reasons he would now have to deal with.

He stood and watched her fuss with the ties of her

chemise. When she refused to meet his eyes, his heart sank. He had to throttle back his frustration. "You need to tell me what's wrong."

She smoothed her chemise, took a deep breath, and raised her eyes. Their usual amber sparkle had disappeared, leaving her gaze flat and bleak. Unease rifled through him.

"I need to tell you something," she said. "You won't like it."

He wanted to sit next to her, to take her in his arms. But her grim expression froze him in place.

"Say it," he replied.

"I've lied to you, Christian. I didn't want to, but I did. It was necessary."

He clamped down on his flaring emotions. "About what? This?"

She nodded, looking miserable. "Partly. I wasn't going to tell you, but I have to now. After this . . ." She gestured at the bed. "I needed you to help me find out what really happened at Badajoz. To help me clear Jeremy's name. After you refused, I decided I had to do whatever it took to convince you to help. I thought if I could make you fall in love with me . . . well, then you would do what I needed you to."

She finished in a rush. Her cheeks were stained a bright pink, and she looked both defiant and on the verge of tears.

Christian had felt such pain once in his life—when a French saber had sliced him open. But this was worse. A physical wound healed, but the wound she'd just inflicted probably never would.

Sucking in a harsh breath, he tried to stem the anger pulsing through his veins. As much as he wanted to explode at her, he couldn't. That kind of reaction would scare her to death, and no matter how much she had earned it he wouldn't do that to her.

After a few moments, he calmed his anger enough to

speak. "What just happened between us . . . was it all a ruse then? Was any of it real, Clarissa?"

She rubbed the corner of one eye, looking ashamed. "Of course it was real. That's why I couldn't go through with my stupid plan. You mean too much to me. I couldn't lie to you any more than I already have."

He stared at her, too baffled and angry to respond. What the hell did she want from him?

"Christian," she said in a pleading voice, "you probably hate me now, and I can't blame you."

He shook his head. "I don't hate you—"

"You should," she interrupted. "If I were a better person, I would leave this house and never bother you again. But I can't. Regardless of what I've done, I still need your help."

She scrambled from the bed and grasped his arm. He clenched his teeth, forcing himself not to respond. But her simple touch burned through him. She was so beautiful, half naked and flushed from lovemaking. She had ripped his heart to shreds, and yet still he wanted her. Needed her.

He didn't hate her. He hated himself for being such a fool. "What would you have me do?"

A faint hope dawned in her eyes. "Christian, you know people, especially soldiers who were at Badajoz and who might know the truth. Could you talk to them? If you uncovered what really happened, then Lieutenant-Colonel Harcourt would have to listen to me."

He cursed inwardly. She asked for the one thing he couldn't deliver.

"Please," she begged when he didn't respond. "If you won't do it for me, then do it for Jeremy. Do it for a fellow officer who deserves help."

Christian pulled away from her loose grip and reached for his shirt. "I can't disobey a direct order. Don't ask that of me."

She yanked the shirt from his hand and flung it across

the room. "Is your blasted career all you care about? Fighting and killing? Does that mean more to you than I do?"

Tears glittered on her eyelashes, but her slight figure radiated fury. He glared back at her, stung by the accusation.

"I'm a soldier, Clarissa. It's who I am. What else should I be? Should I sit at home, the feckless younger son waiting for the crumbs to fall from his father's table? That's no kind of life for a man. This is what I have chosen to do, and I do it well."

When she shook her head, making a disparaging sound, Christian's anger spiked. "And if you think I enjoy fighting and killing, you can go to the devil," he flung at her. "I do what I must to protect my country and my king. I don't like killing, but I'll be damned if I'll apologize to you for it."

He stalked across the room, grabbed his shirt, and pulled it over his head. "And by the way," he added, "your beloved husband obviously thought so, too, or he wouldn't have gone off to Spain and left you."

Her anguished gasp brought him up short. He briefly closed his eyes, suddenly wishing a bolt of lightning would strike him dead. "Clarissa," he sighed.

"No, Christian. Not another word," she choked out, yanking on her gown. "If you feel any affection for me whatsoever, you'll pretend none of this ever happened."

Before he could say another word, she scooped up the rest of her clothes and fled.

An imperious knock sounded on the front door of the Middleton town house, jolting Clarissa from her gloomy reverie. Whoever it was, she didn't want to see anyone. Since she fled Rosedell Manor four days ago—right after that disastrous, earth-shattering encounter with Christian—she had imprisoned herself inside the house. And if not for Colonel Middleton's poor health, she would have already packed up their household and decamped to the security of their Devon estate.

She dropped her needlework in her basket and went to look out the window. A highly polished town coach stood before the front stoop. One of the Montegue carriages, which meant Lillian had come to try to see her. Again.

Clarissa rubbed her temples, trying to ease the headache that had taken up permanent residence in her skull. She hated having to avoid Lillian, but she couldn't face her right now. Not until Christian sailed away to the Peninsula and out of her life for good. Then she would talk to her friend and beg her forgiveness for using her brother in so cavalier a fashion.

Her eyes stung as she imagined life without Christian. Every day she struggled to deny the truth. And every night, alone in her bed, she was forced to admit it. She loved him. How could she not? Even as a boy he had touched her heart, with his intelligence and courage, his kindness, and his sheer joy in life. And now he was a man. Handsome and powerful, whose caresses made her body flare with a passion unlike any she had ever known.

But she had used him and asked him to betray his honor for her sake. Jeremy would have been horrified by her heartless scheme. She understood that now, after four days of thinking of little else. That realization was almost worse than anything.

At the sound of a hasty tread on the staircase, she left the window. A moment later the door to the drawing room flew open and Lillian rushed into the room, as grim as a hanging judge.

Groaning inwardly, Clarissa reached deep for a smile.

"Lillian, how nice to see you. I'm sorry I haven't been well enough—"

"Stow it, Clarissa," Lillian snapped. "No more hiding

away. We're going to talk right now about what happened between you and Christian. And what to do about it."

Clarissa sank into a chair, propping her aching forehead on her palm.

"There's nothing *to* do. He hates me." She gave a bitter laugh. "Not that I blame him."

Lillian rolled her eyes. "You can be such a goosecap. He doesn't hate you. He's been madly in love with you for years."

Clarissa gaped at her friend. "You knew?"

Lillian scoffed. "Of course. So did Father and Mother."

Clarissa groaned and dropped her head back in her hands, unable to conjure an answer to that humiliating revelation.

"Oh, for God's sake! Look at me," Lillian exclaimed.

Cautiously, Clarissa raised her head.

Lillian seemed torn between vexation and sympathy. "Did you really think we wouldn't approve of a match between you and Christian? We'd be thrilled. For both of you."

Clarissa gasped. "Are you insane? I'm five years older than he is. And he's a soldier. I could never marry another soldier."

"You just might get your wish," Lillian retorted. "At this very moment, Christian is destroying his career—for your sake."

If she hadn't already been sitting, Clarissa would likely have fallen down. "What are you talking about?"

"Christian is going on a crusade to clear Jeremy's name. After you bolted from Rosedell Manor, he returned to town immediately and began digging around for information."

"He did?" She was so dumbfounded she could hardly formulate the question. "Why?"

"Because he loves you," Lillian enunciated loudly. "While you've been hiding away, he's been searching high and low for witnesses. He managed to find two crippled veterans of the siege of Badajoz, both in London. According to them, Jeremy's conduct there was brave and exemplary. And they saw everything."

She frowned. "But why didn't they come forward when the rumors surfaced after the battle?"

"They did. They went to Major Blundell, but he ordered them to keep silent. Since he was their senior commander, they felt they had to obey. But Christian promised that he and my father would stand with them. They've agreed to testify to the truth. And they're sure there are others from Jeremy's regiment who would be willing to speak out."

Clarissa's head spun. Conflicting emotions—anger, joy, relief—washed through her.

"That's . . . that's wonderful," she finally managed.

Lillian grimaced. "It is for Jeremy's reputation. But not for Christian. He disobeyed a direct order. He's at the Horse Guards right now, trying to convince Lieutenant-Colonel Harcourt to call Blundell to account."

A jolt of alarm cleared Clarissa's head. "Didn't your father go with him?"

"He didn't tell Father. Christian was afraid he would try to stop him from going to see Harcourt. And he swore he'd kill me if I said anything."

Anxiety and guilt drove Clarissa from her chair. She grabbed her friend by the arm, pulling her to the door. "I never wanted him to do that. I intended to take any information he discovered to Harcourt myself. I didn't want Christian to destroy his career!"

"There's nothing you can do about it," Lillian protested.

Her friend was wrong. Clarissa knew exactly what to do. The thought of it made her stomach churn, but she had no other choice.

"Yes, there is," she said, dragging Lillian into the hallway.

"I'm going straight to speak with Harcourt. I will not allow Christian to do this to himself."

Lillian looked scandalized. "You can't go to the Horse Guards by yourself. Think of the gossip!"

"Yes, Lillian, I can. And you're going to drive me there. Now."

Chapter 8

Clarissa glared at the clerk blocking the door of Lieutenant-Colonel Harcourt's office. The self-important wretch was determined to keep her out, claiming that Harcourt was in an important meeting with another officer.

That officer was Christian, and she had to stop him before he destroyed his army career.

"Stand aside, sir," she ordered impatiently.

The clerk bristled. Puffing his chest out, he pointed to a chair in front of his desk. "Please take a seat, madam. You will wait for the meeting to conclude, or I will call a guard to escort you from the building. I would not wish to embarrass you, but I will not hesitate to do so if I must."

Clarissa suspected he would, too. The very thought of the commotion that would cause made her almost nauseous. But she was tired of everyone telling her what to do, and no priggish bureaucrat would stop her now. Not when Christian needed her. "If you or anyone else touches me, I'll scream. As long and as loud as I can. Please step aside from that door."

The man's face went purple, and he began to bluster. She opened her mouth and took a deep breath.

Grumbling under his breath, the clerk shuffled aside, and Clarissa burst into the room before he could change his mind. She slammed the door and leaned against it, trying to calm her pounding heart.

An imposing-looking officer sat behind a massive desk, his bushy moustache quivering with surprise as he stared at her. Christian stood in front of the desk. He pivoted to face her, and his mouth gaped open for a few seconds before he clamped it shut in a grim line.

Lieutenant-Colonel Harcourt lumbered to his feet. "What the devil is going on here?" he snapped. "Who, madam, are you?"

Praying her legs wouldn't collapse under her, Clarissa crossed the room to stand beside Christian. He gave a slight but angry shake of the head.

Meeting Harcourt's glower, she mentally braced herself and then launched in. "I am Mrs. Middleton, sir. I've come to discuss the harm that has been done to my husband, Captain Jeremy Middleton."

Christian finally exploded. "Good God, Clarissa! You shouldn't have come here. What were you thinking?"

"Hold your tongue, Captain," thundered Harcourt. "I will ask the questions."

Christian snapped back to attention, even though he still looked furious. With her or with Harcourt, she wasn't sure.

The lieutenant-colonel returned his penetrating gaze to her. "Mrs. Middleton, perhaps you'll be good enough to explain your behavior. It's not quite the thing for a lady to be racketing about the Horse Guards without an escort. Your father-in-law wouldn't approve, I daresay."

His scowl twisted her stomach into knots, but she held her ground. "My dear sir, do you intend to offer me a seat, or must I stand all afternoon? Has everyone at the Horse Guards forgotten their manners?" She gave an imperious sniff, for good measure.

Harcourt's ears went red but, to his credit, he wrestled his temper under control. "Forgive me, madam. Apparently I *have* forgotten my manners." He gestured to the chair in front of his desk. "Please, be seated."

"Thank you, but no," she said loftily. "On second thought, I prefer to stand."

She heard a slight choke from Christian but didn't dare look at him. Harcourt's gaze darted suspiciously between them. To her surprise, he gave a grudging laugh.

"Very well, madam. You have bested me, and on my own territory. How may I be of assistance?"

Relief poured through her so suddenly that her knees wobbled. She wished she could sit after all, but she wouldn't show Harcourt any sign of weakness.

"There has been a terrible misunderstanding, sir," she said. "Captain Archer is under the mistaken impression that I wanted him to plead my husband's case to you. That was never my intention."

"That's nonsense and you know it, Clarissa," Christian exclaimed.

"Captain Archer," interjected Harcourt. "Remain silent until I give you permission to speak. Is that clear?"

Christian looked ready to argue, so Clarissa pinched his arm. Harcourt's moustache twitched, but he forbore to comment.

"Yes, sir," Christian replied stiffly.

"As I was saying, Lieutenant-Colonel Harcourt," Clarissa continued, "Captain Archer has made a mistake. I always intended to bring you myself the information I discovered regarding these scurrilous rumors."

"That's odd. The captain seems quite sure of what he is doing," Harcourt replied in a dry voice. "So sure, in fact, that he was willing to disobey a direct order. I find it difficult to believe he could misapprehend such a thing."

Clarissa swallowed her frustration. "That was my fault. I begged him to help me. I gave him very little choice in the matter, I assure you."

Harcourt raised a skeptical brow. "Forgive me for saying so, Mrs. Middleton, but I find your statements contradictory. Did you ask him to disobey a direct order, or did you not?"

Her nerves frayed some more. "Of course I asked him to disobey his orders," she snapped, feeling defensive. "No one else would help me. My husband's good name was being trampled into dust, and his fellow officers didn't seem to care. Not even his superior officers."

Harcourt tugged on his moustache, looking worried. And, she thought, guilty. Resting her hands on his desk, she leaned forward to press home her point.

"It was a matter of honor," she said. "Jeremy's honor. His family's honor. And, once I asked it of him, Captain Archer's honor. How could he refuse me?"

Harcourt emitted an unhappy sigh. "Sit down, Mrs. Middleton. There's no need for us to stand around like we're on dress parade." He frowned at Christian. "Except for you, Archer. You remain standing."

As Clarissa sank into the wooden chair before the desk, she ventured a peek at Christian. His anger had vanished. He even winked at her. Flustered, she turned back to Harcourt, who continued to inspect her with open curiosity.

"Lieutenant-Colonel," she started, hoping to bring the conversation back to the question of Jeremy's reputation. "Will you be able to help us? My husband's good name has suffered great injury. It calls for immediate redress."

Harcourt clasped his hands on his desk, his expression grim. "So Captain Archer and I have just been discussing, Mrs. Middleton. You do understand what you're asking, don't you? There will be risk involved in raising this issue, and the outcome is uncertain. Powerful people will do everything they can to refute the claims regarding Lord Blundell's role in this matter. Captain Archer knows this but you must comprehend it as well, if we are to proceed."

She squared her shoulders. No longer would she be intimidated by Blundell, or by his father, the marquess, or by any other man. "I'm not afraid."

Harcourt nodded solemnly. "So I see. Very well, then. I will proceed."

Her heart skipped a beat. "You will? What will you do?" she asked, hardly believing it.

"I'll make enquiries amongst officers and enlisted men. Quietly, you understand," he said rather sternly. "This is a delicate situation, and there's no point rattling the powers that be sooner than we must."

Clarissa took a deep breath, the first in what seemed like ages. With luck, Jeremy's good name could be restored. And she owed it to Christian.

"Lieutenant-Colonel Harcourt, I can't tell you how happy this makes me," she said. "Please accept my gratitude."

He gave her a brusque nod and rose from his chair. "Mrs. Middleton, I beg you to excuse me. I shall keep you informed of the results of my investigation."

Clarissa stood but didn't move away from the desk. There was another, equally important, matter to be resolved. "What will happen to Captain Archer?" she asked, glancing at Christian. He didn't seem the least bit worried. He gave her a roguish grin, looking so much like the insolent boy she used to know that she almost laughed.

"He'll return to his post in the Peninsula," said Harcourt. "It will be up to Lord Wellington to decide his fate."

Clarissa's relief evaporated as anxiety took its place. "Please, this was my fault. Not his."

For the first time, Harcourt smiled at her. "I wouldn't worry overmuch, Mrs. Middleton. Captain Archer is an excellent soldier. If a bit forward." He finished sardonically, looking down with a pointed glance.

Clarissa followed his stare and gasped. Somehow, her

fingers had become intertwined with Christian's. She'd been so focused on asking for Harcourt's forgiveness that she hadn't even realized Christian had taken her hand.

Her face burned with heat, and she muttered an incoherent apology as she tried to tug her hand away. Christian tightened his grip.

"Christian," she hissed, mortified.

"Yes, Ladybird?" he replied in the most innocent voice.

Harcourt broke in. "I must step out. Please take a few minutes, Mrs. Middleton, to recover your countenance. Captain Archer will escort you home."

He waved away Clarissa's attempt to thank him again and exited the room.

Hesitating, she looked at Christian, who gazed down at her with an adoring smile. She couldn't think of a thing to say, and he seemed in no hurry to break the silence. Her heart pounded like a drum, leaving her breathless. But from what? Happiness? Trepidation?

He took her hands and raised them to his mouth. When his warm lips brushed over her skin, she trembled.

"I'm very angry with you, Ladybird," he said, though his voice held a hint of laughter. "You shouldn't have come down here, flying to my rescue like an avenging angel."

She snatched her hands away, annoyed that he could think of laughing after such a nerve-wracking scene. "And what about you, you foolish man? Why would you take such a risk?"

"Because it was what you needed me to do—for both our sakes. Once you left Rosedell Manor, and after I calmed down, I realized that. You could never let Jeremy go and move on with your own life as long as this cloud hung over your head." He rested his hands on her shoulders, gently caressing. "And you were right about another thing. Jeremy did deserve better, especially from me."

She ducked her head, ashamed to look him in the eye.

"Jeremy would have hated that I tried to manipulate you. I'm so sorry, Christian. I'll never be able to forgive myself."

His leather-clad fingers tipped her chin, forcing her to look at him. She saw only understanding and warmth in his gaze. Her heart cracked under the weight of her own guilt, and the love she felt for him.

"He was your husband. And the army abandoned him after he made the ultimate sacrifice. No woman of spirit could accept such a betrayal. You had no choice but to search for answers."

"I was so angry," she said.

"With me or with the army?"

She grimaced. "With Jeremy. For leaving me." How petty and selfish that anger seemed now.

Christian rubbed a soothing hand along the back of her neck. "He didn't want to. You were in his thoughts every waking moment. Never doubt that."

A rush of emotions tightened her throat. Christian, the most selfless man she had ever known, sincerely mourned Jeremy's death. In a flash, she understood Christian would have spared her the grief of widowhood if it had been in his power, even though it meant he could never be with her.

What a gift she had been given, to have won the love of two such men in a single lifetime.

"Jeremy was a man of honor," she said. "He always tried to do the right thing, no matter the cost. I was wrong to try to hold him back."

"You loved him," he said, as if that explained everything.

She supposed it did, but only Christian understood that. He had never once judged her for hating the war, or for hating what it had done to her life.

"How can I ever thank you?" she asked, fighting back tears.

He lifted his eyebrows, as if surprised by her question. "I should think it was obvious, Ladybird. You can marry me."

The breath rushed from her lungs, and she almost staggered. It just might kill her to refuse him, but she had no choice.

"I can't," she choked out in a miserable voice. "You're too—"

"Oh, Lord," he groaned, cutting her off. "Not that again. You certainly didn't think I was too young when we made love."

She flushed, both from embarrassment and from the heated remembrance of his touch. "Christian! You mustn't say such things, especially not here."

He scoffed, then sat and pulled her onto his lap. He ignored her protests and her feeble attempts to get up.

"Clarissa, you employ your age as an excuse to put me off," he said in a serious voice. "Damn few will give a hang about that, and you know it. Tell me what's really bothering you."

She fiddled with the starched linen of his cravat. His hand covered hers, stilling her restless fingers.

"You *are* too young, but not in the way you think," she blurted out.

He frowned. "What the hell is that supposed to mean?"

"You're still young enough to be reckless. You'll take dreadful risks in battle to advance your military career. Just like Jeremy. I think that's why he volunteered for the Forlorn Hope at Badajoz. I've already lost one husband to that kind of reckless behavior. I couldn't bear the thought of losing another."

Christian rubbed his chin, silent for a moment. "I can't be sure why Jeremy made that choice. All I can do is speak to my own experience. I'm not prone to foolish acts, and I'm not going to risk my life simply to garner notice or glory. I promise you that, love. I've been at war for eight long years. It's a bloody and ugly business, with damn little glory. I do my duty and I do it well, but I seek no honors.

Not ones that ultimately mean little more than a piece of ribbon and a medal pinned to a coat."

Hope stirred in her chest, like the faint hint of the breaking dawn.

"Do you mean that?" She couldn't keep the doubt from her voice.

He captured her face in his hands, feathering a kiss across her lips. She clutched the lapels of his coat, aching for more.

A few breathless moments later, he drew back. "Trust me. I'm very good at soldiering. It's what I do." He rubbed his nose against hers, and she laughed.

"And I promise I'll always come home to you," he finished, making it sound like a vow.

She wanted to believe that was true, but she couldn't. No man who went to war could control his fate. But somehow it didn't frighten her nearly as much as it used to.

"You can't promise me that, Christian," she said, cupping his cheek in her hand.

He kissed her palm. "No. We can never be sure of what the next day will bring. But I *can* promise that I will always love you, for as many days as I have left on this earth."

Tears stung her eyes, but she blinked them back. She had cried enough. If Jeremy's life—and death—had taught her anything, it was that she wanted to live with joy, not fear.

She wriggled off his lap and straightened her gown. "When do you leave for Portugal?"

He hesitated, then came to his feet. "In a week. Why?"

Clarissa studied him. Christian might very well object, but she had no intention of letting him march off to war without her. She had made that mistake once before, and she wouldn't do it again.

"That should give me enough time to pack and get things in order. But just barely," she mused, mentally composing a list of things she needed to accomplish, including settling Colonel Middleton's sister permanently in Brooke Street.

He gave her a puzzled look. "Where are you going? Devon?"

She rolled her eyes. "To the Peninsula, of course. With my husband. Where else would I be going?"

Christian's mouth gaped as if he'd been poleaxed. But then, with a joyful laugh, he lifted her off her feet and into a crushing embrace. She squeaked in protest, but he covered her mouth in a gloriously possessive, toe-curling kiss. When he finally released her mouth, she could hardly breathe.

"Are you sure, Clarissa?" he asked, his voice deep with emotion.

She wound her arms around his neck. "I can hardly believe it myself, but yes. I am. And I want to marry you not because it's what *you* want, but because it's what *I* want."

He flashed a devastating grin. "I love a woman who knows what she wants."

She laughed, her heart so full of happiness she thought it would burst. "I choose you, Christian Archer," she said, holding him close. "I choose you over fear and sorrow and loneliness. I will always choose you."

He nuzzled her mouth, murmuring gentle words of love. Finally, he lowered her to the floor. As he led her to the door, he glanced down at her, his sapphire eyes glittering with mischief.

"You say that now, sweetheart. But wait until you see my bachelor's quarters in Portugal. You may run screaming in the opposite direction."

He was teasing her, of course, as he loved to do. But whatever difficulties lay before them, Clarissa knew there would always be a full measure of love and laughter. Christian would see to that.

She couldn't wait.

The Naked Prince

SALLY MACKENZIE

Chapter 1

"Papa, what the *hell* is this?"

Miss Jo Atworthy threw the package she was carrying at her father's desk; he dove to catch it before it could hit the battered mahogany surface.

"Careful! That's a very rare collection of Catullus's poems to Lesbia, Jo."

"Oh, good Lord." Jo clenched her teeth and counted to ten. Another expensive book, and of dirty poetry, no less. How many times did she have to tell Papa they couldn't afford such extravagances?

She watched him reverently unwrap the book and stroke its leather cover. A thousand times would make no difference. He never heard things he didn't want to hear.

She blew out a short, sharp breath. There was nothing to be done. She'd have to tell Mr. Windley she'd take his youngest little hellion on as a Latin student. She untied her bonnet and jerked it off her head. But she would *not* take Mr. Windley on as well, no matter how clearly he hinted he'd be delighted to hire her permanently—via a wedding ring—to teach his spawn and tend his hearth and maybe even produce a new idiot Windley or two.

Yet the damnable truth was her marriage would solve all their financial difficulties.

She flung her bonnet on the overstuffed chair. Knocking some sense of economy into Papa's thick skull would work as well. He was studying the pages of his newest purchase now, smiling with unadulterated joy and a touch of awe.

"Papa, you *must* stop buying these books. We simply don't have the funds to pay for them."

He didn't even bother to glance up. "Now, Jo, I'm sure we can—"

"We can*not*." She shoved her hands in her pockets to keep from strangling him, and her fingers slid over the letter she'd got when she'd picked up the post. A small thrill shot through her. She'd been waiting for this letter, looking for it each day for the last week. When she'd finally seen it, her address written in the familiar black scrawl, she'd wanted to snatch it up and take it to her room, to curl up in her favorite chair and read it in privacy—but Papa's blasted package had caused all thought of her letter to fly out of her head.

She ran her finger over the paper. Had her London prince found her comments on Virgil amusing? She'd been on tenterhooks waiting for his reaction. Had he—

She snatched her hands back out of her pockets. She was as harebrained as Papa. Worse. Papa's books were real; she'd built her "prince" from air. She'd sent her first letter off to him via his publisher, signing only her initials to hide the fact she was a female. She knew he'd never answer, but when he had . . .

She repressed the shiver of excitement she still felt at the thought. Missive by missive, sentence by sentence, word by precious word over the last year, she'd created a figure of male perfection—handsome, honorable, strong, brilliant, kind, courageous.

She was a fool. She knew nothing about him, not even his name, for heaven's sake. No matter how witty or intelligent his letters, a man who wrote articles as "A Gentleman" in *The Classical Gazette* and signed his letters "K" was probably some ancient don.

She should be inquiring after his gout, not imagining him riding up on a white horse to save her from her boring life. She frowned at her father. "Perhaps *you'd* like to tutor the Windley—"

She heard a sudden banging.

"I say, isn't that someone at the door?" Papa clutched his precious Catullus to his chest and looked over her shoulder, relief evident in his face.

She was *not* going to let him escape. Every time she tried to get him to face their dire financial situation, he found a way to dodge the conversation. Not this time. "Papa, I—"

The banging got louder.

"There? Don't you hear it? Someone is knocking at the door."

"I don't—" Damn, their caller was not going to give up; the fellow risked pounding a hole in the wood. She treated her father to her best glare. "We'll resume this conversation as soon as I find out who that is."

Papa looked so damnably innocent. "I'll come with you."

"Don't think to slip past me and escape. We are going to have this talk."

"Jo, you wound me." Papa tried to look wounded but failed. "Go see who is knocking."

"I *am*." She stalked to the door and threw it open. A haughty-looking footman dressed in Baron Greyham's black and gray livery stood on the threshold, his hand raised to knock again.

He looked her up and down and then sniffed, clearly not approving of what he saw.

She clenched her fists to keep from smoothing her hair or skirt. "Yes?"

"I have an invitation for Miss Josephine Atworthy from

his lordship, Baron Greyham." If the man tilted his nose any farther into the air, he'd fall over backward.

"I am Miss Atworthy."

The footman actually cringed.

She tilted *her* nose in the air. She might not look like the baron's cousin—well, she probably did look like his poor relation. Her dress was showing its age a bit, but, damn it, it was still serviceable. She had no time—or money—to follow the silly vagrancies of fashion.

He addressed a spot above her head. "Lord Greyham sends his regards, Miss Atworthy, and requests the pleasure of your company at a gathering he is hosting in honor of St. Valentine's Day." He offered her a sheet of vellum.

She stared at it as if it were a snake. The Bad Baron was inviting her to one of his scandalous gatherings? "There must be some mistake."

The footman looked as if he thought so, too, but restrained himself with some effort from saying so. "If you are indeed Miss Atworthy, there is no mistake."

He offered her the paper again. She considered rejecting it again, but that seemed rather silly—and she'd admit she was curious. She took it.

"Of course she's Miss Atworthy," Papa said. "Who else would she be—Helen of Troy?"

The footman was not a classics scholar. "Lord Greyham didn't mention a Miss Troy."

Jo perused the invitation. "Lady Greyham writes that one of their female guests came down with a putrid throat at the last minute; they need me to make up their numbers."

"I see." Papa, trying unsuccessfully to hide a grin, shrugged. "Then you'd best go pack your things."

Jo crumpled the note. "I'm not going. What are you thinking?"

Papa patted her arm. "Don't worry. I'll be fine on my own."

She was going to grind her teeth to dust. "I've no doubt

you'll be as merry as a grig, but you know I can't attend one of Lord Greyham's parties. My reputation would never survive it."

Papa laughed. "Balderdash. Everyone knows you're far too full of starch to participate in anything even remotely improper."

She was not flattered. Was she really considered so priggish? Would even her prince think her so?

Damn it, she must cure herself of this silly girlish fantasy. She tried to picture "K" as hunchbacked, balding, and decrepit.

"And you're a bit long in the tooth to be concerned with gossip."

Oh! Insult added to injury. "I am still unmarried; I must concern myself with gossip."

Papa smiled at the footman. "Will you excuse us for a moment?"

"Of course, sir. I'll—"

Papa shut the door in the footman's face.

"Papa!"

He took her arm and led her a few steps from the door. "Jo, think. This is quite the opportunity. It's not every day you get such an invitation."

She jerked her arm free. "An invitation to sin!"

Papa looked heavenward as if requesting divine intervention and then back at her. "A little sin would do you good."

"Papa!"

"Dear God, Jo, I was only funning." He frowned. "Well, mostly funning. The truth is you are twenty-eight years old. You're not getting any younger."

"I'm well aware of my age."

"Oh, don't poker up." He sighed. "I hate to say it, my dear, but you do have a reputation for being . . ." He waved his hand, as if that told her anything.

"For being what?"

"A bit of a prude." He took her hand in his. "Men—except perhaps that idiot Windley—see you more as a Latin tutor, ready to smack them at the least mistake, than a woman."

She jerked her hand back. "That's ridiculous." It might be true that the few moderately eligible gentlemen in the neighborhood had stopped asking her to stand up with them and edged out of any conversational group she joined, but that just saved her from having to stifle her yawns as they droned on about their horses and dogs.

"Frankly you're turning into a shrew."

"I'm trying to save us from the poorhouse. If you'd only exercise a little self-restraint—"

"Jo, men don't like to be berated constantly. If you don't take care, even Windley won't have you."

If only she hadn't sold the hideous bust of Virgil that had graced the table by the door, she could bash him over the head with it. "I'd rather sell myself on the streets than marry that hideous oaf."

"Well, if you're considering that line of work, I don't see how you can take issue with attending Greyham's house party. At least he won't have any Paphians there." Papa paused. "That is, I don't think he will."

Clearly, Papa's obsession with erotic classical poetry had addled his brain. "I cannot go to this party. Mrs. Johnson says all the Greyham gatherings include orgies."

"Really?" An odd expression lit Papa's eyes.

"Papa! Aren't you scandalized?"

"Er, yes, of course." So why did he sound so wistful? "But I think it's highly unlikely Greyham will host anything as exciting as an orgy. And you can't go by what Minerva Johnson says. She'd think a handshake that lasted more than a second was the beginning of a seduction." He snorted. "Frankly, I wouldn't be surprised to learn there never was a Mr. Johnson. I can't imagine that woman ever spread her—"

His eyes met Jo's and he stopped abruptly. He cleared his throat. "Suffice it to say, I don't believe you can put any reliance in Mrs. Johnson's speculations concerning Baron Greyham's gatherings. But if anything of that nature does occur, you can just retreat to your room. I'm sure none of the men in attendance would try to take any liberties with you."

Papa's reassurances made her feel very out of sorts. "Be that as it may, I still can't go. I have lessons to teach to pay for that book you just purchased."

She glared at Catullus; Papa crossed his arms, sliding the tome under his coat.

"I'll teach the lessons."

The footman banged on the door again.

Papa scratched his nose and gave her a speculative, sideways look. "You know, the old baron borrowed a very rare copy of Ovid from me and never returned it. If you found it, we might be able to sell it for a significant sum."

"Ha! As if you would ever sell a rare book." Why wouldn't Papa meet her eyes? He was hiding something.

Still, if there was indeed a rare Ovid in the baron's library . . . Papa might not sell it, but she could. Any extra income would improve their financial picture. "How will I recognize it?"

A small, triumphant smile flickered over Papa's lips. Damn. He did have some plot in his twisted mind, but she couldn't begin to discern it.

"It has a bright red binding with large gold lettering. I'm sure it will almost jump off the shelf at you."

All her instincts told her Papa was setting a trap for her, but what was his goal? Likely all he wanted was to get some days to himself to enjoy his blasted Catullus. "I don't know. I—"

The footman hammered on the door once more.

"Come, Jo. The baron's servant is growing anxious to

hear your decision. I'll tell him you're just packing a few things and will be with him in a moment, shall I?"

"Well . . ." She couldn't believe she was actually considering attending. "You really will teach the lessons?"

"Yes."

"All five Windleys and perhaps the sixth? I told Mr. Windley I wouldn't take the youngest one on, but with your newest purchase"—she glared at Catullus again; Papa moved it behind his back—"I think I'd better agree to give him lessons, too."

"Leave it to me. I've dealt with beef-witted boys before."

Being free of the Windleys for a few days was itself reason enough to accept this dratted invitation. "We can't afford to annoy Mr. Windley, Papa. If he decides to take his boys elsewhere for their lessons, we will be in the briars."

Papa shrugged. "Where else would he take them? Besides, he has his eye on you to be the next Mrs. Windley. He'll put up with me for a day or two, I assure you."

"Well . . ."

"Come, Jo. You need a little adventure in your life."

Unfortunately, that was very true. "Oh, all right. I'll go."

"Splendid!"

Now why did Papa's pleasure sound so much like a trap snapping shut?

Chapter 2

"Can't you see the Widow Noughton wants to drag you into parson's mousetrap?" Damian Weston, Earl of Kenderly, leaned back against the squabs of his very comfortable traveling carriage. What he really wanted to do was grab his friend Stephen Parker-Roth by the shoulders and shake some sense into him.

Stephen laughed. "Good God, Damian, are you going to be a bore about the widow the whole bloody house party? Maria doesn't want marriage. She likes variety in her bed far too much to tie herself to one man."

Damian frowned. "She might like variety, but she wants you. Perhaps she thinks she can have both."

"Then she's an idiot."

"Not necessarily. Many members of the *ton* go their separate ways after producing an heir and a spare."

"And I am not many members of the *ton*. I want a marriage like my parents'. You know that."

"Ah, but does Lady Noughton know it?"

Stephen shrugged. "I don't believe the topic's ever come up." He grinned. "I have far more enjoyable things to do with Maria when I visit her than discuss my views on wedlock."

Damian was sure Stephen did. Maria Noughton's exceptional talent in bed was a frequent topic at White's.

"That may be true, but I assure you Maria Noughton means to have you. She's persuaded herself she's in love with you." Damian glanced out the window. They were approaching the gates to Greyham's estate. "I imagine her sudden interest in wedded bliss may have something to do with her rather spectacular falling out with the current Lord Noughton."

"Well, yes, she told me she'd had words with the fellow. The new baron is a bit of a Methodist; stands to reason he wouldn't care for Maria. But she'll come about."

"As your wife if you aren't careful."

"And how the hell is she going to manage that?" Stephen's voice had acquired an edge; he was clearly tiring of this subject. "It's not as though she's some blushing virgin. She can't claim I've ruined her reputation; she's no reputation to ruin unless it's her reputation as a nimble piece in bed, and she'd be lying if she said I've hurt that."

That was the question, wasn't it? How *was* Maria going to trap Stephen? "I don't know what she'll do, but I swear she's got something planned. She's as thick as inkle weavers with Lady Greyham, you know."

"What of it?" Stephen flicked his fingers at Damian. "You worry too much."

"And you don't worry enough." Though that wasn't true normally. Stephen wasn't careless; he wouldn't be so successful a plant hunter if he were. But he'd seemed on edge—reckless even—ever since he'd got back from his last expedition in the fall. He'd been drinking more. And he usually started planning his next trip almost as soon as he set foot on English soil; here it was February, and Damian had yet to hear anything but vague ruminations of another expedition.

Perhaps Stephen's odd behavior had something to do with

his older brother's marriage and impending fatherhood; perhaps it was due to his thirtieth birthday approaching. Whatever the cause, it was disturbing. It had worried Damian enough to make him leave his comfortable study and current translation of one of Juvenal's Satires to come to this blasted house party and keep an eye on Stephen.

The coach turned and started up the long drive. Stephen leaned forward to tap Damian on the knee. "You *do* worry too much, you know. I'm the damn King of Hearts, aren't I? I'm not about to be caught unawares."

Damian shrugged. There was no point in arguing further. Stephen wouldn't listen, and Damian couldn't blame him. Until he had something more than vague worries to offer, he would do best to bite his tongue—and keep his eyes open.

Stephen sat back. "The real joke here is that I've been worried about *you*."

"You have?" Damian frowned. "Why?"

"Because you've turned into a bloody hermit, that's why. You used to be up for every frisk and frolic, gambling and drinking and wenching as much—or more—than I. You were crowned the Prince of Hearts, after all."

"A nickname I hate as much as you hate yours."

"Yes, but now they've taken to calling you Brother Damian, the monk."

"Ridiculous."

"Is it? You warn me against Maria, but when was the last time you took a woman to bed?"

"That's none of your bloody business." Damian felt a hot blush sweep up his neck; he turned to look out the window. Where the hell was Greyham's damn door?

"Can you even remember the last time?"

Damian kept his eyes on the passing scenery. Thank God the coach was finally slowing and he could escape this inquisition. "I've been busy. This translation is very tricky."

He was afraid he'd see Stephen's jaw hanging if he dared look in that direction.

"A tricky translation," Stephen said. "Good God." He reached over and grabbed Damian's shoulder. "Face it, man. When a jumble of letters written by some dead Roman is more interesting than a tumble between the sheets of a warm and lively lady you need help."

"I—"

Stephen held up his hand. "Say no more. I'm convinced this house party is exactly what you need to cure you of your blue devils."

"I am not blue deviled."

"You certainly are if you can't remember the last time you had any bed sport. But don't worry. Greyham is certain to pair you with a pleasant girl unencumbered by morals. Enjoy her, Damian. Tomorrow is Valentine's Day, and Lupercalia the day after. It's a time for love . . . or lust." Stephen grinned as the coach swayed to a halt. "I certainly intend to enjoy myself—and Maria—to the fullest."

"That's what I'm afraid of," Damian muttered as Stephen leapt from the carriage.

Damian descended more sedately, pausing to have a word with his coachman just as a cart clattered up next to him, blocking his path to Greyham's door. Rude, but perhaps the driver thought Stephen had been the carriage's only occupant. He turned to regard the man and bit back a smile.

The fellow—one of Greyham's footmen—looked harassed, as if he were fleeing the Furies. Or perhaps he'd been condemned to escort one of the unpleasant sisters. The woman seated next to him certainly looked the part of an avenging goddess. Her old, ugly bonnet hid her hair so successfully he couldn't tell its color—or if it were indeed a writhing mass of serpents—but her slightly bushy brows were a golden brown. At the moment, they met over her nose in a deep vee of temper, and her generous lips were pressed firmly together as if she'd just bitten into a lemon.

She wasn't beautiful—her nose was too long and her chin too sharp, and she looked to be far too tall and thin—but she drew his attention like a magnet. Her eyes, even angry, were compelling. They were the same golden brown of her brows and were large and fringed with long lashes. Who was she?

Her worn, unfashionable clothing marked her as someone's maid, but her demeanor gave the lie to that theory. Yet she looked nothing like Maria Noughton and her ilk. She couldn't be a guest.

The footman whose job it was to help arriving ladies alight apparently was of the same opinion. He stayed on the portico, sheltered behind one of the pillars, out of the chill February wind.

"Jem!" The cart's driver tried to get his attention, but the wind whipped his words away.

Well, Damian could help. He didn't care if the woman was a duchess or a dairy maid; she was female and could use a hand in descending. He moved around the back of the cart to reach the passenger side.

The woman made a short, annoyed sound. "I can get down myself, you know," she told the driver and began to suit action to words.

"Miss Atworthy, please—"

Everything happened at once then. The driver, distracted by his passenger, let his hands drop. The pony, beginning to shiver in the wind, took that as an invitation to bolt for the warm barn. Miss Atworthy, gathering her skirts and rising to depart, jerked backward as the cart lurched forward. Her hands flew up into the air, and she screamed as she tumbled over the side.

Damian leapt forward to catch her. A flailing froth of feminine skirts and curves plummeted into his arms.

"*Oof!*" He staggered back a step but managed to keep his feet and his hold on Miss Atworthy. She was not a featherweight. And she was not as thin as he'd guessed, or at least not thin in the important areas. Her bottom and breasts felt very nicely rounded.

She gaped up at him, clearly disoriented by her sudden change in altitude. At this proximity, he saw her eyes had flecks of gold and even hints of green in their depths. Golden brown curls, freed from her bonnet, tumbled over her forehead. He inhaled her scent—lemony, clean and fresh—and it hit his brain like brandy on an empty stomach. He was drunk on the feel and smell of her, and like a drunkard, he acted on his impulses. He bent his head and covered her wide mouth with his.

She stiffened, and he thought for a moment she'd push him away, but then she relaxed, so he let his tongue go where it wished—into her warm mouth.

She tasted sweet, full of promise.

Stephen was right: it had been far too long since he'd been with a woman. Perhaps he *would* enjoy himself at this damn house party—when he wasn't keeping an eye on Stephen, of course.

Her tongue tentatively touched his.

Or maybe he'd let Stephen go to hell with Maria. He had more interesting things on which to focus. He drank in her warmth, her intoxicating sweetness, her maddening mix of innocence and desire.

He was lost in her until his body protested. His cock ached, but so did his back. Standing had never been his preferred position for lovemaking, and Miss Atworthy was far too heavy to hold for an extended period. It would not endear him to her if he dropped her on her delightful posterior.

He eased out of the kiss and raised his head. She blinked at him, eyes wide and slightly bewildered, and her finger crept up to touch her lips. He smiled in what he hoped was a reassuring fashion as he let her legs slide slowly down his body, keeping his arm around her back. She felt very good indeed.

He grinned. "Curls, not snakes."

"What?" She frowned as her feet touched the ground.

"Your hair." He tugged on a lock that had fallen over her forehead. It sprang back as if it had a life of its own. "You looked like one of the Furies, sitting next to that poor footman in the cart."

"I did not."

"You did. You were scowling just like you are now."

Her frown deepened—and then she apparently remembered he still had his arm around her. She flushed and jumped away, catching her heel on her hem.

His hands shot out to steady her. "Careful."

"Miss Atworthy," the driver called as he ran up, having finally got the pony under control and handed the reins off to Jem. "Are you all right?"

"Yes, thank you, but if it hadn't been for Mr. . . ." She frowned again; the woman spent far too much time with her brows lowered. "I'm afraid I don't know your name, sir."

"Damian Weston." He inclined his head. "Earl of Kenderly." He turned to the footman. "I'll see to Miss Atworthy; please have her things taken up to her room."

"Yes, milord."

He offered Miss Atworthy his arm; she took it somewhat gingerly. Odd. She wasn't a young miss, and after that kiss, he wouldn't say she was shy—

No, that wasn't accurate. The kiss had been hot, but not practiced; it had not been the kiss of an experienced flirt. And with the last name of Atworthy . . .

"Are you perhaps Josiah Atworthy's daughter?"

She stiffened. "I am."

Now why the hell did she suddenly look so guarded? He

smiled in an attempt to put her at ease. "I hope to pay your father a visit while I am in the area. He and my father were classmates at Oxford; in fact, my father used to say he had a bone to pick with yours."

"Oh?" Miss Atworthy looked straight ahead, her expression stony. It was hard to believe he'd just been kissing her. "I don't believe I've heard Papa mention your father."

"No? Well, my father claimed your papa borrowed his rare copy of"—he paused; better not be too specific—"Ovid's poems and neglected to return it."

Her fingers tightened on his arm, and she shot him a quick, sharp glance before returning her gaze to Greyham's portico. "That seems very odd. I wonder why your father never came to retrieve it if it was so valuable."

Did the girl think he was prevaricating? "Oh, I rather doubt it's valuable."

She threw him another look. "If it's rare, it must be valuable."

"Not necessarily. A three-legged dog is rare but not valuable."

"A book is not a three-legged dog."

"True." He shrugged. "All I know is my father seemed more amused than anything over the situation. I never asked him about it, though. Perhaps I shall ask your father. Did he not speak of it?"

"N-no."

Now why did Miss Atworthy look so guilty? "Perhaps he didn't think it a suitable topic for your tender ears."

She made an odd gurgling sound. "Trust me, Papa doesn't spare my sensibilities."

"I think you do him an injustice. I've found him to be far more perceptive than I would have guessed, especially from hearing my father's stories."

Miss Atworthy stopped dead and stared at him. "Are you sure you're talking about my papa?"

He laughed. "Well, it did take me a little while to puzzle out who J.A. was."

Her face lost all its color, and she seemed to be having difficulty breathing. "J.A.?"

"Josiah Atworthy." Was she a complete widgeon?

"Ah." She was still staring at him with her mouth slightly ajar, an almost panicky look in her eyes.

"Your father wrote to me last year to comment on one of my articles in *The Classical Gazette*, and we started a correspondence." He frowned. She definitely looked as if she was about to swoon. He shifted his hold to support her elbow. "I say, are you feeling quite the thing?"

"I'm f-fine." She cleared her throat. "Can you tell me—I know it's a silly question, but I'm curious—how did you sign your letters to Papa?"

"With my initial." Her color did not look good at all, though his answer seemed to reassure her.

"Oh. 'W,' for Weston, then?"

"No, 'K,' for Kenderly."

"Ah." Her lips wavered into a smile, and then her eyes rolled up and she collapsed into his arms.

Chapter 3

If it were truly possible to die of embarrassment, Jo would have expired on Lord Greyham's front drive.

She stared up at the bed canopy in one of Lord Greyham's guest bedchambers. She'd not been able to escape her humiliation; she hadn't even been able to maintain a nice, insensate swoon. Oh, no. She'd come to her senses—*all* her senses—almost immediately and had been completely aware of the servants and guests staring at her and whispering about her as the Earl of Kenderly carried her up the stairs and into this pleasant bedroom.

Jo covered her face with her hands. Yes, she'd been aware of the onlookers, but she'd been even more aware of Lord Kenderly—the strength of his arms; the broad, hard plane of his chest; the solidity of his shoulder where she rested her head; the firm line of his jaw with the faintest shadow of stubble against his snow-white cravat; the deep blue of his eyes. When she'd buried her face in his coat to hide from all the people staring at her, she'd breathed in his scent, a mix of clean linen, eau de cologne, soap, and man.

And when he'd laid her on the bed . . .

She bit her lip to stop a moan from escaping.

Dear God, she'd wanted to pull him down on the bed

with her. She'd locked her hands behind his neck and held on a moment too long; he'd had to reach back and disengage her fingers to free himself.

The next moan would not be muffled. She flipped over and buried her face in the pillow.

The prince she'd fashioned out of air had stepped into her life, and he was far more perfect than she could ever have imagined. Her dreams tonight would be much more detailed than ever before.

And he'd kissed her. Heavens! Her very first kiss. She'd been almost too shocked and disoriented to appreciate it at first. Had he actually put his *tongue* in her mouth? It should have been disgusting, but it hadn't been—not at all.

And then she'd tried to kiss him back. He must think her a complete hoyden or worse. What if he—

"Miss Jo."

"Eek!" She turned over and sat up so quickly her head spun. She pressed her fingers to her temples and blinked at the short, round girl who'd come into the room. "Oh, Becky, you gave me such a turn. What are you doing here?"

Becky stared at her as if she'd suddenly sprouted a second head. "I work here; ye know that."

She did know that. Becky was a year or two younger than she and had grown up on the estate; they used to play together when they were children. "Yes, yes, I mean, what are you doing in this particular room?"

"Mrs. Stutts sent me up. She said ye needed help."

"Oh." Mrs. Stutts, a gray-haired, somewhat dour woman, was the Greyhams' housekeeper. "That was very kind of her, but what would I need help with?"

"With yer clothes and hair." Becky was clearly struggling not to roll her eyes.

Jo stared at her for a moment, flabbergasted, and then laughed. "You know I make do for myself at home."

Becky gave her a long look. "Begging yer pardon, Miss

Jo, but ye do need help. All the other guests are from Lunnon. Ye don't want to look a country mouse."

"What do I care if all those London ninnies look down their noses at me?" Jo climbed off the bed and shook out her skirts.

"Oh, ye'll care plenty. I've seen them do it afore. The poor girls those cats turn their claws on end up crying their eyes out."

"Well, I'm made of sterner stuff." She was not some delicate, young debutante, and she didn't care about something as superficial as personal appearance. It was a person's intelligence that mattered.

A certain gentleman's image—a tall, broad-shouldered gentleman with dark hair and blue eyes—popped into her thoughts.

All right, it didn't hurt if an intelligent man was also attractive, but it wasn't important. She'd never have given Lord Kenderly a second thought if he had the mental acuity of stewed cabbage.

Well, perhaps she would have given him a second look. A woman would have to be blind not to—the man was as handsome as sin.

He kissed like sin, too, not that she had any experience in the matter. Still he'd definitely made her feel like sinning. Her breasts and belly . . . lower than her belly, actually . . . had felt very, very . . . odd. She—

She was as bad as a runaway horse, and if she didn't rein herself in immediately, she'd come to serious trouble. Yes, the man was handsome; yes, he was intelligent. But he must also be a rake. He was at this disreputable party, wasn't he? And as far as he knew, she was a complete stranger, yet he'd kissed her in that very intimate fashion. Clearly the actions of a rake.

She flushed. She hadn't known who he was when she'd kissed him.

"Mrs. Stutts told me to tell ye the guests are meeting in the blue parlor before dinner," Becky was saying. "I'm to help ye change." Becky looked around. "Where's yer trunk? I hope we can find one dress that's not too wrinkled."

Trunk? Her entire wardrobe wouldn't fill a trunk. "I didn't bring many clothes."

Becky's eyes had found Jo's bag. "Ye mean this one small valise is all ye have?"

They both stared at the bag in the corner where the footman must have deposited it. It had looked enormous at home, but now in this rather large bedroom . . .

"Yes. You know I've no call for fancy gowns, Becky. I'm a Latin tutor. My students come to me to learn their declensions, not study the latest fashions."

Becky grunted. "Maybe they'd pay more attention to their studies if they didn't have to look at ye in the dowdy dresses ye wear."

Dowdy dresses? She should be insulted, but in the opulent surroundings of Greyham Manor, she was afraid Becky might have a point. The Windley hellions certainly weren't impressed with Cicero or Virgil. "My dresses are perfectly serviceable."

Becky limited herself to an expressive snort and started unfastening Jo's frock. "Ye'll never get through the house party with so few clothes."

Jo sighed and let Becky help her out of her dress. "Unless you are a magician, I shall have to, shan't I?"

Becky considered Jo's poor little case again and chewed her lip. "Let me see what I can do. I think Lord Greyham's sister was about yer size; leastways everyone always said she was a giant."

Was Becky determined to insult her at every opportunity? It wasn't her fault most of the females in the neighborhood were midgets—most of the men, too. "I am *not* a giant; I am merely taller than the average woman."

Lord Kenderly wasn't a midget. He must be over six feet tall; her eyes had been level with his mouth. Mmm, his mouth . . .

She had no business thinking of his height or his mouth. He was an unprincipled rake, like all of Lord Greyham's male guests.

Becky was staring up at her, brows raised, clearly saying—without uttering a word—that Jo was acting like a great ninny.

"And Rosalind married and moved out ten years ago," Jo said. "Even I know any clothes she left behind would be sadly outdated."

"Aye, but I'm very clever with my needle." Becky moved to open the valise and pull out Jo's dinner dress. She shook it out and looked at it doubtfully. "This is yer best gown?"

"Yes." Her poor frock did look a bit woebegone.

Blast it all, she *knew* she should have refused the invitation to this scandalous party, though she hadn't anticipated her wardrobe as well as her reputation would come under siege.

"At least it's not too creased." Becky frowned. "I wouldn't have thought this shade of pink would suit ye."

"It's fine," Jo said, grabbing the stupid dress from Becky and putting it on. She looked in the mirror.

She'd forgotten how consumptive it made her look. She'd bought it because Mrs. Wiggins, the local dressmaker, had purchased too much cloth for another order and so was willing to make her a gown for almost nothing.

"I don't have occasion to wear it often." Jo averted her eyes from the mirror. "It serves its purpose."

"And what would that be? Giving the gentlemen night-mares?"

"Oh, come, Becky." Jo scowled. This was the problem with growing up in the area; the servants had no compunction about sharing their opinions. "I'm twenty-eight years old. I'm sure I don't appear in any gentleman's dreams."

Becky glared back at her. "Yer female—that's enough for most men." She stood back and looked Jo up and down. "And yer not bad looking—or wouldn't be if ye weren't wearing that ugly dress. Ye could even be pretty, if ye made a little effort. Now come sit at the dressing table, and I'll try to put yer hair into some order."

Jo sat and watched Becky brush her unruly curls. She would like to be pretty, just for this house party. She'd like to appear in Lord Kenderly's dreams. . . .

No. She mustn't forget he was a rake. She'd been misled by his letters; apparently scholars could be as scandalous as any man. "I have no illusions as to why I'm here. I'm merely a poor relation invited to make up the numbers."

"Aye, and ye'll never be more than that if ye keep thinking that way."

Jo pressed her lips together. There was no point in arguing further; Becky was—

"Ouch!"

Becky was wielding the brush with a little too much enthusiasm. Her efforts to dispatch one particularly difficult tangle brought tears to Jo's eyes.

"There ye go. At least ye don't look like ye was dragged through a bush backward anymore."

"Thank you. I'm just glad you left a few hairs still attached to my head."

"Aye. I had to leave a few for the cats downstairs to rip out, don't ye know."

Jo lifted her chin, ordered her stomach to stop jumping about like a mouse trapped in the bottom of an empty jug, and headed for the door. "I am not afraid of any London cats."

She stepped into the corridor and closed the door behind

her, but not quickly enough to miss Becky's muttered
words: "Ye should be."

"Who was the Amazon you had in your arms, Damian?"
Stephen took a sip of his Madeira.

"Miss Atworthy. Her father is a Latin scholar and one
of my father's Oxford classmates." Damian surveyed the
room. Miss Atworthy had not yet made her appearance.
Had she recovered from her faint? He hoped so. He couldn't
very well go up to her room and check—well, perhaps he
could at this scandalous gathering.

The assembled guests were an odd assortment of dirty
dishes. Mr. Roger Dellingcourt, Viscount Sheldon's disreputable heir, was laughing uproariously at something Baron
Benedict Wapley had said. As Lord Wapley was not considered a wag, chances were good Dellingcourt had got into
Greyham's brandy early. Sir Humphrey Edgert, baronet; Mr.
Arthur Maiden—an unfortunate surname; and Mr. Percy
Felton, one of the Earl of Brent's many sons, were lounging
by the fireplace and, well . . . giggling was the word that
came to mind.

The women were no better than the men. Maria Noughton sat next to Lady Blanche Chutley, whispering in her ear,
probably trying to get her to lure Damian away from
Stephen so Maria could carry out her nefarious matrimo-
nial plan unimpeded. Ursula Handley and Sophia Petwell,
both nominally widows though no member of the *ton* had
ever met their likely mythical husbands, were standing by
the door, talking to Lord and Lady Greyham. Completing
the assembled guests were the pleasant-looking, portly
Mrs. Butterwick and Lady Imogene Silven, Lady Mardale's
daughter, with, rumor had it, one of her footmen.

"Ah," Stephen said. "So you'd made Miss Atworthy's
acquaintance before?"

"No, I saw her for the first time today." He smiled. She'd looked so fierce and full of passion. His smile broadened. She *was* full of passion. He hadn't been able to get their kiss out of his mind.

"Ha!" Bloody hell, Stephen was almost crowing. "But you're looking forward to seeing her again, aren't you? Seeing and touching and . . . other things."

Damian shot Stephen a pointed look. "Miss Atworthy is not available for 'other things.'"

Stephen grinned. "Oh, don't lose hope. I grant you she didn't look like a highflyer, but perhaps looks are deceiving in this case. She *is* here, isn't she?" Stephen glanced around and shrugged. "Well, not here at the moment, but here at this party." He waggled his eyebrows. "I told you this gathering would be good for you."

"I am not looking for dalliance." Well, he hadn't been, but now—

No. He suppressed his baser urges. He was a scholar; he was used to taming the needs of his body to achieve loftier, intellectual goals.

This time his body grumbled more than usual.

He gave Stephen a long look. "I am here to ensure you don't fall prey to Maria Noughton's machinations. You aren't helping matters, by the way. I noticed how you dashed in to see her as soon as you climbed out of the carriage."

Stephen laughed. "Listen to yourself, Damian. You sound like my mother, though Mama is far less of a wet rag than you."

Damian opened his mouth to blister Stephen's ears with his opinion of that statement but was deterred by Lord Greyham clapping him on the back.

"Kenderly, Parker-Roth, so good to have you here."

"Our pleasure, Greyham," Stephen said.

Damian only managed what he hoped was a civil nod. He was still trying to get his spleen under control.

Greyham dropped his voice and stepped closer. "I wanted to have a word with you, Kenderly, before the party gets under way."

"With me?" Damian glanced at Stephen; he looked mystified as well.

"Yes. It's about Jo."

"Jo?"

"Miss Atworthy."

"Ah." Of course Lord Greyham wished to ascertain his guest hadn't sustained an injury, though it would make more sense for the man or, better, his wife to go up and speak to Miss Atworthy directly. "I was happy to be able to save her from what could have been a very serious accident." Had Greyham heard about the kiss? Better not mention it.

"Er, yes," Greyham said. "Glad you could be of help. Wouldn't want Jo getting hurt, of course."

"Of course." Damian waited. Lord Greyham cleared his throat and shifted from foot to foot. "Was there something else?"

The baron tugged on his waistcoat. The man's belly had grown significantly in the last few years. "Yes, actually. I wanted to tell you—" He coughed. "This is a little awkward, but given your reputation—your *current* reputation, that is, not your old reputation as Prince of Hearts, heh heh."

Damian and Stephen just stared at him.

"Yes, well, given your current reputation, I assumed you wouldn't mind."

Lord Greyham smiled. Damian blinked. "Mind what?"

"That I've paired you with Jo."

An embarrassing bolt of lust shot through him, lodging in the obvious organ. "Oh." It was his turn to clear his throat. "Why would I mind?"

"Well, you see, the thing is we invited Henrietta Helton to be your, er, valentine. She's a knowledgeable widow and would have been very"—Greyham winked—"accommodating. But then she took ill at the very last minute. Literally. By the time I got word, there was no hope of inviting a suitable substitute. The Widow Bellingham, who sometimes attends our parties, was off visiting her daughter in Manchester, and none of the other mature ladies in the area would ever deign to darken our door. They're a nasty bunch of puritanical prudes; they turn their blasted supercilious noses up at us." Greyham shrugged. "My only option was Jo. Her father's a distant cousin; they live on the estate."

"I see. And Miss Atworthy doesn't share the local prejudice against your parties?" Damian asked. She'd looked a bit like a prude in her outdated outfit and severe expression when she'd arrived in that cart, but she hadn't felt—or tasted—like a prude when he'd had her in his arms.

"Oh, she probably does. I took the precaution of asking her father before I sent the invitation. He said he thought he could convince her, but frankly, I was shocked to hear she'd come—I'd expected to get my invitation back torn up into tiny pieces." He shrugged. "Just wanted to warn you, she's not up to snuff, no matter that she's not a dewy young miss. To tell the truth, she's a bit of an ape-leader. Past her prayers, don't you know." He grinned suddenly. "Or maybe that's why she came—to find out what she's been missing all these years. If so, you're just the man to educate her, aren't you, Kenderly?" He waggled his brows. "You two can do a little conjugation together."

Stephen choked on his Madeira; Damian scowled at the baron, even while an evil little voice in the randy section of his brain pointed out Miss Atworthy had shown great promise while kissing him. A confirmed prude would have slapped him soundly.

Greyham looked over Damian's shoulder and frowned.

"Damn." He sighed. "I'm afraid Jo looks exactly like the stuffy, dull Latin tutor she is."

Damian turned and felt another jolt of lust.

Miss Atworthy stood in the doorway, wearing perhaps the ugliest gown he'd ever seen—a hideous pink frothy affair with a high neck, long sleeves, and far too many ruffles. But above the nauseating pink cloud, her eyes flashed with nervous challenge, her firm chin tilted defiantly, and her rebellious curls twisted in whatever direction they liked.

She might be an impoverished Latin tutor, but her attitude was that of a duchess.

Or a countess?

Good God, where had that thought come from?

Her eyes met his, and she flushed a bright red before looking away.

Lust exploded in his gut.

Bloody hell. Perhaps it *was* time he put away his Latin texts to study the needs of his body.

Chapter 4

Jo wanted to hit something, preferably this beautiful raven-haired woman who, like a fox sensing an easy kill, had almost run to her, her equally unpleasant companion close behind, the moment Jo had entered the blue parlor. They'd introduced themselves as Lady Noughton and Lady Chutley.

"What an interesting frock, Miss Atworthy," Lady Noughton said now, derision clear in her voice. "Wherever did you get it?"

Was she hoping Jo would say she'd made it herself? "From Mrs. Wiggins, our local dressmaker."

"You know, I think I once had a gown that was just that shade," Lady Chutley said. "It was a very popular color four or five years ago, wasn't it?"

More than likely, since that was when Jo'd had the dress made. She forced a smile. "Was it? I'm afraid I don't follow the fashion magazines."

Lady Noughton tittered. "That's rather obvious, isn't it?"

Both women tried—not very hard—to choke back laughter.

"What's so amusing, Maria?"

Jo glanced over to see who had spoken. An attractive

man with shaggy, sun-streaked hair was approaching—with Lord Kenderly at his side.

Damn. She felt her cheeks flush again. She looked back at Lady Noughton. Perhaps Lord Kenderly would assume her heightened color was due to anger.

"Oh, Stephen, Blanche and I were just making Miss Atworthy's acquaintance. She is so refreshing—but then, provincials often are, aren't they?" Lady Noughton laughed. "I venture to guess she's never been to London." She glanced at Jo. "Am I right, Miss Atworthy?"

"Yes, I've not had that pleasure." Jo tried to relax her jaw so it wouldn't sound like she was speaking through clenched teeth.

"Then you will have to visit someday, Miss Atworthy," Lord Kenderly said smoothly as if he couldn't tell she wished to kick Lady Noughton in the shins. "If you can put up with the dirt and the noise, London has much to recommend it." The corners of his eyes crinkled in a very appealing fashion. "But I'm afraid my manners have gone begging. Let me make known to you my good friend Mr. Stephen Parker-Roth. I believe he would agree with you that the country is preferable to Town."

Mr. Parker-Roth had been frowning at Lady Noughton, which had put the old cat in a pout, Jo was happy to see. Now he smiled at Jo.

"Most definitely. You show excellent sense, Miss Atworthy, in favoring the country."

"Oh, Mr. Parker-Roth," Lady Chutley said—Lady Noughton was apparently so disgruntled she could only glare—"you must admit society is so much more stimulating in London."

"On the contrary, I find London society too often 'full of sound and fury, signifying nothing.'"

"Oh, but Stephen—"

They were saved from hearing what Lady Noughton had to say by Lord Greyham's booming voice.

"Welcome, everyone! Lady Greyham and I are delighted you could be here to celebrate our favorite holidays of love—"

"And lust!" one of the men standing by the fireplace shouted. Licentiousness suddenly permeated the air. Everyone except Jo—and Lord Kenderly and Mr. Parker-Roth, thank God—cheered and clapped.

"You've heard about our little celebrations, have you, Felton?" Lord Greyham said.

"From my brothers and their friends. It's no secret Greyham Manor's the place for some fun, especially in February."

The other men by the fireplace hooted and cheered. They had clearly been making free with the brandy decanter.

"I'm so happy our gatherings have got such glowing reviews. For those of you who may not have heard the reports Mr. Felton has been privy to, let me explain. Tomorrow is Valentine's Day—"

The men—and some of the women—called out in a completely hurly-burly manner.

"No, really?"

"You don't say!"

"I never would have guessed."

Lord Greyham held up his hands for quiet. "Yes, and the day after we celebrate Lupercalia."

More cheering. Good God, surely Lord Greyham didn't mean the men of the party would run naked over the grounds hitting women with goatskin thongs to ensure fertility? How horrible.

Jo sent a sidelong glance toward Lord Kenderly. Perhaps not *so* horrible. The earl would strip to advantage—

Blast it, what was the matter with her? She'd never had such a shocking thought in her life.

She snorted. Of course not, given the quality of the local males. A naked Mr. Windley, for example; she shuddered. But a naked earl . . .

She cast another glance at Lord Kenderly. His arms and chest had felt so hard when he'd carried her; his shirt and waistcoat must cover muscles as impressive as those of Michelangelo's *David*. And his face, with its strong chin, high cheekbones, long lashes, clever lips . . .

A strange, liquid heat curled through her.

"But first," Lord Greyham said, "we must have the lottery."

"Huzzah!" the men by the fireplace yelled. "The lovers' lottery!"

It was as if a bucket of ice water had been dumped on her. A lottery? Good God! What if she was paired with one of the idiots by the fire? She looked around the room. None of the men besides Lord Kenderly and possibly Mr. Parker-Roth was the least bit acceptable.

Lord Greyham turned to his wife. "The vase, my dear."

Lady Greyham stepped forward with a remarkably obscene bit of pottery: two jugs fused together and shaped like female breasts, with the handles—a hot flush swept up Jo's neck and cheeks—resembling a distinctive part of the male anatomy.

"I will pull a gentleman's name from one side of the vase," Lord Greyham said, "and Lady Greyham will draw a lady's name from the other. The two shall be a couple for the duration of our festivities."

The gentlemen made a number of enthusiastic, if rude, noises; the ladies giggled and preened. Jo swallowed her nervous stomach.

"The gentlemen will have tomorrow, Valentine's Day, to woo their ladies," Greyham continued, raising his voice over the commotion. "If they are successful, they'll have

Lupercalia to"—he grinned and waggled his eyebrows—
"celebrate."

More cheering and catcalls.

Damian flinched, cursing inwardly at the rising chorus
of lewd comments. Why the hell had he let Stephen drag
him to this infernal house party?

His reason was right in front of him. Lady Noughton was
doing a credible impression of ivy, wrapping her fingers
around Stephen's arm and attaching herself to his side. Happily, Stephen didn't look very pleased. Maria had made a
serious mistake in her treatment of Miss Atworthy; Stephen
detested that kind of sly cruelty.

Damian glanced down at the oddly dressed woman. Perhaps she would turn out to be his best weapon in his battle
for Stephen's continued bachelorhood.

Lord Greyham drew the first name. "Mr. Roger Dellingcourt."

Damian saw Miss Atworthy tense. She didn't think
Greyham had really left the pairings to chance, did she?

"Lady Imogene," Lady Greyham called out.

Lady Imogene squealed; Damian cringed. Squealing was
one of the lady's most unpleasant traits, but Dellingcourt
must not mind. The two of them had been scandalizing the
ton for the last six months.

Had he heard Miss Atworthy sigh with relief?

"Mr. Arthur Maiden."

As always, the men snickered and the women giggled at
Maiden's surname. One would think everyone in society
would have grown immune to that feeble double entendre,
but one would be wrong.

Miss Atworthy's face paled. So she did think this was a
real lottery.

"Lady Chutley," Lady Greyham read from the slip of
paper she'd drawn.

"Lucky me," Lady Chutley said, an edge to her voice.

"What's the matter, Blanche?" Lady Noughton asked. "You were singing Arthur's praises to me just this afternoon. You almost made me envious."

"That was before I realized the Prince of Hearts had come out of retirement." She touched Damian's forearm and fluttered her lashes at him. "I'm sure Arthur won't mind sharing, my lord. We might even arrange an exchange with your partner, whoever she may be." She glanced at Miss Atworthy. Blanche knew the pairs had already been decided. "Mr. Maiden takes great delight in sampling a wide variety of female—"

His stomach turned. "Thank you, but no." Even when he'd merited his obnoxious nickname, he'd preferred not to share, and the thought of the disgusting Maiden touching Miss Atworthy in any way was revolting.

Lady Chutley's mouth hung open for a moment at his sharp tone.

"I'd say you've been put in your place, Blanche," Lady Noughton said, her eyes lighting with what looked like glee at the perceived slight.

"No insult intended." Lord Kenderly's voice still had an edge. "I wouldn't want to take you away from Mr. Maiden for a moment; I'm certain he would be most unhappy should I try to."

"You needn't take me away." Lady Chutley smiled. "As I said, Arthur likes variety. I'm sure he wouldn't mind if we all got busy together. He rather enjoys group situations."

"Really?" Lord Kenderly's tone would have frozen water.

Mr. Parker-Roth filled the somewhat awkward pause. "You must know Damian has become a very dull dog, Blanche, though I'm not sure he was ever so exciting as you seem to think. Still, he's been spending all his time in his study with his Latin tomes recently. I dragged him here against his will to shake some of the dust off him."

"Oh." Lady Chutley's full lips curved in the slightest

smile and her eyes slid briefly back to Jo. "I'm the first to admit I'm not a scholar, but my brother always said those Roman fellows were quite, quite adventuresome." She tapped the earl's arm. "If—*when*—you change your mind, I'll be delighted to help welcome you back to the joys of the flesh," she said before making her way across the room to where Mr. Maiden was waiting impatiently.

Lord Kenderly shook his arm slightly and straightened his cuff. He did not watch Lady Chutley's progress.

"Lord Benedict Wapley," Lord Greyham called.

Oh, God. Jo tried to appear calm, but it was difficult when her stomach was shaking like a blancmange. She did not belong here. She was nothing like these other ladies. She didn't even understand what Lady Chutley had been hinting at. A group situation? The only notion that came to mind—no, that *must* be wrong.

And if she were ever in any . . . situation with Lord Kenderly—which, of course, she would never be—she would wish to have him all to herself.

"Mrs. Sophia Petwell."

Thank God. Another nincompoop avoided.

At least it was almost dinnertime. She could get through this evening. She would keep her eyes open for the Ovid; Papa had said it was very distinctive. If worse came to worst, she'd plead the headache and go hide in her room until everyone was in his or her bed. She flushed. Or whosever's bed.

Once everyone was, er, *situated* for the night, she'd creep down to the library and look through the bookcases. And if she didn't find the Ovid, so be it. Her headache could turn into a serious illness requiring her immediate departure in the morning.

Papa had not been at all forthcoming about this Ovid; no, he'd been downright secretive. If Lord Kenderly, a noted Latin scholar, didn't consider the book valuable, it probably wasn't, though she must remember the earl hadn't actually seen the volume. Still, given Papa's behavior, it was most likely all a hum—certainly not worth risking her virtue over.

"Mr. Stephen Parker-Roth."

Lady Noughton could not possibly get any closer to the man without climbing inside his skin. She'd be sadly miffed if Lady Greyham pulled someone else's name.

She didn't. "Lady Maria Noughton."

Lady Noughton whispered something in Mr. Parker-Roth's ear that caused him to smile in an exceedingly warm, terribly unsettling way. Something dark and hot and sinful pulsed between them.

Something dark and hot throbbed deep in *her*. Sin. It was thick around her. And temptation in the form of the Prince of Hearts stood right at her elbow.

She must resist. She must remember her virtue. She would rather die than part with it.

Wouldn't she?

She glanced around the room as Lord Greyham pulled another man's name. Yes, of course. She'd defend her honor to her last breath if any of these idiots tried to take it from her.

"Lord Damian Kenderly."

Oh! Except perhaps Lord Kenderly.

Her palms blossomed with dampness. What if her name wasn't chosen? She had only a one in three chance of being paired with the earl.

What was she thinking? She should be happy if one of the other ladies' names *was* called. Then she wouldn't be tempted to sin . . . but she'd be matched with the fat, balding man or the thin, spotted boy. Her stomach twisted.

"Miss Josephine Atworthy."

She stopped breathing. The dark, throbbing, sinful feeling smoldered deep inside her. She closed her eyes.

"Are you all right, Miss Atworthy?"

Lord Kenderly's voice was quiet, concerned, deep, and male. It acted like wind on coals, causing hot need to blaze and roar through her.

Virtue. She must hold on to her virtue.

She swallowed and cleared her throat. "Yes," she said and looked up at him.

Big, big mistake.

A man should not have such dark blue eyes and such long lashes. And his lips . . .

Dear God! She dropped her gaze to his cravat. She wanted to feel the touch of his lips again so badly she could taste it.

Perhaps a little sin wouldn't be so terrible. She was twenty-eight years old, after all. Her virtue was shriveling inside her like a grape forgotten on the vine. This house party would last only a day or two, and then she'd go back to her old life. If she was going to be condemned to the hell of cramming Latin verbs into Windley heads, she might as well have something interesting to atone for.

No mortal sin; just a few venial ones. What would be the harm in that? She'd get a little experience, a little tarnish on her reputation, but who would care? No matter what Papa said, just her being here would cause Mrs. Johnson and the other matrons to assume she'd done terrible, scandalous things. If her name was to be blackened anyway, she might as well do *something*.

She could further her Latin scholarship. Lord Kenderly should be able to explain the confusing poetry she'd found in Papa's study and perhaps even demonstrate a verse or two.

She flushed. Well, perhaps not.

"And now that our lottery is over," Lord Greyham said—dear heavens, she'd completely missed the last two drawings—"we can proceed to dinner." He wrapped his arm around his wife's waist and bussed her noisily on the cheek. "Gentlemen, though it's not yet Valentine's Day, I'm sure no one will object if you begin your wooing now."

"Huzzah!" Mr. Dellingcourt shouted, grabbing Lady Imogene in a most lascivious manner. All the men in the room except Lord Kenderly and Mr. Parker-Roth embraced their companions. Mr. Parker-Roth didn't have to; Lady Noughton threw her arms around him and pulled his head down for a kiss. His hands landed on her derriere.

Jo looked away. How mortifying. She quickly stepped back from Lord Kenderly. Was he going to maul her in the same fashion?

No, he merely offered her his arm. She took it, swallowing a ridiculous feeling of disappointment. She was relieved. Of *course* she was relieved. "I'm afraid I'm not used to . . ." She waved her free hand, not quite certain how to describe the scene.

"Yes, well, I'm not used to it either." He was frowning at Mr. Parker-Roth and Lady Noughton.

"Then why did you come?" Dear God, Lady Noughton had her hand on the front of Mr. Parker-Roth's breeches.

Lord Kenderly put some distance between them and his friend. "To keep an eye on Stephen. I can't shake the feeling that Maria means to trap him into marrying her."

Mr. Parker-Roth and Lady Noughton appeared to be on extremely intimate terms already. "Would that be such a terrible thing?"

"It would be a disaster." He bent his head and dropped his voice so they wouldn't be overheard, not that anyone was paying them the least bit of attention—everyone else was far too involved in sinful behavior. Sir Humphrey had his hand on Mrs. Butterwick's breasts, and Mr. Dellingcourt was nibbling on Lady Imogene's ear as they made their way toward the dining room.

"Maria is a creature of London. She thinks Stephen

would be happy living in Town; she seems not to have noticed he never stays there more than a few weeks before he's off searching for new plant species."

"Oh." Mr. Parker-Roth and Lady Noughton were strolling toward the door now. "Perhaps she could accompany him."

Lord Kenderly snorted. "Pigs will fly long before Maria will set her expensively shod toe into the heat and mud of South America."

"I see." She watched Lady Noughton's elegant derriere swish out the door. He had a point.

"And Stephen comes from a large, close family. When he does wed, he'll want several children. Maria would never agree to so inconvenience herself or her figure."

"Ah." And how many children would Lord Kenderly like? He was an earl. He must plan to have an heir and a spare at least. She flushed. That was none of her concern. "But if Lady Noughton loves—"

Lord Kenderly scowled at her. "Maria loves no one but herself."

Was the earl a dog in the manger? An unpleasant, but unfortunately reasonable thought. Lady Noughton was very beautiful in a brittle sort of way. "Then why would she wish to marry?"

"I don't know. The current Lord Noughton disapproves of her, so her funds may be in jeopardy. Likely it's desperation that persuades her she's in love with Stephen."

"But how could she trap Mr. Parker-Roth? She's a widow, not a debutante."

Lord Kenderly looked away—and must have realized they were the only people left in the parlor. He started toward the door. "I admit that has me puzzled."

"Perhaps you are imagining problems where there are none."

"I am not. I overheard Maria talking to Lady Greyham at the Wainwright soiree last week."

"Eavesdropping?"

The man didn't even blush. "Yes. Unfortunately, I didn't hear the whole of it, so I don't know exactly what kind of trap Maria plans to set—which is why I'm telling you all this." He looked down at her, his deep blue eyes intent. "I could use your help."

The sinful heat flared low in her belly again. The rational part of her insisted this was none of her affair, but the other part—this strange, needy part that until now she hadn't known existed—was already nodding. "Of course. What do you want me to do?"

He smiled, just the slightest upturn of his lips, and his broad hand came up to cover hers where it rested on his forearm. He squeezed her fingers. "I don't know. Just keep your eyes and ears open. Maybe Maria will let some clue slip."

"Very well." She managed to get the words past her suddenly dry lips. The weight of his hand on hers was doing unusual things to her heart.

She was in very big trouble.

Chapter 5

Jo listened as yet another set of footsteps crept past her door. If the frequent creaking of the corridor floor was any indication, everyone at the party had made his or her way to some other guest's bedchamber. Mr. Parker-Roth was likely already in Lady Noughton's room.

Whose room was Lord Kenderly in?

She tossed his letter onto her dressing table. She'd finally found time to read it, but now that she knew he'd thought he was writing to Papa, his words didn't captivate her as they had in the past. Oh, he was still witty and perspicacious, but she could no longer pretend he was writing to *her*.

She should throw it away. She picked it up again to do just that, but her fingers refused to crumple it. She glanced down at the vellum square. She still felt an odd thrill when she saw his strong, bold handwriting.

She was a fool, but she tucked the letter into the book she'd been reading. She would keep it with all the others, tied in a ribbon in her desk at home.

She turned and frowned at herself in the cheval glass. She raised her chin. She'd put her foolish tendre behind her. Where Lord Kenderly was and what he was doing with whom were none of her concern. She would wait a few more minutes and then make her own surreptitious way through Greyham Manor's darkened halls.

She wrinkled her nose at her nightgown-clad figure. She would not be headed to any gentleman's arms. Oh, no. She meant to search the library. With luck, she'd find the stupid Ovid. She'd like to take it home and wave it in Papa's face. But find it or not, she'd be gone in the morning.

And what about Lord Kenderly? He'd asked for her help. Was she going to desert him?

Yes. She thrust her arms into her wrapper. Indeed she was. He was the Prince of Hearts. She was merely a country spinster, very much a fish out of water at this gathering.

She'd never endured such a shocking meal as this evening's dinner. She hadn't known where to look. To her right, Mr. Dellingcourt was cutting Lady Imogene's food and feeding it to her from his fork. Across the table, Lord Wapley plucked grapes from Mrs. Petwell's bodice with his lips. And on her left, Lady Noughton ate a sausage so slowly and lasciviously, it was as if she were consuming something else entirely. Jo had bolted for her room at the first opportunity.

She glanced at the clock. It was almost midnight. The corridor had been quiet for the last ten minutes. She should be able to make it to the library without encountering anyone else.

She slipped out of her room. Just as she'd hoped, the passage was empty. The candles in the wall sconces provided plenty of light; she didn't need a candlestick.

She hurried past the closed doors, ignoring the laughter and moans that came from behind some of them, and went down the stairs. The library door stood open. Everyone at this party had far more interesting ways of getting to sleep than by reading a book.

She went in, pulling the door closed behind her. Moonlight flooded the room and a glimmer of color glinted in the grate where the fire's embers smoldered, but there was not enough light to find Ovid. She would need a candle after all. Where—

She heard a step in the hall.

Damn! Some randy gentleman was likely on the prowl. She didn't want to be discovered. Where could she hide? He would be in the library in a moment.

The window curtains—they would have to do. She darted behind their generous folds just as the door opened.

Damian stepped into the library. Thank God the room was empty; he'd no desire to encounter any of the other guests.

No, that was a lie. He had a burning desire to encounter Miss Atworthy. Far too burning—he'd been tossing and turning for the last half hour, and hearing people creeping up and down the corridor had only thrown kindling on the coals. He could imagine in painful detail exactly what everyone else was doing in bed, and it wasn't sleeping or reading.

Except Miss Atworthy. She must be lying demurely between her virginal sheets, sound asleep, unless she was bothered by salacious nightmares. The poor woman's eyes had almost started from her head during dinner.

Dinner *had* been quite a deplorable show. Even when he'd reigned as Prince of Hearts, he'd avoided such things. But then again, perhaps the appalling spectacle had done some good. Stephen had looked almost as disapproving as Miss Atworthy. Lady Noughton was doing an excellent job of killing his enthusiasm for her.

Damian frowned. The widow wasn't stupid. She must think she had a solid plan to trap Stephen. What could it be? He kept turning that question over in his mind, but he wasn't coming up with any answers.

Ah well, he wasn't going to solve the puzzle tonight. He needed to get some sleep so he could be alert tomorrow. A good book might distract him—he certainly hoped so. He walked farther into the library, lifting his candle to illuminate the bookcases.

Either the Greyhams weren't readers, or they kept their more entertaining books elsewhere. He had no interest in examining *Recipes to Ensure Improved Digestion* or *A Short Discussion of Sheep Shearing.* Short? This tome was a good three inches thick. A long discussion might crush an unwary reader. Perhaps if he—

Damn, were those voices? Yes, a man's and a woman's, loud and slurred. They were drunk and coming closer. He snuffed his candle. Bloody hell, he'd neglected to shut the door. The moment the couple reached the room, they'd see him. He had to hide and quickly, but where? He looked around. There was only one option.

He jumped behind the window curtain—and into a soft, feminine body.

"Ee—"

He silenced the woman's startled shriek in the quickest, most efficient manner he could think of: he put his candlestick-free hand on her back, pulled her against him, and covered her mouth with his.

She stiffened.

Who the hell was he kissing? None of the women at this party cared whom they frolicked with.

None except Miss Atworthy.

The height and the feel . . . and the innocent taste . . . of the woman were right, as was her scent—clean and fresh with a hint of lemon. His body certainly recognized her. It was reacting most enthusiastically.

She relaxed and opened her lips on a small sigh. He did not need a second invitation; his tongue swept into her warm, moist mouth while his hand slid down her back.

Mmm. It was definitely Miss Atworthy. No one else had such a lovely body. She was in her nightclothes, her stays discarded—and he was wearing only shirt and breeches, pulled on hurriedly over his nakedness. He could feel her every soft curve. . . .

He drew his hips back quickly so she wouldn't feel his suddenly hard curve. She might be older than most debutantes, but she was clearly inexperienced.

He'd very much like to remedy that situation, immediately if possible. He could carry her up to his bed or just lay her down on the couch he'd noticed by the fire and—

And he'd best pay attention to what was happening on the other side of the curtain. He moved his lips to Miss Atworthy's ear. "I think we're about to have company."

"Wha—" She stopped, then stretched to whisper in his ear, "Who?"

He almost missed her question, he was so entranced by the feel of her body moving against his. "I don't . . . ah."

The newcomers' identities required no guesswork.

"I don't see why I have to sneak around my own house, Alice," Lord Greyham said in a conversational, if highly annoyed and drunken, tone.

"Shh, Hugh. It's almost midnight. Maria and Mr. Parker-Roth should be down at any moment. We don't want them to know we're here."

Maria? What was this? Perhaps he'd finally learn the widow's plan.

"I thought they wanted us here." Greyham had dropped his voice slightly.

"Maria does." Lady Greyham whispered loudly. "But we'll be a surprise for Mr. Parker-Roth."

"An unpleasant one." There was the sound of a stopper coming out of a brandy decanter. "No sensible man wants an audience for his proposal, Alice. And why he'd want to come down to the library when he could pop the question in a more comfortable, private location like a bedchamber is beyond me. I imagine he's already in Maria's bed."

"Pour me some brandy, too, will you?" There was the sound of liquid splashing into two glasses. "You're acting just like a man, Hugh. This will be far more amusing."

"Amusing for whom? Not Parker-Roth." Greyham's voice slid into a leer. "And of course I'm acting like a man. I *am* a man, Alice. I'll be happy to give you another, even more forceful demonstration of that fact if it's slipped your mind."

Miss Atworthy made a small sound of distress, and Damian pulled her tighter against him. Fortunately, he'd turned slightly, so she was against his side. She didn't need to have a close encounter with *his* male organ.

"Really, Hugh, you are impossible. Just think how romantic it would be to become betrothed in the first moments of Valentine's Day."

Greyham snorted. "It certainly can't be romantic to have your host and hostess leap up to shout congratulations. I tell you, Parker-Roth can just as easily—far more easily—become betrothed in a nice warm bed and seal his troth with a long, thorough, sweaty bit of lovemaking."

"Oh, pish. I think you must not have a single romantic bone in your body."

"I do have a suddenly bonelike appendage that's very eager to show you how romantic I can be."

Lady Greyham giggled amid sounds of a scuffle. "Mmm. Behave yourself, my lord."

"I thought I was behaving myself."

More giggling.

"Stop, Hugh." Lady Greyham sounded rather breathless. "We have to hide. I promised Maria."

Greyham sighed. "Very well. Shall we conceal ourselves behind the curtains?"

Miss Atworthy sucked in a small breath and her grip on

Damian tightened. It *would* get rather crowded if the Greyhams chose this spot to secret themselves.

"No, I have a better idea," Lady Greyham said. "See, this couch is turned so if we lie on it, we'll be hidden from anyone coming in the door."

"What? You think I can't satisfy you standing up? I'll be happy to show you that you are mistaken."

Lady Greyham giggled some more. "But then we'll make the curtains move. You know I can never hold still."

"And you can never be quiet either, can you?"

"I'll try."

Her accompanying shriek didn't speak well for her success nor did the groaning couch springs.

Frankly they were making enough noise to alert all but the deaf to their presence, but Damian couldn't leave anything to chance. Maria must be planning to trick a proposal out of Stephen—how she thought she'd manage that was a mystery—and by having witnesses, she'd either claim breach of promise or shame Stephen into standing by his offer. A ridiculous scheme, but if she'd managed to get Stephen drunk—a feat in itself—it might work. Stephen was honorable to a fault.

He had to do something, but what? He couldn't risk ruining Miss Atworthy's reputation. If he—

"Why the hell do we n-need to go to the l-library now, Maria?"

Damn it all, that was Stephen's voice. They were in the corridor.

"We have to save Mr. Parker-Roth," Miss Atworthy whispered suddenly.

"Yes, but—"

She didn't wait to hear his thoughts; she grabbed the candlestick from him and stepped out from behind the curtain.

* * *

Jo was lighting the candle in the fireplace when Lady Noughton dragged Mr. Parker-Roth through the library door.

Lady Noughton stopped abruptly and glared. "What are you doing here?"

Jo raised her chin. "Looking for a book." She wasn't going to let this sneaky, unprincipled snake intimidate her. "This *is* a library, you know."

Mr. Parker-Roth laughed. "V-very true. Girl's got you there." His speech was slurred. He must be exceedingly drunk. "F-frankly, I don't know why *we're* here. D-didn't think you wanted to read, Maria."

"No, of course I don't want to read." Lady Noughton patted Mr. Parker-Roth on the arm. "Remember, I wish to show you—"

"Surprise!" Lady Greyham popped up from behind the sofa back, her hair tumbled over her shoulders, her bodice drooping alarmingly low.

"I say, it's a party." Lord Greyham appeared next to her. "And look, here's Kenderly as well."

In the confusion, Lord Kenderly must have slipped out of the room. It looked as if he were just entering the library now.

"Help yourself to some brandy; decanter's on the table." Lord Greyham wrapped his arm around his wife's shoulders. "I have to get back to what I was doing."

Lady Greyham giggled as her husband pulled her down and, blessedly, out of sight.

"You looking for a book, too, D-Damian?" Mr. Parker-Roth wavered a little on his feet. "Should be looking for a l-lady instead." The man winked. "A w-wet and willing woman will help you sleep much better than some dry Latin text."

"And you should be in bed, Stephen"—Lord Kenderly glared at Lady Noughton—"your *own* bed."

Suddenly the couch started creaking in an alarming way;

odd, breathy pants and grunts emanated from the other side, where Lord and Lady Greyham were obviously engaged in some strenuous activity.

"It *is* a bit crowded here, isn't it?" Mr. Parker-Roth executed a wobbly bow to Lady Noughton. "'Fraid my f-friend's right. Not feeling quite the thing. Excuse me?"

Lady Noughton almost growled. "No, I—"

"Oh, oh, *oh!*" Lady Greyham's voice rose, tight and vaguely desperate. There was something intense about her tone that made Jo feel extremely unsettled and, well, *hot.*

"That's it. That's the way." Lord Greyham might have been urging on his hounds. His voice was strained, too. "Come on, old girl. Come on."

"Oh, oh . . . *y-yes!*" Lady Greyham screamed. "Oh, God, Pookie!"

The couch shook more violently in sharp, hard jerks; Lord Greyham grunted . . . and then roared. "Huzzah!"

Jo's entire body flushed.

She glanced at Lord Kenderly; he was grimacing in what looked like pain. Then his eyes met hers, and her temperature shot up another hundred degrees.

A very embarrassing area of her person throbbed, wet and empty.

Dear heavens, was she like a dog in heat—could he *smell* the need consuming her?

"Well, at least someone is satisfied," Lady Noughton said waspishly.

"If you hadn't decided to go h-haring off to the library, you could be, too." Mr. Parker-Roth shifted on his feet as if he was uncomfortable. "*I* could be."

"Yes, well, I believe it's past time we adjourned." Lord Kenderly sounded angry. "I'll see you up to your room, Stephen." He looked at Jo. His face was now expressionless. "Will you accompany us, Miss Atworthy?"

She certainly wasn't going to stay here. Lady Noughton

looked as if she might explode, ripping apart anyone unwary enough to be nearby, and the thought of facing Lord and Lady Greyham after what she'd just heard . . .

"That was splendid, Pookie." Lady Greyham's voice was almost a purr. "But do get off me now. We should attend to our guests."

Jo shot out of the library ahead of everyone.

Chapter 6

Damn. Damian sat up in bed and rubbed his hands over his face. His sheets were a twisted mess. He felt like he'd hardly slept a wink—and every time he had dropped off, he'd dreamt of a certain tall, prickly, *virginal* woman.

She was anything but virginal in his dreams. Those long legs . . . her full breasts . . .

He scowled down at his eager cock where it made an obvious bulge in the bedclothes. Stephen was right; he'd been far too long without a woman. Unfortunately, there was little chance he could cure that problem anytime soon. Miss Atworthy was not a candidate for seduction.

He rubbed the spot between his brows. Listening to Greyham and his wife last night had been torture, and with Valentine's Day and, worse, Lupercalia the focus of the next two days, lust would be so thick in the air, he'd likely choke on it.

He threw off the covers and walked carefully over to the washbasin. Good, the water was cold. He splashed it on his face; he should splash it considerably lower.

He'd tried to talk some sense into Stephen after they'd seen Miss Atworthy to her door last night, but the man had been too drunk to see reason, damn it. Until he could persuade him to look out for himself, he'd have to look out for him, as last night had demonstrated.

He yanked on his clothes and made quick work of tying his cravat. Whether the Greyhams witnessing whatever Maria had had planned would have resulted in her trap snapping shut, he couldn't say. But Stephen was so damn honorable, all the widow need do was convince him he owed her marriage.

Damian was bloody well determined to see to it that that didn't happen.

He shrugged into his coat, straightened his cuffs, and stepped out into the corridor.

"*Oof!*"

Miss Atworthy's delightful body collided with his.

He grabbed her upper arms to steady her and inhaled the scent of lemon and woman. His cock, which had finally assumed appropriate proportions, leapt with eagerness.

"Oh, I'm so sorry." She was babbling, her lovely eyes wide, her cheeks red. "It was my fault entirely. I was wool-gathering."

She was close enough to kiss. He remembered the feel of her last night in painful detail. Her lips were soft; her mouth, warm and wet—

He coughed. "Are you all right?" She seemed to be struggling to get her breath; her bosom was certainly heaving delightfully.

"Yes." She swallowed, and he watched her throat move. Her dress this morning was a great improvement over yesterday's monstrosity. All her graceful neck was exposed to his interested gaze as well as most of her lovely shoulders. And the nicely rounded tops of her br—

"I should have been paying more attention to where I was going," she said. "That was so clumsy of me."

"Don't give it another thought. I should have been more careful myself." He looked down to be certain his wayward body wasn't announcing his admiration too obviously and noticed something had fallen out of the book she was carrying—a letter she'd apparently been using to mark her place. He stooped to pick it up.

He frowned. He recognized the handwriting. "This is one of my letters to your father."

"*Ack!*" She grabbed it and thrust it back in the book. She was even redder than she'd been a moment ago. "Please excuse me. I was just on my way to my room." She stepped to the side as though she planned to go around him.

He stopped her with a hand on her arm. "Did your father give you my letter?" He hoped she couldn't hear the hurt in his voice. He'd saved all the letters Mr. Atworthy had sent him, but if the man didn't value their correspondence the way he did, there was nothing he could do about it. He shouldn't be surprised or offended. It only made sense that what impressed a man of thirty as significant would seem banal to someone twice that age.

"No."

"You just took it?" Miss Atworthy hadn't struck him as someone who had such little consideration for a man's privacy.

"No, of course not." She fidgeted. "I, er, needed a book-mark, and, ah, well . . ." She shrugged.

Very odd. He would try another subject. "Did he tell you I would be here?"

Her eyes snapped up to meet his. "Of course not. Papa didn't know you'd be attending this house party."

Why would she assume that? "Yes, he did."

She shook her head, frowning at him. "No, he didn't."

This conversation was beyond absurd. Certainly she must realize he would know the truth better than she on this subject. "Did a Mr. Flanders not stop to call on your father last week?"

Her brows met over her nose. "Yes, I believe he did. Is he a short man with reddish hair?"

"Yes. He helps with *The Classical Gazette*. He's the one who initially puzzled out who J.A. was; since the letters are sent to the *Gazette* offices, he knew what part of Britain they came from. As he happened to be passing through the area, he thought he should introduce himself. He told me your father was surprised and"—Flanders had said "over the moon," but that had seemed an exaggeration—"pleased that I'd be in the neighborhood, though doubtful he'd be able to see me. I take it he doesn't get out much. Is he perhaps an invalid?"

Miss Atworthy muttered something that sounded suspiciously like "not yet" before she pushed past him and fled down the corridor.

Jo sat stunned among the women in the morning room, the gentlemen having been relegated to the study, and tried to appear as if nothing was amiss. Sheets of red paper, bits of ribbon and lace, and pots of glue were strewn over the tables. Her hand slipped and she cut the bottom off her paper heart.

She couldn't believe it. Papa had known Lord Kenderly would be here. Worse, he must know, after speaking with Mr. Flanders, that she'd been corresponding with the earl for some time.

Dear God, what must Papa think? Well-bred single women did *not* write to single men to whom they were not related.

"How are your valentines coming?" Lady Greyham asked. "You should have everything you need at hand."

"I don't have any ideas." Lady Imogene dropped her scissors, letting them clatter on the table. "I hate making valentines."

"But you like getting them, don't you?" Mrs. Petwell asked as she cut out a large, red heart.

Lady Imogene shrugged. "I like gifts better. Chocolate and flowers."

"Chocolate and flowers *are* very pleasant," Lady Greyham said, "as I tell my dear Lord Greyham every year."

"You just need to let yourself have some fun with it, Lady Imogene." Mrs. Butterwick smiled in a motherly fashion. "See?" She held up the card she'd just finished.

Lady Imogene took it from her. "It's rather an odd shape, isn't it? Like a melted heart."

It looked more like two red mountains decorated with snippets of ribbon and tufts of feathers.

"It's a dress," Mrs. Butterwick said.

"A dress? It doesn't look anything like a dress."

"It depends on your perspective. Open it."

Lady Imogene rolled her eyes and opened the card—it was hinged on the mountain peaks so it lifted up. "Oh!" She started giggling.

Jo frowned. The second layer was all lace. Through the lace one could see the mountain peaks weren't peaks at all, but knees. And the sides were two legs spread—

Lady Imogene lifted the lace, gasped, and then shouted with laughter.

Oh, Lord. A hot blush flooded Jo's face. She must be redder than Mrs. Butterwick's valentine.

"Brilliant," Lady Greyham said, clapping.

Mrs. Handley nodded. "It looks so real. How did you know what to draw? Can't say I've ever seen that part of me."

Mrs. Petwell sniggered. "Sir Humphrey helped you, did he?"

"He did not." Mrs. Butterwick took the card back from Lady Imogene. "I used a hand mirror. Haven't you ever looked at your female parts, Sophia?"

"No, why would I?" Mrs. Petwell grinned. "I'm far too busy examining Lord Benedict's male parts."

"I think it's very clever," Lady Imogene said. "And I'm sure Sir Humphrey will wish to see if your portrayal is completely accurate."

"Of course he will. I'm expecting we'll repair to bed immediately so he can do just that."

Everyone but Jo laughed.

"Well, ladies," Lady Greyham said, "I believe Mrs. Butterwick has thrown down the gauntlet. Let us see if anyone can outdo her in creativity."

"How will we determine the winner?" Lady Imogene asked.

"We will have to observe the gentlemen's falls when they read their valentines," Lady Noughton said. "The card that provokes the largest, ah, reaction wins."

"That's not entirely fair, Maria," Mrs. Petwell said. "We all know men are not equally endowed. I've personally examined both Lord Benedict's and Mr. Maiden's . . . attractions. Bennie is much larger"—she smiled at Lady Chutley—"though both gentlemen satisfy. We ladies know size is not the important issue, don't we?"

Jo ducked her head and pretended to examine the assortment of ribbon in front of her, though what she was really seeing was gentlemen's breeches. Good God.

If she survived this party, writing letters to an unmarried male would be the least of the blots on her reputation. And to think Papa had urged her to attend, had even said a little sin would do her good! Had he had the slightest notion how thick sin would be all around her?

When she'd sat at her bedroom desk, she'd had a vague mental image of the gentleman she'd been writing to all these months. She'd pictured a pleasant-looking, bespectacled man, not young but not old, scholarly, with a gentle voice. But now that she'd met Lord Kenderly, she wanted to touch him, press up against him as she had behind the curtains last night, feel his skin on hers—and, yes, examine his most male organ. The thought was scandalous, shocking—and after less than twenty-four hours at Greyham Manor, it felt oddly reasonable.

Oh, damn, she was throbbing again. She pushed some bits of lace around, praying no one would notice her heightened color.

Of course God didn't answer her prayer. He must be laughing at the old spinster adrift in such sinful waters.

"Are we embarrassing the little virgin in our midst?" Lady Noughton's voice grated.

Jo ignored her and glued some lace to the heart she'd cut. Her valentine was insipid; before she'd seen Mrs. Butterwick's card, she'd thought all valentines insipid.

"Maria," Lady Greyham said, "have done. You know Miss Atworthy is here only because Henrietta Helton took ill."

Lady Noughton frowned and might have argued, but she was interrupted by Lady Imogene waving her valentine in the air for the ladies' reaction.

Jo let the other women crowd around. The tone of their laughter told her clearly she would not appreciate Lady Imogene's imagination.

What was she going to write to complete her boring card? She couldn't just wish Lord Kenderly well. This was a valentine, not a sympathy card. On the other hand, she certainly couldn't mention the odd throbbing heat he provoked in her. She bit her lip. What should she write?

She'd like to write something daring, though not as daring as what Mrs. Butterwick or Lady Imogene had written—or drawn.

She was twenty-eight. As Papa had pointed out, she wasn't getting any younger. She could use a little sin, a little pleasure, in her life. If she let this opportunity pass, she'd have only Mr. Windley at hand—dear God. Mr. Windley was penance, not pleasure.

She glanced over at Lady Noughton's card. The widow had written, *Meet me at the baths at midnight.*

Could she ask Lord Kenderly to meet her somewhere secluded?

No. She hadn't the courage.

"I still don't have any ideas," Mrs. Handley said. "I need some more inspiration."

"How about some brandy? I often find a drop or two of spirits helps me think." Lady Greyham pulled the decanter out of the cabinet. "Oh, bother, Hugh must have stolen the glasses."

"We've teacups, don't we?" Mrs. Petwell said.

"Very true." Lady Greyham passed the brandy around so everyone could fill her cup.

Jo took a splash to be companionable. *Dear Lord Kenderly,* she wrote, *Happy Valentine's Day.* She chewed on the end of her pen. What else?

Her mind was a blank—well, no, it was filled with scandalous things she could never write.

She heard laughter in the corridor. The men were here; her time was up. Her insipid card would have to do. The earl certainly couldn't expect professions of love. They were barely acquainted . . . except she felt as if she knew him so well from his letters. Or she'd thought she'd known him when she'd thought him older and plainer.

She signed the card quickly as the men came into the room.

"Did you miss us, sweets?" Lord Greyham asked, giving Lady Greyham an enthusiastic kiss on the lips.

"Mmm, of course, but we spent our time well, didn't we ladies?"

"Indeed." Lady Chutley smirked. "I think you'll find our efforts most, ah, uplifting."

The ladies giggled; Jo took the opportunity to move toward the windows. She noticed Lord Kenderly was standing a little apart, frowning, his hands clasped behind his back; he looked about as happy to be there as she was.

"And you'll find ours inspiring as well," Lord Benedict said. The men sniggered.

"I'll confess it looked bleak at first when Greyham gave us *The Young Man's Valentine Writer*." Mr. Dellingcourt laughed. "What a collection of trite and saccharine verses! I suppose they might appeal to very inexperienced young ladies, but I assure you there was nothing appropriate for *this* group."

"I should think not," Mrs. Petwell said.

"So then we found Greyham's copy of *Ars Amatoria* hidden behind *A Few Theories on Crop Rotation*." Mr. Maiden grinned.

Jo straightened. Could this be Papa's rare Ovid?

"It wasn't hidden," Lord Greyham grumbled. "You found it, didn't you?"

"Only because of its bright red cover."

It *must* be the Ovid. She had to slip out and get it. With luck the men had left it sitting out in plain sight.

Mr. Maiden's grin widened. "And next to that book was an even more interesting volume, though in some heathen language I couldn't read."

"But you certainly studied the pictures long enough," Mr. Felton said.

"Now, Percy, I gave you your turn." Mr. Maiden waggled his brows at Lady Chutley. "I merely wished to commit a few of the illustrations to memory so I might re-create them later."

"Ha. I'd like to see you try."

"Would you, Percy?"

"Yes." Mr. Felton crossed his arms, a hot, hungry look suddenly appearing on his face. "Now."

Mr. Maiden extended his hand to Lady Chutley. "Are you game, my dear?"

Lady Chutley looked around the room and then smiled slowly. "Of course, if everyone else agrees?"

"Yes."

"Of course."

"Carry on, do."

The chorus of support twisted Jo's stomach into knots.

"Would you like to stroll on the terrace, Miss Atworthy?" Lord Kenderly asked.

"Oh!" The earl was at her elbow, offering her escape. "Yes, thank you. That would be very pleasant."

He took her arm and guided her out the door as the other members of the party whistled, clapped, and cheered Mr. Maiden and Lady Chutley to misbehavior so scandalous Jo couldn't begin to imagine it—and she certainly wasn't going to turn so she could see what they were doing.

The February wind slapped her in the face, and she gasped.

"I'm sorry," Lord Kenderly said. "I didn't realize how cold it was. Would you prefer to go back inside?" He glanced over his shoulder at the room they'd just left. "On second thought, I'll give you my coat."

"Th-thank you." She shivered. She'd rather turn into an icicle than witness what must be going on in the morning room. Well, she'd probably turn into a pillar of salt, like Lot's wife, if she looked. "Aren't you afraid Mr. Parker-Roth might get into trouble?"

Lord Kenderly frowned as he shrugged out of his coat and draped it over her shoulders. Ahh. It was still warm from his body.

"Stephen doesn't care for such public displays." He steered her so her back was to the morning room windows, but he could keep an eye on what was going on. "Making valentines with the other men was bad enough; the level of conversation was so puerile I thought I was back at Eton." He looked at her. "I think if I can just foil

Maria's plans a little longer, Stephen will leave the party on his own, perhaps as early as tomorrow."

And surely Lord Kenderly would leave with him. Fine. She was not disappointed, not at all. She should have left herself. She would go very soon.

His gaze had wandered back to the morning room. "Good God," he muttered, a note of incredulity in his voice, "so that really *is* possible."

She would *not* look. "If you want to save Mr. Parker-Roth, my lord, you might want to watch the baths at midnight."

"What?" His eyes focused on her again. "Baths?"

"Yes. Lady Noughton put it on her valentine. I assume she means the Roman baths." Lord Kenderly's attention had shifted to the action in the morning room once more. His face was rather flushed; perhaps it was due to the wind.

"They aren't Roman baths precisely." Was he even listening? Whatever was happening inside must be riveting. "Lord Greyham's father discovered a hot spring and enclosed it. It's nothing as grand as Bath—at least, that's what people tell me, as I've not been to Bath—but it's pleasant to sit in the warm water in the winter."

"Er, water?" He looked down at her. "I'm sorry; I wasn't perfectly attending."

Jo kept herself from stomping on his toes, but only just. "Lady Noughton and the baths. Meeting Mr. Parker-Roth?" He was looking over her shoulder again. "Oh, I'll go with you. I'll come by your room tonight at eleven-thirty."

"My room?" He had an odd light in his eyes for a moment before he blinked and shook his head. "Right. So we can keep Maria from trapping Stephen."

"Yes." She would *not* feel disappointed that he didn't wish to seduce her. She was a respectable spinster. "Of course." She would not even peek in his bedchamber;

she would merely knock on his door. "Er, which room is yours?"

He was studying the activities in the morning room again. It took him a moment to reply. "Oh, yes, my room. Turn left when you come up the main stairs; mine is the last door on the right."

"Very well. I'll come by promptly. We don't wish to be late." She looked down and noticed she still held the valentine she'd made. "Here." She thrust the poor thing at him, distracting him once more from what was happening inside. She might as well give it to him, even though he'd likely throw it into the fire the first chance he got. "I'm afraid I'm not very talented with paper and paste."

He took it from her and smiled. "I'm not either, as you'll see when I give you yours." He reached for his pocket, and then realized she was wearing his coat. "Pardon me."

He slipped his hand inside his jacket, brushing against her breast by accident. She sucked in her breath. Damn! She hoped he hadn't heard her.

She saw the corner of his smile deepen. He'd heard.

He slid a folded piece of paper out of his pocket and handed it to her. "As you can see, a drunken monkey could make a better valentine than I."

"Oh, surely not—" Jo looked down at the paper. The heart *was* rather lopsided, and the few bits of lace decorating it might indeed have been pasted on by an inebriated animal. "I imagine most men aren't terribly skilled with such things. It's the thought that counts." She opened the card. "Happy Valentine's Day," it read, "K."

She felt disappointment—and then she laughed. It wasn't as if they were lovers; they were barely acquaintances. "You might want to work on your technique, should you find a sweetheart," she said, glancing up at him.

He didn't seem to hear her; he was staring down at her

card, a very odd expression on his face. He looked shocked. Why? She certainly hadn't written anything shocking.

Perhaps it was the primitive nature of the card itself that disturbed him. Well, that was rather a case of the pot calling the kettle black, wasn't it? Yes, women might be expected to have some artistic skills, but she didn't have many of the skills most females had. And, really, the card wasn't that bad. It looked rather good when compared to his effort.

His face had gone from pale to red. Uh-oh. "I told you I wasn't good with paper and paste."

He finally looked up. His eyes narrowed and then swept over her.

She took a step back. "What's the matter? I only wished you a happy Valentine's Day—exactly what you wished me."

His jaw flexed as if he was clenching his teeth. He held her card out to her, jabbing his finger at her signature. He bit off each word. "*You* are J.A."

"Ah." Oh dear. She'd been in such a hurry when she'd signed the card, she hadn't thought. "Y-yes. My name *is* Josephine Atworthy."

A muscle in his cheek jumped. His lips pulled down; his nostrils flared as he drew in a deep, hopefully calming, breath. "You had my letter in the corridor upstairs because I was writing to you, not your father."

"Er, yes." Jo tried to smile. "I hope that's all right?"

Chapter 7

"*All right?!*" Damian took another deep breath. Good God. All this time he'd been corresponding with a female.

He frowned. He hadn't discussed anything he shouldn't have, had he?

No, of course he hadn't. He didn't make a habit of writing about improper subjects and, in any event, he'd thought he'd been addressing an older man. Most of their correspondence had been about Latin, though of late it had begun to stray into more personal topics.

But not too personal, thank God. Not that he had anything of a salacious nature to write about these days.

He scowled down at Miss Atworthy. Damn it all, he'd come to look forward to those letters, reading them eagerly and spending special effort on his replies. He'd thought of J.A. as a friend—but he wasn't. *She* wasn't. It was all a lie. He felt like an idiot. "You should have told me."

She flushed and pulled his coat tighter around her. "Why? My sex wasn't important."

Was she insane? Her sex was extremely important. It was the crucial detail that changed everything.

He made the mistake then of looking away from her toward the morning room. He caught sight of some fat male arse pumping away at—

He took her elbow and hustled her farther down the terrace. The wind tossed her hair about her face and put more color in her cheeks; he hoped it was taking some color from his. He was suddenly very hot. She looked so delicate in his jacket, so damn feminine. "Single young ladies are not supposed to exchange letters with single men to whom they are not related."

God, he sounded like someone's stuffy old, dry-as-a-stick great aunt.

"That's why I didn't tell you. I knew it was improper." She snorted. "Well, improper by society's ridiculous rules. There was nothing really improper in our correspondence. We didn't discuss anything we couldn't have talked about in a roomful of people."

"But we weren't in a roomful of people, were we?"

"No. We were each alone at our separate desks."

He ran his hand through his hair. Didn't she understand? Writing letters . . . sharing thoughts . . . it was very private. Very intimate. He'd let Miss Atworthy into his mind. "There is good reason why society frowns on men and women corresponding."

"Oh, please. I never took you for such a prude."

That stung. Perhaps she didn't understand because his letters had meant nothing to her. Perhaps she wrote to many men—to all the men who had articles in *The Classical Gazette*.

The thought ignited a slow, burning anger in his gut.

She raised her chin. "You are making a great deal out of nothing."

"It is *not* nothing." He clenched his teeth. "You misled me."

"Oh, for goodness' sake, I did not mislead you. You never asked if I was a woman, and I saw no reason to bring it up *because it was not significant*. I never told you I had curly hair, either."

"But I assumed—"

"And whose mistake was that?" She crossed her arms, her chin still at that defiant angle.

"You knew who I was."

"I did not. I only discovered your identity when I arrived at this party and you mentioned you'd been writing to my father."

"Ah." He caught her gaze and held it. "So why didn't you tell me then it wasn't your father I was corresponding with?"

She flushed. "I, er . . ."

Suddenly his anger and hurt coalesced. The fire burned hotter. He wanted revenge. He wanted her to feel something.

Lust. He wanted her to need him, to ache for him.

He hadn't been the Prince of Hearts for nothing. He stepped closer. "You didn't tell me because you knew it was scandalous."

"Improper. Not scandalous." She took a step back. She didn't have much room to retreat. The house was just behind her.

"Did you look forward to my letters"—he dropped his voice slightly—"Jo?"

She took another step back. "I'm sure you shouldn't use my Christian name."

"No? I give you leave to use mine. It's Damian."

"I couldn't possibly call you Damian." She was obviously trying to sound unaffected by his nearness. She wasn't quite successful.

"You could. You can." He bent his head to whisper by her ear. "You just did."

She jerked her head away from his mouth. "Stop."

"Stop what?"

"Stop doing this. Stop making me feel . . . odd."

"Odd? What do you mean?" If he leaned forward just a little more, his body would touch hers. There was only a breath of space between them. But he wouldn't lean forward; not yet.

"Just odd."

The wind blew a strand of hair over her eye and he brushed it away. "I looked forward to your letters," he murmured, sheltering her from the wind and trapping her against the side of the house. They were quite alone. "I was delighted when each one arrived. I thought they were from your father; I'll have to read them again now that I know you wrote them."

"Oh." Her voice trembled.

"I've saved them all." He remembered how her lips tasted. He wanted to taste them again. Now. "They are in a box on my desk." Should he kiss her? "In my bedroom."

He was supposed to be luring her into lust with him, but he was already very much in lust with her. It must be this damn house party. He'd never felt this way before.

"Oh." She sounded quite breathless. "I"—she swallowed— "I don't know what Papa was thinking when he—"

Suddenly her brows snapped down, and her voice lost any trace of uncertainty. She put her hands on his chest and gave him a little shove. "But I *do* know. Damn it, it's all clear now."

Reluctantly, Damian moved back a step. "What's clear?"

"Papa's motives. Why he tricked me into coming to this shocking party. It had nothing to do with Ovid."

"Ovid?" How the hell had they got to Ovid?

"Yes, Ovid." She slipped away from him and began pacing the terrace. "Papa told me some taradiddle about the old baron having borrowed a rare copy of Ovid. He knew that would persuade me to put aside my scruples and attend this, this . . . orgy."

Given what was happening in the morning room at the moment, Jo's description was sadly apt. "You're a fan of Ovid?"

"No. Or, not especially. I find his verse very confusing. I can't understand—" She flushed. "Well, never mind that."

"Ah." He grinned. "I would be delighted to explain any passages you have trouble with."

She answered him with a glare. "No, thank you."

He bit back a smile and shrugged. "Your father didn't make the story up out of whole cloth, you know. I'm reasonably certain the *Ars Amatoria* in the study is the volume he referred to."

Jo looked momentarily interested. "Oh? I wondered if perhaps it was. Is the book valuable?"

He shook his head. "No. Either your father or mine pilfered it from the Oxford library. The margins are full of salacious commentary scrawled by generations of university students."

Jo made a small sound of disgust. "So it is just as I thought. Papa dangled the Ovid in front of me to get me to come to this party." She pressed her lips tightly together for a moment. "I can just see how his devious little mind worked. His Catullus had just arrived, and I was, er, discussing with him how we simply cannot afford for him to keep buying these expensive books." Her voice rose. "He has no sense of economy."

"Oh?" He could see Jo had the bit between her teeth on this topic. She would need to marry a man who knew how to keep a firm hand on the reins or she'd ride roughshod over him.

And why the hell had that thought popped into his head?

"Yes, indeed. He is going to land us in the poorhouse if he doesn't see reason. There are just not that many potential Latin students in the area, and I am *not* going to wed Mr. Windley to produce more."

"No, I definitely think that would be unwise. Who is Mr. Windley?"

"A very annoying widower with six idiot sons all of whom I have the misfortune to teach—to *try* to teach—Latin."

The disgust on Jo's face was rather comical. "He does not sound at all like a good match for you. Is your father pushing you to marry him?" Mr. Atworthy would not be the first man to sacrifice his daughter for the family fortunes.

Jo laughed. "Oh, no. Papa cannot abide Mr. Windley or his progeny either. I think he's afraid I'll marry him out of desperation."

"Come, you're not past your prayers certainly."

She snorted. "I'm far too old to tempt most gentlemen into marriage. And Papa says I've a reputation for being a"—she flushed—"a trifle, er, difficult and, ah, staid."

Difficult he could believe, but not staid. Obviously the neighborhood men were blind to Jo's attractions. She had a lovely mind and an equally lovely body.

She started to pace again, and he admired the way her skirts pulled tight across her hips and teased him with brief outlines of her legs. "After Mr. Flanders visited, Papa knew I was writing to you, and he knew you would be at this party. Having one of Lord Greyham's female guests take ill at the last minute must have seemed like a sign from heaven, a golden opportunity to get me off his back for a few days. I don't doubt he even hoped I'd—" Her cheeks—no, her whole face—turned beet red. "That is, Papa . . . he . . ."

A cold, hard feeling—disappointment with a touch of anger—settled in Damian's gut. He'd been the earl for ten years now; he was very familiar with matchmaking mamas—and sometimes papas. "Thought you could get me to come up to scratch."

Her eyes swiveled to his. "Good God, no. Are you daft?"

His anger turned to pique. "It isn't that odd a thought. You were writing to me. I was answering."

"Yes, but I'm sure he realized if you thought my letters were from him, they could not have contained anything of a, er, warm nature. No, no, trust me. Marriage would be the last thought to cross Papa's mind. I suspect he hoped I would have some kind of small, ah, adventure that would take my mind off rare books and empty coffers for a while." She looked away, her color still high. "He said a little sin would do me good."

Damian's gaze, which had wandered down to her breasts, snapped back up to her face. "What?" Good God, had she read his mind? It was full of sin, lovely, hot, wet sin.

"Yes. I was as shocked as you are."

Now was not the time to point out she had no idea what he was thinking, because if she did she would be having a fit of the vapors. "Um."

"I suppose I will see if I can have a look at the Ovid to satisfy my curiosity, but from what you say, it isn't worth my spending any more time here." A smile flashed across her face, missing her eyes. "I believe I can feel the headache coming on."

He didn't want her to leave, not yet. Things were still unsettled between them. He certainly felt unsettled, and he did not care for the sensation. "But I thought you were going to help me this evening."

"What? Oh, right, Mr. Parker-Roth and Lady Noughton." She backed away from him a step. "I can show you where the baths are now, if you like. You need only follow the path through the garden a bit. You can't miss them."

She was unsettled, too. He could feel it.

Had she truly been interested only in Latin grammar when she wrote to him? Probably the first time and perhaps the second, but something else had crept in by the third letter, he'd swear it. This . . . warm feeling couldn't have all been on his side.

They'd had a meeting of minds; they'd found a harmony of spirit. He'd just been shocked for a moment to discover the mind and spirit he'd been communicating with came in such a delightful package.

He was not going to let her get away. "Thank you, but I think your presence tonight is crucial."

"Surely you can handle the situation yourself." She took another step backward; he followed her.

"I am Stephen's friend. People might not believe me. But you are a disinterested third party and a female."

"Yes." She bumped into the balustrade; she'd backed up as far as she could. Without the building to restrain it, the wind whipped her curls around her face so she did look a bit like one of the Furies, only her expression was uncertain and vulnerable. "I mean no." She moistened her lips. "I mean you don't need me tonight."

"Oh? I think I do." If she had any idea of the need that was pounding through his veins right now, she'd leap over the balustrade. "I need you very much."

"What?" She must have caught a hint; she looked vaguely alarmed.

"And what about sin?" He dropped his voice again and leaned into her.

"Sin?" she croaked.

"Yes. I think your father is correct—a little sin is good for the soul."

She snorted. "You make a far better Latin scholar than you do a theologian." Brave words, belied by the waver in her voice.

"Don't you want to sin a little, Jo?"

"Ah." She had dropped her gaze from his eyes to his mouth, the minx.

He cupped her face in his hands, trapping her wild hair. He bent closer so he could whisper. "I would be happy to teach you how. It would be my pleasure—my very great pleasure."

Her eyes widened. Was that desire he saw in their depths? Desire and uncertainty. He would just kiss her now, just—

"Ah, so here you are."

Damn. Damian spun around to find Stephen and Lady Noughton walking toward them.

"My, my, my," Maria said, looking from Damian to Jo, "what are you two up to?"

Thank God the widow hadn't arrived a minute or two later, when it would have been far too clear what Damian, at least, was up to. "We are taking the air." He took Jo's hand and placed it on his arm.

"It looked to me as if you were on the verge of taking more than the air." Maria examined Jo. "My compliments, Miss Atworthy. I should have said something earlier. That dress is a great improvement on yesterday's gown." She raised a knowing eyebrow. "Out to catch yourself an earl, are you?"

Damian squeezed Jo's hand as he heard her draw breath to answer the harpy. That would be a very bad idea. Maria would tear Jo to pieces; the widow had sharpened her claws in far too many London ballrooms. "You have it wrong, Lady Noughton. It is I who am trying to capture Miss Atworthy's interest."

Stephen laughed. "Bravo, Damian."

Maria glared at Stephen, smiled brittlely at Damian, and then addressed Jo. "I see. Then it was no accident we saw you and Lord Kenderly together in the library last night."

"Oh, no, it was indeed an accident," Jo said. "I thought I'd just run down to find a book; I had no idea Lord Greyham's library would be so crowded." She smiled sweetly. "Were you and Mr. Parker-Roth also in search of some reading material to help you fall asleep?"

Maria made an odd noise, sort of a cross between a gasp and a hiss, but Stephen laughed.

"Touché, Miss Atworthy," he said. "Well done."

Chapter 8

It was almost eleven twenty-five. Jo consulted the clock for the fifth time in as many minutes.

She'd been hiding in her room for two hours, ever since Blind Man's Bluff had become too dangerous. The various blind men—and women—had taken the role as an opportunity to run their hands all over whomever they caught, exploring the most embarrassing parts of their victim's anatomy. Mr. Maiden, not even pretending to be hampered by his blindfold, had taken advantage of Lord Kenderly's brief absence from the room to pursue her, much to the glee of the other guests. She'd been compelled to dodge behind a settee and knock over a chair before the earl had returned and put an end to Mr. Maiden's fun.

She heard giggling in the corridor. Damn. She hoped she'd be able to get to Lord Kenderly's room without encountering any other guests.

Frankly, it was hard to imagine what Lady Noughton could do to force Mr. Parker-Roth into marriage. This party just got more and more scandalous. At dinner the men had decided to get into the spirit of Lupercalia and run naked over the grounds at midnight.

Ugh. The thought of Sir Humphrey or Mr. Felton without

clothes was revolting. She'd shut her eyes at the first hint of bare flesh. But Lord Kenderly naked . . .

She fanned her face with her hand. It was suddenly quite hot in the room.

That afternoon on the terrace, when he'd offered to teach her to sin, she had to admit she'd been tempted.

She bit her lip. She was far too old for such silliness, wasn't she?

Her brain said yes, but her body had a different opinion.

She glanced at the clock again. Oh dear, it was now eleven thirty-two. She was late. She grabbed her dark pelisse and cracked her door open. She listened. All was quiet for the moment.

Cautiously she poked her head out and looked up and down the corridor—no one in sight, thank God. She eased out of her room and hurried as quietly as she could to Lord Kenderly's chamber. She scratched on the door.

"Damnation, Viola." She heard Sir Humphrey's voice as the door to the room across the way began to open. "I don't want to go scampering around Greyham's grass naked as a needle. It's February; I'll freeze my—"

Sir Humphrey and Mrs. Butterwick would see her if Lord Kenderly didn't let her in immediately. What was taking him so long?

She couldn't wait another instant. She turned the knob and scrambled inside, shutting the door behind her just as Sir Humphrey stepped into the passage.

That had been far too close. She turned to give the earl a piece of her mind. "Lord Kend-ack!" She caught her foot on her pelisse and fell forward—onto a naked chest.

"*Oof.*" Lord Kenderly grunted as his arms came around her to steady her.

Her nose was smashed up against warm, hard flesh and soft, springy hair. Mmm. He smelled of soap and eau de cologne.

"I seem to make a habit of catching you," he said.

She felt his words rumble in his chest even as they whispered past her ear.

She'd never encountered a naked male chest before. Men were always covered in layers of fabric: shirt, waistcoat, coat. She slid her hands over Lord Kenderly's hard planes and around to his equally hard back. She'd wager a week's worth of Latin lessons few men had chests as impressive as this one. And had she glimpsed . . . ? She slipped her fingers a little lower. Yes. The man had only a thin towel covering his hips.

Something hard began to press against her belly. . . .

"Jo."

Damian's voice was rough and breathless. She looked up.

The hot expression in his eyes caused her jaw to drop. She watched his mouth descend, and then she closed her eyes as his lips covered hers, his tongue sweeping past her teeth, deep inside. One of his hands landed on her derriere, pushing her tightly against his interesting bulge, while the other skimmed up her side to cup her breast.

Hot, liquid need rushed through her like a stream after a violent summer rain.

She had too much clothing on; he had too much. She slid her hands up his naked back and then down again, lower, all the way to—

He jerked his head up and put both hands on her shoulders, pushing her back. She watched his towel start to slip—

Blast! He grabbed it before it had fallen very far. She caught only a glimpse of a dark thatch of curly hair, and then the cloth was back in place. Well, not quite in place. The hard ridge she'd been pressed against must have grown—was still growing, forming a definite tent in—

"Will you stop that?" Damian grabbed a bright yellow pillow off a chair and held it in front of him like a shield.

"Stop what?" Breathing? She was certainly having a

hard time getting her lungs to work, and her heart was beating erratically as well.

Damian did look like Michelangelo's *David* come to life. His upper arms curved with muscle; his shoulders were unbelievably broad; the short dark hair she'd had her cheek against just moments ago dusted his chest and trailed in a line over his flat stomach down to . . . the pillow.

"Stop looking at me like that."

Her eyes flew back to his face. He sounded as if he was in pain. He looked as if he was in pain—white lines bracketed his mouth and a deep crease separated his brows. "Are you feeling quite the thing?"

"No, I am not. I am feeling . . ." He took a deep breath. "I am feeling as if I should consign my good friend Stephen and his future happiness to the devil so I can attend to my own happiness now. Immediately. With you." He jerked his head toward the bed. "Naked."

"My lord!" The most shocking part of his shocking statement was the way her breasts and her . . . feminine parts throbbed in eager agreement.

"Don't worry, I have myself under control"—he glared at her—"as long as you stop staring at me that way."

"What way?"

His voice dropped. "As if you want to touch every last inch of my person—"

She whipped her hands behind her back.

"—with your lips." She watched his throat move as he swallowed. "And tongue."

Little tongues of flame shot all over her skin. Her nipples peaked into hard, sensitive points; her, ah, nether regions felt as if he'd lit a bonfire right between her legs. She bit back a moan. "I-I'm not."

"You are." He took another deep breath. "Unfortunately, this room lacks a dressing screen. If you will turn around . . . ?"

She stared at him. Turn around?

He made a little circular motion with his finger, but her brain was no longer functioning. The firelight played over his lovely, lovely muscles.

He shrugged. "Very well, if you wish to watch." He dropped the pillow and put his hands on the towel.

Jo spun around to give him her back. She wanted to watch, depraved spinster that she was, but she didn't want Lord Kenderly to think she did. If only there were a mirror handy.

She must stop thinking of Lord Kenderly's muscles and other, er, attractions. "Why in the world did you decide to bathe now?"

"Because I stayed downstairs to keep an eye on Lady Noughton, and Mr. Felton managed to spill a very large glass of ale all over me. To be blunt about it, I was wet and sticky, and I stunk."

"But then why did you leave it to so late?"

"I didn't." The words were muffled; he must be putting on his shirt. "You were early."

"I was not. I was two minutes late."

"Then your clock is fast. It's only eleven thirty-five now. Come on."

She turned to find he was dressed all in black. He picked her pelisse off the floor where it had landed when she'd landed on his chest and helped her into it. Then he put on a black cloak, opened the door, and looked out.

"All clear," he said, taking her hand. He pulled her to the right.

She stopped and tugged back. "The stairs are the other way," she whispered.

"The main stairs are. There are servant stairs here." He opened a door Jo hadn't noticed before.

"How did you find these?"

"I make it a policy to be observant. It's often handy to have an alternate exit when things turn unpleasant."

"And do things often turn unpleasant?" She followed him down a narrow flight of steps.

"Not any longer, but it's a habit I formed when I was younger and more daring." He looked over his shoulder and grinned at her. "And stupider."

Jo put a hand on Damian's arm to stop him when they reached the outside door. "Do you think we'll encounter any of the other guests celebrating Lupercalia? Sir Humphrey and Mrs. Butterwick were leaving his room when I arrived at yours—which is why I came in so precipitately."

Damian laughed. "Sir Humphrey naked—now there's a sight that would turn one to stone. Just the thought roils my stomach. But no, I don't think so. At least not yet." He pushed open the door and a blast of frigid air accosted them.

Jo shivered. "I can't imagine going out without a warm coat let alone without a stitch of clothing."

"They were all gathering in the study to fortify themselves with Greyham's brandy, so they'll be as drunk as emperors when they venture outside. They won't feel the cold—they won't feel anything. Pull up your hood and lead the way."

It was a clear night. The moon was almost full, and Lord Greyham, anticipating the Lupercalia festivities, had hung lanterns from the trees, so it was easy to follow the path down through the garden. They saw the bathhouse as soon as they rounded the last curve. It was a long building with a barrel-vaulted roof. Lights flickered in the windows. Jo stopped short, causing Damian to bump into her. He pulled her off the path behind a tree.

"What is it?" he whispered.

"We're too late. See the lights? They are already there."

He looked at the building. "No, not necessarily. Greyham said the festivities are to end in the bathhouse; he probably sent servants down earlier to get things ready."

"Oh." Jo let out the breath she'd been holding. She was

not used to sneaking around in the dark, and she was still rather unsettled from the events in Lord Kenderly's room. She could not get the picture—or the feel—of his naked chest out of her mind. "You are probably right."

"Of course I am. You said Maria specified midnight in her card, which is shortly before the revelers should arrive. I think she realizes Stephen is becoming disenchanted with her, and she needs to spring her trap tonight if she wants to catch him." His even, white teeth flashed in the moonlight as he grinned. "She's not shown herself to advantage here."

"That's an understatement. I'd say she was a complete harpy."

He laughed. "Exactly."

They continued down the path, approaching the building cautiously. Damian tried the door; it was unlocked. He cracked it open, and they paused, listening. Jo heard the quiet lapping of water against the sides of the pool, the drip of condensation, the hiss and pop of a fire—but no footsteps or conversation. "They aren't here yet."

"No, they aren't." Damian pushed the door open and stepped inside. "Blech, what is that smell?"

Jo wrinkled her nose. "The minerals in the water, I think. I don't remember it being so strong, but then, I haven't been here in probably fifteen years."

"Perhaps the heat makes it worse. Greyham has five—no, six—braziers going."

"It *is* oppressive." Jo unbuttoned her pelisse; Damian helped her off with it and then shed his cloak, coat, and waistcoat. He stuffed all their outer garments in a corner, out of sight behind a large, decorative urn.

They walked farther into the bathhouse, their feet echoing on the tile floor. The room was about forty yards long and perhaps twenty yards wide with large stone pillars along each side. The pool, dark and murky and green, took up most of the space.

Perspiration beaded on Jo's lip, rolled down her sides, pooled between her breasts. It was hotter than Hades—or so she would imagine, not having yet visited that place; however, given her reaction to Damian's broad shoulders, narrow waist, and splendid arse, she might be heading there shortly.

"I suppose Greyham wanted to raise the temperature to thaw the naked idiots," Damian said. He turned and frowned down at her. "Which you should not be here to see."

"I will close my eyes." She should close them now. Damian's fine lawn shirt was plastered to him, revealing his wonderful chest and shoulders. She forced herself to look away before he noticed she was staring at him like a child at a sweets counter. "There aren't any good places to hide, are there?"

"No, unfortunately. We'll just have to stand behind a pillar and hope for the best."

They positioned themselves so they were hidden from the door. Damian was still frowning.

"I do wish I didn't need you here," he said. "If only I could—but it's too late for second thoughts. I don't have time to escort you back, and with drunken idiots running wild, it's not safe for you to go back by yourself."

She had no intention of leaving, but it wasn't fear of naked nodcocks that kept her in the bathhouse. "Oh, I'm sure the revelers would just pass me by. Even Papa says no one would take liberties with me." That comment still rankled, even if it was true.

"What?" Damian's eyebrows shot up. "Haven't I already proved him wrong?"

"Oh. Well, er . . ." Damian *had* kissed her when she'd fallen from the cart and again when she'd hidden in the library. And he'd taken more than a few liberties with her in his room.

Heat that had nothing to do with the bathhouse washed

through her. She was going to melt into a puddle—she felt a distinct dampness between her thighs already.

He took her by the shoulders. "Have you forgotten?" His hands slid down her back, coming to rest on her hips, and he pulled her tight against him. With the heat and the damp, it was almost as if they were naked . . . almost, but not quite, blast it. "Let me remind you."

His mouth covered hers as his hand moved to her breast and his leg . . . oh! His leg slipped between hers so his thigh pressed against her most feminine part. She rocked against him by accident and thought she would faint with pleasure.

Her fingers found their own way to his waistband and started pulling his shirt free. She had to feel his skin again.

"God, Jo," Damian muttered, his lips moving to a sensitive spot just below her ear, "you make me forget propriety. Hell, you make me forget my own name."

"Mmm." She tilted her head to give him more room to explore as she succeeded in freeing his shirt from his breeches. "Mmm." She ran her hands up his back. If only she could—

His fingers dipped below her bodice and rubbed over her nipple. Lightning shot through her body to lodge . . . she pressed herself more tightly against his thigh and moaned. "Damian—"

Suddenly her face was crushed against his chest again. "Shh," he breathed by her ear. "I think they're here."

Her pleasure-soaked brain tried to recall whom they were expecting when she heard Lady Noughton's voice.

"It's Lupercalia, Stephen."

Jo looked up at Damian; he pressed a finger to her lips, and then they both moved to peer around the pillar. Mr. Parker-Roth stood just inside the door; Lady Noughton had ventured farther in.

"Right. Hard to forget after seeing all those naked arses flashing across Greyham's lawn. I'll have nightmares about that for weeks." Mr. Parker-Roth's voice acquired a new edge. "I'm surprised you didn't join in, Maria."

"I might have if you'd done so." Lady Noughton's voice was low and sultry, rather appropriate given the oppressive heat.

Mr. Parker-Roth snorted. "I don't care to have frosted ballocks."

"No, that would never do." Lady Noughton ran her hands down her sides and gave a slow little wiggle—Jo wondered if she should practice such a move.

It seemed to have no effect on Mr. Parker-Roth, however. He turned away to examine the windows. "What did you drag me down here for, Maria? I was planning to spend a quiet night"—he looked at her, his lips twisting into something of a sneer—"alone with a good book."

"I thought we might go for a swim." The woman gave another wiggle and somehow her dress slipped down to reveal she had nothing at all on underneath.

She had a very impressive pair of . . . well, it was quite obvious why she was such a success with the male members of the *ton*. Jo looked up to see if a specific earl was impressed, but Damian was watching his friend.

Mr. Parker-Roth's eyes never strayed from Lady Noughton's face. "It's over, Maria. We had a pleasant association, but it's done. I'll send you a draft on my bank, and you can pick out a suitable bauble at Rundell and Bridge to assuage your wounded feelings."

"But I love you, Stephen." Lady Noughton spread her arms wide in case Mr. Parker-Roth had perhaps not noticed her very large breasts.

He still did not appear interested, but then he'd probably had many past opportunities to examine them thoroughly. "I don't think you do, Maria. It certainly hasn't kept you from sharing your favors with an assortment of men— something I would never tolerate in a wife, by the way."

She dropped her arms and glared at him. "I'll tell everyone you offered marriage, Stephen. Many will believe it; you've been showing me very marked attention these last few months."

"More fool I." He put his hand on the door. "You may do as you like, Maria. I know it is a lie, and I imagine most of the *ton* will know it, too. You will only make yourself look foolish."

"Especially when I corroborate Stephen's side of the story," Damian said, stepping out from behind the pillar.

Lady Noughton spun toward him, sending her large breasts bouncing. "You!"

Mr. Parker-Roth grinned. "Damian, I hate to say it, but you were right. I should have listened to you."

Lady Noughton put her hands on her hips—apparently she was completely at ease with her nakedness—and tossed her head. "People will only say you are supporting your friend."

"They'd best not suggest I am lying." There was more than a touch of steel in Damian's voice. "Dueling may be illegal, but I have many other methods at my disposal to make life uncomfortable for anyone who dares question my honor."

"And I shall support Mr. Parker-Roth as well," Jo said, going to stand by Damian. Not that anyone would care what a provincial spinster said, but it just didn't feel sporting to stay hidden behind the masonry any longer.

Damian scowled at her. Clearly as soon as they were alone he was going to let her know she should have stayed out of sight.

She was rather looking forward to that argument.

"Miss Atworthy." Mr. Parker-Roth's grin widened; he bowed.

"Miss Atworthy." Lady Noughton almost spat the words.

"I don't believe you'll be in a position to say a thing after everyone learns you were here with Lord Kenderly."

Jo shrugged. "Since—as you know—I've never been to London and probably never will, I can't imagine anyone will care what I was doing."

"Ah, there you are wrong, my love," Damian said, putting his arm around her and pulling her scandalously close. "Society will be very anxious to hear everything about the new Countess of Kenderly."

Jo's gasp was drowned out by Lady Noughton's screech—and that was drowned out, quite literally, by the Lupercalia celebrants as they stampeded into the bathhouse and into the pool in all their naked glory.

Chapter 9

"I fear I will go to my grave with the image of fat, balding Sir Humphrey running naked into that damn bathhouse," Damian said, hurrying Jo up the path to the house. Her teeth were chattering. He was damn cold, too, but there'd been no time to collect their coats. With all the naked revelers, a hasty departure had clearly been called for.

"Ah, but then think of Maria's expression as he barreled into her and took her into the pool with a mighty splash." Stephen looked down at Jo. "Miss Atworthy, are you certain you won't take my coat," he said for the third time.

"N-no, th-thank you." Poor Jo was so cold she could barely speak. "W-we are al-almost th-there."

Thank God they were. Damian hustled Jo over the last few yards, through the servants' entrance, and up the flight of stairs. They stopped at Damian's door.

Stephen clapped him on the back. "My heartfelt thanks for all your efforts, my friend. As I said in the bathhouse, you were right about Maria. I shouldn't have come to this infernal gathering." He grinned. "But if I hadn't, you would have stayed sequestered in your study and never met the lovely Miss Atworthy, so I can't repine too much."

Zeus, Stephen was right. Jo felt like such an important

part of his life now, but he'd only known her a handful of hours.

No, that wasn't true. He'd known her for months through her letters.

"I warn you, Miss Atworthy," Stephen was saying, "Damian has the highly annoying habit of being correct in his advice nine times out of ten."

"I d-don't know about th-that."

Jo's teeth were chattering again, damn it. "I need to get Miss Atworthy warm," Damian said, an edge creeping into his voice.

"And here I am, jawing on and on. I will take myself off immediately." Stephen frowned. "I don't put it past Maria to find a way into my room tonight, so I'm going to borrow one of Greyham's horses and decamp to a neighboring inn. Would you take anything I must leave behind with you when you leave, Damian?"

"Of course."

"Thank you." Stephen took Jo's hand in his. "I look forward to dancing at your wedding, Miss Atworthy."

"Oh, I—" Jo shook her head. "There's no w-wedding. L-Lord K-Kenderly just said that to avoid a s-scandal."

Stephen laughed. "Trust me, an earl doesn't 'just say' such an interesting thing to Lady Noughton unless he is willing to have the information spread far and wide."

"Oh." Jo chewed on her bottom lip and shivered some more.

Damian glared at Stephen. Why wouldn't the man move along and let him get to his wooing before he and his bride-to-be turned into icicles? "Didn't you say you were leaving, Stephen? *Immediately?*"

Stephen grinned. "I did. I am." He looked back at Jo. "Don't worry, Miss Atworthy; people really will be delighted. I, for one, must thank you for bringing Damian out of his cave. He'd become quite the hermit."

"I like being a hermit," Damian said. "I hope you don't expect me to start showing up at all of London's inane parties."

"Well, you'll want to introduce your bride to society." Stephen's grin widened. "But if you're absent, I'll know you're at home doing something more interesting than translating dusty Latin texts."

Damian put his arm around Jo as a particularly nasty shiver shook her. "*Good-bye,* Stephen."

"Good-bye." Stephen laughed, looking as innocent as sin, damn him. "But before I go"—he waggled his brows—"does the Prince of Hearts need any advice from the King on how best to get warm?"

"No." Damian jerked his door open. "You may go to the devil with my blessing." He pulled Jo into his room and slammed the door on Stephen's laughter.

"I-I should go to my own room." Jo tried to keep her teeth from chattering. She was cold, but she was also nervous . . . and excited.

She didn't want to leave; she wanted to stay right where she was.

It had been such a bizarre evening, starting when she'd come flying in this door and landed against Damian's chest. His naked chest.

Mmm. She'd like to be up against his chest again, but this time she'd like to be naked, too. He was moving in the right direction: he was pulling off his wet shirt.

To think she'd never seen a naked man before, and then tonight she'd seen a herd of them, pale and hairy with their little dangly bits bouncing as they ran for the pool. They'd looked rather comical, once she'd gotten over the shock.

There was nothing comical about Damian's body. She watched the muscles in his back flex as he yanked the wet shirt over his head. Damian's chest was far more impressive than any of the others she'd seen tonight, and if the sense she'd got when she'd been pressed against him was any indication, his dangly bit was also. She would very much like to inspect it more closely. She'd—

But her feminine bits were not very impressive, especially when compared to Lady Noughton's. Would he be disappointed?

And why was she considering letting him see them at all? God should strike her dead where she stood for thinking such a thing.

"We need to get you warm, Jo," Damian said, dropping his shirt by the fire and coming over to her.

"Ah." She swallowed. Her mouth was dry. He was so handsome. "I sh-should go back to my room. I can g-get Becky to help me."

He put his hands on her shoulders. "Do you want to go back to your room?"

She should say yes. Of course she should say yes. Miss Atworthy, the staid, boring, shrewish Latin tutor would say yes.

She was a twenty-eight-year-old spinster. She might never again get a chance like this to sin.

"N-no." Another shiver set her teeth to chattering.

He smiled. "Good. Now let's get you out of those wet clothes." He turned her around, and his nimble fingers flew down her back, unbuttoning her dress. He tugged it off her shoulders, down her arms, and over her hips. It felt wonderful to get the cold, damp fabric off her skin. She stepped out of it, and he undid her stays. As soon as they hit the ground, he grabbed the hem of her shift and pulled it up and over her head.

She was completely naked except for her stockings. She tried to wrap her arms around herself to hide her poor little breasts and her nether region. She should be mortified, but she was shivering too much.

"Under the covers with you now," Damian said as he lifted her up and laid her on the bed, pulled off her stockings, and tucked her in. He might have been her nurse for all the interest he showed in her body.

She shivered again and curled up, turning her back to him. Apparently, she needn't have worried about sin. She—

She felt the mattress depress, and then a pair of naked arms wrapped around her waist, pulling her back against a very naked male body.

"Sharing heat is the fastest way to warm up," he murmured by her ear as his hands moved, one to cup her breast and the other to rest low on her belly.

"Um." Her temperature was certainly rising. His must be, too. He was like a furnace all along her back.

He stroked the side of her breast and pressed her hips firmly against what felt like a very long, very large male appendage—nothing at all like the small, dangly things she'd seen bouncing on the men in the bathhouse.

"Stephen was right, you know," he said, burying his face in her hair. "News of our betrothal will be all over London as soon as Maria leaves this party—which will be tomorrow, now that Stephen has gone."

"Oh." She found it very hard to care about a place and people she'd never seen. She was far more interested in this warm bed and the very male, very hard person behind her. If only his hands would each move just a few inches. Her nipples had become hard points, screaming—if they could scream—for his touch and the place between her legs was weeping in frustration. She wiggled her hips a little to encourage him, but his hand stopped her immediately. Damn.

"I don't know anyone in London," she said. Her frustration showed in her voice; even she heard it.

"But many people in London know people here. The

news will be all over Greyham's estate and the village in no time—perhaps even before the *ton* hears in Town. I doubt Maria will keep her lips sealed until she arrives."

"Oh." That would be unpleasant, but not fatal. "Then I'll just tell everyone Lady Noughton was mistaken."

Mmm. His lips had found that sensitive place under her ear again. She almost purred, but she caught herself in time.

"Was she? I hope not." He turned her so she faced him, his hand on her shoulder keeping her an arm's length from his lovely body. "Don't you want to marry me, Jo?" His gaze held hers. "I thought you did; I thought that was why you agreed to come to bed with me."

"Ah." Should she admit she'd been willing to sin with him just this once? But that wasn't really what she wanted. Still . . . "Marriage is for life."

"Yes."

"And we hardly know each other."

"On the contrary, I think we know each other very well, certainly better than many of the *ton* do when they wed. We've written to each other." He smiled. "We've shared our thoughts."

He hadn't been smiling on the terrace earlier. "You were angry when you learned it was me you'd been writing to."

He shrugged. "I was surprised. I felt you'd lied to me."

"I hadn't."

"Hadn't you?" Damian raised a brow, and she flushed. Well, perhaps she *had* committed a small sin of omission.

"I'll grant you it took me a moment to adjust," he said, rubbing her shoulder with his thumb in a very distracting fashion, "but once I did, everything came into focus. Don't you feel the same?"

"Er . . ." She did; there was no point in denying it. Even teaching the Windley idiots would be bearable if she had Damian in her life. "Y-yes."

He grinned, so clearly happy it was impossible not to

grin back at him. "I looked forward to your letters, Jo, to reading them and answering them. I admired your mind"—his lips slid into a rather wolfish smile—"but now that I've met you, I admire so much more." He ran his finger over her cheek. "I love you."

Her heart stopped—and then set to beating so hard it threatened to leap out of her chest.

"And I love you," she whispered. She flushed; she might as well be painfully truthful. "I imagined you were my prince who would ride in and deliver me from cramming endless declensions into thick Windley skulls."

He laughed. "Jo! How could you wish to be delivered from declensions?"

She laughed back at him. "It was Windleys I wished to be delivered from."

"And so you shall be. I have no Windleys on any of my estates."

He turned her onto her back then and all thought of Windleys flew out of her head. He was so hard and warm and— "Oh! Yours *is* far larger than the other men's."

He chuckled. "Shame on you for looking! In their defense, I must say they'd just been running in the cold."

"I'm sure they couldn't ever match you." She felt that part of him between her legs. It was wonderful, but it would be much more wonderful if it would rub against a specific point of sensitive flesh. She wiggled.

His wolfish expression intensified. "Eager are you? Then we shall celebrate Lupercalia properly."

"Are you going to strike me with a goatskin thong to ensure my fertility?"

"No, I'm going to strike you with this." He moved his hips and his male organ slid along the wet place between her legs. "And hope your fertility will start the next Earl of Kenderly growing in your womb."

"Ahh." The thought of creating a life with Damian

filled her with warm desire and happiness. "And if you don't succeed?"

He flicked his tongue over a nipple and need streaked through her.

"Then I shall be delighted"—he rubbed against her—"very, very delighted"—he found her entrance—"to try again."

His hips flexed, and he came into her slowly. There was a brief, burning pain, and then an incredible sense of fullness.

He kissed her. "All right?"

"Yes." She loved the feel of him on her and in her, but the sensitive place between her legs demanded that he move. She wiggled her hips to encourage him.

Thank God he took the hint. He pulled back, and then came in again. Out and in; back and forth; slow and fast. Faster . . .

"Oh!" She grabbed his back. She was so tense she was going to shatter. She—

He moved once more and stopped, so close he was almost part of her. Waves of incredible sensation pulsed through her, and under the exquisite madness, she felt another pulse, a spurt of liquid heat, deep inside her.

He collapsed onto her, and she ran her hands up and down his back. "That was wonderful," she said.

"Mmm." He rolled to the side, stretching out on the bed next to her.

"I didn't know what to expect. Frankly, if someone had told me what was involved, I wouldn't have believed them." She turned to look at him. Surely he wasn't asleep? "Is it always this wonderful?"

He cracked one eye open. "Are you always this chatty?"

"I don't know. I've never done this before."

He grunted again and put his hand on her breast. "No,

it's not always this wonderful. It's never before been this wonderful for me."

"Really? You aren't just saying that?" She felt inordinately pleased, but just a little suspicious. "I'm sure the other women—the experienced women—must have done it better than I."

He teased her nipple, making her body hum again in anticipation. "Apparently it's not how it's done, it's with whom it's done that's important. Love is far stronger than lust." He closed his eyes again.

"I'll wager it will be even better next time now that I know what happens."

"Mmm."

She looked up at the bed canopy and tried to determine whether she felt different. Well, of course she felt different—she'd never been so sore *there*—but did she feel *different?* "Do you think we made a baby?"

"Mmm."

"Are you going to sleep?"

He opened one eye again. "I am trying to."

"I'm not sleepy."

"That's clear."

How could he even consider sleep? Her thoughts were darting around like dragonflies on a pond. "When can we do it again?"

"Insatiable, are you?"

"Yes."

He laughed. "Later. You are probably sore now, aren't you?"

"Y-yes, a little." A lot, really.

He stroked his hand over her belly. "If you're looking for something to do, I brought the Ovid up. It's on the night table."

"Really?" She leaned over him to look at the volume.

It was indeed very red, battered, and dingy. "It's rather unimpressive."

"Yes." Damian stroked her breasts as they dangled over his chest. His thumb found one of her nipples and rubbed it. "You know, I'm suddenly feeling more energetic. Perhaps we should read it together. I might even demonstrate a few verses."

"But I thought you said I was too sore."

"For some things." He kissed her nipple. "But not for other things."

"Other things?" This sounded interesting. "There are other things?"

"Of course. You know your conjugations. There are many forms of the verb 'to love.'"

"Oh." She grinned at him. "I think you will find me an eager student."

"Splendid!"

And he proceeded to give her a very illuminating lesson indeed.

A Summer
Love Affair

KAITLIN O'RILEY

Chapter 1

Southern Spain
Summer, 1880

Charlotte Wilton had never seen anything so beautiful.

An azure Mediterranean sea glittered under a brilliant sun, its gentle waves lapping the rugged hills of the coastline. Tall palm trees swayed with careless abandon in the breeze. The expansive blue sky overhead was not blemished by a single, solitary cloud. Charming white houses dotted the surrounding countryside. Exotic flowers and the scent of the sea perfumed the soft air around her. The small balcony on the hillside villa in the south of Spain afforded Charlotte an incredible view.

But it was not the glorious vista of the shore that had captured Charlotte's attention.

What caught her eye so thoroughly was the sight of a man.

A very handsome man. So handsome in fact that Charlotte's normally calm and sensible little heart skipped a beat or two as she stared fixedly at him, unable to break her gaze away from his strapping masculine form.

He moved with a carefree, easy grace for such a tall man. The muscles in his bare, tanned arms flexed and pulsed as he lifted and carried the massive, carved wood chair from one end of the terra-cotta tiled patio to the other. It was not that she had never seen a bare-chested male before, having far too many brothers for that to be the case. The fascination was due more in part to the sculpted beauty and chiseled lines of his broad chest itself.

Her eyes followed him as he finally positioned the wooden chair in a spot that satisfied him and he stood back to admire it. It did not occur to Charlotte to wonder why he was doing such a thing, for she could not see past the perfection of his being. His tousled blond hair glistened in the afternoon sun, giving the effect of a halo around his face. Oh, and his face! He possessed an aquiline nose, a strong jaw, and heavy-lidded eyes. He was clean-shaven and youthful, and she guessed him to be about her age. He was simply the handsomest man she had ever seen.

Indulging in this rare departure of character, Charlotte gazed down from her secluded spot on the balcony on the floor above him. She tried to distinguish what it was about him that so captivated her. She had certainly met handsome men before and some of those handsome men had even fancied themselves in love with her, but never had a man caused her to feel this way. Never had she felt this completely powerless. Watching him was an involuntary reflex. The situation fascinated and flustered her. Not taking her eyes off him, she continued to ignore the breathtaking coastal scenery around her.

Somehow he suddenly sensed her presence and glanced up at her.

A warm, lazy smile, revealing a deep dimple on his right cheek and straight white teeth, lit his face. The effect was astonishing. The charm and humor in his grin sent a thrill of delight through her very bones. He was smiling at her! Almost giggling like a schoolgirl, Charlotte could not help but smile back.

He gave her a nod of acknowledgment. "Forgive me. Have I disturbed you? I was not aware I had an upstairs neighbor. Have you just arrived?" With casual grace, he reached for the white shirt that was hanging on the balustrade and slipped his arms into the long sleeves, obscuring her view of his chiseled chest.

Feeling the deep tenor of his voice vibrate within her, Charlotte knew from his cultured accent he was English, just as she was. And a gentleman. For no man would remain bare-chested in the presence of a lady. At least now she would not be distracted by his rippling muscles. Self-conscious about being caught watching him for so long, she cleared her throat and found the wherewithal to speak. "Yes."

He chuckled at her brief response, while buttoning the front of his linen shirt. "Yes, I've disturbed you or yes, you've just arrived?"

She nodded her head and murmured, "Yes, I've just arrived. And no, you haven't disturbed me at all. I only stepped out on my balcony to admire the view." And what a view it was.

He turned his head toward the sea. "Yes, it's quite a spectacular vista from up here, is it not? That is why I was moving this chair. This way I can sit and enjoy the sea without that cluster of trees obstructing my view." He looked back up at her and smiled. "However, now I see that there is a much prettier view just above me."

Charlotte felt her cheeks redden and her stomach did a little flip at his words. Thankful for the distance of height between them, she tried to breathe. Goodness! Whatever was wrong with her? It was ridiculous actually. She had been through a Season or two and had handsome men making all sorts of fools of themselves over her. And here this golden stranger just paid her a silly little compliment and she fell to pieces like a giddy debutante at her first ball!

"I don't believe we have met," she heard herself murmur, for lack of anything better to say.

He bowed graciously in her direction. "I'm Gavin Ellsworth, here on holiday, as part of a summer tour. And the beautiful blond woman in the room above me must be . . ."

Again her heart fluttered ridiculously. She made a point to ignore it. "If you are referring to me, I am Charlotte Wilton."

"Would that be *Miss* Wilton?" he questioned pointedly.

"Yes," she answered reluctantly. "And I believe you are being rather impertinent."

"I'm more than impertinent, I should warn you." He flashed her another devastating smile. "However, I am very pleased to meet you. I was afraid that this visit might be a bit dull, but now that you have arrived, things are looking up."

"Really? Why is that?" With both hands Charlotte tightly gripped the wrought iron railing of the balcony that held her over his head. It was a flirtatious question, for of course his point was obvious.

"Oh, Miss Wilton, I think you know very well what I mean." Again that lazy, sultry smile flashed at her.

She stared at him, saying nothing at all. Heavens, she had been rendered witless by him! The discovery of this weakness within herself was a revelation.

"Are you here as a guest of Don Francisco also?" he asked.

"His wife is a friend of my aunt," Charlotte explained, surprised that actual words came out of her mouth. "I am traveling with my aunt this summer and we stopped here for a visit." Charlotte was a houseguest at this home and apparently so was this handsome young man. The thought of spending the next few weeks sleeping above him caused her knees to tremble.

"I am most pleased that you have finally arrived."

"Mr. Ellsworth, I believe I shall retire to my room now."

"I suppose I shall see you at supper, then?" he suggested with a hopeful grin.

"I suppose." She would most likely see him at every meal. Charlotte wondered how she would be able to eat anything in his presence. She might perish of hunger by the end of their visit.

"Until supper, Miss Wilton."

Charlotte willed her immobile legs to move and turned from the balcony railing, the spectacular sea view forgotten. As she made her way through the double doors into her room, she suddenly noticed something at the far corner of the narrow balcony. A wrought iron staircase spiraled down to the patio below. To *his* patio. Heavens! A private stairway connected their two rooms!

Gavin watched the vision in blue disappear into the bedroom upstairs and continued to smile, amused by her nervousness. Completely aware of his effect upon the fairer sex, he knew it would be great fun flirting with her and breaking that icy shell of reserve of hers. Miss Charlotte Wilton was certainly a stunning beauty and he wondered why someone had not claimed her by now. She was traveling with a spinster aunt. That was a red flag. Families often sent away troublesome daughters whom they could not marry off. He wondered what she had done to warrant an exile. Whatever the reason she found herself here, it now became his good fortune, for as he had said to her, his stay at the villa would be infinitely more diverting with her there. Beautiful women were always diverting, if nothing else.

Although his hosts seemed like perfectly charming and gracious people, all the other guests he had met were at least a decade older than he and all of them married and some sort of artist, poet, or painter. Pedro Bautista-Martín, his friend from Oxford, had invited him to stay at his home in Spain, and since Gavin had no desire to spend another summer being lectured on his behavior by his father, he had readily accepted Pedro's invitation. It was the least his friend could do considering it was Pedro's crazy scheme that had caused Gavin's expulsion in the first place.

However, when Gavin arrived two days ago he learned that Pedro had been visiting a cousin in Seville, fallen ill with a fever, and would not return to Málaga for another week or two. So here Gavin was in Spain, staying with a family he did not know and his under-the-weather friend in another city! He had a devil of a time understanding Spanish and could only mumble some half-remembered Latin under duress. Fortunately, Pedro's parents spoke perfect English, but they seemed to be the only ones.

He had not even seen one passably attractive woman either since his arrival. He couldn't wait to give Pedro what for when he finally showed up! Leaving him deserted in this sleepy coastal village with nothing to do for fun. Gavin had fumed inwardly for a while and thought of moving on to France before deciding to wait a little longer for Pedro.

Ah, but now there was Miss Wilton. She was just his type, too. Slender and fair with a pretty face. Of course, he preferred actresses and opera singers, women of a certain persuasion with talents for pleasing a gentleman. Miss Wilton was obviously a proper and well-bred young lady and he understood without a doubt the boundaries he dared not cross with her. But she really was quite beautiful and hopefully would provide enough of a diversion until Pedro arrived. Then Pedro could show him around town and Gavin could finally enjoy the summer holiday he had anticipated.

Gavin turned his eyes back to the shore and breathed deeply of the sea air. The view was truly remarkable. Still he could not resist another glance at the now empty balcony above him and the double glass-paned doors that were now shut.

The spiral wrought iron staircase that led from his private patio to the room of the beautiful woman above had not escaped his notice either.

Chapter 2

"*¡Bienvenidos!*" Don Francisco Bautista-Martín uttered with a silky smooth accent as Charlotte stepped into the main salon of his villa. The tall, dark-haired Spaniard welcomed her with a warm smile. She had first met him when she arrived earlier that afternoon and liked him immediately.

"Welcome to my home, Señorita Wilton!" he continued. "I hope you enjoy your visit with us."

"Thank you," she said with awe, looking about the room with wide eyes.

Charlotte quickly discovered that Don Francisco and his wife, Yvonne, were not conventional hosts. The rather late supper that evening was presented in a buffet style and instead of assigned places at the table, guests were encouraged to sit wherever they wished in the sprawling *sala,* which opened onto the veranda outside. Women in rather revealing gowns and casually dressed men lounged atop large, luxurious velvet and satin pillows on the polished wood floor, engaged in spirited conversations. She overheard Spanish, some English and French being spoken, as well as a few other languages she did not even recognize. Scores of flickering candles lit the room while gauzy curtains were draped elegantly about the *sala.* The scents of unfamiliar spices and seafood filled the warm night air, mingled with the heady fragrance of jasmine from the garden. A musician strummed a Spanish guitar, the melody lending romance to the shadowy, candlelit room.

It seemed like anything could happen in a place such as this.

The unusual scene seemed so terribly evocative of . . . *seduction* was the only word she could find to describe the feeling. The highly formal and properly seated suppers back home were nothing like this. She turned to her aunt for reassurance.

"Enjoy yourself, my dear. When in Spain . . ." Louisa Wilton responded to Charlotte's unease with the situation with an indulgent smile, while she helped herself to a plate laden with delicious treats. "Live a little, Charlotte. You are not a babe and your parents are not here," she added in a low whisper.

Surprised, Charlotte smiled back with hesitation, wondering about her aunt.

Louisa Wilton was extremely intelligent and well educated. She was taller than usual for a woman, with thick auburn hair and wide brown eyes. Her bubbly personality and charming ways made her a favorite among her many nieces and nephews. Charlotte was still trying to uncover the mystery regarding her aunt's broken engagement many years ago, but Louisa had yet to divulge the source of her heartache. Although they had grown closer during their travels from London, Charlotte realized there was much about her aunt that she did not know or understand. She had an unshakable feeling she was on the verge of seeing her aunt in a new light since they arrived in Spain.

"But Aunt Louisa, is any of this proper?"

"Of course it is!" She flashed a grin. "It's just a different sort of proper."

Charlotte cast a skeptical eye at the unusually garbed guests and wondered again how she ended up in Spain.

"I would love to paint your portrait," a female voice said from behind her.

Charlotte turned around to see Doña Yvonne Bautista-Martín. "My portrait?" she asked in confusion.

She had met her hostess when they had first arrived that afternoon and had been impressed by her beauty and graciousness. A petite woman with an elegant manner, she was also an accomplished painter. At least that was what Charlotte had been told. Standing there in her flowing gown of red silk, Doña Yvonne seemed out of the pages of a Gothic romance.

"Yes, Charlotte, I wish to paint you," Doña Yvonne said with enthusiasm. "I adore the color of your golden hair. It would look lovely in the morning light."

"I agree with you," Gavin Ellsworth said to their hostess but looking directly at Charlotte. He gave her a smile, flashing white teeth and his engaging dimple. "She is quite beautiful and would be the perfect subject for a portrait done by you."

Charlotte almost dropped the china plate from her hand at the sight of Gavin Ellsworth. She had carefully scanned the *sala* when she had first entered and had relaxed considerably when she had not seen him. Now he was standing right beside her. She could barely breathe. Without the distance of an entire story between them, she feared he could sense her reaction to him. He looked devastatingly handsome, in a clean white shirt and black trousers. He must have just bathed for his blond hair was still damp and combed back. At this close range, she could look into his eyes. They were greenish, with flecks of gold and brown. He stared at her so intently, she had to look away.

Again, Charlotte said nothing but Doña Yvonne smiled, her dark eyes flashing with excitement. "You see, *el guapo* agrees that I should paint you, Charlotte. *Perdóname,* have the two of you been introduced?"

Gavin continued to gaze at her. "We met briefly earlier this afternoon."

Doña Yvonne said, "Then you know that this lovely woman is Señorita Charlotte Wilton, the niece of my dear friend Louisa Wilton. And this young gentleman is Señor Gavin Ellsworth, a school friend of my son, Pedro."

"I am pleased to meet you once again, Miss Wilton," Gavin said, reaching out his hand to take hers.

Charlotte nodded in greeting, the contact of his hand shaking her to her toes. She mumbled, "Pleased to meet you."

Gavin also greeted her aunt. Louisa gave Charlotte a knowing glance. Charlotte wished to roll her eyes at her aunt's insinuation, but she could not. She knew next to nothing about Gavin Ellsworth, yet she could not deny that her heart rate increased dramatically in his presence.

"Yes, let her paint you, Charlotte. Have some fun! Doña Yvonne is a very skilled artist. You will not be disappointed with the end result," Aunt Louisa urged, brimming with enthusiasm. "And it would be a wonderful souvenir of your visit to Málaga!"

Charlotte was a guest in this house and it would be wrong to refuse her hostess. She had sat for portraits before, of course. At this very moment a beautifully rendered painting of her in a stunning formal gown of blue velvet hung in the family gallery of her home, Glenstone Manor, in England. So why did the thought of sitting for this woman fill her with trepidation? She did not know. Looking at the three faces staring at her, Charlotte could do nothing but acquiesce. "If it would please you, Doña Yvonne, I would be happy to sit for your painting."

"*¡Maravilloso!*" she exclaimed, clapping her hands in triumph. "*¡El retrato será magnífico! Ahh, un momento—*"

Doña Yvonne glanced at Gavin and eyed him carefully,

assessing him. Then she looked at Charlotte. And back to Gavin. "I would love to paint you both. *¡Qué rubios!* Yes, that is it. Together. You are both so fair, so blond, and so beautiful. May I paint you also, Señor Ellsworth?"

"You wish for us to pose . . . for you . . . together?" Charlotte squeaked, noting the higher pitch in her voice with mounting alarm. She was making a fool of herself with this man. She had hardly been able to string two sentences together in his presence. The very idea of being in his general proximity for any length of time caused her to tremble.

"I think it's a wonderful idea," Gavin agreed with a winning smile, his dimple playing havoc with Charlotte's heart. "I would be honored, Doña Yvonne, and I am at your disposal for as long as you need me."

"*Muy bien*. Then it is all settled. We shall begin tomorrow morning. Meet me in my studio at dawn."

"Did you say dawn?" Gavin's golden brows drew together in disapproval.

It seemed he had an aversion to waking early. Charlotte silently agreed with him, for she hated arising before ten, but she still could not speak. What had she just gotten herself into?

"*Claro que sí!*" Doña Yvonne exclaimed with a delighted smile. "Of course! We have to be prepared for the sunlight. You will both come on time. It will be perfect, I promise you. Now, you must have something to eat."

Their gregarious hostess began filling two plates with fruit, cheese and ham and then ushered them both to seats in the corner of the long veranda before hurrying off to see to her other guests. Charlotte watched Aunt Louisa sit with a bearded gentleman on a divan inside, while she found herself seated upon a stone bench bedecked with velvet pillows, with Gavin beside her. A small table stood before them. They were virtually alone together in the moonlight. How would she possibly survive such an intimate encounter? *Is Doña Yvonne playing at matchmaker?* Charlotte shuddered to think.

This was exactly why she had agreed to leave England with her aunt, not that she had much say in the matter. The pressure from her family to marry had made her anxious.

"In your brief time here at the villa, what is your opinion of this place?" Gavin asked, his expression full of intent interest in her.

"It is like nothing I've ever seen at home, but I am not sure what to think of all this." She swept her hand across to indicate the sprawling *sala.*

"I am certain I had the same expression on my face two nights ago as you do now."

"Is it so obvious?" Charlotte's cheeks grew warm.

"It's not the calamity you think it is." He encouraged her with a heart-melting smile. "You merely look overwhelmed. And rightly so."

Charlotte understood that most of her nervousness was due to his proximity to her. Yes, the atmosphere at Don Francisco's villa was one of Bohemian indulgence. That was something she believed she could get used to. What rattled her more was Gavin Ellsworth himself. Sitting beside her. Close beside her.

"It's very different from England," she said. In England she knew exactly what was expected of her. Whether she agreed with the social standards of the day or not, she knew how to behave, how to act, and what was proper in any given situation. Whereas here in this villa, she felt unanchored and adrift.

"Yes," he agreed, "but you'll grow accustomed to it. In fact, I'm already quite used to it here. Why this evening I did not even don a necktie."

Charlotte forced her eyes away from the nakedness of his throat and the loosely buttoned shirt, for she recalled all too vividly the chiseled muscles and smooth golden planes of his chest. She breathed in and ignored his necktie-less state.

She *had* noticed the complete disregard of fashion dictates since she'd arrived. Especially Doña Yvonne, wearing flowing robes of colorful silk and her long hair hanging loose. It was quite different here in this house. The rules she was familiar with did not apply here, it seemed.

"How long are you staying at the villa?" Gavin asked.

"A few weeks at least, and then we are sailing to Italy."

"I thought I might leave tomorrow, but then you arrived to alleviate my boredom." He gave her a roguish wink. "You are my saving angel."

Charlotte knew then exactly the type of gentleman Gavin Ellsworth was. She had met enough men like him over the years. He was typically spoiled and lazy and very used to getting his way in everything. Especially with the ladies. Oh, most especially with the ladies. He knew precisely how his charming smile and striking blond good looks left a woman weak-kneed and eager to please his every whim for the chance to see that smile again and with the hope that she would be the one to win his favor. To her great humiliation, Charlotte was fast turning into one of those foolish, fawning girls. Even worse, she could not help herself. Could not stop herself. Where were all her witty comebacks and sardonic remarks that she had readily given other gentlemen of such ilk and for which she was so well known? She was skilled at putting men in their place. And yet now, nothing. She could do nothing.

She realized from the moment she spied his bronzed and bare chest that she was defenseless. She had no resources strong enough to stop his charm.

Now she was *his angel?* She should laugh in his face. She should deliver a quick retort to set him back and show him that she had not the least bit of interest in a man like him. Instead Charlotte grinned, ridiculously pleased by his compliment.

"I don't believe anyone has ever called me angelic before," she said, wishing she could kick herself.

"Well tonight you are an angel to me." His engaging smile lit a fire within her.

"I see," she murmured.

"Am I anything to you?" He eyed her with blatant spec-ulation.

Her heart flipped over in her chest. Oh, she wanted him to be something to her! Wanted to be able to call him by some sweet endearment. "I should think not. I do not even know you."

"Yet."

Her pulse quickened. "Excuse me?"

"You don't know me well enough *yet*. But you will, Miss Wilton, you will. I believe we shall be spending a great deal of time together."

She stared at him. His deep hazel eyes fixed on hers and she could not look away. Indeed, she could barely draw a breath.

"May I call you Charlotte? Miss Wilton seems overly formal given the current surroundings in which we find ourselves." He nodded in the direction of the house.

Through the archway, Charlotte could see various guests coupled together intimately, some seated on velvet sofas and some resting on cushions upon the floor. The bearded gentleman now had his arm around Aunt Louisa's shoulders and the two were laughing together. Another passionate pair was locked in an amorous embrace. In plain view of every-one! The atmosphere in the house was decidedly outside the bounds of propriety.

A heated blush suffused her cheeks. She averted her eyes and asked, "And I am to call you Gavin then?"

"Of course." He gave her another smile. "Unless you'd rather call me darling."

Nervous laughter bubbled up from within her chest at the boldness of his suggestion. It was as if he had read her thoughts! "I don't think I shall be calling you *that*."

He raised and lowered his brows in a devilish manner. "Yet."

"My, my," she shook her head. "Aren't we rather presumptuous, sir?"

He cast her a meaningful look. "Not presumptuous per se. I just hate to waste time."

"I see your point," she responded. He was too charming for his own good.

"Well then, my beautiful Charlotte, would you care for a glass of sangria?"

A servant had approached them with a silver tray of crystal glasses filled with a dark red liquid. Gavin took two glasses from the tray and extended his hand to her before she could respond.

"What is it?"

"It is a kind of fruit punch made with red wine. I think you'll like it."

Normally Charlotte did not imbibe alcohol, but tonight was different. She felt different. She accepted the glass, her fingers lightly brushing his as she did so, and a little thrill went through her. She took a sip, and the rich fruity flavor tingled her throat. She smiled at him. "Mmmm."

"See there. I was correct." He settled back into the velvet cushions. "I know you already."

The soft, jasmine-scented air wafted around them. Charlotte sighed and glanced up at the stars glittering in the night sky. This was certainly one of the most unusual evenings of her life.

"So tell me, beautiful girl, why are you here in Spain?"

She turned to see his hazel eyes sparkling at her. "Why are you here?" she countered.

"Guess."

She smiled at him. Oh, this was far too easy. "You are escaping the drudgery of schoolwork and avoiding lectures from your father on accepting the responsibilities of your position."

His rich laughter caused others to turn and stare in their direction. "You would be correct, my Charlotte. How did you know?"

"Wild guess," she quipped, taking another sip of the luxurious sangria. The possessive use of her name secretly thrilled her and she wondered why that should be so. She knew he did not mean such endearments. He was the type who used such language with casual ease and little consequence. Still . . .

He arched a brow suggestively. "Let me guess why you are here then."

"I bet you can't guess."

"I cannot resist a challenge. Especially such a delightful one."

She took a sip of sangria. "Impress me then."

"Let's see. . . . Your parents have passed away and your eccentric aunt is now your guardian." He gave her a look of triumph.

She hesitated a moment. "Well, you are partly right. My father passed away when I was very young. My mother has since remarried, so I have a stepfather. But both are alive and well and more than able to watch over me properly."

He tapped his finger against his chin. "Ah, well then, it only stands to reason that you are traveling with your aunt until the gossip of some terrible scandal you caused back home dies down!"

Now it was Charlotte's laughter that drew attention. The absurdity of his guess amused her. She shook her head at him. "Oh, I'm sorry to disappoint you, but it's nothing that dramatic. Try again."

He cocked his head to the side and eyed her critically. "You are escaping the overly amorous attentions of an unwanted suitor?"

Charlotte cringed a bit at this. It was not one unwanted suitor in particular but rather all the suitors in general she found completely unsuitable. To put it simply she had not met someone she could foresee spending the rest of her life with. She had been introduced to many upstanding and proper gentlemen during her first Season, as well as her second and third. Some of the gentlemen were even quite charming and attractive, just not attractive to her. No one had met her expectations. Her parents were exhausted and frustrated with Charlotte's excuses for turning down prospective husbands. They despaired of her ever approving of a proposal of marriage, so when Aunt Louisa offered to take Charlotte on a tour of the continent, her parents, overwhelmed with caring for their four young sons, readily agreed to send her off with her aunt for the summer. They hoped a change in scenery might prompt a change in Charlotte's outlook.

So here she was.

"I'm right, am I not?" he boasted.

"On the contrary."

"There is no suitor pursuing you?" There was a note of disbelief in his tone.

"No." Charlotte sipped her sangria.

"How could such a thing be possible?" Gavin's face was incredulous. "One so beautiful as you?"

"I do not lack for suitors, I assure you." Her chin went up. "However, I am rather discriminating in my tastes."

"Oh, I see now." He nodded sagely. "You are one of *those* types of females."

Charlotte bristled slightly at his remark. "And just what type would that be?"

"The very worst kind."

"Please explain."

"I think you know exactly what I am referring to." He drank his sangria.

"I'm afraid you must enlighten me, Mr. Ellsworth."

"Gavin."

She sighed. "Gavin."

He regarded her steadily. "You, my lovely Charlotte, are the type of female who thinks she is too good for any man."

Charlotte gasped. It sounded ridiculous. Was that the way men perceived her? That she was too good for them? It certainly was not how she felt about herself or about males in general. Perhaps Mr. Gavin Ellsworth had a point. Were her standards too high? Had she held herself out of reach? Maybe she had unwittingly been holding out for someone better? Someone perfect? So what if she had, was that so wrong?

If that were not enough, he added, "You've turned down perfectly suitable marriage proposals and your parents no longer know what to do with you."

She didn't say a word.

He folded his arms across his chest and leaned back. "I win."

"It took you three guesses! Besides, I merely know what I like and what I don't like," she countered in indignation.

He leaned in close to her and grinned. "And you like me, don't you?"

"That, my dear Gavin," Charlotte murmured flirtatiously, ignoring her fluttering heart, "remains to be seen, now doesn't it?"

Chapter 3

"Move your lips closer to Charlotte's cheek," Doña Yvonne instructed as she stood behind a large canvas, her colorful pots of paints and her brushes and palettes close by. Her dark hair was swept back from her face and she wore a spattered smock.

Gavin had officially landed in hell and wondered how he had gotten himself in this position in the first place.

He hated posing for portraits, yet here he was, holding the luscious and half-naked Charlotte Wilton in his arms. Under normal circumstances such an arrangement would be quite pleasurable, yet at the moment it was nothing short of torturous agony. Never had he held a woman so intimately before and not been able to further his advances.

He and Charlotte had both arrived at the studio of their hostess just before dawn, as instructed, sleepy but willing to be immortalized on canvas, unaware that Doña Yvonne had envisioned painting them as some sort of ancient Grecian deities or some such nonsense. Using her skillful persuasion and charm, within moments Doña Yvonne had gotten them both draped artfully in nothing but a few yards of pale silk cloth.

The sight of Charlotte's creamy white shoulders and bare arms and legs and knowing there was not a stitch of clothing beneath the silk almost undid Gavin then and there. Doña Yvonne had loosened Charlotte's blond hair from its pins and the silky locks cascaded in golden waves to her waist, glistening in the pastel dawn light. With her sultry blue eyes, she looked as if she had just risen from a passionate night in his bed. Which did nothing to calm him of his already aroused state.

Garbed in his own array of silk, which was wrapped strategically around his waist, leaving his chest and legs bare, Gavin had been instructed to sit upon a marble bench and hold Charlotte in his arms. Charlotte's eyes had widened considerably at Doña Yvonne's request, but she had gamely followed orders, which is how he had come to be embracing the scantily clad Miss Wilton while she lay practically naked across his lap, her gorgeous legs crossed elegantly at the other end of the bench.

Although it was no hardship on his part, he dutifully pressed his lips closer to Charlotte's soft cheek. Her swift intake of breath indicated she was as aroused as he was. He tried not to smile in satisfaction. After their lengthy meal together on the veranda the night before, he had wanted to kiss her, but Charlotte had held herself at a distance and would not allow him an opportunity. He reasoned it had been for the best, since she was not at all the type of woman he dallied with. Or should even consider dallying with. She was too reserved, too British, and in the end too much trouble.

However, he now found himself reconsidering his entire position on the matter.

Charlotte had shocked him by going along with this risqué pose.

Now that he held her this way he realized she was even more desirable than he first envisioned. Consequently, he wanted her more than he had ever wanted any other woman. He ached to caress her creamy skin. God, but she smelled heavenly! An intoxicating floral scent. And she was so light in his arms, petite as she was.

"Gavin, *querido*," Doña Yvonne called out. "Move your left hand up a little bit higher."

A little bit higher? If he was not in hell already, he was certainly on his way now. Never one to miss a good opportunity whatever the consequences, Gavin did not need to be told twice. Slowly he inched his hand along the silk fabric until he cupped the underside of Charlotte's soft, full, and temptingly delicious breast. She sucked in her breath again and trembled slightly. It took every ounce of his self-control not to squeeze her luscious form. His finger brushed her hardened nipple and his groin tightened in response, while his right hand rested possessively on the seductive curve of her hip.

"*Bien*," Doña Yvonne said, looking pleased. "Now, Charlotte, lean back into him and relax."

Gavin's wild heartbeat echoed with Charlotte's against his own chest. He had expected her to protest in outrage, or to stand up and leave, decrying the indecent nature of the portrait session. She did not. Instead she settled into him, resting her head on his shoulder just as their artistic hostess requested.

"That is *perfecto*. Now . . . Do not move," Doña Yvonne ordered them, her hand moving across the canvas.

Do not move. Gavin gritted his teeth. *Do not move while a beautiful and half-naked woman reclines on my lap, my lips are pressed against her cheek, and I cup her breast in my hand.* God in heaven, at this moment he began to regret ever agreeing to come to Spain in the first place!

The exquisite torment of posing in some sort of Grecian tableau continued for some time while both remained silent. All he heard was the pounding of his heart and the soft intake of Charlotte's shallow breathing. The heat of her body permeated every pore of his skin. Caught between heaven and hell, Gavin could do nothing but remain motionless while he held Charlotte Wilton intimately in his arms and tortured himself with vivid images of what he wanted to do to her. The desire to kiss her, to taste her sweet lips, and to remove the flimsy pale silk that barely shielded her naked body consumed his entire being, and he wrestled with the need to restrain himself from ravishing her there in full view of an astonished Doña Yvonne.

After what seemed like an eternity, Doña Yvonne declared, "That is all I can do today. The light has changed. You will both come back tomorrow, no?"

Tomorrow? Gavin groaned inwardly. It had not occurred to him that he would have to endure this intimate encounter with Charlotte for more than one morning. Undoubtedly a portrait required several sessions at least. It was impossible to back out of doing the portrait now without offending his hostess. He would have to continue until it was complete. How would he survive this?

"Of course we will," Charlotte's soft voice murmured, as she began to move from his embrace.

He admired her spirit for agreeing to continue but doubted that she had to fight to restrain her baser urges the way he did. The sessions might be awkward or uncomfortable for her, but they would not be painful, as they were for him. Reluctant to let her go, Gavin let his hands slide from her perfect body. As she stood, a gap in the pale silk draped across her chest afforded Gavin with a brief glimpse of Charlotte's breast. His mouth went dry, but he automatically assisted her to her feet, taking her hand in his. A pair of liquid blue eyes shyly met his as he did so. Something within their depths called to him, causing his heart to flip, and Gavin had to shake himself mentally at the silly perception.

"How long will it take?" he managed to utter somewhat hoarsely, his eyes still locked with Charlotte's.

"Perhaps a week. Maybe more. *Quién sabe?*" Doña Yvonne answered. "I promise I will only keep you for an hour or so each morning; then you shall have the rest of the day free to do as you wish."

Charlotte glanced away and pulled her hands free from his, wrapping the silk tighter around her body. Gavin continued to stare at her, strangely moved by their encounter.

"No, no, you must not look yet!" Doña Yvonne waved Charlotte away from the large canvas. "I shall let you see it only when it is finished completely. *No, todavía no!*"

Charlotte laughed and took a step back, a smile lighting her face. Gavin still could not take his eyes off of her.

"Now, get dressed the two of you." Doña Yvonne gave them a knowing glance. "Why do you not go visit some of the city? It is still early and you have the day ahead of you yet."

Gavin watched Charlotte retreat into the next room in order to don her clothes. Her elegant stride and the graceful sway of her hips mesmerized him. When she disappeared behind the door, he noticed his artistic hostess looking in his direction.

Doña Yvonne winked at him. "*¿Qué hombre más guapo eres tú, eh?*"

He did not know what she said exactly, but he took her meaning well enough to actually blush a little, suddenly realizing he still stood in nothing but his strategically placed silk attire.

"Now go and take that beautiful girl and enjoy the sun," she commanded with a dismissive wave of her hand.

Chapter 4

Charlotte spent the rest of the day sequestered in the safety of her bedroom. She could do little else given how she spent that morning.

She needed to recover her nerve in order to survive another portrait sitting.

Gavin had invited her to tour the city and perhaps visit the shore, but she had politely thanked him and declined. It was far better to retreat to the sanctuary of her little room than spend another minute in his presence, where she might do something reckless and impulsive such as kiss him.

Honestly, what had Doña Yvonne been thinking to pose them in such a risqué fashion? The woman had asked so charmingly and made it all seem so easy that before Charlotte knew it she was wearing nothing but silk, her hair hanging loose. It was hardly what one would deem as decent and Charlotte should have refused to be a party to such a scene.

Yet she could not help herself.

Surprisingly, the idea of the portrait intrigued her. For the first time in her life she felt truly beautiful. Wearing only silk against her naked body and being held by an equally undressed Gavin had been an astonishing pleasure. And wickedly erotic. His muscular arms around her, embracing her possessively. And his hands . . . One on her hip, the other on her breast. She thought she would faint when Doña Yvonne suggested the pose, but she did not. In fact, she reveled in it, much to her amazement. His lips on her cheek, the heat of his breath against her skin, sent shivers of delight down to her toes. Lying against him in the soft morning light, draped in luxurious silk while a sea-scented breeze wafted around them had been nothing less than heavenly. She could have easily remained in that position all day and not minded a bit. Except that she wanted more from him. She wanted him to touch her. Wanted him to kiss her.

And feared that she would kiss him if he did not do it first.

It had been maddening and terrifying and thrilling and wonderful.

And she would do it again tomorrow. And the day after.

Charlotte could hardly contain her excitement over the prospect of another morning in Gavin's strong and muscular arms.

Which was exactly why she could not trust herself to spend another moment in his company. He had already been more intimate with her than any man had a right to be, but she did not think she would be able to ward off further liberties from him. If he were so inclined to try.

And knowing the type of man he was, she did not doubt that he would.

However, it was just that type of man she needed to stay far away from. He would only end up hurting her, breaking her heart. She had seen it too many times before with those spoiled, wealthy, charming gentlemen who took what they wanted and disregarded the consequences. She and her friends had heard the gossip and stories of the rogues who won the heart of a young woman and then set their sights upon the next pretty face. It was the chase that appealed to them rather than the prize itself. And if ever she met a rogue, Gavin Ellsworth was one, and Charlotte had no wish to be one of those foolish young women. She was too smart for that.

A sudden knock at her door startled her. She sat up on the bed where she had been lying and straightened her dressing gown. The late afternoon sun slanted through the wooden shutters and spilled across the rich-tiled floor.

"Come in," she called, assuming it was a servant coming to collect her lunch dishes.

Aunt Louisa entered the room, her kind eyes clouded with worry. "I have not seen you all day, Charlotte. Are you not feeling well?"

"I am quite well, thank you. Just resting a little. I was up rather early this morning," Charlotte explained to her aunt. "Doña Yvonne was painting me."

"Oh yes, of course." Aunt Louisa sat on the bed beside her. She looked at Charlotte carefully. "Still, I am a little surprised you did not join the others on the trip to town."

"The others?" Charlotte asked in confusion.

"Yes, the other young people."

As far as she could tell from supper last night, she and Gavin were the two youngest guests at the villa. "Who are you talking about?"

"Gavin Ellsworth and the rest of them. Don Francisco's son, Pedro, arrived with some friends."

Charlotte shook her head, suddenly wondering whether the friends were male or female. "No, he asked me but I preferred to rest."

Aunt Louisa's brows drew together. "Has Mr. Ellsworth done something to offend you?"

"Of course not!" Charlotte protested. "Why would you think such a thing?"

"Well, the two of you seemed to be getting along quite well last night and I know that you both posed for Doña

Yvonne this morning, and for you not to join him this afternoon . . . I just wondered, that's all."

Charlotte remained silent. Had her name been linked with Gavin's so soon?

"He is a very handsome young man."

"Yes, he is," Charlotte agreed.

"What do you think of him?"

"I think he is used to getting his own way and does not trouble himself with the consequences of his behavior."

Aunt Louisa's brows rose. "You know him so well already?"

"I know his type."

"That's a little judgmental, don't you think? You just met the man."

"Exactly." Charlotte knew all she needed to know.

"How was the portrait sitting?" Aunt Louisa changed the subject.

"Unusual." She hoped her aunt did not notice the blush creeping across her cheeks. She figured the less details she gave about the portrait sitting, the better.

"Knowing Yvonne I can only imagine! I look forward to seeing the finished painting." Aunt Louisa laughed lightly. "My friend is rather eccentric in her tastes. She and I had great fun in finishing school in Paris together back when we were much younger. Then she fell in love with Paco, that is, Don Francisco, and moved to Spain. I make a point to visit them here at their villa whenever I can."

"This villa . . ." Charlotte said, recalling the Bohemian atmosphere in the *sala* last night. "They don't follow the usual conventions here, do they? They prefer doing things their own way, it seems."

"Yes," her aunt nodded in agreement. "That is the wonderful part of traveling, Charlotte, and why I suggested you come along with me on this trip. Women are boxed in and constrained in every way in England. When you see more of the world you realize how much more to life there is than what you are led to believe back home."

"I am beginning to see that," she said, thinking of how her morning was spent.

"Please don't hide away in your room, Charlotte." Aunt Louisa took Charlotte's hand in hers and gave it a light squeeze. "Do not squander opportunities to enjoy your life, for sometimes they do not come again. Your parents entrusted me with your well-being on this trip and wanted you to have new experiences and—"

"They sent me away," Charlotte interrupted, "because they are fed up with my overly selective qualifications for a husband. They don't know what else to do with me."

Aunt Louisa ignored her little outburst. "As I was saying, your parents entrusted me with your well-being on this trip, and as your guardian, I am allowing you complete freedom to do as you wish. Break out of your usual routine, my dear. You need not answer to me or anyone else. You are not here to find a husband, but to let yourself grow. At least, that is how I see it. You are young and beautiful and have your whole life ahead of you. Enjoy yourself now."

Charlotte stared at her aunt, wondering what she would say if she knew that her niece had posed nearly nude in the arms of a half-naked man that morning. She squeezed Aunt Louisa's hand in response. "I was not hiding in my room," she lied, for she had been doing just that. "But if it will make you happy, I will not rest during the day again."

Aunt Louisa sighed. "I just want you to be unafraid and to not regret missing certain opportunities."

Charlotte could hardly be called a coward for what she did with Gavin and she did not regret it. At least not yet anyway . . . But what had happened to her aunt in her past to have her speak so passionately now about wasted opportunities? "What is it that you regret in your life, Aunt Louisa?"

Aunt Louisa pulled her hand away and her eyes clouded. "Oh, too many things to count. I suppose I mostly regret the times I feared doing something I should have done and the chances I lost to do the things I wanted to."

"Who was that gentleman you sat with last night?"

Aunt Louisa smiled and the expression on her face softened. "You mean Carlos? He is an old friend. A very dear and special friend of mine who knew me when I was young."

"Were you in love with him?"

Aunt Louisa nodded.

"What happened?" asked Charlotte, intrigued by this new information.

"I was very foolish and did not marry him when he asked me. So he married someone else."

"That's sad, Aunt Louisa."

"Yes," she agreed, looking toward the window. "I was devastated at the time."

"Is his wife here?"

"No. She passed away last year."

"Oh, then the two of you can now—"

Aunt Louisa interrupted, "Oh well, that is enough about me. I came to talk about you."

And that was all she was going to share with Charlotte on that subject, it seemed.

Aunt Louisa faced Charlotte and said brightly, "Now promise me you will enjoy yourself thoroughly while we are here. No more hiding in your room."

Could she do it? Could she pretend her mother had not sent her here as a punishment? Could she simply pretend the old Charlotte did not exist for the time being and let down her reserve? Could she let go and do as her aunt suggested? Would it be so terrible? And hadn't she already begun?

She whispered hesitantly, "I promise."

"Good!" Aunt Louisa beamed with satisfaction.

The seductive atmosphere of the villa had already begun to work its magic on her, and Charlotte's heart began to race at the prospect of what she just agreed to do.

Chapter 5

Gavin's eyes scanned the room watching for her. Waiting for her.

He had not seen Charlotte since that morning and he wondered with growing impatience where she was and what she had been doing all day. It was the same scene in the *sala* as the night before. Guests were milling about, or seated in intimate groups around small tables or on sofas. Platters of succulent seafood and dishes of exotic fruits and cheeses covered the long table. A guitarist's music filled the room. Gavin was growing rather accustomed to the casual atmosphere in the villa.

"Señor Ellsworth, would you care to sit beside me?"

Isabella Hernandez flashed her dark eyes at him and beckoned to him from a red velvet sofa. Pedro's pretty cousin had been hanging on him all day and the novelty was wearing a bit thin. Accustomed to women flirting with him, Gavin was wise to her bold looks from the moment he met her. Pedro had returned home before noon that day, just before Gavin was venturing into town. Gavin had waited longer than needed, hoping that Charlotte would change her mind and come with him. Then Pedro, along with his three cousins, arrived unexpectedly at the villa, and Gavin allowed himself to be swept along in their plans. He spent the afternoon touring Málaga with them and had a pleasant enough time, although all he could think about was Charlotte.

She was a bit of a mystery. Aside from her reasons for spending the summer abroad, last night he thought he had her all figured out. She was a typically aloof, hard-to-please female, full of high principles and suspicions. But she had proved him wrong on that account this morning in the art studio. Charlotte had not put up a fuss about that pose at all! And she was too delectable to be believed. Her perfectly shaped body, her enchanting scent, the graceful arch of her neck, the silkiness of her creamy skin, the clear blue of her eyes . . . The look in those eyes . . .

He could not get the image of her out of his head.

It seemed, however, that he would not be seeing her this evening. Devil if he knew what she was about! It was ridiculous of him to be thinking of her so much anyway. She was not his type. Charlotte was the sort of girl one married, and Gavin was too young and looked forward to more fun in the years ahead of him to think of getting himself married now. He needed to put the lovely Charlotte Wilton out of his mind.

He flashed a grin at Pedro's dark-haired cousin and joined her on the sofa. Isabella smiled with unabashed delight.

"Did you have a nice time this afternoon?" she asked brightly, placing her hand on his arm possessively.

Before Gavin could give an answer to Isabella, the beautiful object of his thoughts captured his gaze. Charlotte had entered the room and for a moment Gavin could not speak.

Charlotte paused under the archway, looking for all the world like a luscious temptress in an elegant gown of deep burgundy that hugged the curves of her body like a glove and displayed her ample cleavage to perfection. Her blond hair was arranged high upon her head, revealing the graceful curve of her neck. Gavin fought the urge to wave to her, to call her over to him. Instead he watched Doña Yvonne, as the excellent hostess she was, quickly take Charlotte by the hand and draw her into the room. Doña Yvonne then introduced Charlotte to her son, Pedro.

Gavin almost leapt from the sofa at the way Pedro's eyes glittered in appreciation of Charlotte's beauty. Of course his friend would gravitate immediately to Charlotte, for Pedro would never pass an opportunity to be with a gorgeous female. Charlotte reacted with a shy smile to Pedro's charm. He took her arm and then guided her toward the sofa. Gavin stood and Pedro performed the necessary introductions.

"Miss Wilton, have we not met before?" Gavin smiled at Charlotte.

"Yes, I seem to recall seeing you somewhere," she teased, a sparkle in her eyes. "Something about you seems quite familiar to me."

Pedro's face clouded in confusion. "*Have* the two of you met?"

Gavin laughed then. "Yes, we met last night and your mother is doing a portrait of us now."

"*Por supuesto, mi madre.*" Pedro nodded in understanding. "So now we are all friends. *Qué bueno!* We shall eat together. Señorita Wilton, you must come with me. Gavin, will you escort my cousin?" Pedro took possessive hold of Charlotte and moved her expertly toward the table.

Gavin found himself wanting to knock Pedro's hand off of Charlotte's arm and escort her himself. Instead he assisted a beaming Isabella to the massive dining table to fill her plate. He spent the remainder of the supper irritated by Pedro's blatant claim upon Charlotte and growing more annoyed by the clinging Isabella. Every time he caught Charlotte's eye, she held his gaze longer than necessary. Her wide blue eyes mesmerized him. As did her laughter.

And she seemed to laugh at everything his friend said, smiling and fluttering her long eyelashes, apparently

captivated by Pedro's Latin charms. He had not guessed
Charlotte to be a practiced flirt when he met her. She had
been alluring with him and he believed it to be because of
his own magnetic charm.

Yet here she was acting the coquette quite skillfully with
his friend.

He did not like it one bit.

By the time guests began retiring to their rooms for the
evening, Gavin was more than ready to leave as well. As the
group concluded making plans for the next day, Gavin tried
to position himself beside Charlotte, but Pedro had his arm
on hers and he watched helplessly as his friend escorted
Charlotte from the *sala*.

Gavin was left with Isabella, who tugged on his arm and
asked to have a bit of air before retiring. Normally he would
have enjoyed kissing the pretty Spanish-eyed girl on a star-
lit veranda and could not understand why he had no desire
to do so now. She was more than willing and not shy about
letting him know it. Yet, all he could think about was Charlotte. And if Pedro was planning to kiss her.

"I'm afraid I'm not feeling well, Señorita Hernandez."

"The fresh air will make you better," she insisted with a
slight wink.

What was wrong with him? "I am afraid not," he said as
gently as he could, while removing her hand from his arm.
"I think it would be best if I were to sleep. I shall see you
tomorrow, señorita. Thank you for a lovely evening." He
flashed her his most devastating smile.

He recognized the disappointment in her eyes, for he was
sure it was clearly in his own as well.

He fled the scene as quickly as he could. He had to reach
Charlotte before Pedro made an advance on her. Gavin first
searched the walled garden, thinking his friend might have
led her to a secluded and romantic spot in the moonlight,
but he did not find the couple. Although he did happen

upon Charlotte's aunt and a bearded gentleman in a private corner, conversing rather intensely. Luckily, they did not notice him before he backed away. He then hurried through the villa and followed the steps up to the area near Charlotte's bedroom. The long hallway was empty. He paused outside her door but did not knock.

Feeling like a fool but unable to quell the panic within his chest, he descended the stairs and returned to his own room. He flung open the double doors and walked out to the private patio. He stopped before the spiral staircase that led directly to Charlotte's bedroom, glancing up at her balcony.

He took the steps two at a time.

He tapped lightly on the door. Through the gauzy curtains that draped the glass-paned double doors a soft light shone through.

A startled Charlotte opened the doors. Her eyes grew wide at the sight of him. "Gavin!"

"Are you alone?" he demanded.

"What a ridiculous question! Of course I am. What are you doing here?"

He relaxed slightly at that news but still had to know. "Did he kiss you?"

Her elegant brows drew together. "You mean Pedro?"

"Yes." He took a step toward her.

Her chin went up. "Why is that any of your affair?"

"It's not. I just—" He felt like an idiot. He had no claim on Charlotte. Who was he to be standing on the balcony outside her bedroom demanding to know whom she had been kissing? "I just . . ."

Charlotte looked up at him, her expression full of longing. "No," she whispered breathlessly. "I did not let him kiss me."

"Then I will."

Without questioning the impulse, Gavin reached out and drew her into his arms. In a swift motion, he lowered his mouth over hers and kissed her. She melted into him, warm and soft and willing. And he was lost the minute his lips met hers. As their kiss deepened, he couldn't tell who was trembling more, he or she. Her heady floral scent enveloped him and he felt himself drowning in her. The sweetness of her mouth and tongue as it twined with his made him hunger for more. More of her. Her arms reached up and around his neck and he pulled her more tightly against his chest, feeling her luscious breasts press into him.

Gavin had kissed his fair share of women, some far more accomplished than others. Tall blondes, petite brunettes, luscious redheads, stage actresses, ballet dancers, eager debutantes, and young widows. He had flirted with, laughed with, kissed, and enjoyed each of these ladies. They were all beautiful women, just as Charlotte was.

But not one of them made him feel the way he did now with Charlotte.

A soft gasp escaped her lips and his kiss intensified at the sound. His hands moved up her back, along her elegant neck, and splayed into her golden hair, loosening it from the pins that held it in place. Just as it had done that morning, her hair cascaded around her in gentle waves and again she looked like a beautiful goddess.

A faint alarm bell rang in his head and he realized he had to stop now or he would end up with her flat on her back in bed. He cupped her face in his hands, and calling on every reserve of willpower he possessed, he withdrew from the kiss.

Her head fell against his chest and they both sought to catch their breaths. Her arms still around his neck, she held on for support and he cradled her in the circle of his arms. The length of her curvaceous body pressed so intimately against him that it strained his self-control close to the breaking point. Tenderly he kissed the top of her head and breathed in deeply.

Gavin remained standing on the balcony with Charlotte's head resting against his chest, unsure how much time had passed while he held her like that. Both of them were loath to break their embrace.

"Charlotte," he whispered finally, surprised by the hoarseness of his voice.

She did not move a muscle nor say a word.

He cleared his throat and said, "I should go now."

She pulled away from him, her eyes downcast, and stepped backward into the doorway.

"Charlotte." He reached out his hand for her.

She took his hand and gave it a squeeze before letting go. "Good night," she murmured, before quickly retreating into her bedroom.

The double doors closed with a soft click.

Chapter 6

"Gavin, I believe your lips were a little closer to her cheek," Doña Yvonne instructed. "Charlotte, tilt your head toward me. There you go. *Perfecto!* Now do not move."

Once again, Charlotte found herself posed half naked in Gavin's embrace. She had feared seeing him this morning after their passionate kiss on the balcony the night before, but there had been no reason to feel so. The endearing smile he gave her washed away any unease that lingered the moment their eyes met.

She was more relaxed this morning during the sitting. In fact, she enjoyed it more than she had yesterday. There was something special about being held in Gavin's arms and now they had this lovely secret between them. Their kiss last night and this painting. No one but Doña Yvonne knew of their scandalous pose, for the artist kept her studio off limits. Once the painting was complete no one could deny her the pleasure of sitting for it.

And no one knew about their kiss. His kiss had been quite the surprise. A quite wonderful surprise.

She had spent most of the evening on the arm of Pedro Bautista-Martín. He was handsome and charming, no doubt. She had found him to be amusing, had enjoyed his company, and had been grateful for his attention, since

Gavin had seemed to be happily partnered with the pretty
Señorita Hernandez. The feeling of jealousy at seeing the
Spanish woman's hands on Gavin's arm had made her
uncomfortable. Although she had posed for an intimate
painting with him, she had no claim upon Gavin Ellsworth
whatsoever. She had held up her head and taken the advice
Aunt Louisa had given her. She had tried to enjoy the
evening and found herself laughing at Pedro's silly jokes,
but still she had felt Gavin's eyes on her.

Later that night when he had knocked on the door to her
bedroom, she had been stunned, because the look on his
face caused her heart to somersault in her chest. He was
jealous that his friend had wanted to kiss her. The thought
thrilled her! Pedro had not tried to kiss her, nor would she
have allowed him to. Yet when Gavin took her in his arms,
she had no wish to deny him.

She had been craving his kiss since the moment she first
saw him, all tan and golden. And that kiss . . .

Oh, that kiss!

Her stomach did a little flip at the memory of the sensations the kiss had awakened within her. She had assumed
Gavin to be skilled in the art of kissing and she had not been
disappointed. No, not at all. She had never wanted their kiss
to end. But it had to end and she had been grateful for his
self-control, if not quite at the time, then definitely later.

Now, she leaned back into his embrace, enjoying the feel
of his bare and muscled arms holding her. The soft dawn
light spilled around them, bathing them in its pale glow. She
wished she could see Gavin's eyes, but her back was to him
and Doña Yvonne became agitated if her subjects moved
position.

They remained very still until she felt Gavin's hand,
which was resting upon her breast, gently squeeze her
through the thin silk. She held her breath while the tip of his
finger slid ever so slightly over the tip of her nipple. Sheer

pleasure washed over her. His breath was hot on her cheek and sent shivers of delight down her spine. She wished desperately that they were alone and he could touch her without the silk covering her skin.

Charlotte almost bolted off the marble bench at the outrageous thought. Only a few days in the south of Spain with her aunt, and she had lost all sense of decency! Good heavens! What had come over her?

"Spend the day with me," he whispered in her ear.

"Yes, of course," she murmured in return. At the moment he could ask her to do anything, anything, and she would agree to it.

"What are you two whispering about?" Doña Yvonne called out. "*¿Qué es el secreto?*"

"I was asking Charlotte to spend the day with me," Gavin explained, turning his head toward their hostess.

"Do not move!" she scolded him, and Gavin resumed his position with his lips on Charlotte's cheek. Then Doña Yvonne laughed. "And did the lovely Charlotte agree to go with you?"

Charlotte felt his lips and the heat of his breath as he responded, "Yes, she did."

"*Maravilloso!*" Doña Yvonne exclaimed with undisguised amusement. "Just a few more moments of the light and then you shall be free to go."

Only a few more moments! The morning had slipped by far too quickly for Charlotte.

Before she knew it she was dressed in a sweet gown of pale lemon muslin with a wide straw sun hat draped with matching yellow ribbons and on her way to the shore with Gavin. Because they had risen so much earlier than the others, they slipped away before anyone knew they were gone, although Charlotte left a note for Aunt Louisa. Even though her aunt had given her carte blanche to do as she wished, Charlotte did not wish to worry Aunt Louisa over her whereabouts.

One of the coachmen from the villa drove them in an open carriage down to the shore. The warm sun shone brilliantly above and only a few puffy clouds dotted the sky. The scent of the sea invigorated her. Charlotte felt decidedly wicked being with Gavin without a chaperone, something that never would have been sanctioned had she been home in England. Once they reached the shore, Gavin instructed the coachman to wait for them. The beach was empty except for a few fishermen here and there. After assisting her from the carriage, Gavin took her hand in his and together they walked along the sand. How odd that holding his hand now seemed a more intimate gesture than posing for the portrait!

"You are not at all what I expected," Gavin said to her, over the sound of the rolling waves and screeching seabirds.

"Whatever do you mean?"

"You are taking this all very calmly."

"This?"

"The painting and the posing. Most well-brought-up ladies such as yourself would be too mortified to pose in such a manner."

"Do you think less of me then?" she questioned.

He turned to look at her, his lustrous hazel eyes intense. "No, of course not."

"Then why would you say something like that?"

"Because you are more than I expected."

Charlotte remained quiet at that remark, not sure how she should take it.

"Why did you agree to pose for the portrait, Charlotte?"

"When Doña Yvonne asked to paint us, I had no idea it would be so . . . Grecian," she said for lack of a better word, "and then once I realized what she meant to do, it seemed rude to refuse."

Gavin chuckled. "So you are draped in nothing but silk with my hands on your body merely to be polite?"

Charlotte stopped walking and faced him. His blond hair glinted in the sun. "Why are you posing?"

"Because I was ready to accept any excuse to be near you."

He had agreed to sit for a portrait in order to spend time with her. She wanted to believe him, although he probably said such pretty words to every girl. Gavin was outrageous in the things he said to her. But she could not resist the thought that he really meant them. That this handsome, sweet, charming man truly wanted to be near her. She reached one lacy-gloved hand up to touch his cheek. Would she allow herself to believe, just this one time? Just for this summer. Just with him. That his words were true. That his kisses were true. It would be so terribly easy. . . .

She stood on tiptoe and placed a soft kiss on his cheek, near the dimple that so distracted her.

He smiled, revealing the said dimple on the side of his mouth. "What did I do to deserve such a sweet kiss?"

Suddenly feeling shy, she lowered her hand and turned, continuing to walk. He fell into pace quickly beside her, still holding her other hand in his.

"You always smell pretty, like flowers," he said.

"It's lily of the valley."

"I like it."

Charlotte smiled. They walked in comfortable silence, the waves crashing along the shore.

"Where do you go to school?" she asked.

"Nowhere at present." He cast her a sheepish glance. "I was just tossed out of Oxford last term."

"I see." She had suspected this about him from the start. "Dare I ask what you did to warrant such an action?"

"It was a little scheme that Pedro and I concocted. Foolish, but funny. I got caught and he did not. I shall spare you the grim details."

"What will you do now?"

He gave a slight shrug. "I suppose my father is trying his damnedest to find another university willing to take me on."

"Is it so difficult to just do as you ought?" she asked softly. "Wouldn't that be easier than having to hide in shame for the summer?"

"I'm not ashamed," he barked. "And I am not hiding."

For once, Charlotte bit her tongue, feeling his hand tense. "What I meant was, wouldn't it be less trouble to simply follow the rules and get on with it?"

"With my education, you mean?" Gavin's sardonic laughter echoed on the sea breeze. "What do I need an education for? I'll inherit my father's title and lands. I'll become the Earl of Breckinridge, marry well, produce an heir, retire to the country, and become old and fat. What difference does it make if I get an education or not? My future has been preordained."

She paused before responding. "If you don't wish to further your education for the sake of not playing the fool while you sit in the House of Lords someday, fine. But do you have any idea how many men would give all they have for the chance to attend university and never will?"

He remained silent but looked properly chagrined by her words.

"You should not squander such an opportunity, Gavin. It may not come again." Her aunt's sentiment to her the day before echoed in her mind.

"Point taken." He held up a hand in mock surrender and flashed his grin.

"My brother attends Cambridge," she added.

"Have you a brother?" He seemed intrigued.

"I have five brothers. One older and four younger."

"No sisters?"

"No, but I wish I had at least one."

"It must be great fun to be a part of a large family," Gavin said.

"Yes and no."

"No? All those men in the house must treat you like a princess!"

"Not exactly." Charlotte shook her head ruefully. "My older brother is away at school most of the time and my little brothers, well, let's just say they are very energetic. My mother and stepfather have their hands full with raising them."

"I always wished for a sibling."

"I did too. Then my mother remarried after my father died and before I knew it I had a stepbrother and four little half brothers!"

"Poor Charlotte," Gavin said softly, but not at all condescendingly. "You're lost in the shuffle of your new family, aren't you?"

She had never actually put that thought into words before, but she supposed there was a grain of truth in what he said. Since her marriage, Charlotte's mother had not had as much time for her, so consumed was she with raising her sons. Oh, Charlotte loved her younger brothers and helped her mother as much as she could. Still, it was difficult to share her mother when it had been just the two of them for so long. Over the years she told herself it did not matter, but inside she felt a bit of a castoff. Odd that someone like Gavin would pick up on something so insignificant.

He continued, "Still, I wanted a sibling. Brother or sister, it didn't matter. Just someone to take some of the attention and pressure off of me."

Charlotte said teasingly, "I would think you enjoyed getting all the attention."

"That depends on the kind of attention I'm getting."

"And just what would that be?" she glanced up at him.

He stopped walking this time. "Any attention that I get from you." He leaned down and kissed her cheek.

Flustered by his impetuous kiss, she smiled at him. He had the power to send her heart tripping. . . .

"We should head back to the carriage," he suggested. Giving her hand a light squeeze, he turned them around.

Just then a large wave washed ashore farther than they expected. With a startled shriek, Charlotte tried to run so as not to ruin her slippers, but in one swift movement, Gavin swept her up in his arms just as the water rushed in around them. She held on tightly to his shoulders, delighting in being so close to him. She rested her head on his chest as he trudged back through the wet sand carrying her effortlessly.

It was such a sweet and thoughtful gesture that she felt her barriers against him completely disappearing.

Their days fell into an easy pattern. Gavin and Charlotte spent their mornings posing for Doña Yvonne and their afternoons alone together exploring the countryside. Each evening they dined with all the guests at the villa, and everyone was aware that Gavin was openly courting Charlotte. Both Pedro Bautista-Martín and Isabella Hernandez withdrew their attentions, for it was obvious that Charlotte and Gavin only had eyes for each other.

Charlotte knew that it wouldn't last. That it was just for the summer. She knew that Gavin did not truly care for her and was aware that he would lose interest and grow bored with the novelty of her. She prepared herself for that eventuality. In the meantime she tried to figure out, to pinpoint exactly what it was about him that so intrigued her. That drew her to him. The answer never really presented itself. All she could do was let herself be swept up in the giddy feelings that washed over her whenever she was with him.

Chapter 7

"Voilà!"

Neither Gavin nor Charlotte moved. As the last of the morning light faded, they remained in their reclining posture on the marble bench, draped in pale silk.

"*El retrato está completo!*" Doña Yvonne exclaimed from the other side of the canvas. "It is finished!"

It had been nearly two weeks since they began this unusual little venture in Doña Yvonne's art studio. During that time it seemed that Charlotte and Gavin existed only for each other and their days revolved around their intimate sessions together. In the studio they were not Gavin or Charlotte. No. They were not themselves. He was a powerful Greek god and she was a splendid Greek goddess. They lived another life in that studio. There were no limits. They were bare to each other with only a bit of filmy fabric between them . . .

And now it was over. As was her time in Spain.

They still did not move.

"Oh, it is beautiful. Beautiful! *Perfecto.* But you cannot see it just yet. I will surprise you with it. Go and dress now, my dears."

Gavin slowly slid his hands from Charlotte's body, lingering as he did so. Just as reluctantly she moved from his embrace. *Is he sad too? Does he feel as bereft as I do?* As Doña Yvonne chattered away and busied herself with her paints, Charlotte dared a glance at Gavin's handsome face. His hazel eyes were full of longing and the blatant desire that flamed within their depths took her breath away. A burning blush crept up her cheeks and she suddenly stood, clutching the silk tightly against her chest.

When Charlotte returned from the dressing room, Gavin was waiting for her. As was their routine, they had their walk on the beach and a drive through the surrounding countryside. By the time they dined that evening, Charlotte could hardly believe her last day in Spain was over.

And she still had not told Gavin that she was leaving for Italy in the morning.

Aunt Louisa had received a letter from her friend in Italy who was ill and she wished to travel to her as quickly as possible, so they were cutting their stay in Spain a little short and moving on to Venice in the morning. Charlotte did not know if Gavin had heard the news from someone else or not, but she had not mentioned it to him. For some reason, she felt it would break the spell they were under if they spoke of the end of their time together in Spain. She had no expectations from him of what would become of them after.

Gavin took her in his arms and kissed her on the balcony outside her bedroom, as he had done every night since the first time he had kissed her and she had melted into him. Their kisses had grown more and more passionate each night, their hands venturing farther and farther beyond where they should. But as always he stopped before they became too carried away, even though she longed for more, ached for more.

"Good night, my beautiful Charlotte," he whispered in her ear. "I'll see you in the morning."

Yet tomorrow morning they would not meet at dawn in the studio as they had.

It was on the tip of her tongue to tell him then that she was leaving in the morning, but the words would not come out. "Good night," was all she could muster.

And then he disappeared down the spiral staircase.

Charlotte returned to her empty room, blinking back unshed tears and feeling as if someone had kicked her in the stomach. She sat on the edge of her bed, wrapped her arms across her waist, and tried to catch her breath. Finally she stood. With trembling fingers she removed her pretty gown and all its trappings and slipped into the coolness of her white lawn nightdress. She unpinned her long hair, letting it fall to her waist. She turned down the lights and climbed into the tall bed. Restless and anxious and filled with longing, she could not lie still.

Charlotte rose from her bed. She began to pace across the room, her bare feet silent upon the smooth tile. Back and forth she moved, back and forth across the floor. Finally she paused.

She stared at the balcony doors.

Before she could think, before she could change her mind, she slipped out the doors and fairly flew down the iron steps that led to Gavin's room. Her heart pounding an erratic rhythm, she tapped lightly on his door. Without waiting for a response she pulled the double doors open. Her eyes scanned the dimly lit room, focusing in on him.

He turned at the sound of her entrance and froze in place. He had just removed his shirt and stood in only his trousers. The sight of his bare chest made her shiver.

"Charlotte?"

Her mouth was too dry to speak. She closed the doors behind her and stepped toward him on unsteady legs, ignoring the incredible roaring in her ears. Her eyes moved to the large bed that dominated the room and back to Gavin.

He tossed his shirt to the floor and came to her. He gathered her in his arms and she breathed in the clean scent of him. It calmed her. As did being in his familiar embrace. She pressed her cheek into the heat of his bare chest, could hear the beating of his heart. Her arms wrapped around him and her hands caressed the smoothness of his back. He kissed the top of her head over and over, while his hands stroked her hair.

When she could breathe again, he cupped her face in his hands, making her look at him. Charlotte stared into his eyes and was lost.

He knew why she had come.

Without a word, his mouth came down over hers, hot and possessive and demanding. His tongue plundered her. She clung to him tightly and kissed him back as fiercely as she could. She wanted him. She wanted everything. And nothing else mattered at that moment but the two of them. She clung to him, to his soft lips, to his hot mouth.

Finally allowed the freedom to touch her where he wished, Gavin's hands raced over her body, caressing her through her nightdress. He slid his hands down her back, over her hips, then cupped her bottom and pressed her against him. With his fingers he hitched up the fabric of her nightgown, slowly sliding the material up her legs, leaving bare skin in its wake. When he had enough in his hands he pulled the rest of it up and over her head, as she obligingly raised her arms.

A rush of air escaped him in a low whistle. "I've pictured you like this a thousand times, Charlotte, and you are even more beautiful than I imagined."

Naked before him, without the cover of pale silk between them this time, he ran his warm hands over her skin, caressing her shoulders, her arms, her back. Shivers of delight washed over her. Leaning forward she kissed him, her mouth hungry for the taste of him. Effortlessly, he lifted her up and carried her, just like the day on the beach. She loved it when he did that. With a gentle touch he placed her on the bed and positioned himself beside her. He rested his head on his hand and gazed at her.

"You've done this before," she whispered in apprehension, knowing what his answer would be.

He gave a slight nod.

"With very many women?"

"That doesn't matter now."

"I've never done—"

"I know." He kissed the words from her lips and stroked her face in a soothing motion.

Charlotte leaned into him.

"Do you know what torture it was for me to hold you in my arms each morning in the studio and feel your body so close to mine, and yet not be able to do this?"

With the lightest, the faintest of touches, he traced a delicate path from her cheek, to her jaw, down her neck, caressing across her chest until he crested at the peak of one breast. Her eyes fluttered while he stared at her, his eyes heavy lidded with passion.

"Or this?"

He lowered his head and kissed her breast, his tongue teasing the nipple.

Her breathing now began to come in shallow pants and she shivered with pleasure at his intimate touch. It was rapturous, every bit of it.

"Or this?"

He continued to lavish honey-sweet kisses on her other breast.

As she lay naked on his bed, a moment of panic consumed her at the inevitability of what she was about to do. She closed her eyes and pulled him to her, wanting the weight, the solidity, of his body to cover hers. She heard the sound of his voice, soft murmurings of endearments, soothing words. He whispered her name as he kissed her face, her eyes, her cheeks, her throat. She was not afraid, for she wanted this, wanted him too much to truly be afraid. It was the unknown that had her so skittish.

Thoughts, everything and nothing at all, raced through her mind. She could not catch one long enough before another one replaced it. He smelled nice, like spicy soap. His skin was so warm and smooth. His blond hair was thick and silky. She loved the sound of his name. She may have even said it out loud. His touch felt wonderful. Time was suspended around them, for each second seemed to last an eternity. Every caress, every kiss was intensified between them. She could not get close enough and she writhed beneath him. He moved away, and feeling bereft, she pulled him back to her.

She wanted to melt into him, to become part of him. Her mouth sought his and they kissed, their lips searing each other. Tasting, licking, sucking. She splayed her fingers through his thick blond hair, losing herself in the feel of him. She arched her back, pressing against his body, which covered the length of hers. Taut muscle and heated skin, a long, hard penis . . . Her eyes flew open! Unaware of how he had shed the rest of his clothes, she suddenly realized he was as naked as she was. Heavens! She knew it would come to this, and she had four little brothers so she had an idea of what one looked like, but she was not at all prepared for the sight or feel of Gavin's! She gasped and wriggled against the male protrusion that rested intimately between her legs. He kissed her, calming her and enflaming her once again. His molten eyes bored into her and she could not look away, no longer wanted to keep her eyes closed from him.

"Charlotte?" he asked, his voice hoarse with desire. The muscles in his arms tightened.

She knew what he asked. "Yes," she breathed so low she wasn't sure if he heard her.

He kissed her mouth again, his eyes still on hers. He heard.

When he entered her, hard and swift, she cried out before she could stop herself. The pain and awkwardness subsided as he continued to move in a steady rhythm within her. She lay motionless at first, unable to do anything else but accept. But then, oh but then . . . Those sensations began to escalate anew. . . . She had no choice. She had to move then, move with him. The look in his eyes as she shifted her body with his excited her.

Their pace increased, their fervor for each other in a fever pitch. Awash in pleasure and blissful sensations and feelings that had no name, Charlotte thought she would faint. Or scream. Or both. Instead she held on to Gavin's strong shoulders as the only stable element in her spinning world as she was suddenly overcome with waves of the most intense pleasure she had ever known as he strained his body against hers.

Then he collapsed next to her, breathing as heavily as she was.

Exhausted and basking in the delicious lethargy that crept over her entire body, she curled up next to him. Gavin drew her into the circle of his arms and kissed her.

Charlotte closed her eyes then.

Chapter 8

Gavin squinted at the golden sunlight that poured through the tall windows of his bedroom. Glancing at the empty space next to him, he recalled images of the beautiful woman who had been there during the night. Unsure when Charlotte had left his bed, he lamented the fact that she was gone already. He knew she had to return to her own room, but still it would have been nice to kiss her good morning.

Bloody hell! He bolted upright and rubbed his eyes. What the hell had he been thinking? To bed a woman like Charlotte Wilton? There would be the devil to pay now. He knew the consequences of such an act and now he would have to face them.

Charlotte had taken him by surprise, coming to his room in her nightgown the way she had. She had thrilled him, knowing that she had wanted him just as much as he had wanted her. And Christ, but hadn't he been tortured more than a red-blooded male could bear during the portrait sittings the last two weeks? Who could blame him for succumbing to temptation when it came walking in his door, looking like a luscious goddess in the moonlight?

And it *had* been amazing with her. He had sensed that it would be from that first session in the art studio. She had not balked at removing her clothes or stiffened when he had held her so intimately in their required pose. He loved that about her. The naturalness of her desires and feelings. And she had been unabashed and unashamed in sharing them with him last night. Smiling at the memory, he stretched and recalled the taste of Charlotte's sweet lips.

After he had bathed and dressed, he left his room in search of her. The poor girl was probably frantic with worry over what they had done last night. He knew she would need reassurance that he didn't think any less of her. Hell, he thought more of her, if such a feat were possible! For hadn't he done nothing else but fantasize about making love to her night after night? No, the decent thing to do was to find her and tell her he would put everything to rights. He had taken her innocence and now he would have to marry her.

Or he could get out of it somehow. The idea danced around his head, a slight temptation.

He could leave Spain immediately. It wasn't likely he would see her again. He didn't *have* to marry her. But a girl like Charlotte . . . No. He couldn't do it. He liked her too much. Respected her even. She was witty and sensitive and intelligent. They got on well together. Gavin could not do something so low as to disappear on her by playing the cad.

He had been raised to be a gentleman and to behave accordingly.

She must be feeling a little ashamed and fearful about what to do next. He imagined she would be quite pleased with him and grateful for his offer. He was heir to an earldom after all, and as his wife, Charlotte would be a countess.

Marriage was not something he thought he would enter into for a few more years yet. He only had a year of university left, so they could plan a wedding for next summer. Perhaps his father would be pleased by Gavin's desire to settle down with a proper and lovely girl and forgo the pressure for him to finish school. And just what would his dear old father think of the news? Surely he couldn't disapprove of marriage?

"*Buenas tardes, mi amigo!*" Pedro Bautista-Martín called to him.

"Good afternoon to you too." Gavin smiled in return.

"You are up rather late today."

"The portrait is finished and I thought I would sleep in for a change. Have you seen Miss Wilton about?"

Pedro seemed surprised by his question. "I just said good-bye to her."

"Has she gone down to the beach?" Gavin asked, wondering why Charlotte had not waited for him. The beach would be a perfect spot to propose to her.

"No." Pedro shook his head, an odd expression on his face. "She went down to the port. She and her aunt are sailing to Italy."

Gavin felt as if all the air had been sucked out of his lungs. "What do you mean?"

"Miss Wilton and her aunt have left the villa. We all wished them bon voyage. My mother went to see them off."

Stunned, Gavin stared in amazement at his friend, his blood racing. *Charlotte left? Without a word to me? Why would she do such a thing?*

"Did you not know she was going?"

Gavin shook his head slowly. He had definitely not known. If he had known he would have stopped her. Or gone with her.

"I thought you two had grown rather close of late . . ."

He had thought so too. Quite close. Apparently, Charlotte thought something else entirely.

Moving on wooden legs, Gavin walked out to the veranda and stared at the Mediterranean Sea. She had gone. After giving herself to him last night she had disappeared without a word. She wanted nothing more to do with him. He had the oddest sensation that his heart had just been ripped from his chest.

Never in his life had he thought seriously about marrying before. Yet with Charlotte he had. He was on his way to ask her to be his wife. And she was gone. *She'd left him.* Fled the country! He did not even know where she was going. It suddenly dawned on him as well that he had no idea at all where she lived. He had no way to contact her.

Astounded by this bit of reality, he sat on a chair and stared at the sea glittering in the afternoon sunlight. She was out there . . . on a ship . . .

She'd left him.

His mind was not functioning properly. Surely he had misheard his friend and Charlotte had only gone out with her aunt for a while.

Pedro followed him onto the veranda and sat in the chair beside him. "You are in love with her?"

"What?" Gavin stiffened at the question. "Oh, no. No." He liked her immensely. She was beautiful and intelligent and caring. But in love with her? Definitely not. He was not in love with Charlotte. *Was he?*

"I would not have thought this of her." Pedro shook his head in disbelief. "That she would not have told you she was leaving. Was she angry with you over something?"

"Of course not." Unless she was angry about spending the night in his bed, but given how eager and willing she had been, he seriously doubted it. *She'd left him.* No woman had ever left *him* before.

"Women!" Pedro exclaimed. "Who can understand them? Forget about her, my good friend. There is still much to enjoy here and we have a few weeks to go before you return home."

He should take Pedro's advice and enjoy the rest of the summer. Gavin should feel nothing but relief! *She'd left him.* He was off the hook for marrying Charlotte. This development should make him happy. Once again he was a man free to enjoy the delights of pretty women. More than likely he would never set eyes on Charlotte Wilton again. Yet he felt nothing but great disappointment at that prospect. And devastated by her careless defection. He should try to forget her now and join Pedro for a good time, enjoying the rest of a carefree summer.

Yet he had no desire to do that. None at all.

Strangely enough, what he really wanted to do was put all this behind him. He wanted to do something different, something worthwhile. He wanted to start over. He wanted to return home and apologize to his father.

Chapter 9

Four Months Later
English Countryside

"Charlotte!" the young boy cried from his perch on the limb of the oak tree. "Charlotte! Watch me!"

Charlotte saw her younger brother and called out to him, "Addison Forsythe! Don't you dare jump off that branch! It's entirely too high. You'll get hurt!"

"Ah, don't be a stick in the mud, Charlotte! Let him jump!" Allen Forsythe piped up. "Let him jump!"

"Come on, Char!" Andrew Forsythe pleaded, his baby hands pressed together. "We want to see him go!"

She put her hands on her hips in exasperation and stared at her three brothers, their pugnacious little faces set in determination. Adam, her only younger brother who was not vexing her at the moment, ignored the lot of them. Sprawled on the blanket under the shade of the tree, Adam had his nose in a book. The oldest of the quartet of Forsythe brothers at eleven, Adam was studious and quiet and generally considered himself superior to his younger siblings.

"No. It's too dangerous," Charlotte exclaimed. She looked up at the one in the tree. The sunlight sprinkled through the autumn-tinted leaves and colored his brown hair with a red hue. "Climb down a few branches at least, Addison!"

"Well, that's no fun!" snorted Andrew, the youngest at five. His round freckled face filled with scorn at her proclamation.

"Let him jump, please!" Allen tugged on her arm.

"I promised Mother I would not let you run wild if I took you on this picnic. So I will not bring you home with a broken leg or worse, Addison," she called up to him.

"Oh, just jump already, Addison!" Adam called from his position on the blanket, not even glancing up from his book.

"You are not helping me at—Oh!" Before Charlotte could finish the words, her nine-year-old brother came crashing down on the ground beside her amid a flurry of gold and red leaves and broken twigs. "Addison! I told you not to do that!"

He could not hear her reprimands over the shouts of glee from the younger boys.

"That was brilliant!" Andrew cheered, exceedingly delighted with his brother's forbidden descent from the tree.

The wild whoops and hollers even made Adam look away from his beloved book.

Charlotte grabbed Addison's arm, helping him to his feet. "Are you hurt at all?" Her mother certainly would blame her if he were.

Addison, beaming with pride, brushed some dirt from the seat of his trousers. "Course not!"

"Then let's go back to the house," she ordered all of them. "It's getting late anyway and we want to be home before Alec gets there."

"Oh, yes! Let's hurry!" Andrew jumped up and down. "I want to see Alec!"

Charlotte knew that mentioning their eldest brother's imminent visit from university would elicit their compliance in heading back to the house. Her stepbrother's rare homecoming had left the younger boys excited, for they looked upon Alec as an all-powerful hero. And indeed, he was tall, handsome, athletic and excelled at everything he put his hand to. The product of her stepfather and his first wife, Alec was only a year older than Charlotte, with dark hair and deep brown eyes. They had always got on well together and she had been looking forward to his homecoming as well. She had not seen Alec herself since his Christmas holiday last year, because she had been away all summer.

Summer. She tried to block what happened then out of her mind. It was too painful to bring up those memories. And regrets. Aunt Louisa had been terribly wrong about that. Charlotte regretted many things she had done that summer. Regretted one thing in particular.

As much as she tried to forget, it haunted her daily. Gavin Ellsworth haunted her thoughts, her dreams, her every waking moment. The aching loneliness in her heart had not healed and she feared it never would.

"Oh, let's hurry, Charlotte!" cried Allen, dancing a little jig around her.

After they gathered their picnic items, Charlotte ordered the older three to carry the baskets and things and she grabbed Andrew's chubby hand firmly in hers. They set off across the field while the autumn sun sank low in the sky. As they rounded a hedge they spied a carriage coming up the drive.

"It's Alec!" Excited shrieks pierced the air and the boys broke into a run.

Charlotte held fast to Andrew's hand, although he tried desperately to break free. The carriage disappeared from view as it drove to the front of the house. The three older boys raced ahead. By the time Charlotte reached the back entrance, she was exhausted and felt as if her arm were pulled from the socket. She released her impatient charge and Andrew went careening down the hallway in a mad hurry to find his big brother.

Removing her hat, she sighed and followed after the sound of her brothers' wild cries. She always knew exactly where they were simply from the amount of noise they made, and today was no different. She knew her brothers were in the front hallway. As she neared, she could distinguish amid the noise her mother's sweet voice and Alec's laughter. Her pace increased as she turned the corner.

"Charlotte!" Alec cried when he saw her. He broke loose from his little brothers, raced to her side, swept her up in a bear hug, and swung her around. He finally set her down and took a look at her. "You haven't changed a bit, Char. You're as pretty as ever!"

Smiling broadly, she said, "You, on the other hand, look much older!"

"Did you send those little monkeys to attack me?" He laughed and pointed to Andrew, Adam, Addison, and Allen.

"Of course I did!" She gave him a wink.

"Let's not stand here in the hallway any longer," her mother, Elizabeth Forsythe, suggested. "Shall we go into the drawing room? We can't have our guest standing here all day. I fear we've kept you here too long as it is, Lord Langdon."

Charlotte glanced over at her mother and froze at the sight of her standing beside a handsome gentleman; tall, blond, and muscular. Her mind spun and she became slightly dizzy, clutching Alec's arm for support.

"I'm sorry"—Alec tugged her forward—"I should have introduced you."

Charlotte moved on leaden feet, her heart racing so rapidly in her chest, she thought it might very well explode.

With an easy manner and blithely unaware of his sister's reluctance, Alec introduced Charlotte to the man who had turned her life upside down. "This is Gavin Ellsworth, Lord

Langdon, a new friend of mine from Cambridge. Gavin, may I present my sister, Charlotte Wilton."

Charlotte stared into the depths of hazel eyes that were far too familiar. She recognized every fleck of gold and brown.

Gavin's brows raised and he looked at her with surprise, holding out his hand. "I am pleased to meet you, Miss Wilton."

She nodded, unable to form a coherent word, and took his hand in hers. The spark that shot through her veins when they touched almost knocked her to the ground.

"Alec, you neglected to mention that your sister was such a beauty."

She closed her eyes at the sound of his voice and he released her hand. She suddenly felt very cold.

Charlotte heard her brother laugh and say something about Gavin keeping his distance from his only sister. Her elegant mother then ushered them all from the hallway and obediently she followed her family into the drawing room and sank gratefully upon a damask chair. She was vaguely aware that little Andrew had climbed onto her lap. She heard the words that were being spoken, but she could not take anything in except that Gavin Ellsworth was there in her home. *He's here!* Somehow he had become friends with her brother.

And he had pretended not to know her.

He was as shocked as she was. She could see it in his eyes. But he acted as if they had just met for the first time. As if what had happened between them in Spain had never happened at all.

A lump formed in her throat. She did not partake of the tea and cakes and biscuits that were served, although Andrew ate more than enough for her and left the crumbs on her lap as evidence. She did not enter into the conversation among her mother, Alec, and Gavin, nor did she object to the shouts and interruptions from the boys, who were tumbling about on the floor. It took all her energy to keep from bursting into tears.

"Charlotte, are you feeling well?" Alec asked.

She blinked and looked up at the sound of her name.

"She does look rather pale," her mother said, her voice tinged with worry. "Perhaps she was out with the boys too long this afternoon."

"Addison scared her by jumping out of a tree!" Andrew tattled on his brother with no remorse, his mouth filled with shortbread biscuit.

Charlotte leapt at the excuse. "I . . . I do have a dreadful headache. Would you mind if I went to my room to rest for a bit?"

"Not at all, darling," said her mother.

"Excuse me," she whispered. She felt Gavin's eyes on her as she shooed Andrew from her lap and fled the drawing room as decorously as she could manage.

When she reached the safety of her pretty floral bedroom, she flung herself onto her four-poster bed and buried her sobs in the pillows. Wishing she were anywhere but in her home, she could no longer hold back the tears. Hot and stinging, the tears poured down her cheeks while great sobs wracked her body.

It was the first time she cried over Gavin Ellsworth.

Chapter 10

Gavin was stunned. When he had accepted Alec Forsythe's invitation to visit his home, he had never imagined that Charlotte Wilton was Alec Forsythe's stepsister! He was not sure if acting as if they were meeting for the first time was a wise decision or not, but he had been so astonished to see her it was all he could do. She had not rushed forward in recognition nor appeared especially happy to see him. Nothing less than shock had registered on her beautiful face. At the time, his behavior had seemed the best course of action.

He had not said another word to her, and she had grown eerily quiet. She had disappeared to her room claiming a headache, but Gavin's instinct told him he was the reason for her distress. She had remained in her room for supper as well. He idly wondered if she would hide for the duration of his visit. After the pain she had caused him he felt slightly mollified by her obvious discomfort at his presence in her home.

Gavin spent the night in a restless mood, unable to sleep.

He had found Charlotte Wilton and was in her house! After four months of wondering about her, dreaming about her, missing her, and cursing her, she had turned up on a whim. And she was even more beautiful than he remembered. She had looked so carefree when she first entered the hallway, before she had recognized him. She'd obviously just come in from outside, holding a straw hat in her hand and wearing a pink striped dress. Her blond hair was tousled and her cheeks were full of color. The genuine delight at seeing Alec had been clearly written in her expression.

Until her eyes met his. Then all the color had drained from her face.

Meanwhile all he had wanted to do when he saw her was shout for joy. He had believed he would never see her again, so when she appeared before him, so great was his happiness at finding her, it took every ounce of his self-control not to pick her up and spin her around as her brother had done.

The next morning Gavin breakfasted with the family. He was amused by the antics of the four younger Forsythe brothers and noted how much Charlotte and her mother, Elizabeth, looked alike, yet Charlotte was nowhere to be seen. He knew she was avoiding him and it irritated him. He spent most of the day with Alec and his father, the Baron of Glenborough, looking over their estate and learning about their management methods.

Later that day he was returning to his room to change for supper when he ran into Charlotte in the upstairs hallway.

They both stopped walking and stood in awkward silence. Neither of them made a move to pass by but held each other's gaze. Already dressed for supper and apparently willing to be seen by him again, she looked stunning in an elegant evening gown of deep blue edged with black lace, her blond hair swept back from her face. He recalled all too vividly the sight of her with her golden tresses spilling around her naked shoulders, looking like a goddess in pale silk.

Finally Gavin reached out and grabbed her arm, drawing her quickly into his guest room. She did not resist but she did not seem overly eager to go with him either. He closed the door once they were inside.

"Charlotte, this is ridiculous. We can't pretend not to know each other."

She said nothing, but he noticed that her breathing had become more labored and her eyes, the color of aquamarines, were wide with panic. She took a step back from him. He so desperately wanted to hold her in his arms, to kiss her.

"Charlotte," he said again.

"What are you doing here?" she whispered.

"I had no idea that Alec was your brother."

"You must leave." There was a note of pleading urgency in her voice.

"Why?" He stepped toward her and her familiar lily of the valley scent washed over him. The need to touch her became unbearable. "Why? Because you cannot run away from me here?"

She gasped as the truth of his comment hit its mark and her eyes flashed in anger. She made a move toward the door.

He prevented her from doing so by pulling her into his arms. And then he gave in to his desires and covered her enticing lips with his own. God, but she tasted like heaven! How he had missed her. He held her tightly against his chest, feeling her body next to his.

Melting against him, she kissed him back as his tongue delved deeper into her mouth. Her arms went around his neck and the soft sigh that escaped her sent his mind reeling. They moved back until he had her against the wall.

The thrill of kissing her once again excited him more than he could have anticipated. Judging from her eager response she had missed kissing him as much as he had missed her. And he *had* missed her. Not a single day had passed that he had not thought of her, not wanted her, not longed for her.

They continued to kiss and he wanted to devour her. She clung to him, her fingers splaying into the hair at the back of his neck. He wanted her desperately, wanted to strip her of her gown and lavish her naked body with his kisses. As his desire for her grew, he could sense her own heightened passion. Her tongue intertwined with his and her body arched against his. His hand moved to cup one luscious breast and she moaned at his touch.

"Charlotte," he murmured her name into her sweet mouth.

"Charlotte!" A young and quite impatient voice wailed from the hallway. "Chaaaaarrrlotte!"

They both froze at the sound. Her hands fell from his neck and she shoved at Gavin's chest. With great reluctance he released her and stepped aside.

"Charlotte!" the voice called.

"It's Andrew," she whispered frantically. "He's looking for me. What shall I do?" She covered her kiss-swollen lips with her fingers, her cheeks still flushed with desire. Tendrils of her blond hair had spilled from its arrangement atop her head and now framed her face softly.

Gavin wanted nothing more than to carry her to the large bed in the center of the room and make love to her for days.

"Charlotte!" Andrew continued to cry, his five-year-old voice filled with anguish. They heard his little footsteps stomping farther down the hallway. "They're being very mean to me! Chaaaaarrrrrlotte!"

Gavin grabbed her hand and squeezed it reassuringly. She stared up at him but he could not read her thoughts.

As Andrew's childish wails faded, Gavin carefully opened the door and peered down the hallway. He nodded at Charlotte and she scurried out of his room and fled down the hallway in search of her distraught brother. She did not look back at him, but Gavin watched her until she disappeared into the boys' nursery.

Chapter 11

"So what do you think of our estate, Lord Langdon?" Elizabeth Forsythe, her blond hair swept stylishly atop her head, asked her guest.

Charlotte kept her eyes on the delicate china plate in front of her, piled with roast partridge and squash, although she still could not swallow a single mouthful. She had not been able to eat anything since Gavin had arrived yesterday. Her stomach rebelled at the mere thought of food.

"Glenstone Manor is beautiful. I was quite impressed at how well you have been able to drain your fields," Gavin said. "The system you have employed would work well at our estate since we have similar problems with the hills above the fields. I would like to bring my father to visit to see what you have accomplished here."

Charlotte could not suppress a surprised glance at Gavin, who sat beside her at the elegantly set dining table. Since when had he taken an interest in his father's estate? Or in farming? This was a startling change from the indolent and carefree man she met this summer. And Lord Langdon? He never referred to that title while they were in Spain! She remembered him mentioning his father's earldom, but oddly enough she never thought to ask about his title and everyone at the villa had simply called him Señor Ellsworth.

He was still as handsome as ever, though. That had not changed. If anything he had become even more attractive. As he sat at the table in his formal evening attire, the jet black of his jacket and the crisp white of his shirt set in stark contrast to his golden blond hair and tanned skin.

Her heart skipped a beat at the memory of the passionate encounter they had shared in his bedroom not an hour ago. She touched her lips, which were still tingling from his kiss. Being in his arms again had brought to the surface long suppressed memories of their last night together in Spain and she found it difficult to breathe. She trembled to think what might have happened in his bedroom if they had not been interrupted by Andrew's shouts.

"Of course, you and your family are welcome to visit us anytime you wish. How are you getting on at school?" her stepfather, Alexander Forsythe, asked him.

"I'm finding Cambridge much more to my liking than Oxford, but it might be that my change in attitude has more to do with it than anything to do with the school," Gavin explained.

"Why is that?" asked Alec.

"You see, I had a bit of an epiphany while abroad this summer."

Charlotte dropped the fork she had been holding onto her plate. The clatter caused everyone to look at her.

"Excuse me," she murmured in apology, carefully placing her fork back on the table. Her pulse quickened as Gavin continued to speak.

"I realized that I was a very fortunate man, indeed, and I ought not to squander the opportunities I have in my life. Much to my father's delight, I have changed my wild ways and have focused on my studies and placed my energies into improving and modernizing my family's estate."

"That is very commendable," her stepfather commented. "Fathers do appreciate sons who take their inheritances as the serious responsibilities they are instead of spending every last pound on frivolous pursuits."

"You're very welcome, Father," Alec quipped dryly and gave a sly wink across the table to Charlotte.

"Where did you spend the summer, Lord Langdon?" Elizabeth asked with polite interest.

"I spent a great deal of it in Spain."

Elizabeth cried in wonderment, "Why Charlotte was in Spain this summer too!"

The sound of Charlotte's crystal water goblet shattering against the gleaming mahogany table startled everyone, Charlotte most of all.

"Whatever is the matter with you, Charlotte?" scolded her mother, before Roberts, the butler, hurried to clean up the watery mess and glass shards. "That was my grandmother's crystal!"

"I . . . I am terribly . . . I am so sorry," she stammered awkwardly. "I don't know what happened."

"Please be more careful, dear," her stepfather said gently with a pointed look in her direction.

"So what did you think of Spain?" Alec asked Gavin.

Charlotte silently blessed her brother for drawing the attention away from her.

"It was quite beautiful," Gavin began. "I met some very interesting people. In fact, I fell in love while I was there."

Charlotte held her breath. The room began to tilt a little. She held tightly to the edge of the table in order to stay upright in her chair. *Will this supper never end?*

"With a Spanish lady?" Elizabeth asked, intrigued by his story.

Gavin smiled, showing the dimple that so enchanted Charlotte. He said, "No, she happened to be English, surprisingly enough. And astonishingly beautiful."

"How romantic!" Elizabeth cried in delight. "Imagine

going all the way to Spain and falling in love with someone you could have met here at home!"

Charlotte quickly picked up her fork again and stabbed a bit of squash. She shoved it into her mouth to keep from screaming.

"Just a moment." Alec looked confused. "This is not the same woman you just became engaged to, is it?"

Unable to swallow, Charlotte choked on the bite of squash she had just placed in her mouth. Covering her lips with her linen napkin, she began to cough hysterically. *Engaged? Gavin is engaged? He is getting married?* Her coughing increased, growing louder and more violent. She could not stop.

Concerned for her daughter, Elizabeth cried, "Oh my goodness, Charlotte!"

Gavin, who was seated beside her, sprang from his chair and began patting her back. Charlotte continued to fight the terrible coughing spasm and the entire meal came to an abrupt standstill.

"Give her some water!" Alec exclaimed from the other side of the table.

As the coughing fit began to subside somewhat, Charlotte gratefully sipped the water from the crystal goblet that Gavin held to her lips. She gasped and sputtered, her eyes tearing.

"Are you all right, Charlotte?" Gavin asked, his hand still on her back. With one knee on the floor beside her chair, he stroked her with infinite tenderness, his hand moving up and down her back in a soothing motion.

She nodded as the need to cough continued to weaken.

Gavin urged, "Take another sip."

She obeyed his command and drank from the glass he still held for her.

"Better now?"

"Yes, thank you," she finally managed to utter, with another nod of her head.

"Take a deep breath."

She inhaled with a shaky breath and the action seemed to calm her aching throat.

He still rubbed her back, his hand touching her possessively. "Are you sure you are all right now?" he asked, his voice soft and full of tenderness.

She sniffled a little, feeling foolish for her ridiculous display. His hazel eyes were intent on her. "I'm fine now, Gavin. Thank you."

He set down the goblet and touched his hand to her cheek, gently brushing a tendril of hair from her eyes. "You must take more care, Charlotte. You gave me a terrible fright."

She closed her eyes and leaned into his hand. How had he the ability to both calm and excite her with the merest touch?

"Ahem." Alexander Forsythe cleared his throat with a pointed significance.

Charlotte looked up then and her eyes grew wide. Their mouths agape, her parents and her brother were staring at her in amazement. And at Gavin. Who was kneeling on the floor beside her chair and touching her rather intimately. For a moment it had seemed that there were only the two of them in their own little world. She now cringed at the sight of her family.

Slowly and with great care, Gavin removed his hands from her. Without a word he rose to his feet and sat back in his chair. He picked up his linen napkin and placed it in his lap.

An awkward silence fell over the table.

Mortified not only by her own behavior, but by the fact that her family had witnessed the affectionate exchange between her and Gavin, Charlotte avoided the peculiar looks her mother was sending in her direction. She could not face her stepfather or Alec either. She kept her eyes on the dish of barely touched food in front of her. The evening was interminable.

"Now that Charlotte has recovered, shall we finish our meal?" her stepfather suggested, breaking the tense silence.

They resumed eating, although Charlotte could not take a single bite and allowed the butler to remove her plate.

After a sharp look at her daughter, Elizabeth turned her eyes to Gavin. "I believe you were telling us of your engagement, Lord Langdon?"

Charlotte wished with all her might that her mother would close her mouth and cease her infernal questions to Gavin.

"I am not officially engaged yet," Gavin explained, his lips forming a tight line. "I merely agreed to marry the woman my father thinks would be a good match. Her family's estate is adjacent to ours and we could merge the two properties."

"Again, very commendable," Alexander Forsythe declared. "You have a good head on your shoulders, young Langdon."

Charlotte could not believe her stepfather was speaking of Gavin. At least not the Gavin she knew in Spain. She doubted her stepfather would applaud Gavin so heartily if he knew of his affair with Charlotte!

"Yes, but what of the English woman you fell in love with in Spain?" Elizabeth questioned, her eyes moving sharply between Charlotte and Gavin.

A sudden wave of nausea swept over Charlotte. She wondered if she looked as green as she felt.

Gavin paused before answering. "It's quite an unfortunate story, you see. The woman broke my heart. She left the country without saying good-bye. I have not seen her since."

"Oh, how tragic!" Elizabeth said in a clipped tone. "But you're not going to marry the other girl, are you?"

Charlotte definitely wanted to crawl under the table.

"My father would like for me to," Gavin stated simply.

"Do you see how well the boy obeys his father, Alec?" Alexander's teasing voice lightened the mood.

"Really, Gavin, you must stop showing me up in front of my father!" Alec said with a laugh. "Soon he will be choosing a bride for me!"

"Where did you say you were staying in Spain this summer, Lord Langdon?" Elizabeth asked.

"In the south of Spain, near a town called Málaga."

"Charlotte," Elizabeth eyed her daughter with avid interest, "isn't that where you stayed with Aunt Louisa?"

"Yes," she squeaked.

"How funny that you were both in the same place at the same time!" Elizabeth again looked pointedly between her daughter and her son's friend.

"Yes, it's a very small world," Gavin said with charming ease, flashing a smile that revealed his distracting dimple.

"Let's adjourn to the study for some brandy, shall we?" Alexander stood, signaling the end of the interminable meal.

Charlotte would have held a parade in her stepfather's honor so thrilled was she to be released from the table.

"Yes, why don't you gentlemen enjoy your cigars?" Elizabeth stated. "We shall join you later."

Gavin did not glance in Charlotte's direction as he left the room silently with her stepfather and brother. The minute they were gone, Charlotte rose from her chair.

"Sit down, Charlotte," Elizabeth commanded softly.

Slowly she sank back into her seat. The silence between them was palpable.

Her mother folded her elegant hands on the table in front of her. "Is there something you need to tell me?"

Charlotte swallowed. "No."

Elizabeth paused for a moment and tilted her blond head to the side. "I have eyes, you know. You have acted strangely since the moment that young man entered the house. And your behavior this evening—"

"Mother, I'm sorry for how I've acted during supper. It's just that . . ." Charlotte could not bring herself to finish.

Elizabeth waited patiently for her daughter to continue. When it was clear Charlotte would not, her mother said, "It is fairly obvious that you and Lord Langdon already know each other. Did something happen between the two of you in Spain?"

"I would rather not discuss it at present."

A rather long silence ensued as her mother pondered her options. Charlotte wished herself anywhere but where she was.

"Very well." Elizabeth sighed in resignation, clearly irritated. "But we will discuss it at some point, I promise you that."

"Yes, Mother." Charlotte left the dining room on unsteady legs and somehow made her way slowly up the stairs.

Her mother *knew*. Trepidation filled her heart. She would be forced to disclose everything. Yet would that be so terrible? To finally bare her soul? She had never told anyone what had happened between her and Gavin. Not even Aunt Louisa, although her aunt suspected something. Charlotte had fled Spain and buried all her tumultuous and intense feelings for Gavin that day for she did not know what else to do with them.

Now those feelings seemed determined to overwhelm her, to bury her.

On the verge of tears once again, she entered her pretty bedroom and closed the door behind her in relief. Then she almost jumped out of her skin.

"Gavin!"

"I didn't mean to startle you so," he apologized hurriedly.

"I just wanted to see you. Talk to you." He stepped toward her and drew her into his arms. "Are you all right?"

Unable to resist, she instinctively curled her body into his. The warmth of him soothed her agitated state of mind and she breathed deeply of his familiar scent. He was being too nice to her and she did not deserve it. Not after what she'd done. Hot tears ran down her cheeks.

"What are you doing here?" she cried.

"I don't know," he whispered into her hair. "Charlotte, Charlotte, don't cry."

"You must leave." If he left her house right away, she could pick up the pieces of her life and move on. No one would know and she could bury those feelings again. She could forget he had returned. She could forget she wanted him so much. Couldn't she? Had she ever truly forgotten him? "If you don't leave, everyone is going to find out."

He asked softly, "About us?"

She shoved away from him, angrily wiping the tears from her cheeks. "Don't you have a fiancée to go back to?" Her voice was sharper than she intended it to be.

"Don't make this my fault," he ground out.

"Everything was fine until you came here!"

"Was it?" he challenged her. "Was running away from me the right thing to do?"

"I didn't run away from you." Her voice was weak and her protest sounded feeble even to her own ears.

"Didn't you?"

"I don't even know who you are anymore!" she burst out. "Lord Langdon? Who is that? Who is this responsible person who attends Cambridge and does everything his father wishes? Were you simply lying to me the entire time?"

His jaw tightened. "Is that what you think? That I lied to you?"

She glared at him.

"Charlotte?"

"If you won't leave my house, at least have the decency to leave my room." Her hand trembled as she reached for the door.

"I will leave you then." Gavin gave her a cold look before he walked from the room.

Chapter 12

The next afternoon Charlotte sat curled up on a divan in the sunroom, attempting to lose herself in *Wuthering Heights,* which, as one of her favorite novels, usually captured her attention. But she had read the same page at least twenty times and had not moved on. Her mind was a million miles away.

All she could think of was Gavin Ellsworth.

She had barely slept all night, tossing and turning. And crying. Gavin had kissed her and seemed quite sincere in his concern during her choking fit at the table. He had acted hurt that she had left him in Spain and genuinely wished to discuss what happened. Had he truly cared for her? Was he not the rogue she had thought he was? This thought tortured her. As a consequence of her fitful and anguished night, she had slept through breakfast and by the time she had dressed and ventured downstairs, she had learned that Gavin and Alec had already gone out for the day but would be returning for supper. So he had not left to go back to school yet. Relieved she did not have to face him for a while longer, she had hidden in the sunroom, but not before her mother had reminded her that they needed to have a little talk later. Charlotte closed her eyes tight at the prospect.

"There's a package for you, Miss Charlotte," Roberts, the butler, announced as he entered the sunroom. "It just arrived."

"There is?" she said in surprise. "Where is it?"

"Your mother had it carried into the study. It's a rather large box. She asks that you join her while one of the footmen opens it for you."

A large box had arrived for her? How odd! "Thank you, Roberts."

By the time she reached the study, Elizabeth had already instructed the young footman to pry the wooden planks of the crate apart. The inside of the box was packed with padding.

"My goodness, Charlotte!" her mother exclaimed. "Whoever would send you such a large package?"

"I have no idea," Charlotte responded, equally intrigued.

"There was a letter with it addressed to you." Her mother gave Charlotte an envelope addressed with an unfamiliar hand.

Curious, she broke the seal and removed the letter within. In an instant her heart began racing as she read the sprawling script with a mounting sense of dread. Charlotte now knew exactly what was in that large crate. And there was nothing she could do at this point to prevent her mother from seeing it.

"Mother . . . There's something I need to explain to you," she began hesitantly.

Elizabeth was already standing over the crate as the burly footman lifted the enormously framed portrait from within and placed it on the floor, propped against the wall near the mantel.

Elizabeth's shocked gasp echoed Charlotte's own.

Without needing to be told, the footman discreetly left the room, closing the door behind him.

"Good God in heaven . . ." her mother whispered, placing her hand over her heart.

Speechless, Charlotte stood in awe at the portrait that

Doña Yvonne Bautista-Martín had painted of her while she was in Spain.

It was the most beautiful painting she had ever seen.

The pastel colors illuminating the dawn light bathed the scene in an ethereal glow, setting the figures of the goddess and god depicted within to be almost otherworldly in their perfection. Every detail was exquisite. The carefully draped silk seemed to flow like liquid silver over their almost naked bodies, clinging to every curve of their bare skin. Her blond hair glistened in golden waves around them. And the pose! The intimate positioning of their glorious bodies made it difficult to tell where the female form ended and the male began, so close were their arms and legs intertwined.

Charlotte barely recognized herself as the woman in the painting, so lovely was the rendering. How blissful and radiant the expression on her face! Had she truly looked that euphoric? And Gavin! How had Doña Yvonne managed to capture the absolute essence of his masculine features, his perfect aquiline nose and strong chin? His tawny blond hair glowed on his head. There was an amorous gleam in his hazel eyes and a hint of his devilish dimple at the corner of his sensuous mouth, which was pressed seductively against her alabaster cheek. The taut, sculpted muscles in his upper arms held her with such assured possession and his hand gently cupped the underside of her breast. The very strength and handsomeness of him came alive and leapt from the canvas.

But it was the two of them together . . . This was a man and woman passionately in love with each other portrayed with elegance, grace, and mystic splendor.

For days Charlotte had posed for that painting but never had she seen what she and Gavin looked like together from this point of view. Had it been so obvious to everyone else? Never had she suspected . . .

The effect was astonishing. She remained motionless and speechless before the painting. The portrait so astounded her that she forgot to feel embarrassed by the romantic nature of it. Charlotte was the woman in the painting and Doña Yvonne had managed to capture her true essence. When Charlotte had been that woman, it was the happiest she had ever been. It suddenly dawned on her that the woman in the painting was the real Charlotte.

"Good God in heaven, Charlotte!" her mother echoed once again. "What on earth did you do in Spain?"

"I posed for a painting . . ." she offered weakly.

"Yes, I see that! But this?" Elizabeth cried, scandalized. She gestured angrily to the painting. "This is indecent, Charlotte!"

Charlotte turned to face her mother. "You are only saying that because I am in the painting."

The painting was beautiful. That point could not be disputed. It was a true work of art. Anyone with eyes would have to agree.

"Yes! My daughter is undressed with an equally unclothed man!" Elizabeth looked distraught enough to faint. "And that young man is now a guest in my house! Lord Langdon! What is the meaning of this? What if your brothers see this?"

The thought of Adam, Addison, Allen, or Andrew seeing this painting made her very uneasy. She wasn't comfortable having her mother see it right now, let alone her stepfather or Alec. But it was simply because it was *her*. Her emotions and her body were on display for all to observe, yet the portrait was not in bad taste or offensive in any way. If it had been a pair of strangers in the scene instead of her and Gavin, she would still find it artistically appealing. Elizabeth would most likely hang it in the gallery. Or in the main parlor. But it was probably not the best time to bring up that point to her mother right now.

"What possessed you to do such a thing, Charlotte? And

where was Louisa while this scandalous picture was painted? How could she have allowed something like this to happen?"

"Aunt Louisa did not know that Doña Yvonne was painting us in that way, so please do not blame her." Charlotte defended her aunt instinctively.

"It was her responsibility to know about it! You were under her care!" Elizabeth exclaimed, righteous anger shaking her voice. "I knew we never should have let you go with her!"

"*Let* me go?" Charlotte burst out. "You sent me away!"

Her mother came up short and looked at her oddly. "Is that what you think, Charlotte?" Her face softened, as well as her tone. "That I sent you away?"

"Yes." She blinked back the tears that suddenly threatened.

"I thought that you wished to go," Elizabeth said in confusion. "That you were tired of another unsuccessful Season and wanted a change of scenery, a bit of a break from the business of finding a husband."

"I did . . . I just thought . . . you were weary of me and too busy with the boys . . ." Charlotte's voice trailed off.

Her mother put her arms around Charlotte's shoulders. Together they sat on the leather sofa. "Oh, Charlotte. I *am* very busy with the boys and I am *quite* weary with your stubbornness at not choosing a husband from an array of suitable gentlemen, but I would never send you away from home because of that. I am sorry if I ever made you feel that you were not wanted. I love you, darling."

"I love you, too, Mother."

Elizabeth glanced at the painting. "But what are we going to do about that?" She shook her head. "Alexander is going to be fit to be tied when he sees it. I don't know what he will do to Lord Langdon."

Charlotte cringed. She had not considered that prospect.

Her mother gave her hand a squeeze. "Did you really pose for this? She didn't simply paint your face on someone else's body?"

"No, it's all me," she admitted. "I posed every day for over two weeks." And they were the happiest two weeks of her life.

"With Lord Langdon as well?"

"Yes."

Elizabeth shook her head. "I never would have expected behavior like this from you. You've always been so steady and responsible and this painting is so out of character for you. Wasn't posing like that"—her mother actually blushed—"rather . . . awkward?"

"That was the most remarkable part," Charlotte explained as she recalled those early morning sessions in the studio, being held securely in Gavin's arms. "It was not the least bit awkward posing with Gavin."

"Is that when you fell in love with each other?"

Charlotte remained quiet.

"It was obvious to everyone at the table last night that something happened between the two of you," Elizabeth said gently. "You're in love with him."

"I don't think I admitted it to myself at the time, because I was too afraid, but yes, I fell in love with him."

"I never suspected something like this happened to you in Spain," Elizabeth said in disbelief. "You never said a word about it. Why didn't you tell me?"

"You never asked me what I did in Spain, Mother," Charlotte stated quietly, "or anywhere else I went this summer."

Elizabeth looked crestfallen. "Didn't I?"

"Not once." Charlotte shook her head.

"Oh, Charlotte, I am sorry. I just don't know what to say. The boys occupy so much of my day, but that is no excuse for ignoring my daughter." Elizabeth looked contrite. "Can you ever forgive my thoughtlessness?"

"Yes." Charlotte squeezed her mother's hand.

They sat in silence, staring at the portrait together.

"What shall I do?" Charlotte finally murmured. "I didn't

think I would ever see him again and then he happens to befriend Alec, of all the people in the world! And here he is at our home."

"Have you spoken to him about any of this?"

"I've only asked him to leave."

"Do you want him to leave?"

"No." The truth was she wanted to be with him always.

"You tend to push people away, Charlotte, if you haven't noticed. You had better think long and hard about what you want. I like this young man and have an idea you will be very happy with him, if that portrait is any indication of your feelings for each other." She looked toward the painting again and shook her head in wonder. "It's amazing. I've never seen you look so full of joy, Charlotte."

"I was." At the time she had attributed her happiness to the seductive atmosphere of Don Francisco's villa and the carefree environment of Doña Yvonne's art studio, but now she realized it was simply being with Gavin that had made her feel so alive and joyful. She recalled what her Aunt Louisa had said to her in Spain about not wasting opportunities for happiness. She did not wish to follow in her aunt's footsteps.

Elizabeth continued, "If you love him, I suggest that you let him know it. Men have their pride, after all. You have already left him once and he has another woman willing to marry him. He won't wait for you forever." Her mother gave her a hug of reassurance. "Perhaps you should talk to him about the—"

"I believe the ledger we need is in this desk."

Elizabeth was interrupted by the arrival of Alec Forsythe and Gavin Ellsworth. Both young men entered the study clearly under the impression the room was unoccupied. They both stopped abruptly when they saw Elizabeth and Charlotte on the sofa.

"Oh, excuse us—"Alec saw the painting first and his mouth dropped open.

Charlotte kept her eyes on Gavin, her pulse quickening at the sight of him. He truly was too handsome for words.

"What in blazes is *that?*" Alec cried.

Gavin was as riveted by the painting as she had been. A look of wonder lit his face. He glanced at Charlotte with appreciation, and without words they both understood that the painting was incredibly special. She gave him a tentative smile.

"In the picture . . . It is Gavin and . . . good God!"—Alec turned with eyes bulging toward his sister—"Charlotte?"

Elizabeth rose from the sofa and went to Alec. "Yes. It was painted while they were both in Spain this summer. Isn't that remarkable?" She took his arm and led him toward the door. "Come with me, dear. We're going to give these two a bit of privacy." Elizabeth gave a quick smile of encouragement to her daughter before exiting.

Now that she was alone with Gavin, Charlotte's mouth went dry at what she was about to do.

Chapter 13

As the door to the study closed, Gavin remained still. Judging from the hasty retreat of Charlotte's mother and in light of the arrival of the painting, he surmised that their ruse of not knowing each other had come to an end. The stunning portrait that leaned against the wall quite clearly indicated in no uncertain terms that he and Charlotte knew each other on an intimate level.

Doña Yvonne had outdone herself. That creative, vivacious woman possessed an amazing talent. The painting was beautiful. There was an incandescent quality to the colors giving their human forms a touch of the divine. Charlotte was mesmerizing in her beauty, and even he had to admit that he looked more handsome than he imagined himself to be. It was quite flattering. But it was the deep emotions portrayed within that astounded him. These two people were undeniably in love with each other.

"It just arrived today."

Charlotte's soft voice broke his concentration on the portrait. She had risen from the sofa to stand beside him.

"Was your mother horrified by it?" he questioned.

"Yes, at first she was terribly upset to see me posed in such a way. But I think now she sees that it is simply an incredible work of art."

Gavin nodded in agreement. "I had no idea it would turn out so fine."

"Neither did I."

"Honestly, I never thought I would ever see it." He tore his gaze from the framed portrait once again and focused on Charlotte. His heart skipped a beat. Her natural beauty was more than any artist could capture. "I am happy she sent it to you."

"The letter she sent said she hated to part with it, but she thought I should have the portrait. She also said she hoped that you found me." She paused a moment and there was a catch in her voice when she asked, "Were you looking for me?"

"Yes," he admitted. "When you left me that day in Spain, I realized I did not know how to reach you. I asked Doña Yvonne if she knew where your home in England was, but she only knew where your aunt lived. I wrote to your aunt, requesting your address, but I never heard from her."

"You wrote to Aunt Louisa about me?"

"Yes, a few times."

"Aunt Louisa has been away. She married while we were in Italy and has been traveling with her husband—"

"She married?" he echoed in amazement.

"Oh, yes, it was quite romantic." Charlotte's blue eyes sparkled. "She married the man she was in love with her entire life. But she has not been home in London at all. She more than likely has not received your letters."

"Well, that explains not getting an answer from her," he said ruefully. A thought perplexed him. "But then how did Doña Yvonne know where to send the painting to you?"

Her elegant brows drew together. "Perhaps Aunt Louisa gave Doña Yvonne my address when she visited Spain on her way to Egypt with Carlos."

After a thoughtful moment, she asked, "Why were you trying to find me?"

"Do you really have to ask why? I should be asking you

why. Why you left without saying good-bye, Charlotte. Without even a word to me. After that night we—" He broke off, unable to speak.

She whispered hurriedly in explanation, "I didn't think that you would care if I left, that it would—"

"What?!" he boomed. The girl was batty. "Why would you think I wouldn't care that you left?"

Her chin went up. "I know how you are. You've done *that* with other women and I thought it would be best if I just went on my way—"

"For your information, I have never done *that* with a woman like you before, and I wanted to marry you," he ground out between clenched teeth.

The color drained from Charlotte's face and she stumbled back to the sofa, sank into the cushions as if her legs would no longer support her. "I had no idea."

He moved to sit beside her. He took her warm hand in his as she spoke.

"When I woke up the next morning I was afraid. I couldn't face you after . . . after what we did that night and I didn't know how to tell you that my aunt and I were leaving. I didn't want you to feel bound to me or obligated to marry. I just had to get away . . ." Her voice faded.

"What had I done to make you flee from me?"

"I thought . . . I thought you were a rogue."

"I was." He flashed her a grin.

"I felt that I was merely a summer diversion for you."

He took in the meaning of her words. He asked softly, "And what was I to you then, Charlotte?"

There was some hesitation before she responded. "I think what I feared most of all were my feelings for you."

"Why?" He waited for her to continue, holding his breath.

"I had never done any of the things I'd done with you in Spain before. Posing for the painting, kissing you, being with you . . ." Soft color suffused her cheeks now. "I'd never felt that way about anyone before, the way I felt about you."

"And how did you feel?"

"Happier than I'd ever been in my life."

He grinned. "That's how I felt being with you."

Her blue eyes clouded with doubt. "But, Gavin, I didn't think you truly cared. You are not serious about anything and I—"

"I was serious about you." Gavin squeezed her hand.

"I wish I had known that," she murmured.

"You never gave me a chance to tell you that, did you?"

"I suppose not."

"Meeting you changed everything for me, Charlotte. Losing you just about destroyed me. Do you have any idea how thrilled I was to find you here? I had no idea that Alec was your stepbrother when he and I became friends. I did not know your stepfamily's name was Forsythe. What are the chances of me discovering you this way?"

"It is remarkable."

"It is more than that, Charlotte. It's fate."

She raised her eyebrows.

He pressed on. "And the painting of us arriving while I was here? More fate."

"What does it mean?" she ventured.

He leaned in close to her, his lips brushing the silky softness of her cheek. The scent of lily of the valley wafted over him. "It means that you cannot run away from me this time, because we were meant to be together."

She pulled back, her eyes searching his. "I wish I hadn't run from you, Gavin. I regretted leaving you the moment I was on that ship bound for Italy. I was such a fool. It was too late then and I didn't know how to get back to you. I tried to forget you. I really tried. I thought that if I didn't speak of you to anyone or tell anyone what happened you would cease to exist. All I succeeded in doing was making myself more miserable each day with longing for you, because I thought of nothing but you all these months. I missed you more than you can imagine." She finally paused for a breath before she confessed, "Gavin, I won't run away from you this time."

As he lost himself in the blue depths of her eyes, his heart turned over in his chest. Unable to resist any longer, he lowered his head to hers and kissed her sweet lips. She responded with undisguised ardor. It was heaven to feel her this way again. Their arms found their way around each other and he held her tight.

He had finally found Charlotte and he was never going to let her go.

"You couldn't run away now, even if you wanted to," he whispered in her ear.

"Why is that?"

"Because I am not going to let you. In light of our little scene at the table last night, your stepfather and I had a bit of a chat this afternoon. I asked his permission to marry you."

She blinked at him. "You did?"

"Yes." He kissed her again. He would never tire of kissing her. "Yes, and it's a good thing I did it before he sees that painting." He imagined Alexander Forsythe being none too pleased over Gavin's intimate relationship with Charlotte. It was bad enough to have her parents suspect the worst. It was something else to have blatant proof of how far their love affair had progressed.

"What did he say?"

"He consented to the match as long as it is your desire to marry me. Then he wished me luck, informing me that you had turned down numerous offers of marriage in the past."

Charlotte laughed ruefully. "My reputation precedes me."

"It's no laughing matter. You may have refused the others, but not me. I'm not going to lose you again, Charlotte, in spite of your trying to get rid of me."

"But you are already engaged to the woman your father approves of."

Enjoying the touch of jealousy he detected in her words, he shook his head in reassurance. "That was never official. In truth, I did not wish to marry her. I was merely at a loss to find you and thought I would please my father. I haven't even seen the woman since we were young children."

"Oh," she breathed, and he noted the relief in her expression as she grinned. "So, are you going to ask me?"

Thrilled, he moved to the floor and knelt on one knee, taking her warm hand in his.

"Gavin!" A smile of delight lit her beautiful features.

His heart thudded loudly, but he had never been more sure of something he wanted before in his life. And he wanted this beautiful woman with him. Forever. "Charlotte Wilton, will you do me the great honor of becoming my wife?"

"Yes, I will marry you," she whispered, squeezing his hand, "because I love you."

Gavin moved back to sit beside her and drew her into his embrace. "I love you, Charlotte." He held her close to his heart for some minutes. He could not believe his good fortune at finding her again.

"Let's hang the painting in our bedroom," she murmured.

He laughed low in his throat. Most women would immediately be thinking of wedding plans, but Charlotte was decorating their bedroom. *Their bedroom.* His heart began to pound again. "Yes, that is exactly where that portrait belongs and that is exactly where we shall hang it. After we return from our honeymoon trip."

"Our honeymoon . . ." she said in a soft whisper. "Spain?"

"Where else would we go?"

Charlotte gave him a seductive little smile. "Maybe Doña Yvonne could do another portrait of us?"

"What a brilliant idea. . . ." Gavin kissed her.

Books by Bestselling Author
Fern Michaels

___	The Jury	0-8217-7878-1	$6.99US/$9.99CAN
___	Sweet Revenge	0-8217-7879-X	$6.99US/$9.99CAN
___	Lethal Justice	0-8217-7880-3	$6.99US/$9.99CAN
___	Free Fall	0-8217-7881-1	$6.99US/$9.99CAN
___	Fool Me Once	0-8217-8071-9	$7.99US/$10.99CAN
___	Vegas Rich	0-8217-8112-X	$7.99US/$10.99CAN
___	Hide and Seek	1-4201-0184-6	$6.99US/$9.99CAN
___	Hokus Pokus	1-4201-0185-4	$6.99US/$9.99CAN
___	Fast Track	1-4201-0186-2	$6.99US/$9.99CAN
___	Collateral Damage	1-4201-0187-0	$6.99US/$9.99CAN
___	Final Justice	1-4201-0188-9	$6.99US/$9.99CAN
___	Up Close and Personal	0-8217-7956-7	$7.99US/$9.99CAN
___	Under the Radar	1-4201-0683-X	$6.99US/$9.99CAN
___	Razor Sharp	1-4201-0684-8	$7.99US/$10.99CAN
___	Yesterday	1-4201-1494-8	$5.99US/$6.99CAN
___	Vanishing Act	1-4201-0685-6	$7.99US/$10.99CAN
___	Sara's Song	1-4201-1493-X	$5.99US/$6.99CAN
___	Deadly Deals	1-4201-0686-4	$7.99US/$10.99CAN
___	Game Over	1-4201-0687-2	$7.99US/$10.99CAN
___	Sins of Omission	1-4201-1153-1	$7.99US/$10.99CAN
___	Sins of the Flesh	1-4201-1154-X	$7.99US/$10.99CAN
___	Cross Roads	1-4201-1192-2	$7.99US/$10.99CAN

Available Wherever Books Are Sold!
Check out our website at www.kensingtonbooks.com

More by Bestselling Author
Hannah Howell

__Highland Angel	978-1-4201-0864-4	$6.99US/$8.99CAN
__If He's Sinful	978-1-4201-0461-5	$6.99US/$8.99CAN
__Wild Conquest	978-1-4201-0464-6	$6.99US/$8.99CAN
__If He's Wicked	978-1-4201-0460-8	$6.99US/$8.49CAN
__My Lady Captor	978-0-8217-7430-4	$6.99US/$8.49CAN
__Highland Sinner	978-0-8217-8001-5	$6.99US/$8.49CAN
__Highland Captive	978-0-8217-8003-9	$6.99US/$8.49CAN
__Nature of the Beast	978-1-4201-0435-6	$6.99US/$8.49CAN
__Highland Fire	978-0-8217-7429-8	$6.99US/$8.49CAN
__Silver Flame	978-1-4201-0107-2	$6.99US/$8.49CAN
__Highland Wolf	978-0-8217-8000-8	$6.99US/$9.99CAN
__Highland Wedding	978-0-8217-8002-2	$4.99US/$6.99CAN
__Highland Destiny	978-1-4201-0259-8	$4.99US/$6.99CAN
__Only for You	978-0-8217-8151-7	$6.99US/$8.99CAN
__Highland Promise	978-1-4201-0261-1	$4.99US/$6.99CAN
__Highland Vow	978-1-4201-0260-4	$4.99US/$6.99CAN
__Highland Savage	978-0-8217-7999-6	$6.99US/$9.99CAN
__Beauty and the Beast	978-0-8217-8004-6	$4.99US/$6.99CAN
__Unconquered	978-0-8217-8088-6	$4.99US/$6.99CAN
__Highland Barbarian	978-0-8217-7998-9	$6.99US/$9.99CAN
__Highland Conqueror	978-0-8217-8148-7	$6.99US/$9.99CAN
__Conqueror's Kiss	978-0-8217-8005-3	$4.99US/$6.99CAN
__A Stockingful of Joy	978-1-4201-0018-1	$4.99US/$6.99CAN
__Highland Bride	978-0-8217-7995-8	$4.99US/$6.99CAN
__Highland Lover	978-0-8217-7759-6	$6.99US/$9.99CAN

Available Wherever Books Are Sold!

Check out our website at
http://www.kensingtonbooks.com